The Adventure
Stolen Days

Mark K. Vogl

The
Scuppernong Press

Wake Forest, NC

Dedicated to my wife Barbara,
Lt. Colonel, Ret. Barbara Vogl, U.S.A.R.
a remarkable woman

The Adventure – Stolen Days

First Printing

The Scuppernong Press
PO Box 1724
Wake Forest, NC 27588
www.scuppernongpress.com

Cover and book design by Frank B. Powell, III

Cover sketch of Thomas J. Jackson, Robert E. Lee and J. E. B. Stuart
on horseback from an 1893 drawing in the Library of Congress.

International Standard Book Number ISBN 978-1-942806-42-4

Library of Congress Control Number: 2022907453

Table of Contents

The Adventure – Stolen Days

From the Author

A great deal of time and effort was taken investigating the details of history that are the framework for this story. Special care was taken to provide the essence and character of the past in terms of daily life, people and events. Every effort was made to include life as it actually occurred for Mrs. Jackson, the people of Mt. Airy, North Carolina, Richmond, Virginia, and the Army of Northern Virginia, for the weeks in 1863 in question.

The personal recollections of Anna Jackson, Henry Kyd Douglas and Reverend Lacy and *All Things for Good, the Steadfast Fidelity of Stonewall Jackson* by J. Steven Wilkins provide integral contributions to the story, particularly concerning the days Thomas, Anna and Julia spent together leading up to the Battle of Chancellorsville.

Providence has a special role in the story. General Thomas J. (Stonewall) Jackson had a strong belief in Providence, best expressed in his statement "Duty is ours, the consequences are God's."

The West Point Atlas of the Civil War, Mighty Stonewall by Frank E. Vandiver, *Stonewall Jackson & the American Civil War* by Lieut. Colonel G.F.R. Henderson, C.B., *Mapping for Stonewall, The Civil War Service of Jed Hotchkiss* by William J. Miller, *Chancellorsville* by Stephen Sears, and *Chancellorsville 1863, The Souls of the Brave* by Ernest B. Fergurson were studied concerning the military aspects of the battle.

Much thanks is offered to the Park Rangers at Fredericksburg – Chancellorsville National Battlefield for their assistance concerning the battle, and to the Museum of the Confederacy, and Tredegar Iron Works in Richmond, Virginia, and the Chamber of Commerce at Mt. Airy, North Carolina.

Additionally, much time was spent researching time travel in order to develop a working theory for this adventure.

Ellis County Courthouse, Waxahachie, Texas and Pilot Mountain, near Mt. Airy, North Carolina are featured photographs.

The Adventure – Stolen Days

Gettysburg, Pennsylvania
July 1, 1863

President Davis and General Lee had spent months since the Battle of Chancellorsville reinforcing and supplying the Army of Northern Virginia for its maximum effort in the summer of 1863. Time was running out for the Confederacy, the forces available to the South would never be as much as they were now. The blockade was strangling the South, immigration from Ireland was providing endless manpower to the North for her armies. The campaign in to Pennsylvania by Lee, riding on the miraculous victory and the regretful loss of Stonewall Jackson, was Lee's most audacious strategy to win the war.

Contact with Meade's Army of the Potomac had begun earlier this morning when Confederates moving from Cashtown ran into Federal cavalry west of Gettysburg. Though Lee had ordered his generals to avoid a major engagement, both armies rushed reinforcements to the sound of the guns. The Confederates moved on Gettysburg from Cashtown and from Carlisle to the north. Four divisions of two different corps marched and fought throughout the day, first against Federal cavalry, later against the infantry of General Reynolds First Corps.

The Yankees set up a defensive line on the high ground north and west of Gettysburg and held out most of the day, until they were overwhelmed on both flanks by superior Confederate forces. By four thirty in the afternoon the Yankee line had been forced back, and then broken, retreating through Gettysburg.

The fighting in the hot summer's heat of central Pennsylvania had been ferocious. Both sides had endured large numbers of killed and wounded, and hundreds of prisoners taken. Confederate forces were exhausted from marches as much as twelve miles, and then heavy fighting. But they had cleared the field north of the town, and from Lee's position, a mile or so in the rear, it appeared the Yankees were shaken badly, ready to break.

Lee turned to Lt. General Ambrose Hill to ask whether his forces could continue the attack to take the dominant hills, Cemetery and Oak, south of Gettysburg. Hill said he could not do it, his forces were exhausted and in great disarray. One of his divisions was not yet on the field.

Lee called for a rider, he penciled a note to Lt. General Ewell, the other Corps Commander on the field, directing him to take the hills to his front, if practical. The message was delivered, but no attack was organized.

And it is this lack of audacity and perseverance by the replacements of Stonewall Jackson many argue was a missed "moment of decision" in the War of Northern Aggression. Many military historians and analysts, and modern day "Secesh" have proclaimed had Stonewall been there at Gettysburg, the outcome of the war could have been much different.

Ft. Stockton, Texas
November 19, 1961

Nash loved his father's office. It was so different from everything else in the house or outside. It was wood paneled with bookshelves on two walls. His father organized the books by topics, most of them about medicine. He served as both a doctor and veterinarian to the people of Ft. Stockton. But there were sections of his father's bookshelves dedicated to history, especially World War II and the American Civil War.

Nash was in sixth grade and they were studying American history. He was excited because the teacher had said they would be getting into the Civil War after Thanksgiving. Nash's father had said this next four years would be the 100th Anniversary of the War, and that he would take Nash east to Vicksburg, Shiloh, Chattanooga and all the way through Virginia to Gettysburg if Nash did well in school. "Not just history," his dad had said, "all the classes."

Nash loved the smell of the library. It smelled old. And was dark. His favorite spot was a big brown leather chair in front of his dad's desk. It was big enough to sit sideways in … with his feet over one arm. He could put the light on next to the chair and be almost directly under it. There was a blanket over the top of the back of the chair, in case it got cold. And Nash's dog, a border collie named Dixie, would come and lay down near him, and sleep while he read or looked at the pictures in the books.

Sometimes, Nash would sit or end up laying on the floor, Dixie somewhere nearby, and his father would sit in the big leather chair and read to him. His father picked out stories he thought Nash would enjoy, but more would light the imagination of his young son. It started when Nash's father read to Nash the complete volume of Sherlock Holmes by Arthur Conan Doyle. The boy's imagination would fly when his father read those stories. To help, there were pencil drawings in the book: pictures of Sherlock, Dr. Watson, 201 Baker Street, Dr. Moriarty and landscapes of London, and the country in England and Scotland.

Presently, when there was time, his father was reading a new book to Nash by someone without a first or middle name. Strange, Nash thought. This person's parents only gave him initials, H. G. Yep, Dad said he was H. G. Wells. The story was interesting, it was about time travel. Something Nash had not even heard of until his dad began reading this book. It was amazing.

But today, Nash was reading a book he had found. It was smaller than the others, so it gave him more confidence he might be able to get through it.

This book was about the Civil War. His father said the man who wrote the book actually rode with "Stonewall" Jackson during the war, and so this would be more like a long letter than a book. And it was all true!

Nash got a personal feeling for the author Henry Kyd Douglas, for Thomas Jackson, and the members of Jackson's staff. The book really was more like a letter, or a series of letters telling about the Shenandoah Valley and the different battles. And since Nash was not yet familiar with war, he did not know what would happen at Chancellorsville in late April, early May, 1863. The only loss of life he felt was when Colonel Turner Ashby, one of Jackson's favorites had been killed.

Today Nash was reading about May 2, 1863. Jackson had proven to be a remarkable commander, fearless on the field. For Nash it seemed Jackson had a special protection draped over him by God. So when Jackson was wounded, Nash was stunned, and moved. But he had hope. They were only wounds to an arm and hand, and he had been evacuated without further injury.

Jackson's wife and daughter had returned and things seemed to be going in the right direction. At least it seemed that way, until Jackson's cold turned into pneumonia and Jackson died. For Nash, it was the first time in his life he experienced death.

As he sat in the chair … he thought how could this happen?

Henry Kyd Douglas wrote of the night of May 1st in his book *I Rode with Stonewall*:

"The night was clear and cold. The General had neither overcoat nor blanket; for his wagon was far in the rear. Lt. J. P. Smith, aide de camp, offered him his cape, which the general at first refused and then, not to appear inconsiderate of Smith's persistent politeness, accepted. But he did not use it long. Waking up after a short doze, he observed Smith asleep near a tree and went up to him and placed the cape on its owner so quietly that he was not aroused and slept on in comfort. When Smith awoke, the General was asleep in his old position. It was a sad as well as tender incident for the General caught a cold that night, which predisposed his system to that attack of pneumonia which ended in his death."

The sequence of Jackson's death stuck in the mind of the young Nash and the seeming realization of how easily history could be changed.

Photo by Stephen McNierney

Pilot Mountain, North Carolina

The Adventure – Stolen Days

Pilot Mountain, near Mt. Airy. North Carolina
December 23, 2011

"I got it Dad, don't worry." Michael said.

"Michael, this is very important. It's the only sure way you will be able to communicate to us, once you've gone. And, it's one of only two possible ways we will know you made it." Michael's father was insistent.

"I know, Dad."

"Michael, this is perfect. A geographic formation this large is not gonna change in one hundred and fifty years." Pilot Mountain, North Carolina outside of Mt. Airy is a dominant geographical feature. Its strange shape is accentuated by its towering elevation. Both men felt sure they could find the spot they had chosen to bury what would be the world's strangest mail box, even at night under very unusual circumstances. At that spot Michael would be able to place messages for his father.

They had rented a private plane and flown at night to check its silhouette.

It seemed hard to believe, after decades of work on a mission no one ever thought could actually happen, the adventure was about to begin. Michael was not even a gleam in his father's eye when Nash Laurent first started working on this project.

Now, the village of Mt. Airy, North Carolina was a key, an important part of the plan to change history. Pilot Mountain was nearby, and because it stands alone with no other mountains near it, it is a good nighttime landmark from the air. And Pilot Mountain is where Michael would bury a box at the location they just found. That box will help Michael pass messages to his father, though they will be more than one hundred fifty years apart.

"We can't depend on trees being in the same place or even streams. I can only hope that the maps we were able to get are reliable."

"I know Dad, but the small dose of radiation we used on the box should help you find it," Michael said, "and you have a real good idea of where it will be." The two men had identified a place on the mountain both of them thought they could find again. Of course, for Michael it would be more difficult because they could not know what plants were in the exact area a hundred and fifty years ago.

"True, this is really better than anything I could have hoped for, amazing how the exact thing we need is precisely where we need it. Only God could have put it there."

The two men took one last look around, and then headed back down the mountain to the car. Michael would try to find the location tonight, walking from a spot in town. It was a rehearsal, a way to try to build some confidence that you could find the same location under different conditions.

As they drove northwest to Mount Airy both men were in deep thought. Nothing like this had ever been tried before, at least not to any one's knowledge. The Norman Rockwell settings passing by were wasted on these two men, their minds in a different time, traveling through dimensions no man had visited before.

This part of North Carolina was beautiful, even in the twilight of dusk. The foothills of the Blue Ridge running down from Virginia, this land was not easy to farm, or to develop and so had not been overly built upon. In addition, it was some distance to the metro areas of Winston–Salem and was not yet the spillover of a large city called a bedroom community.

"Are you sure we don't need to take the airplane up again, Michael?"

"No Dad, I know there are an awful lot of lights now, but I worked very hard to try to memorize the skyline. But I do think Jeanne Marie definitely should go up a couple of nights. …"

"Yes, Michael, you are right. It's too critical to the mission. We head back to Texas tomorrow, and begin our final work on your craft."

It would be months before Michael's travel back in time would occur, the window and space-time arc back to 1860 would not be at the Rebel Mountain entry point until about a month before the second group, led by Michael's sister Jeanne Marie, would follow.

Ranch near Mt. Airy, North Carolina.
December 22, 1860

The rain was falling in torrents, lightening ripping through the sky, flashes revealing the gray clouds and large pieces of something foreign to the time, broken and resting in many pieces on the ground. Thunder cracking in huge booms, and it was cold. The crash had left Michael unconscious, sprawled across the control board, the ship split into several pieces, parts of it on fire. Michael woke up to find his clothes torn, a cut on his head, and soaking wet. The visible smoke of his breath indicated how cold it was.

Michael stumbled out of the wreckage, branches slapping him in the face. He was confused. What had happened? It took him a while to remember what exactly he was doing. He had a headache and was freezing. He looked through the wreckage by the light of the fire, and flashes of lightening for the overcoat they had packed for him. Then he remembered the bag.

Panic struck Michael. The bag had 1,000 dollars in 1859 Federal currency, about 4,000 in Confederate dollars which hadn't even been issued yet, a small bar of gold, some maps which he had to have and the metal container his father had made in order to pass messages through time to the future. He turned his attention from the coat to the bag. It was so dark. The rain pelted him, he started to shiver. He could not find the bag. Tired, he thought I will return tomorrow.

He stood up straight and looked around. Through the woods he thought he could make out a light glimmering. Michael decided to make for the light in hopes of finding someplace to get out of the rain. He stumbled through the woods tripping over vines and tree fall, stepping into holes in the ground and sliding on the wet leaves. Again and again he got up and took a couple of steps before he fell to the ground once more. It took him ten minutes to go ten yards. But finally, he was at the wood line. He gained some mental relief, it looked like a clear meadow between him and the house. He took off at a run and seemed to be making good progress when one leg and then another caught and he fell forward onto the ground his leg torn open. It hurt bad, and he realized that he had run into a low chicken wire fence. He had landed in a chicken roost, next to a pigsty. He thought he was lying in mud until the smell got his attention.

He worked to stand up, looked to his right, where he thought he saw something in a small lean to type shed just feet from him. It wasn't moving, but it was making some harsh threatening guttural sounds. The house with the light was in front of him. The rain continued to pelt him. Michael sloshed forward through the pig pen slowly. He didn't want to run into another fence. A flash of lighting gave him a moment or two to see a gate for the pen and he made his way to it, and through it.

The house was in front of him, but there was a barn to his right. Michael decided to make his way towards the barn just as a dog started barking inside the house. Michael made his way to and inside the barn. He was out of the rain, but soaking wet and freezing. He looked around, was there a blanket in here? The dog kept barking.

Michael could hear a horse in the barn, off to his right front. This made him cautious. He could not see; it was so dark. He felt around the wall searching for a blanket. He stepped on the prongs of a pitch-fork and it flipped up, its wooden pole handle hitting him in the face. Michael laughed, things can't get much worse, he thought.

But they did. All of sudden he heard the barks of the dog get a lot louder and coming towards the barn. He scrambled looking for somewhere to go, to try to get some height. He didn't want the dog taking a bite out of him. Michael's luck changed when he found a ladder and started climbing it just as the dog burst into the barn. He had gotten about half way up the ladder when he heard a female voice; "Stop right there, mister, who are you? Karl David, come on with that lantern."

"OK Mom" Michael heard the voice of a young male. The dog kept barking and jumping up on the ladder trying to get to Michael's legs.

"Come on down you," the woman said in a commanding voice, "or I will splatter you with this bird gun." The dog kept yapping, but there was more light as a young boy entered the barn with a lantern.

"I can't with that dog down there," Michael replied.

"Hold that lantern up, Karl David," the woman commanded. A pale-yellow light increased in most of the barn, creating flickering shadows.

"Moses, stop the barking, come here," the woman said. When the dog kept barking, the woman repeated her commands louder. "Karl David, go grab Moses." The boy put the lantern on a barrel, walked over and grabbed the dog by the excess skin on his neck.

"Come here Moses." The boy dragged him back away from the ladder.

"Now come down," the woman commanded again.

The two negotiated back and forth, Michael expressing concerns about the dog, the woman expressing concerns about her safety and demanding he come down. Finally, Michael made his way down the ladder a step at a time. His feet reached the ground and he turned to face the woman. He was a mess, soaking wet, blood on his face from the cut caused by the crash, dirty from his fall in the pig pen and bleeding from the cut on his leg. His clothes were shredded. He was covered in pig dirt.

"What have you been up to?" the woman asked with a hint of sympathy in her voice. The wind kicked up behind her, blowing her dress enough to push her forward.

Hypothermia started to set in and Michael started shaking. The shaking started slowly and with his legs, then spread to his arms. The shaking started to become more intense; "My name is Michael, I am freezing, ma'am." He stood there for a moment shivering wildly, uncontrollably. Michael collapsed.

* * * *

The sun hit Michael in the face. He was lying on the ground, covered in a coarse blanket, but still in wet clothes from last night. The morning noises of a farm filled his ears. Chickens were clucking, he could hear strange voices outside. Behind him he heard the sound of a strong stream hitting metal for a second or two, then silence, then the sound repeating for a second or two. He looked around to see a large black and white cow behind him. A second was further away. A person sitting on a stool on the far side was milking the cow into a metal pale. There was a strong pungent smell of cow manure present, a pile of it not too far from his head, glistening with steam rising off it.

His physical condition dominated his thoughts, he stank, was wet and though warm under the blanket, as soon as he moved to get up clean cold fresh air surrounded his body sending a jolt through him.

Outside he heard the lady's voice: "Micah, take these clothes to the man in the barn, but make sure he takes a bath before he puts them on. Take him down to the stream."

"Yes, Miss Hattie," a black voice said to the lady. A few moments later a younger, well-built black man carrying clothes walked into the barn. "Suh, we needs to go down to the creek. The mistress wants you washed up."

"OK, who are you?"

"I am Micah, suh." He walked closer and saw the evidence of dried blood on Michael's head and leg. "Here, let me helps ya, suh." Micah moved closer and put his arm around Michael so he could lean on him.

"Is the creek far?" Michael asked.

"No suh, it's just down over that way aways, a couple of good stone throws from here."

The two men hobbled down the road in between the house and the barn to a wood line. "We ain't got fer to go suh."

Once they got to the stream Micah said, "It's gonna be cold suh, but you do needs a bath. She sent you these clothes to change into." Micah held up some long johns, a pair of pants and a shirt in his other hand. "Mr. Tucker is 'bout your size."

"Tucker?" Michael asked

"Yes suh, Mr. Tucker, he's the Misses, mister. But he ain't been here for a couple of years. We don't know where he went off to."

There wasn't much left of the clothes Michael was wearing so it didn't take long to get them off. He had pealed or tore everything off, but decided to keep his brogans on since he didn't know what the bottom of the stream would be like. Naked except for his shoes, he walked into the creek and shivered as the icy water slammed into his lower legs.

"Best to get right in suh." Michael knew he was right, and fell forward into the water. The shock took his breath away. "Wash yaself good suh, Miss Hattie has breakfast inside for ya, and ya don't wants to stink when ya go inside the house. It's warm in thar, and maybe you can stay in thar for some time and heal some."

Just then two boys came a runnin' down to the creek. Laughing and racing each other, the smaller boy, maybe five years old, yelled out "Is he here, Micah?"

"Yes suh, Mr Jimmie Earl, he taken a bath like ya momma said."

"Momma told us to bring this to him," the larger, probably around eight, said, "he can use this to dry off with."

"Ain't you freezing, mister?" Jimmie Earl said.

"Yes," Michael never looked up but was scrubbing his body as hard as he could.

"You might want ta wash yer head sir, there's a lot of blood in your hair," Karl David said.

Michael reached up with his hand and felt his head; it was matted and sticky. He bent over to stick his head in the water, and when it hit the ice-cold water, it jarred him; he fell forward into the water. He fought to stand up quickly and actually felt warmer when he rose from the dunking. He worked to wash his head but it hurt any time he pulled at the blood in his hair. A trickle of blood started running down his face.

He had done about as much as he could do, so he walked towards the bank, his body rising from the water. The extreme cold of the water had all but castrated him. The two boys pointed and laughed.

Micah looked at them "You boys go on back up to the house and tell yer momma we will be up in a little while. And tell her his head is bleedin' some."

Karl David threw a large piece of cloth material at Michael and the two boys took off back up the hill and through the woods towards the house. They were laughing all the way 'til they were out of sight.

"They just boys, suh." Micah said.

"Micah, I am Michael," Michael stuck out his hand towards Micah as he dried himself with the other hand. Micah took his hand and shook it. A big smile appeared on his face.

"Pleased to make your acquaintance, suh."

"I appreciate what ya done for me, Micah."

"Just doin' what the mistress ordered suh. She is hospitable to most, once she knows who you be."

Michael looked up at the sky, there were gray clouds up there with the sun. "Do you know what day it is, Micah?"

"Yes, suh."

Michael looked up as he was dressing. "What day?"

"It's Sunday, suh. We will be heading to church this afternoon."

"I see, and would you know the date, Micah?"

"Hmmm, let me see now. Well the 14th was Ms. Hattie's birthday, and that was last Saturday, so I believe it's the 22nd."

"Thank you Micah. Guess we can head back up to the house now." As they walked back up to the house, Michael noticed a lot of activity in the woods and around the house. There sure were a lot of black folks around he thought. "Who are all these folks Micah, and what are they up to?"

Mark K. Vogl   *13*

Before Micah could say a word, a large, older black man with white hair walked up to the two of them. Micah backed away a bit, and kind of bowed to the larger man.

"We live here," the man said, "I am George Washington Taylor, suh. I am the head man on this farm. We are fixin' to get ready for the Day."

"George Washington, I am Michael." And he stuck his hand out, "Michael Laurent." George's huge hand took Michael's and he squeezed 'til he saw a look of pain on Michael's face. "Sorry, suh." George said.

"It's OK," Michael said. "George, may I say that Micah has been a real help, I was a mess this morning, pretty beat up." Micah's head rose up some, and he looked at George with a sheepish smile hoping for a sign of approval from George.

"Yes, suh, you was a mess, no doubt about that." The three started laughing as they walked towards the house, "Well, I am glad to hear Micah was earning his keep. He's my oldest boy."

"Well, you have a good son there, sir." Michael said.

"Thank you sir, Miss Hattie is waitin' on ya," George said.

"Ya'll fixin'to get ready for Christmas, George?" They came up on the front steps to the gray wooden porch.

"Just go on in, suh, Miss Hattie is waiting on ya. Micah, come on let's go get the axes and go find some green to cut down." George turned and walked away, Micah following him.

Michael stepped up on the porch, crossed it to the door and knocked. "Come on in," he heard a female voice say. When he opened the door, he felt a blast of warmer air and the smell of food and coffee. A little slow in closing the door he heard the woman say, "Close that door, it takes a long time for the stove and chimney to get some warmth in this house."

Michael quickly shut the door and walked towards the voice. "It's Michael, ma'am, the man you have been so kind to."

Stepping out in to a small hallway was a tall thin woman dressed in a white blouse with lace neck and long sleeves and a grayish long heavy skirt. "I am Hattie, Hattie McMichaels." She stretched out her hand and Michael took it gently. "How are you feeling, Michael?" She stepped forward and reached up towards Michael's head to inspect the wound that seemed to still be bleeding.

"I am OK ma'am, a bit worse for wear, but much better because of you. I will repay you for the clothes you have leant me," Michael said.

"Tut, tut there's no call for that now, Michael. Reece won't be using them and it will be awhile for the boys are big enough for them," she said with an Irish brogue as she made her way back into the kitchen. The smell of the food was intoxicating to Michael. "I hope you are hungry?" she said as she turned some white gravy.

"Famished," Michael replied.

"Well then, have ya's seat in the dining room," she pointed across the hall to a table and chairs, "and I will bring ya some biscuits and gravy to start."

When Hattie came in, she had a plate filled with a split biscuit covered with white gravy. She set it in front of Michael and watched as he bowed his head to pray. "Lord, thank you for a safe trip and for placing Hattie on the road of my journey for you. Thank you for this meal, and please let me use its energy for Thy will. Amen." Hattie echoed, "Amen."

"Well, I will be, I don't think I have heard a man pray at my table in several years. And such a lovely prayer it were, Michael," the Irish was coming out in Hattie.

Michael stood, "Will you join me, ma'am?"

"Sit down, Michael, and eat. You have to be starving after the night you had last night. Your body had to burn all night long, lying in them wet cold clothes. I just hope you don't get the fever." Hattie was back inspecting Michael's head as he took huge bites of the food before him.

The combination of the heat, the food, and being dry, except for his feet in the wet shoes was quickly bringing on a feeling of exhaustion. Hattie could tell it and decided not to wait. When Michael finished his breakfast, Hattie handed him a glass of water and said, "Follow me." She led him back up the hallway to the front of the house and into the parlor where she made a right and headed down another hallway 'til they came to a door. She pointed into it.

"Take them shoes off and sit on the bed. I will be right back."

Michael sat on the bed and removed his shoes, his feet shining in the wetness. Hattie came back in, got on her knees and lifted each foot to dry it.

"Ma'am," Michael tried to pull away.

She looked up with scorn on her face: 'You'll catch your death if you don't get out of them shoes and get your feet warm. This is the boys' bed, get under them blankets and get some sleep." Hattie picked up Michael's brogans, "I am taking these out to the stove to dry 'em out."

Michael was asleep before his head hit the pillow.

Paradise Ranch, Nevada
July 11, 2012

D r. Nash Laurent had been a pest about me visiting his daughter. He had given me a wrapped package for her. I told him I would stop by and visit her on my way from Area 51 in Nevada to the Space Center near Houston.

Nash was about the age my father would be. A geologist, he had either worked for NASA, or been a consultant for them, for much of his life. I had recently met him at Paradise Ranch, a.k.a. Area 51, while training for a high-altitude flight intended to test a new bird we hoped might be able to lift us from the stratosphere into space.

Nash was not working on my project, but we met in the cafeteria one day by accident, I thought. He was a kind of odd-looking duck. Tall, maybe 6' 1", with round wire rim glasses, and white hair, kind of like Santa Claus. He always wore a white dress shirt, white slacks and red suspenders. And he wore a red baseball cap, the Razorbacks of Arkansas. To top it off, he wore red and white wingtip shoes.

He got his undergraduate degrees in Mechanical Engineering and Geology at the University of Arkansas. And he earned his Master's in Physics from the University of Chicago. I never did ask him what discipline the doctorate was in.

Nash and I ended up sitting at the same lunch table one day. He was eating and buried in a book. When he put the book down to take a bite, the book closed revealing the cover page; "*Dick Dowling and the Boys of Erin.*"

Of Scot-Irish decent myself, the book caught my attention. I took the opportunity to introduce myself, reaching out with my hand I said, "Hi, I am Parks Walter, sir."

He looked up, smiled, a twinkle in his eye. Taking my hand, he said, "I thought I would meet you today, I am Dr. Nash Laurent," his voice wandered off. He had a Southern accent.

"So, what's the book about, Doc?"

"Ah, it's a little-known story from the war," he said, as if there had only ever been one war. He went on; "It's a story about an Irishman named Richard O'Dowling, or Dick Dowling as history records it now."

"Dick Dowling?" I said, "don't believe I have ever heard of the man."

"Not likely you would, Parks, he was a Southern hero, and though he saved Texas from Yankee occupation, he did it out west, and not in Virginia or the Carolinas. ..." Nash said as he picked up the book and started reading again, he mumbled "... so no one ever heard of him."

Dick Dowling. Will have to google that name I thought to myself.

The rest of lunch was quiet until Nash was about ready to get up and leave. He turned to me and said, "I hope we can get together for dinner tonight, round 6 pm, we have quite a lot to talk about."

He got up and left. I was a little perplexed. I had never heard of Dr. Laurent, the meeting was accidental. What would we have to talk about?

Area 51 is a strange place. A lot goes on there. One of the basic rules is you don't ask people what they are working on. So, I wondered how did he know me, and what did we have to talk about? I headed back to the hangar for my afternoon briefing, and some work in the simulator. I reminded myself not to forget to google Dick Dowling.

Sim. Tech. (short for Simulator technician) Dr. Lisa was just inside the door as I entered the hangar. "Hello, Colonel Walter," she said with a smile. They still used my former military rank, despite my no longer being on active duty. I worked for an aerospace company, space being their priority, and the reason for my present training here.

She was a looker. Tall, thin, great physique, and a full head of thick red hair. A really pretty face, high cheek bones and glasses, she oozed sensuality. I had been told by another Citadel grad when I first arrived at Paradise Ranch that Dr. Lisa was a confident lady who wasn't shy. He said she usually dated the hottest pilot at Area 51. I was hoping my airborne wings and Ranger tab might mean something to her. But they didn't. From her perspective I wasn't really a pilot, after all I only flew Cobra attack helicopters before entering the NASA program!

I guess she thought a Citadel helicopter pilot was second string to an academy anything.

Now she was beside me, her heels clicking on the cement as we walked through the hangar.

"Say, Colonel, what do you say we have dinner tonight?" she said.

Boy, that wasn't expected.

"Uhhh," my mind was thinking fast. "Well, maybe later, around nine? Maybe ..." I said.

"Nine suits me fine, I'll pick you up at the BOQ," she said, as we went through the heavy metal doors into the air-conditioned portions of the hangar. Her hair swung as she turned her head over her shoulder and said; "By the way, I understand you maxed out that test this morning," she turned away with a wave.

Gosh, she looks great from behind, I thought to myself watching her rear end sway from side to side as she made her way down the hall. Was she adding a little for me as she walked away? Hope so, I thought.

The test she was talking about was a test no pilot had ever successfully completed before. So to hear I maxed it out was quite a boost. The test evaluated a pilot's ability to handle four axes of flight simultaneously, something not found in nature, since we live in three dimensions, allowing for three axes.

Dinner time came pretty quick and I found myself headed back to the cafeteria about quarter of six. Tonight was chicken fried steak and mashed potatoes. My favorite! One thing I always loved about the military life was the chow. You eat good, none of that chick food. Instead, plenty of meat and potatoes. Too much physical labor required to eat less.

Dr. Laurent was there when I got there, and had already been through the serving line and gotten his meal. It didn't take long for me to join him; "Hello Dr. Laurent."

"Hi Colonel, have a seat."

"Thanks, so what can I do for you, doctor?"

"Parks, may I call you Parks?" he said.

"Sure"

"Parks, I read your book, *Ten Moments of God in the Civil War*, the one about the ten small things which could have changed the outcome of the American Civil War. Very interesting. I found it very well researched, and your sources were not the traditional P.C. sources. I think your use of first-person accounts and period news reports were especially enlightening. Took a lot of revisionism out of the history and added things hidden from most of us."

"Thank you, Dr. I appreciate your compliments. Not many people have ever indicated they knew I wrote a book, no less read it."

"Have you written any other books?" Dr. Laurent asked as he continued eating.

"None that are published, but I do have a couple manuscripts I am working on." I said.

"What are they about?"

"The war. I am fascinated by that era, and the untold stories of the South." His ears seemed to perk up when I said that.

"Where are you from, Parks?"

"Ummm, well that's a little complicated," I said. "I was born in the northeast, but I kind of feel like I was a born in a foreign land. I am a Southerner by blood, spirit and outlook. My mother's side of the family is from Carolina, near Charlotte."

"I see." Dr. Laurent did not seem to look up when he was eating. He devoured his chicken fried steak, French fries and corn on the cob like a man who had not eaten in weeks.

"So, you think the South should have won?" He asked.

"Well, I don't know, but I do think how things turned out is not the only possible outcome."

"Parks, your identification of such simplistic alternative outcomes was really brilliant. Which of the ten events do you think had the most real chance of changing the course of the war?"

"Doctor, that's difficult to say. Some of those events would not have, by themselves, changed the final outcome. My general thesis was that a combination of two or three of the ten could very likely have changed the war. But, that Providence, God's Will, manifested itself to guide history."

"Yes Parks, but if, for example, Johnston and Beauregard had energetically followed President Davis' order to pursue the Yankees after First Manassas, don't you think the Confederates could have taken Washington, and possibly ended the war right then and there?"

"Wow, you really did read my book. Well, as I wrote, they probably could have taken Washington, but whether the North would have surrendered, or whether that would have brought England and France to the side of the South is very problematic." I went on, "I don't think Abraham Lincoln was a lightweight. He was very committed, and after the initial shock he probably would have been able to rally the Union."

I went on, "Now, if St. Louis had been taken by the Confederates first, and then Washington taken, well that really changes both the military situation and the politics."

"So that is one of the combinations you were talking about?" Dr. Laurent asked. Not waiting for an answer, he went on, "Hmmm, so you have given this quite a bit of thought."

Our conversation moved from my book, to general discussion. Dr. Laurent said he had been at Area 51 for quite some time. Since there is a blackout of news, and limited outside telephone use, he had little knowledge of what was going on in the world. He didn't know his Razorbacks had won a national championship in football.

"You might find my daughter Jeanne Marie interesting to talk to," Laurent said, 'She too is very interested in the war. In fact, she has quite a collection of artifacts at her library in Mayberry, Texas.'

"Really?" I said, thinking about my upcoming date with Dr. Lisa.

"Yes, Jeanne Marie has always wanted to travel back to that time, she was smitten by *Gone with the Wind* as a child."

"Well, Dr. Laurent, I have to be getting back to the BOQ. A lot of studying to do you know?"

"Quite," he said without looking at me, "maybe we can get together again before you leave?"

"Sure, why not," I said, as I got up and picked up my tray. "Have a nice evening."

The walk back to the B.O.Q. took no time. Still had plenty of time to shower, clean up, put on a khaki safari short sleeved shirt, some tan pants and pair of dockers. I even had some time to think of ways to impress Dr. Lisa. Though she seemed pretty aggressive so maybe she was going to do the heavy lifting! Type A ladies have been known to do that. I smiled.

It was a pleasant evening. A thick velvet darkness with a sky full of stars, and the surreal lights spread across the desert floor inside the mountain range which created the bowl that was Area 51. I sat on the trunk of my Corvette waiting for Dr. Lisa. Red and white exterior, with a removal top. I loved my car. A red interior, the cars made in the sixties were so much better than what is available today.

I had bought the Corvette from a farmer in central South Carolina twenty-two years before during my junior year at The Citadel. Sitting under a magnolia, it was rusting, topless, the interior a disaster worn by the weather, the sun, and animals' droppings. It even housed a bees' nest. But I saw its potential. I had some cousins who lived near New Port Richie, Florida. They rebuilt old cars. I knew if I could get it to them, they could conduct major surgery and bring life back to this car.

It wasn't a quick fix, and in fact I wasn't sure they would ever get it back to me. But when I returned from Desert Storm, there she was, along with my cousins and the rest of my family at Charleston Air Force Base.

The 'vette is the best investments of my life. I have been offered a quarter of a million dollars for this car. But I will never sell it.

The mechanical work they had done was unbelievable. Much more difficult than the body work, or the interior, they had to rebuild the motor, the transmission, the brakes, the whole mechanical "enchilada" had to be redone. But this car purred. The power was amazing, and I could get through the gears and up to a hundred miles an hour in about eight seconds!

No computers, no GPS, no means to track me, or artificially restrict the performance of this car. My cousins were wizards. And when I tried to pay David, the oldest of the cousins, he wouldn't take it. "You did your thing in Iraq, we did ours at home," he said.

Dr. Lisa pulled up in her dark blue Mercedes, top down, hair blowing in the wind. "Hi Parks, let's go," she said

I walked around, got in the passenger side and was looking for the seat belt when she stomped on the gas and the car took off, literally. The "g" force slammed me back in my seat. I looked at her; she was smiling as she shifted through the gears.

"So, where are we going for dinner?" I honestly had no idea. It's not like you can just take off out the front gate of Area 51. Heck, I wasn't even sure Area 51 had a front gate.

"I know a place … "she said as we sped off towards Groom Lake.

Tank top, shorts, and sandals she was showing off everything she had, and I was glad I hadn't over-dressed. Tonight was going to be fun.

She turned the radio up, or maybe it was a CD player, 70's Romance songs blared out the speakers into the open sky. So, I just sat back and enjoyed the ride. The further you drive out from the small cluster of buildings, the brighter the stars become. It's hot, but dry, and the air rushing over the windshield and into the car was almost cool.

Lisa drove to a spot she must have been to before. Got out, and started unloading things from the trunk. She had brought a blanket, a bottle of wine, glasses, a serious candelabra, a basket full of food, and even a rolled-up wire fence and battery. "This is an electric fence; I lay it on the ground circling around us to keep away the snakes and scorpions and other unwanted visitors."

Wow, I thought to myself, this lady has a plan. I helped her lay out the blanket, and the fence, and the rest. It wasn't long before the candles were lit, and she was busy getting out the food. "Here," she said as she handed me the cork screw, "make yourself useful."

Dinner went great. She had made some kind of chicken with cheese and a really good, cold salad. The wine was great, and we did some small talk about who we were, where we came from. She had more or less settled at Area 51. She had one of the few homes built out there, even had a pool. And living there was how she rated a car. She enjoyed her work, though she didn't tell me what it was.

We lay back on the blanket looking at the stars. Groom Lake, though pure white sand, did look different at night, especially after a couple of glasses of wine. I almost thought I saw small waves with the moon shimmering on them. She asked, "So why do you think you did so well on the test?"

"Huh?"

"Parks, no one has even come close to passing that test, and you maxed it out. How did you do that?" Her voice got a little sharper, her head turned to me as she said it. Her eyes were looking at mine as if she wanted to cut through to my brain.

"I don't know, it didn't seem that hard," I said. "It's not much different from the tests they give us at aviator school at Ft. Rucker."

"What?" she said with an even sharper voice.

"Yea, if you are flying a helicopter you have to do more things, use more limbs than the pilot of an airplane. We are used to thinking about more than one variable at a time, and coordinating several aspects of flight and power at the same time."

"Really?" she said, almost as if it were too easy.

"Lisa, if you fly an airplane and take your hand off the controls, it will fly itself. That's the aerodynamics of a plane. But, in a helicopter, if you take your feet off the pedals, and your hands off the controls, torque will immediately fill the void and the bird will spin faster and faster, falling and careening!"

Fear is a great place to make your move. Us guys learn that in Gender Relations 101. When a lady understands you face death, she tends to be more vulnerable to your needs. I made my move.

I tried to kiss Lisa, she coyly pulled away. "I am not really much on the first date," she explained.

"But there may not be another," I said. "I won't be here that much longer, I am off to Houston in a couple of days. And, well, you know we don't know how this ship will fly, no one's ever tried what I am going try. Could be my last mission. ..." I looked away, playing it for everything it was worth. I saw Tim Hutton use this approach in an old John Wayne movie, *The Hellfighters*. It always worked great in that movie!

"I know," she said, almost by rote, as she sat up and started picking up plates and the silverwear and placing them in the basket. Well, that didn't work, I thought to myself.

This lady knew precisely what she was doing. She reminded me of some Canadian ladies I met on the beach in Ft. Lauderdale during spring break, my senior year at The Citadel. About eight of us drove down to Florida and stayed in a vacant home one of our parents was selling as a realtor. We were just across the bridge from the beach. It was perfect and cheap.

The second day we were there a group of ladies were on the beach. One of the guys, Reece, pointed to half a dozen lovelies sitting not far from us. They were cute and happy, talking and laughing.

Reece said, "Parks why don't you go over there and see if those girls will go to dinner with us tonight?" I guess it was a dare, or maybe he didn't think I would do it. But I did.

I got up, walked over to the girls, sat down on the pure white sand of the Florida beach and started talking with them. After some small talk with them, I signaled to the rest of the boys to come on over.

The two groups kind of merged on the beach, and we talked. We decided to go back to our respective lodgings, shower, dress and meet for dinner. The girls were from Canada, had terrific accents and were really gorgeous. So, we took 'em to a Steak and Ale. Bought 'em a nice dinner and moved in for the kill. That's when they told us we had to take them to the bus station, they were headed back to Canada that night! Boy, did they play us.

Seems Dr. Lisa and those girls had the same course on the martial arts of romance. They knew how to use our own psychological momentum against us! LOL

Lisa and I rolled up the electric fence after we had picked everything else up. Lisa had a system. You have to, to fit all that stuff in the trunk of a two seat convertible.

The drive back to the BOQ wasn't exactly as I had thought it would be. But it had been a nice evening, she was a really intelligent lady, and good company, and well, you don't win 'em all. When we pulled up to the BOQ, I got out, turned and said; "Lisa, you might want to take a look at the Army Field Manual Fundamentals of Flight, many of the answers you are looking for are in there."

I think she could tell I was disappointed. She put her finger up in front of her face, and bent it towards her, indicating, come here. When I bent over it was the closest I had been to her breasts, what a view. She reached up, grabbed my head and kissed me. And I mean a kiss. She smelled terrific.

"Parks, you are a nice guy, good looking, and sexy. If you head back this way, and want to do more than a night, look me up." She turned and drove off.

Except for the dust kicking up into my face, it was a 1950s movie-like ending to a nice night.

Paradise Ranch, Nevada
July 12, 2012

The next morning I headed over to the cafeteria for breakfast. Dr. Laurent was already there. He had finished his breakfast and was drinking his coffee. "Get your studying done?" he asked in a mildly sarcastic tone.

"Ah, yea ..." I said as I sat down. I wondered why I had come over to his table. Interrogation wasn't something I needed first thing in the morning.

"Parks, you are going to be leaving soon. I was wondering if you could stop by my daughter's on the way to Houston and give her this." He pushed a small package towards me. "Her name is Jeanne Marie. First name is on the package in case you forget."

His voice drifted off as I spoke over it. "Well, I don't know, I mean it's a good two-day drive from here to Houston, Dr. Laurent. I don't know if I will have time," I said.

"You will have more than enough time, Parks, and it's on the way, and I really need to get this to her." The tone of his voice was urgent, and he seemed confused when I didn't just say yes and pick up the package.

"Parks, Jeanne Marie is expecting you. I told her about you, and well. ..."

"Dr. Laurent," I said sternly, "don't you think that was a little presumptuous, dang we just talked a couple of times?"

"Parks, yes it was. And I am sorry. But this is important, and I am sure when you meet Jeanne Marie and find out more about this, you will be glad you helped us out."

"Before I take the package, let me look on the map and see where she is, and see if it is on the route."

"Her town, Mayberry, is not on the map," he said nonchalantly. "But it is on the route, only four miles off US 280, maybe one hundred and fifty miles east of El Paso."

"It's not on the map? Well, I could use my GPS to find it," I said.

"No, you wouldn't find it that way either," he said. "Parks, we could get together later and I could bring you a map of Texas with the route designated on it."

"Dr. Laurent, there's almost nothing not on the GPS."

"I know Parks, but trust me, Mayberry and Rebel Mountain aren't. Now will you help me out here?"

"OK, how 'bout we meet for lunch, you bring your map, and I will take a look at it. I am leaving tomorrow."

"Fine," he said as he pushed the package to me again, "don't forget this, it's critical." And he got up … "see you at lunch and thanks."

I headed over to the hangar for some more simulator work. When I got there the place was a filled with Sim. techs scrambling. Something was wrong. "We are having some trouble, Colonel, why don't you take a seat over at one of those desks and we will call you when we have this thing working."

I headed over to the desk he had pointed to, placed the package down and cued up the computer. After I checked the route to Houston through Phoenix and El Paso, it was about the same.

I remembered Dick Dowling, the man Nash had told me about when we first met. I figured I would google him while I waited for the sim. techs to fix the glitch.

It didn't take long for Google to produce its list of sites on Dowling. Dick Dowling, or more properly Richard O' Dowling was quite a man. Born in Ireland, he had traveled with his family to New Orleans when just a child. His parents died of yellow fever and the kids decided to move to Houston.

By the time Dowling was 19 he owned a saloon and had met the woman he wanted to marry, Elizabeth Ann Odlum. When Dowling saw Elizabeth Ann walking in town he quickly learned her name and found out her uncle was the commander of a local militia unit. He decided to join the militia so he could meet Elizabeth Ann's uncle. Dowling joined the local militia, composed of recently immigrated Irish–Catholics. Once comfortable with Captain Odlum, Dick would work for an introduction to his niece Elizabeth. His plan worked. Captain Odlum introduced Dick to Elizabeth and their romance started almost immediately. They were married before the Civil War started.

When Texas seceded from the Union, the militia became part of the Confederate Army. Dowling was made a lieutenant. After an initial posting down by Brownsville, the Irish were moved up to Houston to take part in the successful Confederate combined arms (Navy–Army) offensive to retake Galveston on January 1, 1863. Dowling did well in that fight, but he earned his fame at the little-known battle of Sabine Pass. In this battle in September of 1863, Dowling and less than fifty

Irish Catholics beat a Yankee fleet of more than twenty ships and five thousand Yankee soldiers! It was a remarkable feat. President Jefferson Davis himself described the battle as the South's Thermopylae, a reference to the Spartans victory over Xerxes.

"Colonel ... Colonel," I could hear a voice ... "Yes," I said,

"We are ready for you, sir," the tech replied.

Hitting the clear button, I got up and headed towards the simulator. Dick Dowling, gonna have to go back and do a little more work on him I thought.

Interesting, there was no Dr. Lisa to meet me this morning.

As we walked to the simulator, the Sim. Tech. asked; "Colonel, the MIG 29UB is up there, do you think they will be able to break the stratosphere with that?"

"I don't know, I don't think that's what they are trying to do." I said. The MIG was an advanced version of a high-altitude fighter, but it did not have the life support or space navigation systems to survive outside the earth's atmosphere.

Other commercial outfits have been trying to find the key to penetrating space without the traditional rocket launch seen at Cape Kennedy, but there are so many different problems to deal with. The costs are huge. And even though wealthy people all over the world are willing to throw down money for tickets for a craft not yet designed, only governments can make the long-term financial commitments necessary to resolve all the challenges.

Parks was the first of a new breed of pilot astronauts and the first flight could still be years in the future.

Lunch time came and it was back to see Dr. Laurent one last time.

"Hi ya doc, what's up?" I said as I put down the tray on the table. I don't think I will ever get over how good government food can be.

"Not much Parks, are you about through with your training?"

"I am for this trip. Probably be back here a bunch more times before I ever really see space."

Dr. Laurent's one eye brow rose just a tad. That man could eat. I thought I was the king of mashed potatoes and cream gravy, but Dr. Laurent could put them down.

"I took a computer recon of the route to Houston, there sure is a lot of Texas out there!" I said sticking my fork into the Chicken Fried steak.

He pushed a folded map towards me. "The route is outlined in red.

You won't have to travel much off the straight line. It won't take you but a couple of hours, unless you decide to spend a couple of days with Jeanne Marie. …"

"How's that?" I said. "Dr. Laurent, I do have a week to report, but I figured I would check in to Houston and then go down to Galveston for a couple days. Maybe do some work on Dick Dowling, (Laurent looked up) and I do know a lady down there to walk the beach with." I smiled.

"Well, I am not trying to fix you up with my daughter, Parks," he took another bite of steak, and he got hard to hear …" it's … just …" crunch, slurp … eating sounds.

"What?"

He finished chewing, swallowed, took a good strong pull on his sweet tea, "Well it's just that Jeanne Marie is very interested in the Civil War, and well who knows, the library she works at might even have a copy of your book."

I was jealous of Dr. Laurent. He always drank Southern sweet tea, even though they didn't serve it in the government cafeterias anymore. Michelle Obama's health craze had removed that from the menu and we were sure more pain was to come. We joked it was done on a Madame's Executive Order. "Doc, could I have some of your sweet tea?"

Laurent reached down with his left hand and pulled up a jug, "Sure son, help yourself," he said.

I had to go dump the "nothing tea" they served, so I could get some sugar back in me bones. Ahhh … I love the tinkling sound of sweet tea pouring over ice into a glass.

"So Jeanne Marie is a buff?" I said.

"Um, you might say that, Jeanne Marie believes our entire history as a nation begins there."

"Really, so she's a fan of Lincoln?"

"Not exactly."

"How's that?"

"I think you should meet her; she has developed some theories about Post Civil War history you might find worth a listen," he said. He sounded confident, like my interest in the Civil War would keep me with a librarian when the lady in Galveston had been Miss Texas.

"OK doc, I look forward to meeting your daughter," I said. All I had to do was drop off a package. After that, I could get on the road and off to my adventure in Galveston.

"Let's look at this map a minute," Nash said as he unfolded it. Pointing to an empty space on the map off US 280 he said, you will see a sign on the road that points you towards Mayberry, just follow the sign. When you have gone a few miles, you will see Rebel Mountain."

"Rebel Mountain?" I said.

"Yep, you'll know it when you see it. Now look here," Nash pointed to a scratch drawing he had made on the map off in central Texas, "See this circle, that's Rebel Mountain, and the road you will be on will take you right to Mayberry, here." There was the old symbol for a town, drawn inside the circle that represented the mountain. "If you can't find Jeanne Marie at the courthouse, drive around and leave the town headed south and it will take to our place, Three Pines. Got it?"

"Yep doc, I got it."

"Ok, see ya soon." Dr. Laurent said as he was turning to leave.

"Uh huh …" I said, looking at the map, then realizing what he said … wondering when would I see him again?

Mayberry, Texas
July 15, 2012

In Texas, the state highways often resemble interstates. They are four lanes, with a wide median between the two-lane roadways. These medians fill with wild flowers in the spring. Depending on where you are in the state, the flowers could be Bluebonnets, Crimson Clover, Indian Paintbrush, or a wide variety of others. They spread like a carpet before you as you drive. Large parts of Texas can be a very bland landscape, with sparse vegetation, or orange land structures rising. But, in the spring, areas of Texas are simply beautiful. And the beauty contrasted to the starkness helps create a surreal environment of mystery and wonder that rivals Erin for its legends and magic.

I had already covered about 900 miles in a day and half, and was on the last leg. U.S. Highway 280 headed east towards Fredericksburg, Texas, the back door to Austin.

On this road the landscapes are huge, barren, dominated by the colors of the desert. It seemed like you could see a hundred square miles when you looked in all directions. While driving, I saw what appeared to be a smoke tail rising from the ground. The tail was moving very fast and looked more like a car traveling at high speed across country. Boy, was that thing moving, whatever it was. I thought it might be someone crazy driving a motorcycle, or some four-wheeler at top speed. Whatever it was, it was approaching the road ahead of me. We seemed on a collision course, though it was going to cross in front of me, maybe two hundred yards or less, ahead of me. It turned out to be a wild dog, but its speed and stamina were unbelievable. It never stopped at the road, but crossed it in two or three strides and just kept going. Must have an appointment, I thought.

Long before the Alamo, Texas was a place of enchantment and unusual occurrences. Men and women, Indian or white lived large in Texas. The place required it. Texas is not a land for the timid. The creatures who inhabit Texas, from bug and spider, to coyote and rattlesnake are lethal. Introduced later, wild boar and others just got a little meaner after their arrival, and made the place even more challenging to the newcomer, or unsuspecting wanderer.

I had been driving for several hours when an odd sign read Mayberry 4 miles. The sign was not the usual highway colors, but instead a kind of faded orange sign with black writing. I did not see the poles holding it up, it almost appeared to be suspended in air.

I didn't pay too much attention to my hallucination; I had been driving a while and didn't see the sign until I was almost on it.

I had never heard of Mayberry, Texas. But having blood from North Carolina, and having grown up with Andy, and Barney, Aunt Bee and Opie, I remembered the fictional place from my childhood. It was nearing lunch, so I decided to see what this Mayberry would be like by eating there.

I don't think I went a half mile before I saw another sign, again seemingly suspended in midair, with Mayberry and an arrow to the right. Strange because the road it pointed to was dirt! Not macadam or anything else, just dirt. But my mind was made up, so I turned onto the dirt road. I looked down at my odometer to check the mileage. The first sign said four miles, if I went that far on this dirt road and didn't get to Mayberry, I would turn around and resume my trip to Houston.

Though the dirt road was unusually smooth I began to grow anxious when I had gone about two miles. And, when I glanced in the rear-view mirror to see what type of tail I was sending up into space, I saw nothing, the road was not there. Must be dust obscuring the road from my sight, I thought; except, I saw no dust either.

There was no sign of dust and no sign of the road I was driving on. The road seemed to be disappearing under me as I drove it.

Then in the distance, on the horizon, I saw what appeared to be a mountain rising sharply out of the ground. It was a fairly substantial mountain, more than a mile in width at its base. And it was green, in sharp contrast to the desert brown and orange surrounding the mountain in all directions. I smiled to myself, it looked like a Salvador Dali painting I had seen in my History of Art Class at the Citadel. The mountain was covered in trees and had the usual sharp point a couple thousand feet in the air.

What a contrast, green against the endless and naked orange and light brown of the land, and clear blue of the sky above. It did take my breath … what was I getting into?

And, the sky. It had been clear and endless all morning. But over this single rising mountain was a large white fluffy cloud, which by its location seemed to be providing shade onto most of the mountain.

Well, I could use some shade. It gets to more than a hundred and ten Fahrenheit this time of year in west Texas.

I felt a mild bump as my vehicle reached the base of the mountain as the road switched to macadam and was engulfed in large pines. These pines reminded me of those in the northwest, much larger than what you find in East Texas, or anywhere else in the Lone Star state. My vehicle started to climb the mountain. Pine trees and other woods shaded the road, and the temperature dropped rapidly. The thermostat in the car said 75! I had to look again, because just moments ago it had read 107.

Right at the four mile mark I entered the town of Mayberry. To say the least, it relieved my anxiety. People were doing all kinds of daily activities. Cars were pulling into and leaving parking lots, or the driveways of homes. The local school was on the right, a playground in front. A little further up the road was a feed store, pickups parked in front. All seemed right with the world.

Somebody was going to have explain this, I thought to myself.

And then, there was the town square.

Texas is known for its town squares and especially its county court-houses which dominate the center of each square. And while I have driven through many towns, and seen many courthouses, none of them compared to the one I was looking at now.

This courthouse looked like a Bavarian Cathedral on high. Its colors were a mixture of the pinkish orange seen so often in Texas and a cream-colored white, topped off with a black roof. The central foundation of the building was lifted so there was at least one-half story below ground and another two stories above the half-exposed ground floor. The wide steep black roof made the overall structure seven stories tall.

Round columns divided the front in equal thirds, and appeared to enclose spiral staircases within the building. Tall thin windows dotted the columns. And these columns framed the broad stone staircase that led from the road in the square to the central entrance of the building. Black, rounded cones topped each of these columns. These staircase enclosures had five tall thin windows on each floor. Another column emerged from the roof in the center joining the two rising from the ground. This column was squared off, mostly in white stone and had the shape of a German home. It rose only two more stories and stopped. The last tower crowned the center roof and was an additional two stories. In its center, on the top story was the clock.

In front of the courthouse stood a simple, single soldier Confederate monument. Its slim light-colored profile was in sharp contrast to the huge size and complexity of the building behind it. The entire square was in the shade and it really was a comfortable seventy-five degrees. Three flags flew to one side, between the Confederate statue and the main entrance. The U.S., Texas and Third Confederate national flags were all flying. Unusual I thought, since not many Southern towns flew Confederate flags any more.

I turned right on the town square, keeping the courthouse on my left and pulled my 'vette up to a place in front of a western antique store, where I slide into the space and shut down the powerful engine. Looking at my 'vette I thought; I bet she's loving this coolness after weeks in the desert. The red exterior glistened, damn I loved that car.

I picked up the map laying in the passenger's seat on top of the package for Dr. Laurent's daughter. Besides the red line which traced the route to Mayberry, was Jeanne Marie Laurent's name, a phone number, and Dr. Laurent had written "she works in the library which is housed inside the courthouse in the center of the Square."

I checked my watch and it was about 12:10. Oh great, lunch time I thought, somewhat disappointed. I could not just run into the library, and drop the package. She probably wasn't even in there now, the sign on the door clearly said "Closed for Lunch." Maybe I should go find a place to get something to eat and come back at one.

I got out of the car, shut the door and started to walk the square to see if there was a restaurant or luncheonette open. The square was filled with an odd, but usual, assortment of places you will find in a Texas town square. Attorney's offices, a pharmacy, a dance studio, a pawn shop, the local newspaper, a vacant store, a couple of antique stores, and then I came upon an old hotel. The smell of food seemed to be coming from there.

I opened the door, and there was just inside a large dark wood counter for check in, giving the room its purpose. Dark and quiet, there was no one there. It was almost as if I had stepped into a time warp. Framed in dark wood with a tall ceiling, a spittoon sat on the floor in front of the check in bar and an ash tray on the counter. Behind the counter were the old small boxes on the wall that held the keys, and might have a piece of paper or letter for the room's occupants.

There was the smell of cigar, unusual in this time when smoking indoors could lead to castration. But then again, this was west of the Brazos, … as a cowhand told John Wayne in a movie "there ain't no law west of the Brazos," or did John Wayne say Pecos? I don't remember.

Large leather chairs with small tables were spread across the room. A fan hangin' down from the ceiling was twirling slowly.

I could hear voices, and noises, and followed them and the smell down a narrow, dark hallway to a room filled with diners. Across the room was a large glass window. Through the window there was a large tree and a lush green garden completely enclosed by the walls of rooms surrounding it. The hotel was at least two stories tall, though I could not see above that to know for sure.

The room was busy, the tables were filled except for one in the far corner at one end of the window. The sounds of chatter, tinkling silverware, and an occasional burst of laughter helped ease my spirit. Over there, a table in the corner had a woman sitting at it, reading something. I thought to myself, I guess I will wait 'til someone gets up. Just then one of the waitresses came up and said with an Irish accent; "Can I help you sir?"

"Oh, it's no trouble," I said, "I will just wait 'til a table clears."

"No reason for that sir," she said, "Follow me please."

I took only one step before I realized she was headed to the table where the lone woman was sitting. I slowed, and the waitress, almost as if she sensed it, turned her head and said, "Now follow me sir, no reason to be shy, deary."

We made our way through the crowded floor and as I got closer, I could see the woman a little better. She had blonde hair, up in a bun. She was wearing black glasses and had on a white blouse with long fluffy sleeves and a high neck. That's about all I could make out as we got close to the table.

I thought I heard the waitress say; "Miss Jeanne Marie, this lad needs a seat, would it be alright to park him with you?"

Without looking up she waved with her hand and said, "Of course." I could barely hear her. The noise in the room and the noise coming from a fountain outside under the tree, and the waitress in front of me, made the woman's voice slight, like the sound of a light breeze.

The waitress handed me a menu, pointed at the chair, and made a sharp turn to begin her rounds.

I moved to the seat opposite the lady to sit down. The table was filled with books, and notebooks, and newspapers and photographs. I smiled to myself, where did the waitress think she would put any food I ordered? I figured she knew, and sat down.

Whatever this lady was reading must be something. She still had not looked up. I studied her blouse. It had small round black shiny buttons down the center and the front was pleated. The neck was high with lace. If this was Jeanne Marie, she looked like a librarian, kind of frumpy.

The books on the table were the strangest arrangement. There was a large book on Stonewall Jackson, another titled *Until the Sun Dies* by Robert Jastrow, and Stephen Hawking's *A Briefer History of Time*. She had a map stretched out, and though upside down the area was easily recognizable as Chancellorsville, Virginia. When she moved to rearrange herself in the chair, I could see she was reading *I Rode with Stonewall* by Henry Kyd Douglas.

A frump maybe, but a smart frump. The books this woman was reading were not lightweights. Kind of made sense that Dr. Laurent's daughter would be a nerdy type! LOL.

Ah hummm. … I tried to cough to get her attention. Didn't work.

A second cough had no effect.

Finally, I reached out my hand over the crowded table and said; "Hello, I am Parks Walter."

Slowly she raised her head slightly, turning towards me her blue eyes peering over the tops of her glasses. She didn't say anything.

"May I assume you are Ms. Jeanne Marie Laurent?" I said with a smile.

"And why would you presume that?" She snapped.

I didn't expect that. "Ah, I am sorry, ma'am I would not have come over here if the waitress had not insisted. I am here to meet some old librarian, and well I thought I heard the waitress call you Jeanne Marie. …" I started to fumble with the chair, trying to get up.

"So, you are not Sherlock Holmes then?" She said with a slight smile.

Dang, another lady that could shift gears quicker than my 'vette.

I fell back into the seat. "No, I am not Sherlock Holmes. However, some of your reading materials kind of gave me indications you might be Dr. Laurent's daughter." I said hoping a return smile would be accepted. I couldn't tell what this lady would do next.

I picked up Hawking's book, "But this is not easy reading and not something most women would be interested in."

She slapped my hand, knocking the book from it. "Oh, that's just something I toy with, when I don't have anything better to read."

Then she extended her hand and said, 'Colonel Walter, I am Dr.

Jeanne Marie Laurent, pleased to meet you."

"And I you, ma'am. Have you ordered yet?" I asked.

"No," she said curtly with a kind of a giggle, "I don't eat lunch."

"You don't eat lunch?" I asked, "So what are you doing here?"

She had already returned to reading *I Rode with Stonewall*, "I had to, to meet you at the right time and place. ..." Odd answer I thought. She was gone, lost in the book.

I looked at the menu and decided on a Mexican lunch. When the waitress came back, I ordered, and when Jeanne Marie didn't look up, I asked the waitress if she knew what Miss Jeanne Marie drank? "Sweet tea," she responded. "Fine, please bring her one," as I handed the waitress the menu, "And a tall one for me too."

She stayed in the book. So, I wondered. Long ago in Gender Relations 101 I had learned that women are very cagey about looking at men. While men will just flat out stare at an attractive woman, women have learned never to reveal they are studying their prey. Was she lookin' at me?

After we exchanged first names, things loosened up a little. She asked about her father, Area 51, and what I did for a living. She seemed particularly interested in my experience as a Cobra pilot, and not really that impressed with my selection BY NASA for the astronaut program.

Finally, by the end of the meal she was looking me in the face. I could see her pretty features; her tanned skin, steely blue eyes behind her glasses, and a face that lit with a smile. She had a thin cute nose, and an almost angelic look about her. Her hair, in a bun, was blonde.

Just as the waitress brought up the ticket, which I took, Jeanne Marie asked;

"Parks, did my father give you a package for me?"

"Yes, it's in the car."

"Parks, if you could live one adventure, I mean one not presently on your schedule of space launches and all that, what would you choose?"

"Well, I have always been fascinated by the American Civil War, so maybe I would want to go back to that time."

"Hmm, interesting," Jeanne Marie said, "I think I may have read your book, *Changing History* — a thin line," she said, as she took a sip of her sweet tea.

"Really, you might be my second reader!" I said with a smile. I was surprised she would even know about my book. "Your father thought it had merit."

"I don't know if I buy your foundational premise, based on Providence, that God willed the South to lose," she said, "but of the ten events you identify which could have changed the course of the war, you certainly demonstrate a thorough knowledge of their consequence, and demonstrate it was a lot closer run affair than many people, even historians realize. You do a very good job of not saying which changes were most likely to result in victory for the South?"

I decided to parrot her dad, "Well, if Beauregard and Johnston had done what President Davis had ordered on the late afternoon of the Battle of First Manassas, we might be living in an independent South today."

"Yes, I thought that too," she said gathering her things, "but is there any other event you think could have changed the war?" She started to rise from her chair, not giving me a chance to answer her follow up question, "I really have to be getting back to the library. And, I have to pick up the package from you." She said with a sense of urgency.

I rose, left a tip on the table, and picked up the check quickly but was still several steps behind her when I turned to leave the table. She had darted elegantly through the complex of tables, chairs and customers to the hall that led to the front of the hotel.

The room had cleared some since I first arrived more than an hour ago, and the view of Ms. Laurent from behind was quite stimulating. She was slim, short, maybe 5' 4", wearing heels with a strap across the back, and black slacks to compliment her white blouse. The outline of her bra barely shown through, or was that my imagination? In that kind of outfit, the curves of a woman's body can be revealed, and in Jeanne Marie's case, she possessed a marvelous slim, but curvy figure. Her hips and shapely behind swayed to and fro when she walked. And, I even picked up a light perfume scent in her trail.

She waited for me at the register with a slight hint of impatience. But I had intentionally not closed the distance between us as she walked in front of me.

After paying, we walked down the dark corridor towards the lobby and the front door. I guess I was just used to it, but I prepared to be blasted by the heat I expected to feel when I opened the door. However, when I opened the door for her, it was still in the mid-seventies, with a slight breeze. I could not believe it.

"Which way is your car, Parks?"

I pointed off to the left, "Would you like me to carry some of those books and maps and things?"

"No, I got it." She said, almost pulling them away from me.

As we walked, she said almost in surprise, "Look at that 'vette, what a car!"

"That's mine," I said.

As we got closer, she could see the brown paper wrapped package in the passenger seat. She screamed as if she had been stabbed or something; "Parks!" She dropped her books and ran to the car.

"I don't believe you left that in an open car!" She yelled almost wounded, and bent over, reaching in to the car to grab the package.

Meanwhile, I was down on my knees picking up the scattering papers and the books, and maps.

She didn't even look back, walked straight across the road and up the stairs to the building that I thought was the courthouse. I was still down in the street picking up the last of the papers when she pulled a key from her pants, opened the door and went in.

After I collected everything, I rose and started on the same path, but when I got to the door it was locked. And though there was glass in the door, it was dark and I could not see in. I stood there waiting, assuming she would come back for me. When five minutes passed, and she hadn't come back, I figured I would start a reconnaissance around the huge building and look for another entrance.

I found the main entrance on the other side of the building, where the flag poles were, across the street from the hospital.

Up a half a story of stairs and into the front door I went. Again, my eyes had to adjust to the darker light. The inside of the building was a large cavern. Lights on iron arms stood out from the wall, just above the level of the top of the doors. A walkway of marble went all the way around the building, with office doors along the wall, and a stone banister of Texas pink marble on the inside. Titles for mayor, city manager, councilman in large dark lettering were printed on smoked glass on the upper half of the door. The door handles were a shined brass.

This was a sharp looking municipal center.

But in the center was a large hole. Looking over the banister you could peer down one floor to what looked like a library. In the center there appeared to be a glass room, with large leather chairs and antique looking furniture and books. So now I had to walk the halls, searching

for the staircase that went down stairs. Fortunately, it was easily identified on the other side of the building.

A sign extended out on the wall right at the stairway.

The Library
Mayberry, Texas
July 15, 2012

I started down the stairs as they curved around and when I came out at the bottom, there was the library. An older woman stood behind a checkout counter. "Is Ms. Ah, I mean Dr. Laurent in?"

"Right here," she popped from behind me, "Follow me Parks," as she walked past me towards an office across the floor. The door was open and she went straight in and behind her desk, where she sat down. I followed, placing the books on her desk, some of them falling off the pile along with papers and the map in front of her. "Jeanne Marie, do you always run away from men?" I asked.

"Depends," she worked on straightening her papers. "Some men don't seem to know what's important," she said in a hushed sound.

"If you are referring to that package, you are right. Your father never told me anything about it. I assumed it was a book, or gift or something."

Jeanne Marie glanced up, a little startled. "Well, it is a family heirloom, worth a lot of money and more emotion; I thought Dad would ask you to take good care of it?"

"He did, Jeanne; it was in my front passenger seat, wasn't it?"

"Yes, in a car with its top off!" She said, obviously upset.

"OK, … sorry, no one told me it was a national treasure." I started to get up, figured this was over and I had done my duty and now could head off to Houston.

"No, don't go Parks, it's just I have been a little nervous lately, a lot going on. Wouldn't you like to look through the library?"

"Well, I don't have much time, Jeanne, I figured I would try to get to Dallas tonight, and then on to Houston tomorrow."

"What, no … that won't do," she said. You would think she was my mom or a schoolmaster.

"Parks, I have been looking forward to your visit, there is a lot to talk about. I was going to make you a steak tonight out at my place, and you could stay in the bunkhouse." She said.

"Ummm, Jeanne, I never thought of. …"

"Parks, Dad told me you have like a week to get to Houston. I was really hoping you would talk to me about your book. You never answered my question about the battle. …"

Just then the phone rang on her desk. It was an old rotary phone. Not something you see too often anymore. Jeanne picked it up; "Hello? Oh, that's right, I will be out in a minute."

"Look Parks, there is a lot to see here. If you will walk out with me, I will ask one of my girls to show our Civil War collection upstairs. I have something to take care of, and then I can show you some other things I think you will be very interested in. And then we can go to my ranch Three Pines for dinner, what do you say?"

I wasn't sold yet, "Jeanne. …"

She looked at me, batted those baby blues, smiled and said, "Good, we can take a dip in the pool before dinner. Follow me, and I will have Kelly take you to the collection."

This lady was something. I was saying no, she took it as yes, and before I knew it she was introducing me to Kelly. "Kelly, take Colonel Walter to the Civil War Collection, and make sure you show him all the original books, and the artifacts. Stay with him, 'til I can get up there." And with that Jeanne Marie turned and headed to the front desk where some men were waiting for her.

Kelly was another blonde, thirty something, slender with long blonde hair on her shoulders. She put her arm through mine and said, "Let's walk this way. …" It was that easy, and I was hooked. Southern women have several weapons in addition to the usual woman. We learned that in Gender Relations 201 (Advanced) for the gifted learners. Southern ladies could sweet talk you out of an air conditioner in August. That sweet Southern accent, when deployed with batting eyes and a smile, was lethal.

"So rumor has it you are an astronaut, is that right noble sir?" Kelly said, her Texas twang as sweet a molasses.

"What?"

"Yes sir, people saw your car when it came into the square. We have seen those type tags on bumpers before. The town cop ran your plates, and within the first hour you were here we knew you were Colonel Walter," she said it so matter-of-factly, like you can't put nothin' past us here on Rebel Mountain.

"I see," I said as we walked up a pair of stairs catty corner from the one I came down. "This leads to the Civil War Collection?"

"Yes, two stories up! I like getting my exercise this way." And, so we walked up two flights of steps. The exit on the first floor was not there, just a wall. When I pointed to it, Kelly said, "You have to understand the Civil War Collection is extremely valuable. There is only one way in and one way out."

As we topped the stairs, we walked through a doorway into a small two story room. On the second floor was a walkway all the way around which provided access to four walls worth of book shelves. On the first floor there were a number of tables and chairs, large old books, and in the far corner a tall four-sided glass display. Inside the display was a Confederate officer's uniform. I immediately started walking towards it.

"I thought that would catch your eye, Colonel," said Kelly.

The jacket was obviously an infantry officer's because of the blue collar. Two gold stars on the collar and the gold braid on each sleeve indicated it was a colonel's blouse. At the base of the display was a brass metal plaque inscribed;

Presented to Mayberry Library, Mayberry, Texas
By Andy Griffith
May 3, 1987 to commemorate the 125th Anniversary of the Battle of Chancellorsville.

"What is that doing here?" I said. "Andy Griffith, are you kidding me?"

"No Colonel, that coat has been here from long before I got here. Look at those buttons, those are North Carolina buttons on that jacket!" Said Kelly. "And lookie here on the wall, in this framed photo is Dr. Laurent, Ms. Laurent, and Andy Griffith and the coat. I am told they placed that coat in there that day, and it has never been removed since."

That's what the article kind of indicated. It didn't say why Andy Griffith had traveled all the way to Mayberry, Texas from North Carolina to bring the jacket. It only said that Andy Griffith and Nash were friends.

On one of the walls was an original painting of the tragic night Stonewall Jackson was fired on by troops from the 18th North Carolina Volunteers. I had never seen that painting before in all the books and museums I have ever been in. Underneath the painting was a plaque reading:

"A night that will forever live in infamy in Dixie."

The paintings had two focal points, the flash of rifles and the image of the mounted Jackson in front of others on his staff. Around the dark picture were scattered lights, cannons firing, individual rifles going off, all seeming like stars around the central image of a calm Jackson.

I stood there in disbelief. Every Civil War buff or student knows the incident well. Chancellorsville, the greatest victory for Lee, but the cost, … the loss of Stonewall and the war.

"Colonel, … Colonel" Kelly was trying to bring me out of my stupor.

"Ah … yes," I looked at her confused.

"Colonel, should I get you a glass of water, maybe some iced tea?"

"Sweet tea," I heard Jeanne Marie's voice as she entered the room.

"Yes ma'am, anything for you?"

"No Kelly, thanks."

Kelly skedaddled out of the room as Jeanne Marie walked up to me. "Now aren't you glad you came up here?"

"I can't believe this, Jeanne Marie, I still have not accepted it all. Let me sit down."

The room looked like an old English study. Thousands of books stood silent, paintings which told the glory, deep sadness and tragedy of the South. Around the room, scattered here and there, were sabers, pistols, a parched document. In one corner hung a portrait of Major Dick Dowling, in another a painting of Sam Houston.

There on one wall, a large painting of the bay side of Galveston, showing the Yankees fighting from their dock fort, while their ships fired on the city and engaging the two Confederate Cottonclads built near Houston. Those two Cottonclads would drive the Yankee ships out into the Gulf of Mexico and secure the victory on the morning of January 1st, 1863.

And then of course, a painting of the Battle of Sabine Pass where Lt. Dick Dowling and the forty-eight Irish Catholic Texans, with only six cannon, defeated a Yankee invasion fleet of five thousand soldiers and twenty two ships. Hanging off the walls above were banners of Texas during the war.

You could smell the history of the books, the oldness, the slow decay of ink and paper.

"Here's your tea, sir," Kelly said as she handed it to me.

"Now don't set that down on the wood," Jeanne Marie warned, "I never allow drinks in here, but you are a special guest." Here, she drew a white lace hanky from her sleeve and placed it on the cherry wood table next to me.

"Jeanne, this is amazing. I mean I have never seen so much present-ed in such an overwhelming fashion before. …"

"My name is Jeanne Marie, Parks, and you have not seen even half of it yet. We have original letters from the sailors on the C.S.S. *Alabama* after its fight with the U.S.S. *Hatteras* off the Texas coast. We have a great painting of Admiral Semmes after the war, which is being re-framed."

"I could stay here for days," I said.

"Now that's what I was hoping you would say," Jeanne Marie said as she sat down in a leather chair beside me. Kelly had left the room while Jeanne Marie was talking about the *Alabama*. "You may stay in the bunkhouse out at our ranch as long as you like, Parks. You can start your research in here tomorrow if you want? You will have free access to everything we have."

In my mind somewhere there was a date in Galveston, not one I was going to make.

"Our afternoon is nearly half shot, Parks, and there is another room I want you to see. Are you OK to get up?" She said almost as if she were a nurse in a senior citizen home.

"You have more?" I said.

"Yes, downstairs, let's go."

We got up and headed down the stairs I had first walked up with Kelly. "Jeanne Marie, what's up with Andy Griffith, why was he here? How would your father know him?"

"My father met Andy in North Carolina before Andy was Andy. Though my dad was younger than him, maybe five years, Andy took a liking to my dad. When Andy made it big, my father got to go on the set for Mayberry. He met little Ronnie Howard, and Uncle Jimmy Neighbors. My dad and Don never got along too well, but dad always spoke well of Don as a professional actor."

Our feet made sounds as we tramped down two floors of steps back into the main part of the library.

"Parks, I want to take you into a vaulted area where we have some of our most precious items."

More precious than what I just left, how could that be I thought.

Jeanne Marie took me to a special room, the glass room which sat in the middle of the main library room the one I had seen from the hallway of the floor above.

It had a large door with smoked glass and ornate etching. The door was made of brass, or bronze and I thought it would be very heavy to open, but surprisingly it was not. The scent of cigar filled my nostrils as I entered the room, but there were no ashtrays, or any evidence of recent smoke.

The room was cool, and dry, the carpet a dark red. Dark, highly polished wood dominated the room. Bookshelves filled with what appeared to be old classics. Off in the far corner was a piece of furniture dedicated to just one, rather large, old, closed book and a large metal magnifying glass, held by a chain.

On a platform, under glass, was an open newspaper. A quick glance told me it was the *Carolina Gazette* from Salem, North Carolina, dated in April, 1861.

Jeanne Marie led me around the table and chairs to this distinct piece of furniture.

"Parks, I believe this is a book you will find most interesting," she said as she pointed to it. "During lunch you told me if you could live one adventure, one unbelievable, unimaginable trip it would be back in time, to witness history. This book may have been written for you."

Jeanne Marie's voice drifted away to quiet, the thoughts hanging.

I looked down on the book, almost afraid to touch it. The cover was an old, darkish red cloth with words written in some kind of gold. It was hard to make out the words. Except for the bottom where the name Dr. Nash Laurent was still visible.

The pages were no longer perfectly flat, but rather seemed to have a kind of bumpy, sharp surface, almost as if they had been wet, and then dried. The words were written in long hand rather than neat print. I thought this could be some kind of diary, or notebook.

I began reading Dr. Laurent's notes.

In 1901, divers were working off the coast of the Greek island Antikythera, near Crete, found the hull of ancient Greek ship and were excavating the find. After weeks of diving and the work it took to remove the almost two millennium of sand and debris from inside the wreck, they found a large rusted metallic device. They took great care to bring it to the surface making every effort to preserve it in the condition found.

They had no idea what they had discovered. The item was named the Antikythera Mechanism after the location of its discovery. (Throughout his work, Laurent referred to this as the Alpha M, or

Alpha Mechanism.) This ancient piece is believed to have been constructed in the second century B.C. It is made of bronze and is a primitive computer — calendar used to forecast the astrological movements of some planets and stars. The complexity of this device would not be matched for almost twenty centuries!

The remains of this treasure are at the Greek National Archaeological Museum in Athens. It is alleged to be the most complex machine of antiquity ever discovered. Mainstream science believes the mechanism is used to predict the motion of the planets.

Dr. Nash Laurent, an American geologist, saw the Antikythera Mechanism, or Alpha mechanism while he was working in the Middle East. He was very interested in a symbol that had seemed unimportant to others. He took notes, in his personal notebook, and did drawings in his own hand of the Mechanism, including all the identifiable symbols.

Dr. Laurent had made extensive drawings of this mechanism. It was rectangular in shape with a number of bronze discs, or gears, with symbols adorning each disc like the numbers on a clock, though the symbols were more like drawings then numbers. His drawings below the largest one, were the individual discs, with great detail in the drawing of the symbols.

Jeanne Marie saw me looking at the drawings and jumped in to explain: "This mechanism does more than predict the alignment of the planets. The previously unrecognizable symbol (she pointed to it) was studied by Dad and others; they determined its purpose. This purpose is a very tightly held secret."

She went on, "The symbol appears only in a very few analogs, and when scientists originally identified this symbol, it was thought to do no more than fill a place in the order of alignment to make the rest of the calculations work. It would be years before the meaning of the symbol was understood."

"So, what are you saying Jeanne Marie? What does this predict?"

"Parks, this tool predicts the coming of a wormhole to earth."

Silence. Wormhole? You mean those things theoretical physicists talk about that no one has ever seen?

"What Jeanne Marie? What the heck are you talking about?"

"My dad discovered the meaning of the symbol. It represents a wormhole event on earth. One that touches earth on a predictable basis in terms of when."

Staggered again. How many times in one day? Getting a little hard to breath in here.

Jeanne Marie kind of laughed a little, I guess when my skin turned pale she found it amusing. "Parks, I am giving you a lot to absorb in a real short period of time. The day's about over, maybe we should head to Three Pines?"

"Three Pines?"

"Yes, Three Pines, my ranch? Remember, dinner? A bunkhouse? The pool?"

"Oh yea, sure. Uh huh … yea I got all that." I was shaking my head. No day in NASA introduced as much new reality to me as hit me in the face today. And the day wasn't over yet.

"Good Parks, let me go get my things in the office, let the girls know I am leaving, and we can be off." Jeanne Marie guided me out the door of the glass room, and out, sounded like it locked when the door closed.

"Be right back." She went off towards her office.

I had never had an afternoon like this. Even at Area 51, even when they told us they had actually produced anti-matter, and discovered the God particle at CERN in Switzerland. Nope, nothing like this before.

When Jeanne Marie came back, she was struggling, trying to carry the books, and the package from her dad. I grabbed the books from her and followed her up the stairs to the first floor. She did have a nice posterior. I always wondered what women were thinking when they had a guy walking behind them, walking up stairs.

We walked around the building and out the door.

She walked out towards a Jeep, while I headed for the 'vette. I watched from behind, smiling and thinking I thought she was a "frump," what a fool. She turned and looked towards me standing by my 'vette when she got to her truck. I waved, she waved back, and pointed in the direction she was heading.

Three Pines
Rebel Mountain, Texas
July 15, 2012

I followed Jeanne Marie in her green Jeep out of town on a lazy, shaded country road. It was so weird; you would have thought you were in the mountains in Carolina in the spring. It was mid-seventies, shady; a nice drive after the hours and hours in the unbearable July heat of Texas and the sparse geography from Area 51 to Mayberry.

She turned left off the road at an iron gate sign, Three Pines. There were several horses in a pasture off to our right as we drove down the path further into her property. The horses didn't even look up, just kept munching on their dinner, lush green grass.

As we made a wide left turn around a stand of three full blue spruce pines, Jeanne Marie's home came into sight. It was a beautiful old Southern mansion. Not something I would have expected in west Texas! At least two stories, white with four white Greek columns spread equally along the porch. A balcony ran across the front and down the sides of both floors. A Confederate Third National flag snapped on a pole off one of the center columns.

The doors were open on the second floor. Someone seemed to be moving around up there. By the time we pulled up to the front steps leading to the door, the front door was opening. Low and behold it was Dr. Laurent.

The drive ran right up to the front of the house and then looped back on itself. Jeanne Marie pulled right up to the front steps. I pulled up behind Jeanne Marie and shut down the 'vette.

I got out of the car before her, stood and stretched. I took a look around, trying to get a visual map in my mind, a layout of the place. Off to my left rear was a stable and corral we had driven by coming in. Off to the right front, some distance from the house, was a barn and a windsock, indicative of a runway or landing zone. Have to go take a look over there some time.

"Hi honey, I see you brought him home just like you said you would." Dr. Laurent walked down the steps to Jeanne Marie and gave her a hug.

"And how are you, Colonel Walter?" His hand outstretched towards me.

Stunned too many times to care, "I am fine, Dr. Laurent. ..."

"Call me Nash, son. Too many titles here for no purpose."

With one of us on each arm he said, "Let's go sit on the porch and partake of a Mint Julip, I just made a pitcher myself. Jeanne Marie had called in time to let me know you both were on your way."

I looked at Jeanne Marie, boy was she sly; always a step ahead.

"Dr. ... Nash, after today I do need a drink, maybe a couple."

Nash and Jeanne Marie laughed as we walked arm in arm up onto the porch. The breeze was blowing and it was still in the mid-seventies. The sun shown bright on the pasture with the horses, but there was no sun on the porch as it was blocked by the trees we had driven around.

"Just a regular day..."

Cool and calm was gone: "Dr. Laurent, are you kidding me? I start off driving down a road that disappears under my wheels as I drive over it. Then I am on a green mountain in the middle of the desert, and the temperature drops twenty degrees ..."

"Thirty ..." leaning in, Jeanne Marie sneaks in a word.

Almost like a queue, I turn towards Jeanne Marie; "Then I meet Jeanne Marie and she shows me the Civil War Collection, and Andy Griffith, and then she takes me into the glass room and I read your diary. ... "I collapse into a chair and take the tall glass being handed to me by Dr. Laurent, filled with ice, a green mint leaf and whiskey and take a long pull. And then cough ... not used to drinking straight bourbon without a water cutter.

"Well Parks, if you are up for it, there's a lot more to learn???"

No doubt it was a question. But more? What else? Now I finally understood Alice in Wonderland. For me, that was always just a little too far. But this beat that by miles.

"Doc, I got one question. ..."

"Yes" he said with a smile as he took a draw on his drink.

"Is there a large rabbit in this?" I took a drink as he almost choked on his. Jeanne Marie kind of giggled and then laughed out loud. I think they both got it.

The two of them sat down at the table and Jeanne Marie told her father about our afternoon and added; "The men we expected did show up, Dad, I will tell you about it later." The two chatted while I drank at least two tall ones.

"Let's head to the kitchen and start dinner." Jeanne Marie said as she rose from the table and headed towards the front door.

When I stood up the impact of the straight whiskey, combined with the long drive and the afternoon's events hit me. I wasn't drunk, but I was exhausted.

"Woow," and I fell back into the chair.

Nash turned to see me, my head in my hands.

"You have had a long day, boy. Maybe we should change direction and head for the bunkhouse. You can crash there."

Three Pines
Rebel Mountain, Texas
July 16, 2011

I woke up the next morning spread over the made bunk. I had on only my pants, and it took a minute to remember where I was. I didn't have a headache, so I didn't think I had a drunk the night before. In fact, I felt pretty good, refreshed. Opened my eyes and kind of looked around. It looked like, and smelt, like a large log cabin. There were three double bunkbeds, a table with some chairs. There was a refrigerator along the wall, over by a sink and some cabinets.

My bag was over on another bunk, and my shirt hanging on the back of a chair.

Opps, need to see if they have a restroom in this place?

The restroom was complete and I took the opportunity to shower, shave and clean up. It was only a little before eight when I heard a car leave. I finished dressing and headed out the door towards the main house. There on the front porch I could see Nash seated at the table drinking a cup of coffee. As usual he was in his white slacks, white shirt and red suspenders.

"Good morning Parks, feeling better?" he said in a kind of chipper way.

"Yes sir, fine. I can't believe how pleasant it is here, after months in the scorching heat of Area 51."

"Yes, there are real advantages to Rebel Mountain. How 'bout we move inside, you can get a cup of coffee while I make some breakfast?"

As we walked through the large white door into the plantation-like home I had to ask: "Nash, tell me about this strange place. If I remember right, and didn't drink too much last night before I passed out, I would swear I remember turning off US 280 onto a dirt road that literally disappeared as I drove it. But that can't be. ..." I shook my head.

We continued to walk through a large central hallway, past a central staircase, back through an entrance way into a modern kitchen.

"Parks, Rebel Mountain and Mayberry are a very special place. I think Jeanne Marie showed you my first diary in the glass room, didn't she?" Nash was getting out the eggs, butter and other things it takes to make breakfast.

"Yes," I answered as I sipped coffee. "That's some story, but I was asking you about Rebel Mountain. ..."

Nash was a master of getting the kitchen ready to cook, looked like we were having bacon and eggs … but the eggs were being made a special way: "I know and that first diary leads to the second, the one which explains Rebel Mountain."

Nash was buttering bread on both sides, cutting holes in the center and then placing the bread on a flat griddle he had made the bacon on. He then broke the eggs into the holes.

"The story goes like this: I was working in South America in the 1970s, when I happened to cross paths with a little-known German writer and explorer, Erich von Daniken. We spent some time together taking in the culture and women, and drinks. von Daniken and I discussed the Alpha Mechanism you read about yesterday. He was intrigued. Maybe to one up me, Erich revealed to me his discoveries on the Nazca Plain."

With a twinkle in his eye, Nash said "Jeanne Marie found it interesting that von Daniken estimated the Nazca Lines to be constructed between 200 B.C., and 700 A.D., about the same time as the making of the Alpha Mechanism."

He went on: "But the real prize was yet to come. Erich made the startling proposal that because the lines could only be clearly seen from the sky, that these lines could be directional, or identification markers for extra-terrestrials."

Nash explained that the lines, which had been built in the desert between the towns of Nazca and Palpa, (80 Km apart) on Pampas de Jumana in Peru, held the secret to the second part of time travel. Nash had taken the compass direction of the east and west exterior lines of the plain.

"These lines" he said, "crossed the equator and intersected north of the Rio Grande. The point of intersection of the lines was here, on Rebel Mountain, not too far from what is now Mayberry." He finished flipping the eggs held in the bread, and placed them on the plates. He then added the bacon, and pointed to the table. He had a plate in each hand. "Grab some silverware" he said, pointing to a drawer with his head.

I opened the drawer grabbing the silverware quickly and said; "So the lines at Nazca intersect here?"

"That's right," as he placed the plates on the table and sat down.

"And time travel?" I asked, looking at him with a dropped jaw.

"Oh sorry," he said, "I got ahead of myself. Let's pray … "he bowed his head "Almighty Father, for what we are about to receive may we be truly thankful, amen."

"Amen," I echoed quietly as he invited "dig in."

I was hungry so I dove into the eggs in toast or whatever it was. Mmmm, delicious. This was one big cholesterol bomb. Nash or Jeanne Marie had anticipated we would be eating breakfast there, a pitcher of ice-cold orange juice and some juice glasses were already on the table.

He looked over, "Like your bull's eyes?"

"Delicious"

It was Dr. Nash Laurent's work that finally established the meaning of the symbol on the Antikythera Mechanism. The symbol actually identifies precisely when an intra-dimensional worm hole, which allows a ship to enter the Time River, will appear.

"Time River?" I asked.

"That's what I call it," he said, "… more accurately it is the Dark Matter Universe."

These conversations just keep getting wilder and wilder. The look on my face must have told him he would have to do better than that.

"Parks, this gets very … almost unbelievable, but we had the best minds we can find on this for years. It turns out at least two different universes are intermingled … the one we know, and the one we don't know. And in places they seem to cohabit in the same space. Where there are galaxies, we can see they rest co-mingled with a Dark Matter universe that is everywhere."

Dark Matter and Dark energy are not new concepts for me, but what Nash is explaining are concepts I have never heard before.

Nash went on, "Parks, think of a piece of paper … and then a coffee stain on the paper. The paper is complete from end to end, but the stain is part of the paper where it exists on the paper. That's best way to understand this … and it's why the planets and asteroids and other space materials could hit your ship when you are inside the reverse neutron shield in the Time River."

And now I find from Nash that it was the Nazca Lines which brought him to Rebel Mountain.

He looked at me. I put my hand up to indicate to him, give me some time to absorb and consider what you have said. After some time I asked: "So Doc, what's up with this place. I mean you have to admit there are some strange goings-on here."

"I can't argue with you there, Parks. All I know is when I need a road to leave here there is one, and when I need a road to get back, there is one. The weather is always perfect as long as I count occasional rains as a good thing."

"So how come no one knows about this oddity?" I asked. But I knew when I asked, he wasn't gonna say anything. I could just feel it. Moments passed in silence.

"OK what will you tell me?"

"Parks, I have been working for most of my life on this project, one that has already begun. It took decades to create a large organization to solicit the finances necessary to bring together the minds and technologies necessary to travel back in time. What you are seeing is the culmination of all the work," Nash said.

He went on: "The third part of the time travel is a device, or more like a series of devices that provide propulsion, navigation in the river of time and a shield around the craft to deal with forces inside this new dimension," Nash said.

"This device is what will allow me to go from Three Pines here, to my destination, to another specific point in space-time." Entered Jeanne Marie. Her shoes were so quiet. She had a large smile on her face. "Hi Dad," she gave him a hug.

Nash picked it back up, "The specifications for the system came from the original, unpublished, handwritten manuscript of H. G. Wells story, *The Time Machine*. In this manuscript, Wells attributes the drawings, specifications and calculations required to make the devices to travelers whom he met while touring Europe".

"He met these travelers in the Alps, but he does not provide much information about them or the meetings he had with them."

According to Nash the travelers told Wells that the information they were providing about the device was incomplete because the ship required a portal for travel which they could not tell him about. The travelers also told Wells that the other information necessary for space-time travel was available on earth. They indicated that the first pieces of information had come to earth around the 2nd century B.C.

The story was amazing!

If true, time travel might be possible.

"So how did you get the Wells' manuscript?" I asked.

"It gets a little complicated here, but interesting. H. G. Wells, when he was ten, had met the famous Admiral Raphael Semmes, of the Confederate States Navy. Wells was fascinated by Semmes, and the South. The Admiral is the one who made Wells aware of the power of technology. Though this is not generally known, the Confederacy was very interested in the cutting-edge technologies of the time. Did you know the Confederacy was the first nation to use the micro dot to transmit secrets?" Nash laughed, "Parks, do you know what a micro dot is?"

"No, I think that was before my time," I answered.

"Well, the Confederacy was like one hundred years ahead of its time," said Nash.

Nash went on to explain that after Wells' time travel story made it big, he ran into one of the Admiral's adult children in Britain. As an expression of Wells affection and respect for the Admiral, he gave the original manuscript to the Admiral's son.

"The Semmes family retained the book until they became aware of my work. They contacted me, and generously offered to loan it to the Mayberry Library for as long as we needed it." "

It's still there if you want to look at it," Jeanne Marie said.

"So, could you make out the device?" I asked.

"Devices," Nash quipped.

"Devices?" I said.

"The drawings were so precise; it was as if someone intended them to be the actual plans, to be used by a mechanical engineer to construct the various devices." Nash said, "When I realized these were real, or at least appeared to be real, my life changed."

"So, is that what you were working on back at Area 51?" I asked, expecting nothing less than an affirmative.

There was a silence. I looked up.

Nash nodded, no. Perplexed, I continued to look at him.

"Parks, this is not a government op. Great pains have been made to keep this out of the federal loop."

Why would I think anything different … I thought to myself.

"But I thought you said this was a big operation?"

"It is."

"Private sector?" I asked

"You could say that," Nash got up, picked up the dishes and headed for the sink.

"And what did you mean by devices?" I asked.

"There are many aspects to time travel, Parks. First you have to access the time-space dimension, or river; that requires the window the Alpha Mechanism predicts, but to survive there requires a reverse neutron field, to remove you from this dimension, while maintaining a habitable environment," Dr. Nash said.

"A reverse neutron field?"

"Yes, Parks. All neutrons in this reality spin in one direction. The reverse neutron field is composed of neutrons spinning in the opposite direction ... create a field of those, step inside it, and poof ... you are out of this reality ... for the most part."

"OK," I said, acting like I understood what he just said, "... and what are the other devices?"

A female voice went on: "Direction and speed, moving forward or backward in time, and at what velocity? Velocity relies on a harmonic propulsion system, the higher the harmony you move forward, the lower, you move backward. The degree of higher or lower increases or decreases your speed of travel."

Jeanne Marie must have tiptoed into the kitchen as her dad finished his sentence. "Did you sleep well?" Jeanne Marie asked me as Nash walked away.

"Like a rock," I said ... not even really hearing her, and completely mesmerized by the stuff I was trying to comprehend, but didn't. Dr. Nash had just given me the short course in time travel ... equal in complexity to quantum physics, and yet ... it sounded almost simple.

"Did Dad show you around the house?"

"Huh, Noooo."

"Well, let me have that pleasure, I am pretty proud of our home." With that, Jeanne Marie got up and motioned for me to follow her.

"Dad, you gonna take care of the dishes?" She patted him on the head as she went by him.

I followed Jeanne Marie out of the kitchen into the main hall. Today she was in a summer dress which flowed easily as she walked. She was wearing heels, and I found myself surprised that I didn't hear her coming earlier.

She pointed to a large painting of a Confederate officer on the wall. "That is my great-great grandfather Major Laurent of the Louisiana Tigers! They served with ..."

"General Lee," I said.

She turned smiling, her dress flaring out as she swung around, "That's right Parks. I forgot about your expertise in the war."

Jeanne Marie grabbed my arm and led me to a large doorway

beside the painting: "This is our formal sitting room or parlor, some of this furniture is more than a century old." The room was filled with several formal couches and chairs, end tables, vases, and paintings on the wall." Three tall rectangular windows, each with white sheer curtains running down the side of each gave the room its own open character. The view out the windows was beautiful, a rose garden, further out the trees swayed in the breeze.

The rest of the tour I was only half there, though I do remember walking down the staircase.

I was thinking about everything Nash had told me, trying to figure out exactly what he was doing, and how far along this project he was. Time travel was something you only ever heard about in the movies, or on Sci Fi shows on television.

We ended up back in the central foyer.

"Dad, I have to get back to the library," she yelled towards the kitchen as she led me out the front door. "Sorry Parks, but I have things I have to take care of. If you need anything just ask Dad. As you saw from my bedroom, the pool is in the back, take a swim if you like. I will get back here as fast as I can. I still owe you a steak." And with that she was in her Jeep, started the engine and sprang around the loop and down the driveway behind the trees and out onto the road.

I decided to head to the bunkhouse, change into my swim suit, and head for the pool, might as well take advantage of the offer. I spent the rest of the morning in the pool or laying on one of the chase lounges enjoying the sun and the mid-eighties temperature. Every once in a while, the breeze would kick up, I would hear the whinny of horses and feel the cool air against my tanning skin. I dozed off for a while.

The next thing I heard was glass on metal; it was Nash bringing out a pitcher of lemonade and some glasses.

"Hi Parks, thought we could have lunch out here."

"Fine sir," I said instinctively, I wasn't even awake yet.

"Be right back." Nash had turned, headed into the house and came back out in moments with two plates. "We will probably have a heavy dinner, so I thought some cold tomato and bean salad would work."

"Fine with me, sir."

"After we eat, if you want to we can go catch us a couple of horses and go for a ride this afternoon. Do you ride?"

"A couple of times," I lied, "but I am no cowboy."

"That's OK, Parks," I will talk you through it. We have some good horses here, I think Whiskey will work fine for you," he said with a smile.

"Whiskey?"

"Yes, he's a solid mount, strong headed, but a good horse. He matches your personality and can carry your weight."

We finished lunch, and Nash told me to go and change. I started towards the door which would lead me through the house to the front door: "Do you have a pair of boots, Parks?"

"Uhhh, not with me,"

"What size are you?"

"8 ½"

"Close enough." He chuckled some. Under his breath I heard him say, "We are going to have to get him some boots."

I heard his comment as I started through the kitchen. Figured I would shower and change into jeans and a golf shirt. Never had ridden before, so this would be an experience, I thought.

The Stable, Three Pines
Rebel Mountain, Texas
July 16, 2012

Ten minutes later I was heading out the door in my dockers, no socks headed to the house. When I got there, Nash was on the porch sippin' a lemonade, a pair of high black boots on the table. "Where's your socks?" Nash said.

"Don't need 'em."

"Ok but these are nines." Nash said.

'That's OK, they should be big enough." I said, "I could wear my dockers?"

"Nah, I don't think that's a good idea. We'll just have to work with what we've got. I could get a pair of my socks?" He offered.

"No."

"OK," he said with a kind of exaggerated voice, "You may wish you had considered them. Let's take a walk down to the horse barn, grab the boots."

As we walked, Nash decided to give me a quick course on horse psychology.

"You ever ridden before?"

"No." I replied, forgetting my previous white lie.

"Well Parks," Nash said, "you have to understand that a horse is a creature with a mind of its own, especially Whiskey, so in one sense you are going to have seduce him like you would a woman. You are gonna have to win his confidence."

"OK"

"Don't do any sudden movements. When you walk up to Whiskey be in front of him, and be deliberate. Oh, and a horse can sense fear, so you have to submerge that."

"Should I be afraid?" I asked. "Is the horse broken?"

"Of course he is, Jeanne Marie rides Whiskey all the time, but she smells better than you." Nash went on, "Whiskey knows Jeanne Marie, he don't know you. So be easy at first, you are gonna have to let him get used to you first."

We came up to the barn and out in the corral was a really beautiful horse, tan, strong looking legs. "That's Whiskey there." Said Nash. The horse kind of turned its head towards us when Nash said that. "Horses can sense mendacity, Parks, so always treat a horse nobly. They are a noble creature."

"Get that blanket over there," Nash said.

Nash led me to his horse," We'll work together on my horse, and then you can saddle yours up." It felt like he was teaching me or something. We got his horse done in a few minutes. Then he gave me a bridle and led me outside into the corral to Whiskey and the fun started.

I circled around Whiskey to get in front of him, and then approached him at a slow but deliberate pace. He was munching on some hay and didn't take much notice of me. I started rubbing the large flank of his neck. "Hello Whiskey I am Parks," I said. He kept eating. While I rubbed his neck I observed the flank of this horse. He was good sized, I figured six or seven hundred pounds, maybe more; and in great condition.

Finally he turned towards me, and I rubbed the top of his head between his eyes; "Hi, you are a fine one aren't you?" I rubbed behind his ears and figured maybe I could try to put the bridle on. I put the bit to his teeth. I was surprised without too much protest it slid right in his mouth.

But when I attempted to pull the harness up over his head he stepped back and pulled his head away. I stepped forward, tried again, and he stepped away again. He led me around the corral. Nash stood off watching, smiling. "Just stay with him, he likes you."

He evaded me a couple more times before I finally got it. His eyes were constantly on me and I remembered Nash telling me a horse could sense your fear. I was a little nervous, but tried to chase those bugs out of my mind. Once bridled, I threw on the blanket and threw the saddle on Whiskey. He moved around a little, but not too much. It took me a little while to thread the girt through the d ring, and then had to tie it off.

"Good job Parks, you need to get them boots on so you can mount him, and I can help you set the stirrups."

"How 'bout I just go with the dockers."

Nash frowned, looked like he was thinking, and then said, "Your call. Think you can get your left foot up high enough to get it in that stirrup?"

Nash mounted first easily, I watched, and followed his example. "Got the reins in your hand?"

"Sure." Didn't look that high. But when I raised my leg I found it was a lot higher than I thought. Had trouble getting my foot to the stirrup, and when I did I felt exposed, off balance and unsure. The first time I kicked off with my right leg, I wasn't even close to getting high enough to swing my leg over Whiskey's back, and my foot came down to the ground. Whiskey made a kind of sound, I could see him thinking, "oh another first-time rider!"

"Try again," Nash said with encouragement, "think yourself up."

I understood what Nash was saying. I visualized myself rising off the ground and swinging my leg over the horse. I took a breath, up and over, my butt seated in the saddle for the first time. It took a minute to find the stirrup for my right foot.

"Nice job." Nash said, "OK, now, we will go for a ride right here in the corral." Nash talked me through controlling Whiskey with the reigns and my feet. It didn't take long before I was directing Whiskey around in a circle. After a couple times around the corral Nash asked; "OK, ready to head out on the trail?"

"Sure," I said keeping my eye on Whiskey's neck.

"OK, follow me," Nash headed to the gate, lifted the rope off the fence and pushed open the gate, slowly walking his horse out. I followed with Whiskey. At first, I followed but after a time Nash dropped back beside me.

"How do you feel?"

"Well, OK, I guess," I said, "I have a bad left knee and I feel some real strain on it."

"Should have had the boots," Nash said. "We will just do a brief ride this afternoon. Maybe I can get Jeanne Marie to get you a pair of boots."

"Maybe I could do that this afternoon?"

"Fine, I think Jeanne Marie wants to ride with you tonight." Nash said.

We rode through the greenish gold pasture, grasses up to the flank of the horse. The dockers had been a mistake as the sheaves of grass reached up and cut my legs, and bugs would get on my bare skin. I tried not to say anything. Couldn't help but think to myself there is more to this cowboy stuff then they let you know in the movies.

After a short while we turned around and started back. Off to my right I could see a runway, the plane, and a large barn. "You fly, Nash?"

"Yep, we all do." He said.

"Yep?"

"Yes, me, Jeanne Marie, and my son Michael."

"Where's Michael?" I asked.

"He's in North Carolina." We rode through the open gate and when Nash dismounted, he saw the mess that was my lower legs, the blood and bugs. "Well, I will give you credit for handling discomfort and not saying anything. Parks, why don't you head to the bunkhouse and get cleaned up. I will take care of the horses."

He didn't have to ask me twice. When I dropped off Whiskey I almost fell to the ground. The muscles in my thighs and behind were tight, and aching from being stretched and my left knee was out of place. I had blown that knee out playing football, and never had it reconstructed.

I almost ran, hobbled fast from the horse stable to the bunkhouse, the last couple steps barefoot on rocks and dirt. I stripped down my jeans as I went through the doorway, and headed straight to the showers, pulling off my shirt. The blood trickled down my legs as I swatted at the bugs on lower legs.

The shower took a while, I even stepped out of it to get a wooden chair to put it in so I could sit and wash off the lower parts of my legs real good and inspect the damage. It wasn't as bad as I thought. Razor cuts by the grass. The bug bites were swollen and red. When I got out of the shower, I searched the medicine cabinet above the sink and found Corn Huskers Lotion. What the heck, I applied it liberally to my legs.

As I dressed, I decided to put on a pair of socks, and decided it might be smart to listen to Nash if he recommends something. I was feeling the ache everywhere I walked. I finally understood why cowboys walked the way they did and were bow legged. I decided to head to town to see if I could find a place to buy a pair of boots. I grabbed my keys, and walked out the door towards the house. Nash was coming up from the stable.

"I am headed to town to go get me some boots, Nash, wanna come?"

"No, thanks, think I will go up and take a siesta. See ya when ya get back, Parks."

"OK," I jumped in the car and started her engine up. She sounded great. The trip in didn't take long at all, and I found a shop right off the square. Of course there was a pretty lady working the shop and she had to help me make the correct choice. I saw the ones I wanted in the first fifteen minutes, but it was an hour of trying different pairs on and talking to Mary Frances, the pretty girl, before I settled on the ones I first saw. I don't think it took me all of two hours to get my new boots and get back to Three Pines. As I pulled into Three Pines and drove up the long drive towards the house, I saw that barn and windsock again.

Pilot Mountain Photo by Stephen McNierney

The Alabama *approaching Pilot Mountain.*

The Adventure – Stolen Days

The Barn, Three Pines
Rebel Mountain, Texas
July 16, 2012

My curiosity was up to see the barn. I got out of my 'vette, left the boots in the car, and decided to take a stroll and check it out.

The barn was at the end of the runway. Beside it sat a fairly modern two engine Piper Navajo airplane, which I could only assume Jeanne Marie, or her father flew. Its colors were patriotic, red white and blue I thought, until I saw the Confederate Naval ensign and the words Confederate Air Force had been only lightly painted over, but not so much so that you couldn't see their shadows.

I had heard of the Confederate Air Force when I was a boy. It no longer existed because of a streak of political correctness. However in my childhood many of the planes in the Confederate Air Force were World War II vintage, and were flown at air shows.

The barn was old. The wood was a grayish color, no paint that I could see. And it was large. Larger than what you usually see in Texas, more like something in North Carolina. I peered in through one of the cracks. It was dark, and at first I did not see much. The glare from the sun required time for the eye to re-adjust when looking into a dark area. But as my "night vision" came up I started to make out a familiar design inside.

No, it couldn't be?

Sure looks like one. Dang, that's a Hind helicopter! What the heck is that doing in there?

I started to work my way around the barn. I wanted to find a way in. It couldn't be. How could the Laurent's have an old Soviet Hind helicopter? I moved faster and faster around the building 'til I finally came up on the front doors. They were closed, but no locks. I pulled one back, and when I did the shafts of sunlight hit the nose of the bird. Almost sixty feet long, the Hind could travel above 200 miles per hour. This is a war bird, what are they doing with it? I continued my walk around the bird doing a pilot's inspection.

The Alabama

Modified HIND HELICOPTER Space–Time Ship

Now wait a minute, that's not a Hind nose, looks more like the nose of a space shuttle.

As I walked towards the craft, the prop hung down over the front confirming it was a helicopter. And while the front had been changed, the front was still mighty close to a Cobra. Except the nose, and then along the body, the bird was covered in the heat squares that they use on the Shuttles for re-entry into the earth's atmosphere!

Weird.

Still, it looked in tip-top condition. The prop material looked and felt different. But I am no mechanical engineer. And the front seat area of bird was filled with some kind of instruments.

In the location where the armament pods were normally attached, there were smaller, black boxlike attachments on the wings. These boxes had small red lights in the front, and what appeared to be almost porcupine hairs extending out of them.

There was a square like lump in the frame behind the rotor, and there seemed to be a hose which ran into the rotor which I had never seen on any version of a helicopter I had flown.

Off in the corner of the barn was a blackboard, a desk, a light. They must have used this area as a kind of office. I walked over to look at the diagrams drawn on the black board. Blackboard and chalk I thought to myself. I didn't think anyone had those any more.

The diagrams drawn on the blackboard were not easily read. I never saw some of the symbols before.

$T(p) = E$ reconfig $+ AE$ to/thru T (c)mirror $+ E$ for RN field for TR $+$ Nav./Propulsion to $T(p)$mirror $+ E$ reconfig.

$T© = AmE$ to/thru $T(p)$ mirror $+ AmE(-)$ for Nav./Acc to $T(c)$ mirror $+ E$ reconfig

Angle of exit $T©$ mirror 60% climb$(+)$

After looking at the formula for some time, I decided it was time to move on. I didn't get it. I found out later it was the transformation procedure for the ship.

I headed back towards the house, and my car.

My mind went back to time. Is time only one dimension? Is time only real in the present, now? Does the past disappear forever like a vapor that is gone? Is the past just a memory? If there were no one to remember it, or discover it, would it be gone forever? And the future, will it stop when we aren't living? I had never thought about time like this before. Everything else seemed to have more than one dimension, more than one way to look at it, experience it. Is time the only exception?

Walking back, I saw Nash was on the front porch sitting at the table with a couple of glasses and a pitcher.

"Parks, you looked at a one of kind, jerry-rigged machine intended to make a very unique trip. We have been working on it for years, decades actually in design. The tiles you saw on that bird are similar to the tiles on the space shuttle. They are put together tongue-in-grove, like putting in a floor with no spaces. And the propeller is so sophisticated, it is made from an advanced memory metal, something few people have even heard of. ..."

"Memory metal?" I asked almost silently, revealing I had no idea what he was talking about. I thought my clearance and work in NASA had me on the forefront of flight technology. But this thing, this contraption was way beyond any briefing I had, or any piece of machinery I had ever seen."

"Well, it's built to do something no one has ever done before. Memory metal can reshape itself back to an earlier state, shape."

Just about that time, behind me I heard a car coming up the drive. When I turned, it was Jeanne Marie. She pulled up, got out and grabbed a bag of groceries. "Could you grab that second bag, Parks? Hi, Pops! There's a package in the back seat for you, Dad."

"Sure, Jeanne Marie." I went down the stairs to the car, saw a fairly large box-like package, wrapped in brown paper. I picked up the bag, and turned and headed up the stairs following Jeanne Marie's wake.

We spent the next couple of hours fixing up dinner, steaks, a salad, corn on the cob. We talked about the Hind in the barn.

"Have y'all flown that bird?" I asked.

"Sure, plenty, at least ten hours," Jeanne Marie said, "Though only in the conventional mode."

"Conventional mode?"

"Yes, we are only getting the final components. ..." Jeanne Marie said.

"Did you understand the formula on the board, Parks?" Nash said.

"Not at all, never saw most of those symbols before," I said.

Jeanne Marie and her father Nash sure had guts, or faith in their minds. She was going to pilot a craft she had less than ten hours in, dive it into a hole in the side of a mountain they believed to be encasing a wormhole at certain times, based solely on their own investigative work. And then she would have to change the configuration of the Hind into a sort of time craft, navigate through time space, and then re-configure it back to a helo just to land it back on earth.

When I came back to this reality, they had started preparing the food, Nash shucking the corn, Jeanne Marie preparing the meat.

"Umm, looking forward to dinner," I said looking over Jeanne Marie's shoulder.

"Supper," Jeanne Marie said, "… only Yankees would call it dinner. Say it, Parks, supper," she almost commanded.

"Supper." I said.

"Thought you would have learned that at THE CITADEL," she said.

"Maybe I did, but that was a lifetime ago." I replied.

"… A lifetime ago, ma'am." She said with emphasis on the ma'am.

"Are you trying to teach me how to speak?" I said with a note of indignation in my voice.

"Maybe I am, Parks," she said not looking at me. She sounded serious.

"Did you go riding today?" asked Jeanne Marie.

I said "Sure." I told her I had gone and bought some boots.

"Yes ma'am," she said, and she looked at me.

I did not say anything.

By this time water was boiling for the corn, Nash had taken the steaks outside to a chimney and fireplace where he was cooking the steaks. "How do you like your steak?" he called to me.

"Well done," I replied.

It didn't take long before both the steaks and corn were done … I thought they must have done this together a hundred times, and were able to make sure both steak and corn were ready to eat at the same time. After grace we were all quick to focus on the chow … there wasn't much talking.

When we were all done, pushing our plates away, talk went back to my boots.

"Well go get 'em and bring them in here, and let's get 'em on and see how they look and fit. You know you need to wear them awhile," she said.

I went and got them from the 'vette, sat down and put them on. After some joking around Jeanne Marie looked at me and said, "You ready?" I smiled, I had no idea what she was talking about.

She turned to Nash and said: "OK Dad, I am taking him down to the stable, we will back in a couple of hours. I think we will go down the lake. I am taking a bottle of Cabaret. Parks, there are some glasses up there in the cabinet."

All of sudden she looked down at herself and realized she wasn't dressed to go riding. "I'll tell ya what, Parks. Just leave the glasses on the table by the door and go own down to the stable and saddle up Whiskey and Star, she's the mare, black and white. My saddle is on her stall. I will change and meet ya down there. OK?"

Perfect, hadn't seen a woman do that to me that good in a long time. It's called manipulation, and she just did it perfectly.

"OK, Jeanne Marie." I turned, headed to the door, dropped the glasses on the table and went out the screeching, swinging screen door out the kitchen. I walked down to the stable as the shadows cast an early darkness on the ranch. You could see sun rays blinking through the trees occasionally, but it was gonna be dark soon. This should be fun.

I got to the stable and it was still light. The first thing I did was look for a light switch, which I found and turned on. I decided I would work with Whiskey first since he knew me. I walked up to him, and started talking to him. The stable had the pungent smell of both urine and manure. It was strong. Whiskey cooperated and I was able to get him bridled and saddled pretty quick. Then I turned to find Star. She had been watching me with Whiskey. She didn't move when I walked into her stable. I decided to try to get in front of her before I moved towards her. As I walked along her flank she started to whinny and back up.

"That's OK, Star." I put my hand on her back and rubbed her flank as I walked towards her head.

I took a little while to let her get used to me, and then bridled and saddled her. It took me some time, but repeating the process did help me gain a little confidence. Jeanne Marie walked into the stable, flicked off the light, "Parks, it's not dark yet."

Maybe not to her, but my eyes had grown accustomed to the light so when she turned it off, it took some time for me to gain my night vision. She was right though, it was only dusk, there was still some light, though more outside the stable then inside it.

"Parks," she pointed towards the wall, "grab them saddlebags for me. We'll need them for the wine, and glasses."

"I like the way you think."

"Well let's see if you, did you roll a blanket?"

I laughed, "You got me! Where's a blanket?" Bringing the saddle bags over to Star.

"I will take care of this, you roll the blanket." She said. She pointed to a large chest like box at the foot of Star's stable, "one's in there."

"You do this often?" I asked.

"Usually by myself, the lake is beautiful when the clouds clear. And they have tonight."

She took care of stashing the glass items in the bag and tying on the bags while I rolled the blanket. Once I had it rolled, I stood up and looked at the rear of the saddle on Whiskey. Jeanne Marie looked over, giggled, walked over and said "Parks, the straps are right there," reaching over Whiskey's hind quarters towards the saddle and pointing. I saw them, pulled them out and tied the blanket roll to the saddle.

"OK, we're set, let's go," the excitement in her voice made it sound like she was a kid going to the beach. She smoothly mounted Star, and grabbed her black Cowboy hat hanging on a post in the stable as she guided Star out. They moved smoothly.

I placed my left foot in the stirrup, visualized mounting, took a breath and pushed off with my right leg while pulling with my left hand and swinging my right arm in hopes of adding some momentum. It worked. I was up. I pulled left, spurred his flank and Whiskey turned and took off a little quick. I think he sensed I wanted to catch up to Jeanne Marie. I had never seen a woman from behind on a horse. And even in the dusk you could see the V shape of Jeanne Marie as her butt shifted with each gate of Star. She looked cute with the black cowboy hat on.

I think she heard me coming because without turning her head she said, "The stars are starting to emerge, watch for the moon over that way." She pointed. When we got to the gate at the fence, she reached for a long stick that had been pre-placed and used it to lift the rope which held the gate closed. She then pushed the gate open with the stick and placed the stick on the opposite side of the post. She did it so smoothly without any hesitation. Star just kept walking as if the gate wasn't even there.

"Do I close it?"

"No need" she said as she headed into the pasture, the last of the sunlight — dusk gone. It was dark. "Come on up here beside me, Parks. I don't get too many chances to ride side by side with a man through this pasture at night."

I spurred Whiskey pulling slightly to the right and we came up on Star's right.

"How ya feeling?" she said.

I laughed, "Well I am sore, but the boots help a lot. There is no pressure on my left leg like there was this afternoon with your dad."

"Good," she said. "If you make the trip with me you are gonna have to do a lot of riding. Going back in time takes a heck of a lot of planning and preparation."

I had only heard the first sentence, so that's what was going on today. They were trying to see if I could handle a horse, and trying to help me prepare for the trip. I started to get mad, they had set me up, and didn't even tell me.

"Jeanne Marie, I don't know that I can do this trip with you, I mean I am not sure, it's very crazy. I mean just you and your dad. …"

"It's not just me and my dad," she responded sounding hurt, "there's hundreds of people who have helped with this.

"Hundreds? Where are they? Who are they?"

"Parks, this has taken two score years to get together. There is a lot of money invested in this trip. People all across the South have been involved in this effort." Jeanne Marie was more animated, more excited than I had seen her to this point.

"OK, OK, but how do you folks even know if this will work? This is one far out, never been done before, mission."

"Not quite never before." Jeanne Marie said quietly. "Parks, whether you go or not, I am going, and time is growing short, so do you mind if I enjoy the night?"

That was final. She rode on. I saw no point in debating her. But on the other hand, this was a beautiful, intelligent woman. And Nash, as eccentric as he appeared, sure was a calm together man who seemed to know precisely what he was doing.

The sky was a velvet dark black, the stars beyond count. I don't think I had ever seen the stars so thick. And the moon had risen, a full moon. It was bright. You could see. We were riding towards a tree line and there seemed to be a silver pond glistening through the trees.

"Is that the lake I see?"

"It is." She said. "Sometimes, I can't believe I live here. Life is so special here."

We hit the wood line. These were old trees, the ground between them cleared of any brush. "Don't over guide Whiskey, he knows where we are going, he can probably smell the water now."

"Got it," I said. While Whiskey knew how to navigate around the trees and avoid branches at his level, he didn't pay any attention to my level. So I was trying to duck under branches as they came up, and once or twice I had to pull hard one way or another to avoid being knocked off my mount. All in all, it wasn't a bad ride, though by the time I made it to the clearing on the lake Jeanne Marie had already dismounted, tied off Star, and grabbed the saddle bag with the wine and glasses.

"Was wondering if I had lost ya?" She was poking fun at me.

"Ah, I wasn't that bad." I protested weakly.

"No Parks, actually you did pretty well. Hand me down the blanket." I did. "And you can dismount and walk Whiskey over there with Star. Tie him off on a tree branch."

I dismounted, and this time because my knee had not been stressed, I landed squarely on my feet. I walked past Jeanne Marie, who had thrown the blanket out and was laying it down on the ground, Whiskey following me. The lake was really beautiful. It was smooth and looked like glass. Star did not even look up when I brought Whiskey over and tied him off to a branch.

Moonlight always surprises me. I could not believe how much you could see. Of course it wasn't sunlight, and was more dreamlike than daylight, but you could see a good distance, all the way across the lake to the far wood line.

"Want to open the wine, Parks?" Jeanne Marie handed me the bottle and bottle opener. She took off her cowboy hat and shook out her golden hair. It fell on her shoulders. She was sitting on the blanket. While I took off the metal wrapping at the top of the neck and opened the bottle, she took off her boots.

"Are we staying awhile?" I asked.

"Hope so." She said.

By the time I had pulled the cork she was holding both glasses up. I poured both, then got down on my knees and looked for something to lean the bottle against so it would not fall on its side. I placed it against a fallen log and when I turned to her she handed me a glass.

"Here's to adventure," she said.

"Adventure," I echoed.

We both took a sip. "Make yourself comfortable, Parks." She took the saddle bags and placed them long ways across the top of blanket, like a large pillow. And she pulled out another piece of folded linen, looked pale blue in the light. Looked like a light blanket or sheet.

When finished she turned sitting with her legs out, holding her glass. She patted the blanket beside her, hinting I should be sitting there. I moved to take the spot.

"Jeanne Marie, I guess you have been working with your dad since childhood on this, where's your mom? Bet she thinks this is nuts."

"Maybe, I know she didn't believe in it when she was alive." She went quiet. I always step blindly in to emotional minefields, it must be an art or a talent God made me a master at it.

"I am sorry, Jeanne Marie, I didn't know."

"Of course, you didn't know. Divorce is so common today, it was very likely she could have left the marriage. But she didn't. She loved Dad. She supported him, moved here to Rebel Mountain from Tyler. She had been a Rose Queen, a dancer, an Apache Belle, and a choreographer. But she loved Dad and me and Michael."

I thought about it, but didn't ask what happened. To be honest, this was just too romantic a time and place to go into that.

"Parks, do you find me attractive?"

This girl doesn't fool around, but on the positive side, there was a lot of her to be attracted too.

"Jeanne Marie," I turned her face towards me and leaned in to kiss her. She smelled so good and her hair blew against my face with the breeze. The kiss was not overly passionate or long, but it was a lot more than a peck and her hand reached for mine on my leg. I pulled away slowly from her face.

"I would have to answer yes to the question," I said.

"I think I got that," she said with a smile as she took a sip of wine. "Want to do that again?" She turned towards me.

I did, and I closed on her and this time reached around her shoulder with my right arm as I kissed her. This one was a little more passionate and I could hear her breathing get a little deeper as she pressed towards me. But sitting side by side doesn't work well when trying to kiss so I pressed her down so that she was laying on her back. I was over her, but on one side. I let my wine go … really didn't think about. She held hers in her right hand out from her body resting on the blanket.

She kissed back. We lay there kissing and finding each other, but not free to range across each other's bodies. I think we both enjoyed just the first kisses. It's a special time when you become vulnerable to another; when you taste someone for the first time, when you break from the kiss and stay so close you can look in the other's eyes and see the fire there.

"You can kiss, Colonel," she said.

"Ummm, well actually it depends on the woman a lot." I said. "I think you are someone I want to kiss."

Just then a shooting star crossed the sky and Jeanne Marie caught it despite my face being so close to hers. "Look at that," she said, pointing with her face and eyes. I had to back away, lean on my elbow and turned away. There was a star shooting off to our right. She pulled her glass to her, and was able to prop herself up enough to take a drink.

I leaned back away from her enough to feel something on my left butt cheek. It wasn't cold, but it was wet. I jumped a little, turned and saw it was some wine from the glass I had let go of. "Damn," I said, "I am wearing the last part of my wine." Jeanne Marie laughed, "I made you wet your pants!"

"Nah …" I laughed; it was funny, what she said.

"Don't worry, Parks, I was gonna get you out of those pants anyway." She said.

"Oh yea?" I said, she was a really attractive woman, and in this light at this place, it was the things you have fantasies about.

"Yes, we are going skinny dippin'" she gulped down her wine. Stood up, and started unbuttoning her Cowboy shirt. "Come on, Colonel. …"

She had caught me totally by surprise. I couldn't help but think she had planned this whole thing as I sat there pulling off my boots. "Hey, Jeanne Marie, what about snakes?"

"Parks, we don't have many here, it's too cold for snakes. And we don't have any water moccasins." By this time her shirt was off and she was pulling down her jeans. I had to work fast, pulled off my socks, as she pulled hers off. But I was working on my jeans when she reached behind her back, unhooked her bra and dropped it on me as I slide my jeans off the bottom of my feet. She placed her hand on my shoulder as she dropped her panties and they slid down her legs, while I tried to unbutton my shirt.

"Beat ya," she giggled as she made a run for the water. The view of her from behind was like an Italian painting. She ran into the lake splashing the water around her and then dove in. It took me time to get my shirt off, stand, drop my briefs and run towards the water. She was already out far enough that only her head was above the water line and she was looking right at me. "Colonel, I don't think you did too well on this first reaction test!" She laughed as I splashed through the water and finally dove in. I came up a few feet in front of her, my feet searching for the bottom. There wasn't any.

"Did I surprise you, Parks?"

"You could say that, Jeanne Marie, but it was a surprise I don't think I will ever forget or regret."

"Isn't this lake great?" She said her arms moving constantly to keep her afloat and in place. It was dark enough I could not see any of her body below the waterline. Every once in a while, her foot would kick my leg.

"It's amazing, it's cool but not cold and I don't know, it seems to add energy to me or something." It really did. I felt like I was being recharged or something.

"Like I said before, sometimes I can't believe we live here."

"It does seem kind of magical," I said, "almost like something out of Erin, or the Hobbits or something? I mean Rebel Mountain, and Mayberry, and the whole thing."

"I know," Jeanne Marie said. "There were not many people here when we first got here. Dad brought a lot of the people here through his travels and different adventures."

"Really?"

"Yes, not everyone can come to Rebel Mountain, in fact, only a few can."

"Jeanne Marie, if we do this, if we go back in time and get back here, then what? What do you want for your life?"

"You have got me there, Parks, I never really thought about that. We have worked for this all of my adult life. If everything works out, I guess I would like to live here and raise a family." She moved closer to me and grabbed me, making me have to work with my legs even harder to keep us both up. She wrapped her legs around me. "Keep going, Colonel, you are keeping me above water."

I couldn't stop myself, and I kissed her. And despite kicking with my legs as hard as I could we sank while in each other's arms and kissing. I really can't tell you how long we kissed, or how deep we sank but when we finally broke the kiss and released each other we had a ways to swim up to get back to the surface.

We both broke the water at the same time, just in time to take deep loud breaths.

"Wow," coughing she said, "I don't think I want to do that again! I am headed for shore." She took off swimming, me following behind her, her feet kicking in the water, and occasionally her bottom glistening in the moonlight. After some time she was, close enough to get her feet on the bottom, stand up with half her body out of the water, and walked in. I followed. When she got ashore she walked to the blanket, bent over and picked up that blue linen which turned out to be a really large bath towel. She invited me in and wrapped it around us. We kissed again.

"Let's lay down on the blanket and wrap ourselves." She said. "Parks, this can't go where I know you want to go right now." She looked at my face. That wasn't exactly what I thought was coming, and I was disappointed. She could see it on my face. "Parks, I have a mission, maybe we have a mission. I just don't want to complicate that right now."

"OK," what else could I say?

"You are one hunk of a man, and I don't think this will be our last time seeing each other in this way," she kissed me.

"OK, but can we lay here awhile? This is something pretty special I think."

"Me too," she said as she placed her head on me and I felt her pinch me. This lady was so unpredictable, I loved it.

We laid there for a while, just holding each other, looking at the sky. She asked about my life, and that started me telling her about a lot of adventures I had been on. She was quiet, but I could see her eyes, and knew she was listening. But then clouds started to roll in, light, almost like a high fog at first. "We better get dressed Parks, clouds at night usually mean rain's coming."

I kissed her again, "OK" and released her. She stood up and finished drying herself with the towel before she threw it on me. She started dressing, while I used the wet towel to dry off. Did the best I could and then started searching the blanket for my underwear, socks and everything else. Needless to say, she was dressed long before I was.

She picked up the glasswear, put it in the saddlebags and walked over to Star. After a couple moments she walked back leading Star and Whiskey. I was rolling the blanket. It was getting darker fast as the clouds got thicker and blocked much of the moonlight. "Let's walk through the woods, it's only about 50 yards, and we can mount after we get out of the wood line." I said.

"Good plan, you lead, and I will follow." She said.

When we came out of the wood line we mounted and rode slowly across a much darker meadow towards the stable. We couldn't see it, but we could see the lights inside the house and I knew about where the stable was in relation to the house. Rain drops began to drop as we made it through the gate. I dismounted and told Jeanne Marie to take Whiskey and head for the stable, I would close the gate and follow her on foot.

The rain started to fall more consistently as I made it to the stable. But by that time, Star was in her stall and Jeanne Marie was working on Whiskey. It didn't take her but a minute or so to get Whiskey free of his saddle, blanket and bridle.

"Let's go, its coming." She said running right by me. It wasn't raining too hard when we ran to the house, but it was at that moment that I realized the top wasn't up on my 'vette. Jeanne Marie laughed as she ran up the stairs on the porch, hearing me cuss as I stopped to open the trunk of the 'vette to pull the top out.

"See ya in the morning," Jeanne Marie said as she went through the screen door and closed the front door.

I couldn't help but smile as I was pelted by rain while I wrestled with putting the top to on the Corvette and securing it. I looked up at the house, completely soaked, then I turned and walked to the bunk house. What a night.

The Kitchen, Three Pines
Rebel Mountain, Texas
July 17, 2012

The gray clouds overhead filled the sky as I went out the door of the log cabin.

I walked briskly towards the house knowing that this morning would very likely change my life. It had rained all night so the road from the bunkhouse to the main house was wet, with puddles and the rain splattering on the ground. There was a great smell in the air, and every once in a while, lightening would flash.

Nash had been clear that this morning the three of us would have breakfast and I would be given a detailed briefing on what was going on. To be honest, I was kind of surprised I had gotten such a good night's sleep. Clearly, they were thinking of traveling in time, and though I had not said it, in my mind I had already agreed to be a part of the journey, despite knowing only fragments of their plan, and nothing about the science or aeronautical skills required.

Maybe that is the core of anyone who thinks himself an adventurer. We will try something just because we can. We don't know the odds, or the likelihood of success. We really don't have any idea of the dangers we will face. But we do know one thing, we do know the scent of adventure, we know it when we smell it. And like a good hunting dog, once we are on the scent we won't leave it 'til we find our prey.

I literally bounced up the steps, across the porch and through the screen door into the foyer yelling out "good morning" as I entered the house.

From the back of the house, the kitchen I supposed I heard Jeanne Marie; "Good morning, Parks, come on back for some coffee. Dad's upstairs." I walked into the kitchen and Jeanne Marie was in a light-colored pastel t-shirt and shorts. Barefooted, her hair was up.

"How are you Jeanne Marie?" I gave her a gentle pat on the behind.

She looked at me cross, and then smiled, "Oh I am fine, really pretty good. I enjoyed our ride last night, and our swim under the stars."

"Yes, I did too."

"You have had a really interesting life Parks, almost as good as mine!" She said with a giggle. "Of course I had the advantage of my father." Her voice fell off as she said, I guess realizing the double entendre of her comment; I had no father.

"I am sorry, "

"It's no problem Jeanne Marie, you should be proud of your father, and the love the two of you have. Believe me, because of my life I can appreciate it. But God has taken care of me, and I have had my share of excitement and challenge."

"Yes, and now it will get even better!" She said as the bacon started to crackle in the frying pan.

"Morning Parks," Nash said as he walked into the kitchen and directly to Jeanne Marie who he gave a hug. "Hi hun, how'd you sleep?" Nash released Jeanne Marie and headed to the coffee pot for a cup of coffee.

"Hi dad."

The smell of bacon filled the kitchen.

"Can I ..." before I could finish Jeanne Marie said; the OJ is in the refrigerator, and the glasses and plates are in the cabinets, and the silverware is in that drawer." She pointed with her free hand as she focused on turning the bacon with a fork in her other hand.

"Dad, can you do the toast?"

"Parks, you go get the butter." She was so smooth and easy in her directions, a lady who felt sure of herself and the people she was with. No hesitancy or doubt.

I thought to myself, it's funny how the simple things in life are the best at showing you the real person; the self-assuredness of a person.

For a few moments the kitchen hummed with activity. It's really amazing how fast eggs and bacon and toast all come together. If you do it right, while everything is hot and fresh. But if you miscalculate, you either have cold toast, or your bacon is cold waiting on the toast. I wondered if this was one of the tests given to prospective flight coordinators to see if they could deal with multiple vectors of activity, like a plane landing on a carrier.

I took the initiative to get the jellies from the refrigerator just as Jeanne Marie brought over the eggs on one plate, the bacon on another. Nash had the toast. Maybe this was a sign.

We all sat down, Jeanne Marie said "Dad would do grace this morning?" She extended her hands to each of us. I took hers, Nash did to, looked to me, and extended his. I took it.

Nash bowed: "Almighty God and Father, thank you for what we

have and for bringing Parks to us. Please help us to know and do your will oh God. We join to make the work of decades come true, if it be your will. Amen." We echoed, "Amen."

Without a word, the plates started moving around the circle, and in no time we were enjoying breakfast. A light rain began to fall outside. There was no lightening or thunder, no heavy winds, just the occasional splash of a rain drop against the windows. The tempo of the splashes increased.

We really didn't chat much through breakfast. Every once in a while, Jeanne Marie would glance over at me. Maybe she was just checking to see if I was still there.

"Good breakfast, don't you think?" Nash said, looking for consensus agreement. "Honey, could you fill our cups with coffee before we get started?"

Jeanne Marie got up and walked across the room to get the coffee pot. Dang she looked good in anything. Slim with a terrific figure and as she walked away, I could not help but look at her behind remembering the night before. The time we had spent the night before was important to me. Affection for her had grown during our few hours together. I liked her, maybe more. She was easy going, fairly confident in herself, funny, and bold. I don't think I had ever met a woman like her before, except in the military.

Jeanne Marie returned, filled each of three cups and turned away.

"So Parks, would you like to hear how simple this is going to be?"

"Nash, you have my undivided attention." I heard the chair beside me slide back, and when I glanced, Jeanne Marie was there, sippin' her coffee.

"Parks, did you read the National Science Summary Brief on Dark Energy and Dark Matter?" Nash asked, sipping his coffee and looking at me.

"I did"

"What do you remember?" Nash said lifting his eyebrow.

"Well, current theory uses dark matter and energy to explain why the expansion of the universe is accelerating, instead of slowing, if I remember right."

"Excellent Parks, you have a fine memory."

"Sure do," Jeanne Marie whispered under her breath. I turned to look at her puzzled.

"If I remember right, even though physicists cannot prove the existence of either, they estimate that the combination of dark matter and dark energy comprise something like 95 percent of the universe!"

"That's right Parks, and it is the combination of the two which I believe make a dark universe, something I don't think the consensus has come to yet. In fact, to this point I have never heard any credible scientist even propose the idea."

"Nash? A dark universe?"

"It gets better," Nash kind of chuckled, this universe and the dark universe co-mingle and co-exist in the exact same place."

"What?"

"Parks, look, I am not proposing any science you already know is wrong. I am trying to expand your base, to bring you up to speed on the science you don't know, and very few others do." Nash went on, "The dark universe adds additional dimensions in the same space. The two universes are everywhere and 95 percent of what we would consider real exist in the other universe. In that universe things have not only slowed down as we thought they would, it is actually collapsing on itself. Well, theoretically anyway."

Nash said with a kind of puzzled look on his face. He did not try to pass off the last statement as fact.

"So how does that have anything to do with what we are talking about?" I asked.

Nash looked at me, and passed me a yellow legal tablet and a pen. "Pictures tell a thousand words, Parks. Would you do me a favor and draw a large rectangle on that piece of paper."

Why not? I picked up the pen and drew a medium sized rectangle on the paper.

"Great, now right here," he pointed on the piece of paper along one of the shorter lines of the rectangle, "draw a small square box."

I did.

"Excellent, now, let's move over to the other side of the rectangle and put a small box over on that side. Oh, I forgot something. ..." Nash said with a smile, "go ahead and make your second box."

I did.

Now at the top of the page, just to keep us all together please write Flight path.

I did.

"Great. We are making some real progress here; don't you think Parks?"

"Dad, should I get the Crayola's?" Jeanne stuck her elbow in to my side with a smile on her face.

"Parks, don't mind Miss know-it-all over there. We are doing just fine. Now, by each of the two small square boxes please write "window." And now, under the box on the left, write Rebel Mountain. In the large rectangle write Dark Universe, and over there. ..." He pointed to the small box on the right under the word window, "please write Mt. Airy, North Carolina." I did.

"So do you see, Parks?" He looked at me with a broad smile, and an expectant look.

"Ah, I see a bad drawing." I said.

Jeanne Marie laughed, but Nash lost his smile. "Parks, do we need to go through this again from the top?"

"Did I misspell flight path? I don't think I. ..."

Jeanne Marie giggled, but Nash was disturbed. "Parks, stop kidding around, on that paper is your flight plan ... oh, I am sorry, please write under Rebel Mountain, 18 July 2012, and over under Mt. Airy write: circa April 12, 1863."

"There ya' go Parks, now do you get it?"

I picked up the paper, turned it one way, then another, hoping something would jump off of it and make this all clear. Nope, nothing. "Nash, I am sorry. Why don't you walk me through this again?"

"OK, fair enough. We have been working on this for a score of years, and you have had about 24 hours."

Using the drawing to illustrate the flight mission, Nash started on the left side of the picture, pointing to July 18. "Parks sometime tomorrow afternoon you will take off with Jeanne Marie as your engineer in the *Alabama*. ..."

"The *Alabama*?" I interrupted?

"Yes, the *Alabama* with Jeanne Marie, and you will fly into the mirror. ...

"The mirror?"

"Yes, Parks the time mirror, you will dive down a shaft, and into a wormhole and through a window inside Rebel Mountain. That will pass you through to the Dark universe. You will fly through the Dark Universe and space-time back to around April 12, 1863 where you will find another mirror and wormhole that will deliver you within 50 to 100 miles from Mt. Airy, North Carolina."

"Uh huh." I said acting like I was still with him.

"You will then fly nap of the earth to a beacon in the vicinity of Mt. Airy where my son Michael will have created an LZ for you, and you will land completing the first half of the flight mission. See?"

He looked again with an expectation of understanding.

"Nash, are you saying this helicopter in your barn is going to fly through space-time?"

"Good question, yes and yes. Jeanne Marie, since you will be the engineer for the flight how 'bout fill in the pilot. I am headed to the head for a minute." Nash got up and left for the toilet.

Jeanne Marie backed her chair up a little and turned towards me. "Parks," she extended her hand, "I will be your flight engineer for the flight portion of this mission." When I did not take her hand, she moved it towards me and nodded, take it. I took it, but said "Jeanne Marie, how many hours do you have as the engineer on this contraption?"

Jeanne Marie responded without blinking, "Good question, I was designated the pilot for this mission, and dad was going to be the engineer for me. If you asked me about pilot hours, I have about twenty. But as the engineer. ..."

"Yes," I said with a little more force.

"Well, we are hoping to get an hour or so in this afternoon."

What, you have not been the engineer on this? Well maybe that is not too bad since the engineer really doesn't usually have too much to do."

"Usually is right," she said, "but on this flight it's a little different since the bird has to be re-configured in flight."

"I pushed my chair back hard; "reconfigured?"

Just at that point Nash returned, "She'll be a helluva engineer, I just know it."

"You know it?"

"Yes, we have done about a dozen dry drills of the reconfiguration protocol."

"OK, but how many in flight?"

"None."

"That's what this afternoon is for?"

"No." Said Nash

"We can't do an in flight reconfiguration; we would splatter all over the ground." Jeanne Marie got up nonchalantly to take her coffee cup to the sink.

"What? What kind of reconfiguration are we doing?"

"Jeanne Marie, come back here. Talk Parks through the reconfiguration."

She walked back over at a kind of easy pace, sat down and crossed her legs. Yes, that did draw my attention; she sure did have some legs; tanned, and very shapely. She got a girlish smile on her face, and even blushed a little. I think she liked me looking.

"Parks, pay attention." Chastised Nash.

Once she got composed, "Parks, this bird has two completely different propulsion systems for two very different environments. One is for the environment on earth, the other for the environment in the Dark Universe. These systems not only use different power sources, but one uses the other to help sustain a magnetic field in the Dark Universe. So, for this to work, the transition from one system to the other has got be smooth and sequential."

"What does that mean Jeanne Marie?"

Nash moved as if to start speaking, but Jeanne Marie gave him a look, and he stopped.

"Parks, when we take off you will be flying a chopper. When we dive into the shaft in Rebel Mountain you will be flying a chopper, but on our immediate approach to the window we will disengage the rotor, retract the blade, create a metal core from the blade for the magnetic field, and engage the neutron field and antimatter propulsion system."

Silence.

Silence.

I tried to assimilate what she had just said. Hell, I could not even remember everything she just said.

"Doc, I need another piece of paper for this."

Nash pushed the yellow legal pad over to Parks.

"Parks, you are right in wanting to write this down, but maybe we should do that when we go out the ship and work our way through a couple of dry runs." She leaned forward, reached out with her hand and looked me in the face.

I was caught like a deer in the headlights. But not for long, I pulled away from her hand and looked at Nash.

"Nash, this is a lot of stuff. Why are we leaving tomorrow? Give me a couple weeks. I will have to call NASA and ask for some time off. But they will. …"

Quietly he said speaking over my words, "The window is closing."

" … probably let me … the window is closing? I asked.

"Yes, we either go tomorrow, or we don't have another shot for a decade." He answered bluntly. "We can't do that. I know this is a lot, but if you are not up to it, then you can head on out to Houston and we will do this as we originally planned it. Jeanne Marie can pilot and I will engineer." His voice faded.

I looked at Jeanne Marie, I could not let her do this alone. "OK, when did you figure to get to the bird and do some dry runs?"

"Maybe this afternoon, I have to go in this morning. You can use the time to check out the bird, maybe fly if it you want too. I better go get dressed. Dad, can you. … "

"We got it hun," Nash was including me in the "we."

"Nash, I don't understand how you think this crazy plan can work? You are a scientist, there are so many holes in this, it's more like a kid's tree house fantasy, than an actual mission that grown people would try …"

Nash lifted his hand and tried to insert a thought, but I was on a roll and figured once I told him my thoughts, I would head towards the bunk house pack my stuff and get out of here.

"Nash," I put my head down and shook it left to right, "I can't believe you are going to allow Jeanne Marie to fly this mission, your own daughter?!" The volume of my voice rising.

He kind of bent his head and said quietly, "I know, my son is already there. …"

"And this thing has no chance, how do you even know traveling through time is possi …" I kind of lost my train of thought as it registered in my mind what he just said.

Nash looked up.

"What do you mean your son is there?" I said.

"Parks, my son Michael is already there. He went there about a week ago, and has been there three years."

"What?" I stood up… almost as if I was shot up like a rocket.

"Sit down Parks, I told you, there is a lot to this. Yes, in some ways we are flying by the seat of our pants, but that's when being Southern is most helpful, you learn to do things in unconventional ways, where ingenuity and persistence are paramount to getting things done."

I understood what he meant there. Because the Confederacy had less industry and money, less manufacturing, less access to iron and the pharmaceutical processes of their day, they had to come up with innovative ways to try to implement new technologies. Ingenuity was a strategic asset of the South and we have always exercised it to a remarkable degree.

"Parks, to make the kind of trip we are going to make, we needed to make mission essential tests on core components. I could not risk my daughter, or the monies necessary to build a returnable time ship unless I was certain we actually could travel in time, and that our navigations systems and aides would work. I mean we were literally going where no man had gone before. And though we had help from ancients not from this world, still, who knew if we were interpreting everything right?"

"Parks, my son Michael was willing to take the first risk. He volunteered to travel first, in a much smaller, one-man, disposable craft. He was our test monkey. Oh, we did have one unmanned flight, and the evidence of the flight was found about where we thought it should be. …"

"What, you have had two trips back in time already? What do you mean disposable craft?"

"Parks, look you are going to know everything we have done. You are going to know all the science. This project is much larger than I can tell you before launch. There simply is not enough time to read you in on every aspect of the organization and the mission, we have been working on this for decades. …"

Decades, well that was kind of soothing, but how the heck. …

"Parks, I need to know, are you in, or do I go as Jeanne Marie's engineer?"

The last words echoed around the room. What a question. My whole life had been an adventure, but this. This was out there. And I barely knew these people.

"Nash, give me some time. …"

"Parks there is no time. If you are not going there are some things I have to work out with Jeanne Marie and I. …"

"How come you need me, where's Michael? Why can't he go with Jeanne Marie?"

"Because he is there now. We sent him as the pathfinder for the larger insertion. He went to prove we had unraveled the mystery of time travel and to prepare the landing site for a returnable ship. He has been there for about a week our time, but three years his."

"How do you know he is there? How do you know he made it?" I asked.

"He has sent us messages, and we have received them?"

"You have radio communications through time?"

"No Parks, we can't communicate with him, but he can with us through a methodology we worked on since last Christmas season."

"How's that?"

"We set up a means for him to pass messages to me. The key is in Mt. Airy, North Carolina where we agreed on a drop off point, where he would place messages for someone to find one hundred and fifty years later. We know he is there, and we have a map and coordinates for the LZ at his farm. The map was delivered just this past week to Jeanne Marie at the library."

"Those men?"

"Yes," Nash said surprised, "yes those men. They are part of a larger infrastructure, a Southern infrastructure that is part of the mission support. Parks, I can't tell you more without a commitment. Are you in?"

There didn't seem to be any more time to think or to stall. The mission was a go whether I went or not. I was falling for Jeanne Marie and knew it. I liked Nash, and so far he had answered every question. This was unbelievable, but I like unbelievable.

"Yes. I'll go." I had said it my whole life. I was one of those kids you never said "You can't do that." I would do it just to prove you wrong. A lot of times I got hurt with that approach, but I always did "it," whatever "it" was.

"Parks, the stuff I am going to start telling you is above classified, there are only a tiny handful of need to know people who know everything, even though hundreds of people have helped in this mission. If you say you are in, you are in. This is the darkest black op possible, and like the Mafia there is only one way out of the project once you are in."

"Nash, I said I am in." I was angry, I don't commit to things lightly.

"Good," he said.

"Nash, why isn't the government doing this?"

"The government has nothing to do with this Parks," Nash said that with a firmness in his voice I had never heard before. "Parks we are doing this to change history, we are going back in time to save the life of Stonewall Jackson."

The silence following his statement allowed time for me to consider what Nash had just said.

"But, if Stonewall lives ..." before I could finish the thought.

"We could have a new world." Nash completed the sentence, not the way I would have, but there was the purpose for this trip as clear as day. "We could have our South, the one that should have been a nation from the very beginning."

"Nash the thought of this is. ..."

"Like nothing anyone has ever considered, the entire world will be a very different place if we are successful. Parks, the main stream scientist have long avoided this field because of the lesson they learned from nuclear weapons. Once you open the bottle for the genie, you can't put it back." Nash said as he washed the dishes.

"So how will you control it Nash?"

"Precisely, we will control it. We will take the steps necessary to make sure only we have the technology, and that others never even know it's even possible. By being first, we can prevent others from ever getting this power."

"Nash, if you change history you may never be born, and all of this that you are doing now may never happen."

"That is a possibility Parks, we thought about that." Nash said, "if history is changed, if the Confederacy is successful in its effort to create a new nation, we are willing to trade never being here for that."

He looked up to see my reaction. What he just said was that I was going on a mission which could mean Parks Walter is never born. Or I could be born into a world so different that I might never fly. Certainly, there would be no NASA.

I was never much of a poker player, but I instantly realized that to show any emotion could be a deal breaker. Right now, I had to stay at the table if I was going to have any influence on what was occurring. I could think about options later when I was in the bunk house. But right now, stupid was probably the best response.

"Some of the stuff I read on time travel says history can't be changed, and others say that if you do change history, all you are doing is creating a new parallel universe, a new time line, but that the original time line would continue." I said.

"That's true Parks, the only way we will know is if we proceed," his voice sounding sincere and accepting my doubts.

"Well, we don't have much time. Let me go out to the bunkhouse and wash up, and then maybe we should head out to the bird and. ..."

"Take her for a test spin." Nash said with a smile. He almost looked like Santa in his white shirt, white slacks and red suspenders. His sleeves were rolled up as he did the dishes.

As I walked through the main hall of the house towards the front door Jeanne Marie came down the stairs.

"Jeanne Marie I have to ask you something. Your dad said Michael had gone ahead, that he is in North Carolina in 1863 now?"

"That's true Parks. He is the pathfinder for this mission. I am sure you are familiar with that concept of Pathfinder as a chopper pilot." She walked toward a painting beside a large open doorway that led into another room.

"I know in the Army they are the advanced men for an airborne operation. …"

"Exactly," she said, "and he even attended the U. S. Army's Pathfinder school as a part of his training for this operation."

"Aren't you worried about him? I mean how do you know he is in the past? He could be gone for all you know?" My voice rose with excitement. I just could not believe how calm Jeanne Marie and Nash were about this entire operation. And as I spoke, Jeanne Marie had even gotten a little smile on her face.

"Parks, he's fine." She said softly.

"How can you possibly know that?"

"Because he has dropped us a few lines," she said without any emotion at all.

"He dropped you a few lines, how's that?"

"I will let pops tell ya 'bout that. He worked real hard on that aspect of the operation."

We headed out the front door. We stopped on the front porch; Jeanne Marie looked up at me, got up on her toes to give me a kiss. "I am off to the library. See ya' later." And she was gone. She was like some kind of tornado, always moving somewhere. I shook my head and walked down the stairs and headed to the bunk house.

Back to the Barn
Three Pines Ranch, Rebel Mountain, Texas
July 17, 2012

I had grabbed my flight suit from my duffel bag in the trunk of the 'vette before I headed off to the bunkhouse to shower and shave. Might as well take that bird up and see how she handles. I guess Nash saw me take the flight suit out because he was on the porch in his when I emerged out the bunkhouse.

"Going somewhere Nash?" He didn't look right in clothes different from what he always wore. Here he was a man with a Santa Claus looking face, with white hair and beard with aviator sun glasses on, in an olive-green flight suit with different tools like a small pen light, pen, compass, and other items hanging off his suit. He was in combat boots.

"You bet, figured I would go up with ya. Since you are gonna be flying my daughter around I figure I should see what you got."

We headed off down the stone road towards the barn. "Where'd you get this bird, Nash?"

"Well the Soviets owed me, I helped them with something they were working on connected to the launching of their Space station. They were happy with what I did and asked me what I needed?" Nash smiled, "It was funny, they didn't think a helicopter was a big deal at all. They asked if I had a preference, I said an MI-24 Hind?"

Nash went on. "They nodded, and you know what they said?"

"No, what?"

Nash said: "And what else?"

"They thought the helicopter was the first thing on a long list!" Nash chuckled, "wish I had known that before they asked me. I was caught flat-footed, and they closed the door."

We made our way down to the barn. Nash got a tractor, hooked up a chain between the tractor and the *Alabama* and pulled it out of its "hangar" and out on the tarmac. "We can take this up and fly over to El Paso to fill her up!" Nash said with a smile, "Want to make sure you have plenty of fuel for the trip."

Out in the sunlight the *Alabama* took on a different look, more threatening and lethal. Yet, the black boxes were where the missile pods should be. Sure were curious. "Aren't you afraid someone will ask about these?" I said pointing to the box.

"Weather data collection gear," Nash responded without even looking. He pulled the side door back. "Come on Parks, get in."

The HIND helicopter is Russian or Soviet invented. It was a kind of heavy combination version of a Cobra and a Huey. It could carry a wide variety of weapons and a small band of men. The cabin of this HIND was filled with a whole bunch of strange equipment. There were several computer screens, extra wiring and even something that looked like a pump and industrial weight tubing. There was a single rotating seat near the screens and keyboard which I assumed was the engineer's seat. There were a bank of lights and gages across the wall opposite the door. The modifications to the inside cabin of this bird were extensive, and took up most of the room.

"All of what you are looking at Parks was put in here by Michael, Jeanne Marie and myself. Some of the component pieces are one of a kind items designed and built in small shops across the South."

"Looks like a lot of bucks went into this, Nash," I said.

"It did, and this is just the tip of the iceberg. It took a great deal of fund-raising support from a whole set of people you will never see or know. At least not before you two go." Nash said as he sat into the chair and flicked on some switches. "You enter the cockpit that way." He pointed to a small opening which went straight up through the front wall and ceiling of the cabin. There were two-foot bars protruding from the front wall. It was different. "We had to make some modifications to the internal structure."

I went up and through the hatch into the cockpit and took the sole seat. Nash yelled up through the hatch, "Headset should be on your right, put it on so we can talk."

It was there, I put it on. He must have already put power to it as I heard a buzz. "This is Nash, do you read? Over"

"Roger over." There was no need to push a button, or in some other way activate the mic.

"In the area in front of you, where their gunner, or weapons officer would sit, we have stripped out the seat and all the weapons control equipment and put in a lot of equipment for this mission. Over" I guessed we were using over as the means of signaling the end of our thoughts so we would not step on each other blocking out messages back and forth.

"This thing was built to 12 metric tons for the Russians, and I believe that's about the weight we have in it. On a full tank you can cruise

280 miles. Over" Nash knew the specs for this bird. "The flight pre-ops checklist should be hanging off the canopy. Over"

"Got it over," I replied.

"Give me a minute to look over their instruments, this configuration is not American! Over" We had looked at some Soviet stuff but that was a long time ago, and taking this up without any instruction did pose some danger. Before I even turned the key to start the engine I wanted to have a good understanding of the controls and instruments.

"It's safe to fly Parks, Jeanne Marie has about twenty hours in this thing. Over" Nash said with some confidence in his voice. "I am powering up back here, you are cleared to start the engine at your pleasure. Over"

"Parks our mission today is twofold; to familiarize you with the bird, and to refuel in El Paso. There should be plenty of fuel, so use what you need to be fully confident in your ability to fly this thing. over" Nash said. "Forget to shut the door, ..." I heard the side door being pulled shut and locked.

"OK," he said.

This is going be fun I thought.

I set the appropriate levers in place, and switched the toggle to start the engine, the blades began to move slowly after the high-pitched whine of the engine start. All the gages had popped up, needles going to the right place on the dials, light indicators coming on. I could smell the JP4 fuel, what a smell for any helicopter pilot or infantryman who had flown in these things.

I was thinking, I want to put some distance between me and the ground quickly in case the feel isn't right, or there is a center of gravity issue, the worst thing you can do is be indecisive in the takeoff. We had a long runway in front of us, no obstructions or tree lines to worry about.

As the rpms rose the bird came to life, and you could feel it was ready to lift. When I pulled on the stick we started to slide forward and rise, the power kicking in quickly, we were off, rising and moving forward.

"Smooth, over" Nash said.

I pulled to the right and tried to push her to see what kind of climb rate I could get. We rapidly rose away from the ground and Rebel Mountain. I started with easy maneuvers, increasing and decreasing elevation and speed. The bird had a good feel to it, a tight feel. "Do you have a heading for El Paso and the frequency of Air Control? over"

Nash came back: "Freq is already set on the radio, heading coming up in a minute."

I turned the *Alabama* to a heading generally northwest at 2,000 feet, and waited for the heading from Nash. "Heading two one four degrees over," Nash said

"two one four," I repeated.

The rest of the afternoon went pretty well, the bird and I seemed to have a psychic connection or something. It was a little slow in response, probably due to the weight she was carrying. From my perch I could see the equipment Nash had mentioned. Lights on the boxes were constant, probably indicating the equipment was in a rest mode.

After we fueled up in El Paso, we headed back to Rebel Mountain. About five minutes out Nash came up on the system: "Parks, I want you to see something, please take her up to 4,500 and slow down, hold a position southwest of Rebel Mountain. Over"

"Roger." I started a climb and a right turn to circle to the southwest. Once we got into position: "OK Nash, what am I looking for? Over"

"Engaging DU optics, give me a minute, over" Nash came back. "Set your heading on three five degrees north and approach at 100 KPH. over"

"Heading three five north, 100 KPH. Roger, over"

The view from this height was really something. Rebel Mountain was the only green object on a desert floor. To the south, way off on the horizon was some rising ground, but not as high as Rebel Mountain. As I approached the mountain, I saw a large black orifice about two-thirds up the mountain. "Nash is there a cave on this mountain? Over"

"Look over this area; look for land marks you might make out at night that could lead you to the orifice Parks, the window for your entry into the Dark Universe is in that cave. Over"

"Are you saying I have to fly in there? Over"

"About 100 yards, Parks and you will have to dive into it to generate enough kinetic energy to carry you through the window. Want to circle around again? Over"

"Nash, are you kidding me?"

"No Parks, I am not. Please take her around again, and look for a point on the ground that we should mark to give the starting point for your approach and dive. Over"

We flew a wide circle back out from the mountain into the desert to the southwest. I went out about five miles from the mountain, turned and looked. I started looking for a land mark visible from up here at night that would be on the azimuth I would be flying. At a little over three miles out I found a road intersection. "Nash, mark the spot, there's a landmark. Over."

"I can see it on the video, I will have someone come out and mark it, put a beacon on it. Jeanne Marie should be able to find. Let's head to Three Pines. Over."

"Roger. Over" We weren't far from Three Pines and I found it pretty easily. The runway stuck out like a sore thumb. I could set this thing down on a dime, but used the runway as the approach for my landing point. She set down easy, and we started shutting down systems, the engine first.

I took off the headset and as I switched things off, I heard the door open, slid back and locked.

Now I had to descend through the hatch into the cabin. Good thing I was slim, this wasn't built for a big guy. When I made my way out of the door, Nash was standing there.

"Nash, every time I start to warm up to this idea you throw another hand grenade. You want me to dive into that cave with this? What happens if the window isn't in there? How do you know this is going to work? You are betting our lives on this."

"I told you before Parks, we have done this twice before, once unmanned, once manned with Michael. We know it works." Nash said unzipping his flight suit.

"How do you know it works?" I was getting irritated with the same responses.

"Let's walk to the house and get some sweet tea." Nash said. He started walking. I took a couple brisk steps to catch up to him. "I am listening." I wasn't going to let him dodge me again.

"Parks, first we sent through a small unmanned craft. We know it made it to North Carolina because we found debris within miles of where it was supposed to land."

"Miles?" I said.

Nash laughed, "We are going back 150 years in time, to a location almost two thousand miles from here, to an earth in a completely different place in space, hell we were thrilled we hit the same continent!"

"How do you know it hit in North Carolina?"

"Because we had recovery teams in North Carolina look for it! It had a transponder on it, which helped them find it. We were not sure the batteries would run for 150 years and kick on the transponder in the right space time. But they did."

"OK, then what."

"Well, we needed to send in an advance party. There are a lot of missions for a Pathfinder, you know that. But in this case, our Pathfinder would also be a test pilot of the system, and tell us if man could live through space time travel. Michael volunteered and trained for years. He went, and he's there now. We know that he made it." Nash said, the pride too hard for him to control, it was all over his face and in the tone of his voice.

Nash, was his wreckage found?" I asked.

"No, we have gotten messages from him Parks. Hand written messages."

"How's that?"

"Parks we made a trip to Mt. Airy North Carolina back in December last year, Michael and I. We selected a specific location in the ground on Pilot Mountain where Michael was to place a mailbox. Michael was to place messages there 150 years ago, and we would pick them up out of a special designed metal box 150 years later. That simple." Nash said. He was pouring sweet tea in two glasses full of ice. He had my attention so glued to his words I didn't remember walking up the porch steps, through the front door, through the great hall and into the kitchen.

"What did he say?"

"Well his first note was that he was in 1860, it simply said I am alive, Michael, '60." Nash said. One thing we had discussed was what if someone found the mailbox anywhere along that 150 years. So, he had to keep his messages simple and non-indicative of what they were."

"You went to North Carolina to get the messages?" I asked, not believing he could be in so many places on such a tight schedule.

"No Parks, I did not. One of our couriers checked the mail box daily, picked up any messages left, and forwarded the information to me."

"Gosh Nash, how many people are involved in this secret!"

Nash chuckled. "Well, if I said a couple hundred in the outer-inner circle I would not be lying. But things are very compartmentalized, and most of that number have no clue what our mission really is. I would say a dozen people may have complete knowledge, probably less than that."

"I guess the big money people know?" I said.

"Hmmm, not really. And I am not going into this anymore then I have. Parks, I know you need to feel confident, so talking you through any of the science or engineering is no problem. And, I know you have to have an understanding of the mission once you get to the other side, because you have the central role in it. So again, I would tell you anything you asked." Nash looked up at me, "But you don't need to know the size, scope and breadth of our support organization. So, I think I am about done here."

He took his glass of iced tea over to a cabinet and broke out a small bottle of bourbon; "Would you like a touch?"

Just about that time I heard a car pulling up the drive to the house. A few seconds later I heard the screen door open and shut, and heels clicking on the wood floor in the central hall coming back towards us; "Anybody home?" Jeanne Marie yelled out as she entered the kitchen. Jeanne Marie was carrying a Confederate Colonel's blouse on a hanger. "Thought we should try this on you," she said.

"Me?" I responded with a squeaky voice.

"Yes sir Colonel, you!" She said with a bright Sarah Palin like smile!

She took the coat off the hanger and started to walk around behind me. "Hold on a minute," I said, "I have a flight suit on, that thing looks small, I don't want to tear an antique worth a lot of money."

"Colonel, OK, unzip the flight suit and get your arms out of it, tie it off at the waste, or let it drop to the floor for all I care." Jeanne Marie said with a really brash and bold tone.

Nash, who was sitting at the table taking all this in, looked a little startled at his daughter.

"Only kidding dad." She said in a sarcastic tone.

I unzipped my suit, got out of the top portion and used the sleeves to tie it off at my hips. By then Jeanne Marie was standing behind me and touched my right hand with the blouse. I reached back and inserted my arm in to the sleeve; then did the same thing with my left hand. She lifted the coat up to my shoulders brushing off the shoulders of the coat. Surprisingly it was bigger than it looked, and though unbuttoned it felt comfortable.

Jeanne Marie walked around me to my front; "Not bad, not bad at all, what do you think dad?" She asked as she straightened the blouse and started buttoning it up.

"By crackee, he looks like the real McCoy in it, don't he?" Nash said sounding like Walter Brennan, an actor of the mid twentieth century. "Andy Griffith would be proud to see you in that coat."

"Nash, Jeanne Marie showed me the plaque and the news story at the library. How did Andy Griffith get this coat and why did he bring it to you?" I was puzzled.

Once buttoned, Jeanne Marie stepped back and put her hands on her hips; "Well, I will be danged ... you look just like the pictures in them Civil War books," she was trying to deepen her Southern accent and practice her grammar.

"Parks, Andy told me that the jacket had been passed down in the Taylor family to his grandmother and that she had given it to him and told him it had a role to play in the future, a role that could be important in history. He was to look for someone who wanted to change history. Andy said when he heard of our work he knew where to take the coat." Nash said.

She took a step forward and hit my chest with her hand, "You'll do."

When she did that, we both felt something in the coat. It kind of crackled. We looked at each other. She started unbuttoning the blouse and once it was undone, I reached in with my hand and found a pocket in the coat. In the pocket I felt paper. I was worried I would tear it, so I took extra care when removing it.

What I pulled out was an envelope. I walked over to the table, Jeanne Marie following and I placed it on the table with the back side of the envelope up. After a few seconds Jeanne Marie reached down and flipped it over. We all froze, looking at the handwriting on the envelope. It was handwriting which had been placed on the envelope with an old quill pen, one dipped into a bottle of ink. The writing had broad clear strokes. On the envelope in the center it read:

Lt. General Thomas J. Jackson, C.S.A.
In the left-hand corner of the envelope it read:
Zebulon Vance, Governor, Mt. Airy, North Carolina

It appeared that this might be official correspondence. "Whose gonna open it?" I said.

"I am not," Nash said taking a good draw on his spiced up iced tea.

"Babies," she looked at me and Nash, "Dad, I guess this is why you sent me off for my Masters." She picked up the envelope and separated the leaf from the rest of envelope and looked in it. There was a folded

piece of paper inside. She pulled out the folded paper carefully unfolded it and laid it on the table. The hand writing was clear as day. The
letter said;

General T. J. Jackson,   April 11th, 1863
Sir,
It is my great honour to write a field commander of your renown
and success. As the governor of the great North State I knew that the
men of this fine state would acquit themselves well in battle if given
good military leadership. On behalf of the people of North Carolina I
gratefully commend you for the skilled leadership you have provided
and for your relationship with our Almighty Father. Only the beneficence of Providence can explain your miraculous victories.
Sir. With this letter I present to you Lt. Colonel Parks Walter who
I am sending to you as a liaison between myself and you to insure that
the soldiers of this great state are provided with every possible convenience and supply. Please allow Colonel Walter to fulfill this small duty
so that we in Caroline can be assured we know the needs of our men
have been met. And feel free to utilize Colonel Walter as you see fit
when he is unencumbered by his duties on my behalf.
May I add my congratulations on the birth of Julia, and allow me to
pray for you, your wife and child that this tragic event should soon end
in the favor of the right. I am, sir,
                        Zebulon Vance, Governor
                        North Carolina

Jeanne Marie and I stood paralyzed; Nash didn't move. How could
this be I thought to myself, how could this …
Just then, Nash's arm hit his partially filled glass of iced tea and
it fell over, the ice racing out over the table like small rocks, with the
alcohol mixture traveling behind more slowly. The tea headed towards
the letter like a guided missile and quickly overwhelmed any resistance,
soaking the 150-year-old paper. We watched the paper dissolve. The
letter that seemed a miracle, provided by God, to help get me get in the
vicinity of Stonewall Jackson was gone.
Silence pervaded the room. Nash looked distraught his right hand
clutching his thick hair.
"It's OK dad," Jeanne Marie moved to comfort her father. He re-
coiled.

"Nash, we now have a plan, a story, an idea of how I am to reach Jackson. OK, we don't have a letter from the governor, but at least I have a story I can tell."

"And get shot as a spy when they ask for your orders and you don't have any." Nash said.

"They won't shoot me Nash, I will get behind Jeanne Marie," I said jokingly. The letter was just too perfect. Who could ask for such a trump card in this great gamble. "Nash, we are gonna be lucky not to end up buried in the cave. Don't worry about this."

Nash got up and left, walking into the central hall, and we could hear him headed up the stairs.

"There has been a tremendous amount of pressure on dad for years. And each day it has grown and gotten more massive. I don't know how he has stood the pressure so long." Jeanne Marie said with tears in her eyes. I walked over, took her in my arms to comfort her.

"We have a plan," I whispered quietly.

"We always had a plan, now we just have more of one." She looked up, tears in her eyes. She was hurting for Nash.

"Let's sit and give him some time." I said, taking off the Confederate blouse and laying it on the counter.

"You said you had a plan, what's the rest of it?" I asked.

"Well when we get there, we will meet Michael, rest and assimilate into the time, and then split up." She said.

"Split up?"

"Yes, you will go to find Jackson, meanwhile I will go to Richmond to find Mrs. Jackson, try to befriend her, and place warnings in her mind. If you don't reach Jackson, the back-up is that his wife will talk to his aides and ask them to be even more protective of the general!" She said matter-of-factly.

I nodded, pushing my lips up and out, the secondary plan made sense.

"I have studied Anna's trip to visit Stonewall in April, and I will try to get in her path, probably at Richmond, but maybe before, if I can. She will have Julia so she might like some help." Jeanne Marie looked up, Nash had come back.

"Your daughter has been telling me about the secondary plan, Nash." I am impressed. I was trying to lift his spirits.

"This whole mission could not have been done without Michael and Jeanne Marie." Nash said.

The Adventure Begins
July 18, 2012

"Jeanne Marie, Parks it's time for you two to get dressed for the mission. Remember, empty all your pockets. You can't take anything with you. I know there is all of kinds of 21st century secrets in the *Alabama* that would have to be destroyed if something goes wrong. You can't take anything except what is in the different elements of fleeing back in time, OK?"

"I know dad."

"OK Nash. I looked at Jeanne Marie, I will meet you here in twenty minutes, OK?"

"Sure." Jeanne Marie sounded a little nervous for the first time.

Nash was on the porch waiting when I got back. I always felt right when I was wearing my olive-green aviator's flight suit. "Are the communication wires in the *Alabama* compatible with my helmet?" I asked. The one in the chopper I had used yesterday worked fine, but I thought my helmet more appropriate, it had my call sign, JOHNY REB written in white across the front.

"No problem," Nash said. "I guess I don't have to tell you to watch out for my daughter. And my son." He added.

"She's something. I wonder if she will be taking care of me?" I said with a smile.

"This is a lifetime's worth of work coming to fruition; it was back in the sixties when this all first started. I am having trouble accepting that we are about to begin a new future."

"Dr. Nash, don't get your hopes to high. I believe in God's plan. As General Jackson would say; "The duty is ours, the consequences are God's." I was hoping God was listening.

"Maybe this is part His plan Parks." Nash said as he took a sip of a mint julep he had setting on the table.

Jeanne Marie came out the screen door in her orange jump suit carrying a pair of flight gloves. It's hard for someone to look good in a jump suit, but Jeanne Marie did. She put a pair of aviators sun glasses on. "So, what do you think?" She did a series of poses, smiling.

"Looks pretty good," Nash pulled his daughter to him for a hug.

"Ah pops, not in front of the help, will ya?" She said pulling even closer to her dad, "I will be OK, dad," she purred.

"Guess it's time to go," Nash took a last swig of his drink, picked up his red baseball cap and put it on, and we walked down the front porch steps, wheeled left and started towards the runway. A few white clouds spotted the blue sky. It was comfortable, maybe the low 80s. Hard to believe it was July in west Texas. But this whole thing was hard to believe.

"We'll use the Jeep on the far side of the barn to pull the *Alabama* out from the hangar, uh barn. Once we get her out, it's your job to take off the safety lines from the blades darling," Nash said to Jeanne Marie. "And you ..." he looked at me.

"Nash, I have been to this rodeo before, I will do the pilot's exterior inspection."

You would have thought we were a practiced crew. Everyone focused on their different roles, no laughing or even talking. When your life is the price for even a moment's distraction, it puts a special intensity into what you are doing, you stay focused. Once the safety ropes were off, Jeanne Marie opened the side door and jumped into the cabin to begin her pre-flight checks. She really did have a big job. The engineer's pre-flight for the Hind was relatively simple and did not take her long. But, then she had to do the pre-flight on the space time aspects of the ship ... something I had no clue of.

When I jumped into the cabin, she had finished her pre-flight, had her helmet on, and was working through her protocols for the Time ship controls and checking gages and lights. As she hit toggle switches, lights started to come on, some permanent, some blinking. I climbed through the hatch and got myself into the cockpit, I saw Nash outside the bird, directly in front of me with the canopy open to the front seat, checking out the equipment in the stripped-out weapon's officer's cockpit.

"Test, this is a comm check, do you have me Parks,? Jeanne Marie's voice came alive in my ears.

"Sweet voice, never had a better comm check, roger." In my mind's eye I could see Jeanne Marie blushing. I hoped it, anyway.

Nash finished his checks, pulled his head out of the forward cockpit, gave me a thumbs-up, and pulled down and secured the canopy in front of me. He walked back past me on my left towards the open door to the cabin. After a few seconds Jeanne Marie came up on the system: "Pops gave me an up on all systems check, my pre-flight is complete, over."

"Roger, is the door secured and has Nash cleared from the craft? Over"

"Roger, we are clear for take-off." She said her voice sounding confident.

"Roger, still going through my second check list." I replied. The one big difference with this mission was that we were actually two different craft in one ship. First, we were an MI 24 Hind helicopter and then we were the Time Ship *Alabama* with a whole different set of propulsion and navigation systems. A system that scared the heck out of me, because my check flight would be our first operational mission. But it was kind of like the C.S.S. *Virginia*, and many other ships of the Confederate Navy that were forced to sail into battle without a single test of any of their systems.

As explained to me by Nash and Jeanne Marie, when we went through the "window" that was the entrance to an inter-dimensional wormhole which would take us from this reality and move us to the new Time River reality, the propellers would be reconfigured, turned into a molten metal mass and brought into a storage tank where the contents would serve as the core of a magnetic field. Something never done before, this was the one thing they could never do in flight in this reality, so we just didn't know if this new process would work. The process would have to be reversed when we passed through the second window, the exit from the wormhole, back to this reality but in North Carolina, 150 years in the past.

Too much to do right now, I wasn't even gonna think about the other things Jeanne Marie had to handle.

"Starting power plant, over" I said, the whine of the engine starting low hum over my voice, but quickly rising. The blades started to move slowly.

"Parks, this is Nash, over," he was coming up on the FM, not the internal system.

"Go."

"Don't forget, when you get on the other side, and catch up with Michael, send me something."

"Roger, over"

"Love you babe," Nash said. That obviously wasn't for me.

"Love you too, dad." Jeanne Marie.

"Mission's a go, good luck, out." Nash said, He saluted the bird. I returned the salute.

By now the propeller was closing on its optimum pre-flight rotation. The power of the engine was being felt inside the craft.

"All secure back there, Jeanne Marie? Over."

"Thumbs up," she said, "let's do it." I could see the smile on her face. This girl had guts, something I really like.

"Ally oops," I said as I lifted the bird into the air, "God be with us."

The ship was in really good shape and she lifted off the ground effortlessly. Nash had moved away from us, but not so far that the blade wash did not blow the baseball cap off his head as we took off.

We lifted past the tree line headed to the southwest. "Starting up my Time Navigation equipment for a test and to identify the window, over." Jeanne Marie was straight to her job.

"Roger, over." I looked around at the beautiful scene. Rebel Mountain was behind us. I was looking out at West Texas. El Paso was off beyond the horizon. I might see her lights, but doubted it, as the sun was not going to set before we dove into the cave. Nash anticipated our flight to be somewhere between two and half and three hours. Most of that flight time would be in the next dimension. The plan was to travel 100 years per hour. Anything faster could make it very hard to avoid collision with something.

The issue we didn't even discuss was how harmonics worked as the directional force in time. He only told me that the lower the harmonics, the faster we would move back in time. On our return we would be in the higher harmonics moving forward in time.

Suddenly I realized I was sweating. Normally, I loved flying and had absolutely no fear. Felt no pressure or strain. This time it was a little different. The plan was to dive into a cave at more than 200 KPH. If this "window thing" dad and daughter talked of so confidently was not there, we would be history in a fiery explosion. But, if the window was there, we would have passed through into another dimension placing our lives in untested equipment in an unknown environment. There was no way to anticipate how dying would occur in a strange dimension. And, if we made it back to the second window we would emerge over strange ground, at night, and not having any idea whether the reversed reconfiguration of the propeller had occurred properly. This was a flight full of unknowns, something I was not used too.

"Starting up DU power plant, and engaging Time navigation system, over" Jeanne Marie's voice came up. She sounded solid.

In the distance I thought I could see the crossroads Nash and I had identified as the mark for the final approach on the cave.

"Do you have the beacon for the crossroads, over" I asked.

"Roger, you are about 1/2 mile dead on. You need to be gaining altitude, over." Jeanne Marie was reminding me we had to get to 4,000 feet so as to use the kinetic energy of our dive to penetrate the window.

I started a wide circle to come back onto the marker from the South. "Climb to 4,000, and heading will be three five degree north when we cross the marker, over"

I like someone who does their job, "Roger, climb to 4,000, will try to approach marker at or near three five degrees north, give me a bearing check at the marker, over"

"Roger."

"All DU systems engaged, and standing by, remember to shift to Time Ship controls once we are in the cave, online with the window, over."

I just about had her on three five degrees, increasing speed to two hundred KPH, "You are at the marker, over" Jeanne Marie said, her voice not quite as strong as before, the ride was beginning.

Tried to boost her confidence "three five degrees north, at 4,000 feet, 200 KPH, here we go," I said. We were covering about a mile every 20 seconds. Rebel Mountain was on the horizon even at the marker.

"Two miles out, "Jeanne said.

"Lights visible, over" I told Jeanne, the lights Nash had said would be around the mouth of the cave. This bird was moving, it didn't take long to halve the distance, "Will commence dive at half mile out. Grab on to something. Over"

Barely a whisper, "Roger over"

We dove towards the cave accelerating as we fell. Just as we hit the mouth of the cave the propeller started to shrivel and almost like the rain drops on a windshield. "Retracting blade, over" Jeanne Marie reported.

I let go of the controls, though my feet stayed on the petals, force of habit I suppose. I hit the toggle and the Time Ship control swung up, and the three Time Ship navigation screens dropped in front of me. The canopy was covered over by a dark, seemingly molten material, like liquid rubber or something.

"DU systems fully engaged," as she said that the *Alabama* rocked hard, I heard a loud crashing sound below and behind me, and felt the rear of the craft coming up on the right. The screens lit up. I could feel the tension within the controls which told me I did have a force operating against me.

It took a moment to adjust. One screen had the four axis of flight, vertical, horizontal, lateral, and the time axis. "Reversed neutron field engaged," Jeanne Marie reported. She sounded weak.

"Roger, are you OK back there? over."

"Took a spill, back at my seat, over."

As we entered the new environment, we had to engage the propulsion system, which sounded much different from the Hind's engine and blades. We had to accelerate. We were no longer in an MPH, KPH reality. Now were moving in time space, and our speed was measured in years per hour ... but distance was also a factor.

The second screen displayed objects in space and their trajectories. This screen looked like a pin ball machine as objects were moving at quite a rate because it was like driving in the wrong lane, their approach velocity added to our own.

The third screen displayed the truest course to Mt. Airy, North Carolina, April, 1863.

"How you doing back there Jeanne Marie?"

"A little better, had the wind knocked out of me, but I am OK now, over."

"You did a great job engineer, all systems a go." I thought some positive news would help.

Once we had our routine set the flight actually became more like a traditional one. No doubt it was different, but almost like a computer game, it was addicting. It did require uninterrupted focus.

The first hour flew by pretty quick. Everything was new, and we were both working to make sure everything was functioning properly.

"Have a fix on the exit window, over" Jeanne Marie reported. "You will have plenty of energy to pass through it, so we don't need to dive, over."

"Do you know how we will re-emerge? Over"

"Not yet, over" Jeanne Marie said, a sense of urgency in her voice. I didn't want to bother her if she was doing something that could save our lives.

"I will add the window to your first and third screens when we are fifteen minutes out, still working on its location on the other side. Over"

"Roger."

A few minutes later the window came up on both screens. The approach to the window was not gonna be fun. Because of where the moon was, we would have to skirt around it, seconds before we passed through the window, and it would require a tight turn to make that.

"Make sure you are strapped in tight Jeanne Marie, don't want another accident. Over"

But as we got closer, on approach the real power of the *Alabama* shown. We were powered by anti-matter in this configuration, which provided power at an exponential rate to carbon-based jet fuel. It was actually easier to make very difficult aerobatic moves because we were in space, gravity was a lesser factor, and the power to alter course nothing like I had ever known before. We just glided past the moon and made a sharp descending turn towards the window and earth.

"You should come out about 1,500 feet above the Appalachians, over" Jeanne said. "I will track your approach to the window and reconfigure the propeller as we pass through. I will reconfigure and engage the engine and propeller just as we go through. Over"

Nothing had been easy in this flight, but engaging the engine and propeller in flight was not something I looked forward to. Hell, we could hit the ground in that time.

"We are about ten years out," Jeanne Marie said, "starting engine." As she said the whine started up. It would take a minute or so to get her up to operating power.

I had to keep her tightly focused on the window now.

"Thirty seconds to window," Jeanne Marie said, "reconfiguring now." I could feel a drop in power in my controls as the magnetic field was dissipating with the expulsion of the memory metal back out of the tank and outside the aircraft to form the propellers. Now I had to wrestle with the control to stay on the trajectory.

"Engaging engine. over"

My one hand reached down to grab the stick, my feet on the petals felt tension, we were through the window, more smoothly this time. The shield protecting my canopy almost seemed to melt away. We were right side up in a dark sky, the stars above me. We were back on the planet earth.

I hit the switch and Time ship screens pulled up and to the right, the controls retracted to my left front. We were back to being a Hind helicopter.

"Any idea where we are?" I said.

"No, but I am looking." Jeanne Marie said. "Computer is matching topography below to maps in the hard drive. Would suggest heading east, til we have a fix."

I was soaking wet. I felt relieved, we had done it. Whether we were in Virginia and whether it was 1863 I could not tell you, but it sure did look like earth, even in the darkness of night.

"Wow hoo, picked up a beacon …" you could hear the excitement in her voice, "Way to go Michael! … Should have you a fix, but come to eight three degrees east."

"eight three degrees east, roger, over"

"I think we are about fifty, five zero miles to the beacon." Jeanne Marie said.

"Taking her down to nap of the earth, less signature, do you still have the beacon? over."

"Weaker, but we are on it."

"Closing, five miles, you may want some altitude and to slow down I expect there will be lights at the LZ. over" Jeanne Marie said. Sometimes a woman anticipates a man's thoughts and when she does, it is both annoying and funny. You always wonder, did she know I was already thinking that?

"Rising to 200 feet, slowing to 80 KPH over" As we rose above the tree line I did see a single weak ray of light, almost like a light house beam, except rising from the ground and pointed up into the sky, moving in front of me and across the sky. A few seconds more and I picked up a series of four fires in a straight line along a wood line in a clearing. It was the same clearing where the light was emanating into the sky. The light shut off. He must have heard us coming in I thought.

As I approached the clearing, I could see two flashlights pointing at me and lined up with them. Michael was bringing us in. He used the proper hand movements to bring me to him, and then to indicate descend until he flattened out, meaning touch down. And boommm … we felt it. We were down.

"Touchdown, Jeanne Marie," I relayed to her.

"Shutting my systems down, will get out and see what the plan is, over." Jeanne Marie said.

I put the engine on its lowest cruise and waited. There were no exterior lights on, I could only see what the star and moonlight allowed. I did see Jeanne Marie run in front of the bird and jump up into Michael's arms. They hugged even in rotor wash. I could see them yelling at each other. He pointed to me with his flashlights, indicating to follow.

We probably moved less than 100 yards when he turned and indicated stop. A few seconds later Jeanne Marie came up on the intercom. "The hangar barn is directly in front of you. Once the prop has stopped moving, we can coast her in."

"Roger, shutting down prop. Over"

We could get some power to the wheels from the engine for a short move. The barn was large enough, but I was afraid I might push her too hard and slam into the back wall. So when I did kick her forward it wasn't with all the power. We slid forward, and in. I started my shut down procedures.

I took off my helmet, undid my belts, and shut down the last power. This was a flight I would never forget. I stepped down, through the hatch behind me into the cabin. Jeanne Marie had turned everything off except her lamp and was outside the bird talking to Michael.

I jumped out, nice to feel earth. The two walked over to me, Michael extending his hand. "I am Michael, thanks for bringing my sister home." He said, "Great job getting her into the barn, just made it."

I took his hand, smiled but exhaustion had caught up to me.

"We have to get you guys out of those clothes, and load your trunks in the wagon, so we can be on our way." Michael said as he climbed into the cabin in his 1860s outfit. "I will leave my flashlights and strobe in the *Alabama*."

The two chatted and laughed, spoke about their father, and were thrilled that they had actually done it. Michael grabbed the trunks with our clothes in them, and pulled them out of the ship. We took off our flight suits and threw them in a laundry bag, along with our boots. Jeanne Marie went back in the cabin to take off her 21st century underwear and get dressed in her 1860s clothes. I stood outside with Michael doing the same thing. The plan was that all 21st Century gear would be left in the chopper. We could not lock it, but assumed Michael had thought through the security aspects of what we were doing now.

Once we were dressed, we looked around to make sure everything was inside the bird and we shut the door. It had a discreet outside handle and we thought it unlikely that anyone who found it would be able to open it. At least not right away.

We walked out of the barn and Michael pulled the doors closed. "We don't have too far to ride to the house, but I do have to make sure these fires are down before we go." He was pointing to the four fires which had been used to get us to the clearing. We got up in the wagon. The bench was too small for three, so I climbed over it into the back and stood behind them. When Michael snapped the reins and the horses pulled forward, the force was enough to spill me backwards into the wagon crashing onto the trunks. The corners were sharp and stuck me in the ribs. "Ouch"

"Sorry about that." Michael said. Jeanne Marie spun her head around looked back at me and smiled.

"So how do I explain him?" Michael said.

"Explain him to who?" Jeanne Marie said.

"Hattie, my … uhhh, the woman I have been living with, and her sons, and her slaves?"

"He's my husband," without a moment's hesitation, "he is Colonel Parks Walter, my husband."

"Husband?" We both said in unison! and then laughed.

"Yes, and you best behave yourself, husband." She said. "But not too much." She winked. Michael didn't say anything.

We went from fire to fire, doing what we could to separate the burning logs and take the energy out of the fire. I really don't think they would have spread, even if we had done nothing. But Michael was right for being sure. Still it took some time to do it, and I was really tired.

The moon was rising and we got more light the later it got. Finally, the fire detail was over and we were headed towards the road that sat on the western side of the field. "Home is just a little more than a mile down the road. My lady's name is Hattie. She is expecting Jeanne Marie and my dad." Michael said. "We do have a room for you two?" There was a definite question in his voice.

"You don't have anything to worry about from me," I said, "I am bushed."

We traveled down the road, the stars sparkling in the sky above us. It smelled country. You could smell pine and honey suckle. Off to my right I thought I heard a brook, the water slapping over rocks. It seemed like it only took minutes 'til we were in sight of a house, the lights on inside. As we turned off the road into the yard you could see a woman sitting on the front porch. She got up and stepped down onto the ground as we came up.

"I see you have them, Michael," she said waving at us.

Michael pulled up on the reins stopping the wagon. He jumped down, walked around in front of the horses to help Jeanne Marie get down. I was climbing out the back when I heard Michael say: "Hattie this is my sister Jeanne Marie."

Hattie took a step forward and gave Jeanne Marie a big hug. "I am so glad to meet you, Michael talks about you all the time."

"He does?" Jeanne Marie said.

As I walked up to them Hattie said, "This must be your …"

"My husband," Jeanne Marie interceded, "this is Parks Walter, Colonel Parks Walter, Hattie"

Confused, Hattie extended a hand. "Michael told me …"

"He didn't know, Hattie. Parks and I are both headed to Virginia, though different places. But we figured we could at least come this far together."

Michael grabbed my arm, "Let's grab the trunks and carry them upstairs and let the women get acquainted." We each grabbed one of the trunks and put it on our shoulder and headed to the house. "The boys are sleeping, so do the best you can to be quiet." Michael said as he started climbing the porch steps. The wood creaked and there was nothing either of us could do about it.

Candlelight is strange, dimmer, flickering. I could see inside the house, but because it was not as bright as lighting in the 21st century, it wasn't as hard on the eyes when you came in from the dark. We headed up the stairs just inside the door, and Michael went into a room on the left just at the top of the stairs. He placed the trunk on the floor quietly, and I did the same.

"Knowing Hattie they will be visiting for a while. I am headed to bed. Morning comes early here Parks," he said, "I am so glad you two made it safe."

"Thanks Michael, I think I will just lay down a minute and catch my breath." I said as he left the room. I don't remember another thing.

Photo by Stephen McNierney

Looking towards the farm near Mt. Airy from Pilot Mountain.

The Farm, near Mt. Airy, North Carolina
April 10, 1863

I slept forever. The sun was up towards noon in the sky when I finally awoke. I don't know if it was the stress of the trip, or the hundred and fifty years we had traveled without sleep, but when I hit the bed last night, I was too exhausted to feel the ropes under the mattress. I didn't even take my clothes off.

It was warm and kind of humid, but I could hear the trees rustling through the open window, which told me there was a breeze. Outside I heard Jeanne Marie's voice as she was being introduced by a woman to some people. While I could plainly hear Jeanne Marie, the woman was a little harder to understand, and the other people were almost impossible to make out.

I could smell coffee, a stronger smell than I was used too ... time to get up.

Ouch, as I sat up on the bed my back hurt. Everything was sore; my arms, my hips, everything. Was that the after effects of the flight, or this bed? I put my feet over the side of the bed to learn that this was a high bed. I had to slide off the bed some for my feet to hit the floor. Where were my brogans?

Ah, there they are across the floor. I was surprised how comfortable they are. No laces, just a buckle. Not much of a sole though and no heel to speak of, I wondered how long they would last. Walking any distance in these could be tough.

Ummm, have to pee, wonder what they do? I laughed to myself. Doubt they have an upstair's bathroom here! Later I learned there was a pee pot under the bed.

I made my way through the doorway to the hall, and then down the stairs to the first floor. The front door was there at the bottom of the stairs, and I walked out onto the porch, my shoes making an awful racket.

The ladies heard me and turned.

"Morning Parks," Jeanne Marie said with a huge smile. "This is Hattie, Michael's wife."

Hattie curtsied and when she rose, walked towards me extending her hand. The wind blew pieces of her reddish-brown hair across her face. "Hello, Colonel Walter, I love your wife, Jeanne Marie, she is so fresh and alive. And it's so nice to hear a wife speak kindly of her husband. She really loves you."

Caught by surprise at Hattie's remarks, I looked at Jeanne Marie who was blushing a bright red.

Hattie was a fine lookin' lady in her own right. Her dress went to the ground, was tight around her waist. But she was a buxom lass. She had pretty brown eyes, and high cheek bones.

I glanced back at Jeanne Marie before I bowed to Hattie, took her hand, "Hattie, I am so pleased to meet you. Please ma'am my name is Parks. "

"Ma'am, I don't know how to ask this …"

Hattie turned back towards Jeanne Marie and the slaves who were standing with her, "Micah, come here." One of the blacks quickly moved towards us. "Micah, take the Colonel to the outhouse." She looked over her shoulder towards me, her eyes flashing, to confirm her guess.

"Yes, ma'am" Micah said. "This a way suh" he said as he pointed around the house.

As we walked around the house and towards the back you could see a small building with several doors, off maybe forty yards in the direction of the breeze. It didn't take long before the smell reached us. Micah was about to turn to return to the group when I heard a low hum in the outhouse which seemed to be growing. I grabbed Micah's arm.

He jumped to the unexpected touch, and looked at me, then smiled realizing that I heard the sound.

"Oh suh, that's just the beez. Ya know they love them shit holes, don't worry none, they won't bother you. And they's sure do make us some good honey." I let go of his arm, he tipped his straw hat and headed off.

Hummm, hadn't even considered sharing my private moments with bees.

After my initiation to old world, I walked back around to the front of the house to find the ladies and Micah moving chairs and a small table on to the front porch.

"Ah there you are darling," said Jeanne Marie, "will you join us for some coffee and biscuits?"

"Absolutely, I am starving. Will Michael be joining us?" I said loud enough for Hattie to hear.

"Not likely," Hattie said without stopping her work, "he's out on the west field with the field hands checkin' the tobacco and weedin'. We just had a rain the last couple of days and if'n we don't weed quick, the weeds will bury our corn."

"Oh"

"Michael will be back this evening, Parks. We have the day to get our bearings and visit with Hattie." Jeanne Marie said as she stood behind a chair indicating she wanted me to take a seat.

Two black women brought out cups, a pot, a plate full of biscuits and set the table. "That is very kind of you," I said.

One of the ladies curtsied and bowed, before saying "Suh, its no trouble t'all. If'n we wasn't here we'd be in the hot field, so we's 'preciaten' y'all's visting Miss Hattie."

"Yes suh," said the other younger lady, "I am Mary, suh.

As Mary poured the coffee, Hattie sat down to one side of me, Jeanne Marie on the other, "So how is the war going Colonel?"

Not a question I had ever anticipated, and thought slowly how to respond. "Well, Miss Hattie, they ain't whopped us yet, and we are finally getting things organized. This coming campaign season could be the teller on how this is going to turn out."

Hattie smiled, "Amazin'."

"How's that?" I said, frowning. Inside I was scared to death I said too much or the wrong thing.

"Well," she said with her sweet Southern tongue, "I think it's amazin' that lil' ole me told Michael just about the same thing last night, after we got to read the paper from Richmond."

"Would you still have that paper Miss Hattie?" I asked.

"Thelma, would you get the paper in the sittin' room for the Colonel?" Hattie said.

The older of the two women sitting on the porch just some feet from us got up and went into the house, came back out with the paper and handed it to me. "Thank you, Thelma," I said.

I looked at the paper, the *Richmond Examiner*, April 4th, 1863. "April 4th?" I said to Hattie.

"Yes, we got that one pretty quick, just six days." Ah ha, it was April 10th I thought to myself. Was wondering how I would confirm what the date was. I have about two weeks to get up to Lee's Army.

"Hattie, we have been on the road a couple of days, what is today?"

"Why it's Thursday, Thursday, April the 10th."

I took a sip of my coffee, looked at Hattie "Quite good," I smiled, "thank you." I looked back down at the paper.

The paper was cluttered with stories in tiny print. I remember looking at examples of these old papers way back on the other side of time, and wondering how these people could ever read these things, the print was so small? The ladies started talking lady talk as I read, drank my coffee and ate a biscuit. The paper was full of war news, politics, and advertisements. One of the stories was a follow up about an explosion at the Confederate Ordinance Laboratory on Brown's Island, near Richmond which occurred on March 13th, 1863 and the 69 casualties were all women; I thought to myself, the manpower shortage was already showing itself.

Another story reported on the bread riots that occurred in Richmond on April 1st.

Jeanne Marie looked at me, got up and walked around the table, "Parks, you look a sight, sir. I think we need to clean you up after you finish eating."

"Please dear," I tried to brush her away, I wanted to finish looking at the paper.

"Parks you need a shave, and to refresh your tie, and to wash your face, and ...."

I laughed "OK Jeanne Marie, as you say dear. But, let me finish this coffee first."

"There is a bowl and a mirror in your room," Hattie said, "Thelma can you make sure there is water in the pitcher for the Colonel to use?"

"Yes, ma'am"

"Jeanne Marie, I think we need to start thinking about your trip to Richmond." I said, not thinking anything of it.

"What do you mean?" Hattie said

Jean Marie turned towards Hattie; "I am meeting mother in Richmond on the 19th."

"The 19th?" Hattie said with a sense of urgency, "We have a couple days, but we must start planning this right away" Hattie got up from the table and went to the front door. "George Washington!" She yelled out.

In a couple of moments George Washington appeared. "Yes, ma'am."

"We have to get Mrs. Walter to Richmond, would you please give some thought as to how to get her there, and who will go with her and let me know."

"Yes ma'am." Hattie turned and came back to the table. George Washington will tell us how to get this done.

* * * *

That evening, about five o'clock, we were out in the front yard when we heard some noise approaching the cabin. It was a group of people, one white man and a bunch of slaves. Jeanne Marie yelled out "Michael," and took off like a bullet towards them. The man who was mounted on a horse, dismounted, handed the reins to a man next to him, and ran towards the oncoming Jeanne Marie, like something out of a movie. They ended up in a big hug on the side of the road while the slaves rode in a wagon or walked past them.

"Evening suh," they said as they passed me. I was walking towards the brother and sister. The smiles were large on their two faces and they were both talking about as fast as they could get words out when I approached them. Jeanne Marie saw me coming, stepped back from Michael, put her arm through mine and said; "Michael, this is my husband Colonel Parks Walter of the North Carolina Volunteers."

I looked at her sideways with a smile, looked back at Michael and extended my hand, "Walter, Michael, pleased to meet you. Heard a lot about you from Jeanne Marie and Hattie."

Michael smiled, shook my hand, then scratched his head and said, "I ain't heard nothing about you!" We all laughed.

"This is some place you got here." I said.

"Ah, you ain't seen the half of it. We were out working one of the smaller fields, one hundred acres. Got tobacco out there."

"Well hush my mouth," Jeanne Marie said lifting her hand to her mouth. She was teasing Michael. "I didn't know my brother was a propertied man such as yourself. That looked like a dozen or more slaves with you, when you came prancing in here."

"It was." Michael said smiling.

We started walking down the dirt road towards the home. Hattie was standing on the front porch, her hands on her hips, her apron cross the front of her long dress. She had been shucking corn before the entourage approached.

"I really did not get a chance to commend you last night for the organization of the landing zone, and the beacon, and having a place for us to hide the *Alabama*." I said to him.

"Hey that's why dad sent me in early. I have been here for three years because there was a lot to do." Michael said.

"It's still hard to accept that you left about a week before us, and you have been here three years." Jeanne Marie said.

I said, "I guess you could say he has stolen some days, Jeanne Marie."

Michael took off his hat to wipe the sweat off his brow as we walked, "Well sis, I can tell you it has been almost three years and I have worked my can off just about every day. So, what do you think of Hattie and the boys?"

Both Jeanne Marie and I started to talk at the same moment. We looked at each other, "You first," I said.

"Michael, she is wonderful woman. She was very kind to us today, thoughtful, and easy to talk to." Jeanne Marie said.

"And, she's in charge." I added.

"In charge is right. She had been running this whole place for a couple of years before I arrived. Her husband had left her, with two boys, twenty slaves and a farm of almost a thousand acres."

"Michael, the home is pretty … but well isn't it kind of log cabinish for a thousand acre place, isn't it?" Jeanne Marie said.

"You are right, sis. You see her husband owned the house and about two hundred acres and didn't have any slaves. Hattie brought almost eight hundred acres and fifteen slaves as her dowry." Michael said.

"Wow." I was impressed, "Comes from a wealthy family, does she?"

"Yes, she does, and well, she is the second sister. She was in a hurry to get married and took the first man to come along. Seems it didn't work out, and he skedaddled after they had Karl David and Jimmie Earl. Hattie's father said he sensed mendacity in Tucker, but not enough to block the marriage."

Just about that time we were walking up on the house and Hattie. There was a flurry of activity around the house. Some of the slaves were over near the barn, doing the afternoon milking of the cows, the slave children were chasing the chickens trying to get them into their chicken house. The kids and chickens were making quite a racket, between the clucking and the kids yelling and laughing.

Michael explained: "The chickens are let out each morning to wander the yard and find food. One of the slave children go in and collects the eggs from the night before."

Other slaves were taking the bridle and gear off the horses that had been pulling the wagon. And I could smell food cooking when a breeze came up from the east. When I said something, Michael replied; "The slave village is in that direction on the other side of the creek. Some of them have to do the cooking for the rest, and also the maintenance and care of their homes, plus work their gardens. Each winter we have worked to improve their conditions. There is even another barn over there."

"This is really a huge operation, isn't it?" Jeanne Marie said.

"Yes, it is, and George Washington. ..."

"We met him," both Jeanne Marie and I said at the same time.

"Great, I am glad you did," Michael said, "he has a lot to do with how efficiently this place runs. He has been with Hattie since she was a newborn. He is like an uncle to her. She trusts him completely, and so do I."

Thelma came out on the porch, "Miss Hattie supper will be ready in about twenty minutes, ma'am." When Hattie heard that she turned to us out in the yard. "Time to wash up!" She said in a commanding voice. She looked at me and Jeanne Marie, "I had a basin and a pitcher of water placed in your room. Sorry there isn't a mirror. Jeanne Marie, you can use this." Hattie handed her a hand mirror. "Now go get cleaned up quick so you can eat the food while it's fresh. And then we have something to tell you."

We went to the room prepared for us and got washed up. It was one of the first moments we were alone since we had arrived. I wanted to steal a minute with her, just to be alone. After we both washed, we came back down to the dining room which was a little tight for six people and for the room necessary for servants to serve.

Hattie was already there, her apron removed and Michael came in. "Michael, would you offer the Blessing?" Hattie said. Karl David and Jimmie Earl ran to the doorway, each running his hand to slick back his hair. They then calmly walked in to the dining room and ended behind their assigned seats at the table.

"Let us bow, Almighty Father thank you for another day and for the health of all. And thank you for the land we steward for you, and for the help you have given us with George Washington's family. Thank you for the safe travel of Jeanne Marie, and Parks. God please let us do Thy will and be satisfied with your plan. Amen." We all echoed and then pulled our chairs back and sat down.

"Thelma," is all Miss Hattie said and servants began bringing in the food.

"How was your day, boys?" Michael asked.

"We didn't see a thing." Jimmy Earl said with a frown on his face.

"They must have known we were coming dad," Karl David said to Michael.

"Who knew you were coming?" Jeanne Marie asked.

"The critters," Jimmy Earl said.

"The critters?" Jeanne Marie said looking down on little Jimmy Earl who was sitting right beside her.

Karl David intervened "We were hunting today Miss Jeanne Marie, and we didn't see nothing worth shootin'."

"That happens," Michael said, "but did you see any sign?"

"Oh yes suh," Jimmy Earl said, "there's a herd of hog out there I'm certain."

"Yes suh, and we did see some dear skat too. Just didn't see any critters."

Jimmy Earl reached up and tugged on Jeanne Marie's sleeve, she looked down at him. Jimmy Earle smiled, a gaping hole 'tween his teeth, he said almost in a whisper "I am pretty sure I heard a turkey out there. Pretty sure," he nodded his head.

"Ohhhh" Jeanne Marie whispered back.

"Well, maybe next week then," Hattie said.

"You gonna tell 'em mom?" Karl David asked Hattie.

"Hush child." Hattie said not wanting to be pushed.

"Tell us what?" I asked.

"Ah go ahead Michael, now's as good a time as any." Hattie said, a little miffed at her son.

"Well with you two being here, we decided we would get married tomorrow."

There was a moment of silence. It hit Jeanne Marie the strongest.

Then the table burst forth with talking, Jeanne Marie reached over to Hattie and touched her arm. The random chaotic talk went on for a couple of minutes before Hattie held up her hand. The table got quiet.

"Jeanne Marie and Colonel, my family will be coming over tomorrow afternoon and we will get married around four o'clock. Jeanne Marie I would be honored if you would be one of my bride's maids …" Hattie said.

"Colonel, would you be my best man?" Michael asked, not knowing what I would say.

I looked at Jeanne Marie, "Sure would sir, it would be an honor."

"Momma, can we go out and play?" Karl David asked.

And how do you ask that Mr. Karl David?" Hattie looked at him sternly.

"May I be excused momma?" Karl David said.

"Yes, you may"

Karl David pushed back his chair and got up and left. "Can I be excused momma?" Jimmy Earl jumped in before Hattie's first reply had finished. She looked at Jimmy Earl.

Jimmy Earl bowed his head; "May I be excused too, momma?"

"Yes, you may." Hattie said again. And Jimmy Earl disappeared in a flash.

Once the boys were gone, Hattie decided she wanted to explain what was going on.

"Uh, hummm," she kind of coughed to get our attention. "Colonel, Jeanne Marie this is kind of embarrassing, but family is family and I know you have to have questions, and I want to answer them right here and now. You probably thought based on the arrangements and all that we were already married." Hattie's face turned a little pink, then a brighter shade of red.

"Well, ..." Hattie started to say something.

"Folks, I love Hattie and have, almost since the moment I first saw her," Michael intervened. "I would have married Hattie six months after I got here, but couldn't because of state law. Where ever Tucker went, he had to be gone a certain amount of time before a divorce due to abandonment could be legal."

"But we fell for each other, and circumstances kind of led from one thing to the next." Hattie interceded. "We went to my father and explained everything. He wasn't convinced at all. But he did come over to the farm one day, and he saw how everything was running and he talked to George Washington."

"And well, I guess he didn't like it, but he said things would be alright, and that we would pretend to have a wedding at his home for the boy's sake. But it wasn't legal." Said Michael, "But the appropriate amount of time has passed, and unless Tucker shows up tomorrow to object, we will be getting married."

"I should like to propose a toast to you two, would we have something appropriate" I asked. Jeanne Marie reached for my arm with her hand. She was beaming.

"Let me see," Hattie said.

Hattie, followed by Jeanne Marie went out of the dining room towards the parlor. "God Bless you Michael, but how we going to make this work?" I asked.

"Easy," Michael said in a low voice, "I am staying when you two go back."

Just then the women walked in with a mostly used up decanter of wine, four crystal glasses and a jug!

"They will have the wine, we get the White Lightening," Michael said with a big smile. We stood up. Michael took the jug and poured two glasses; Hattie poured two glasses of wine.

We lifted our glasses to the center, "May God bless your home, your children, and your love." I said. The tinkle of crystal touching led to a drink by each of us, and some hugs all around. I watched Jeanne Marie and she was so happy, like a little girl.

"Let's move out to the porch," Hattie said. As we walked out, Michael peeled off, but came back quickly. He handed me a cigar we walked out into the yard while the ladies sat at a table on the porch.

"You can see Hattie has some serious good upbringing," Michael said as he lit a match and applied it to the end of his cigar. The flame rose when he inhaled, the tobacco glowing red as it caught fire, "We already have plans for another home, more like the plantation you two probably think we should be in. Give us enough time and this will look like a real plantation." He blew some smoke out in front of him.

"You sure put the wedding together quick!" I said.

"No, not really, we had talked about this and she knew my family was coming. I thought it would be dad and Jeanne Marie that was the original plan. So, we kind of preplanned everything and talked to the Taylor's, Hattie's parents, about trying to do something when my family showed up. I know you two don't have a lot of time to visit with us, so we had to have a plan ready to go on short notice." Michael said looking out towards the front of the property. I could see he was envisioning the future, trees cleared, lawns in place. Michael seemed very content with his new life here in this place.

"I will be sleeping in the barn tonight." Michael said.

"Huh?"

He laughed, "Yes, I spent my first night on this farm sleeping on the floor in the barn. The night my time ship crashed into the woods over that way." He waved his hand off towards the left. "God that was a terrible night, I don't remember most of it."

He went on, "The afternoon of the first day I was here the boys had found my bag out in the woods near the wreckage of my craft. They had carried in the bag …"

"Your bag?" I questioned.

"Yes, dad had gotten an old bag from this time, and he had filled it with old federal money, about one thousand dollars, a bar of gold, and a lot of Confederate currency. It was to help me get a place where the *Alabama* could land. I was supposed to look closer towards Petersburg, and I did. But in the end, I thought this was too perfect both for me, and for the operation."

"What about the bag?" I said.

"Well the boys couldn't open it, and when I told them it was mine, they looked at me funny but gave it to me. It helped me help Hattie, and kind of made me respectable to the people in this area. Money does that." He said

"And what about the wreckage?"

"Interesting thing there, a couple days after I arrived, and after I had regained my health George Washington came to me and said that he thought there was a mess we should clean up. I didn't know what he was talking about, so he said he would show me. We walked out that way," Michael pointed to the woods again, "and George Washington led me to a pile of debris, it was the remnants of my craft. He said, "Should we burn it suh?" I said, "yes." That's the last anyone has spoken a word about it."

"George Washington, huh?" I said.

"I think mine is not the only secret George Washington knows. He is truly a splendid and caring protector of Hattie and the boys." Michael said puffing on his cigar, "He is as much a part of this family as anybody else, and so are his family. It's something not taught in 21st Century schools."

Dusk was settling on the farm when we heard the thunder of hooves in the distance. They were getting louder, indicating they were headed in our direction. Everyone froze, none of us knowing what this sound meant. In a moment we made out the lead of a cavalry column approaching us. As they got closer, we could make out the Confederate Battle Flag and could be a little more at ease.

But, as the group pulled into the yard in front of the house tensions rose as the soldiers dressed in gray had the appearance of Indians, long hair, some with feathers in their hair. The ranking officer dismounted and walked up to me and Michael and presented his compliments. "Would this be Hattie Taylor's place?" He said.

Michael taken back that the officer would know Hattie's maiden name answered cautiously, "Yes it is, sir."

"Fine, fine, my name is Colonel William Thomas, commander of the Thomas Legion and I would like to spend the night in camp with my escort, would that be alright, sir?"

"Yes sir, I am Michael Laurent, Hattie's husband-to-be tomorrow, and it would be quite fine for you to camp on our property." Michael turned looking for George Washington. Michael waved to Micah to come over, "Micah, could you fetch your father and tell him I would like to speak to him?"

"Yes, suh" Micah turned and headed off towards the slave cabins on the other side of the creek.

Michael extended his hand to Colonel Thomas, "Pleased to meet you Colonel, this is my brother-in-law Colonel Parks Walter."

The two shook hands, he then turned towards me extended his hand and said, "Please to meet you Colonel Walter, I see I am not the only the officer ordered here to meet Governor Vance." He smiled.

"What?" Michael said

"Sure Michael, didn't you know the Governor would be attending your wedding?" The Colonel took pleasure in the surprise he had just brought to Michael. "Didn't you know he was staying at the Taylor's plantation?"

"No, I did not," Michael said in a huff, he turned sharply and walked to the house. About that time, George Washington met Michael halfway to the house, out of hearing distance. I turned to talk to the Colonel, "Fine looking body of men and mounts sir, but they have a strange look about them." I said.

"Colonel Parks these are men from the Cherokee Battalion of my legion." He said.

About that time George Washington walked up to us, "Colonel," he was looking at me, then he looked at Thomas, "Colonel, suh, I am George Washington Taylor, and I have been directed by Mister Michael to lead you across the creek and past our village to a place for you and your men to camp, suh."

"Is it far George Washington?" Colonel Thomas asked.

"No, suh."

Thomas turned towards his escort, "Sergeant, have the men dismount and follow us in a column of twos."

"Yes sir." I heard as we turned and started walking behind George Washington, "Dismount." I could hear. The clanks and jingles of solders dismounting from their horses filled the air.

"The Governor is really coming tomorrow?" I asked.

"Sure is," Thomas said, "I know because I have to report to him tomorrow about an event that occurred in my district back in January."

"Oh?" I said.

"Yes, and I will be glad to do it and get this done with. The supposed massacre at Shelton Laurel in Madison County of Confederate deserters and Yankee bushwhackers has been a thorn in my side for too long. I hope to make this my final report to the Governor about that distasteful event." Colonel Thomas never looked at me as he spoke.

"Understandable," I said. We followed George Washington across the creek and past the slave village on the left. About a hundred yards down the road there was a clearing, spotted with a couple large oak.

"This is it suh," George Washington said to Colonel Thomas. "Make yourselves ta home."

"Colonel, I believe I will head back to the house, I am sure there is probably some excitement about the news. Good night, sir." I saluted.

"Good night, Colonel." He returned the salute as the dismounted troop walked past the two of us.

As I walked away, I could hear the sergeant organizing the encampment, giving instructions for a picket line to tie the horses to, the building of a camp fire, and the watering of the horses. It didn't take me long to get back to the house. Jeanne Marie had come out looking for me. When she saw me walking up the road from the creek, she came a running.

"Did you hear, Parks? Governor Vance will be here tomorrow ..." Her excitement faded with her last words as she realized the potential for trouble. Her smile went to a look of concern, "I wonder if he will have any questions about who you are?" She said.

"I don't know," I said as I took her arm in mine and walked back to the house. I didn't realize it, but George Washington had followed behind us. As we came up to the front porch Hattie was coming out the front door.

"GW, poppa is bringing the Governor tomorrow."

"Yes ma'am, I heard." George Washington said from behind me.

"Well, I guess you know this means we all have to be on our special behavior." Hattie said. "I can't believe it, Governor Vance at my wedding!" She threw her hands in the air, turned around, her hoop skirt spinning behind her, she headed back into the house giving orders like a ship's captain.

Jeanne Marie took off after her.

George Washington stepped forward; his mouth close to my ear: "Don't worry 'bout the Guvenor suh. Masser Taylor is a good friend of his, won't be no troubles tomorrow." With that, GW said good night and headed back towards the creek and his village.

The evening went by very quickly as preparations dominated all the activities. The women were busy talking when I decided it was time to turn in. I walked into the parlor where they were talking, "Jeanne Marie, I am gonna say good night darlin'."

Without even looking, she waved at me nonchalantly and said, "I will be up after a while, dear."

I went upstairs to our room, got undressed to my long johns and got into bed. The room was dark. I lay thinking how strange this was. There was no electricity, only a window. From my place I could see the stars in the sky. The night sky was sparkling like a bowl of a diamonds poured onto a black velvet cloth. This adventure was really unbelievable. We really were one hundred fifty years in past. The smells, the sounds, all the animals and activity were engulfing me. Meeting Major Thomas tonight and his Confederate Indian escort was not something I could have ever imagined. But it happened.

I started to doze a little bit when the door opened and Jeanne Marie came in. She started to undress, "Are you awake, Parks?" She said almost in a whisper.

"Yes," I said in a low voice. It took her awhile to get her dress off, and like me she kept her long undergarments on. I was a little surprised when she moved close to me after she got under the covers. She reached around and pinched me on the behind. She searched in the dark with her lips, to find mine, then she kissed me. I started to kiss back, but she pulled her head back; "Can you believe this? I mean we are here! What a day." She snuggled next to me. It wasn't long before she was out.

Wedding Day
April 11th, 1863

"Karl David, Jimmy Earl, let's go it's time to get up, we have a lot to do before grand pa Taylor gets here." It was still dark, but Hattie was up and I wondered if she would be coming in to wake us up. I nudged Jeanne Marie who had not moved since she fell asleep. She moved slightly just as Hattie spoke even louder; "Jimmy Earl, Karl David up boys, now. First thing head down to the creek and bring me up a couple of pales of water. Now let's get going."

Hattie's voice sparked life in Jeanne Marie, and she raised her head slightly, opened her eyes slowly and smiled. "Good mornin' " she said.

"Morning."

Jeanne Marie leaned towards me, and I moved towards her pulling her close and kissed her. She was the first woman I ever slept with and didn't sleep with. She was as much as I thought she could be when I watched her in the library. And she kissed me back. But then she pushed away, "Parks this is gonna be a day to remember, let's get moving." Her brother was getting married and she didn't want to miss a second.

With that she popped out of the bed, and started dressing. "Oh, I wish there was a potty," she said.

"I can step out of the room, and you can use the pee pot. It's under the bed on your side," I said. I had my pants already on, and though the room was only slightly lit by the pre-dawn light coming in the window, I grabbed my brogans and made my way around the bed and out of the room. "I am gonna go find me a tree." I said quietly.

I don't know why, but I tried to be quiet as I made my way down the stairs to the first floor and went into the parlor to put my brogans on. In the kitchen I could hear the boys grabbing the pails. "Karl David, I want you to pour your first pail of water into the pot. Then go upstairs and get the pitcher in Jeanne Marie's room and bring it down here. Then head back to the creek for a second pail of water. Jimmy Earl, I want you to pour some of your pail into the pitcher when your brother gets it down here. And put the rest in the sink, OK?"

"Yes momma," Jimmy Earl said. The boys took off running out the back door towards the creek.

I decided I would sneak out the front door headed for a tree. As I got to the front door, it opened inward and Michael came in, "Morning Parks, headed to the woods?" He said holding the door open.

As I walked out, I smiled. There were routines back one hundred and fifty years ago, they just weren't the ones I had ever read about in a history book.

By the time I got back Jeanne Marie was downstairs, lanterns had been lit in the kitchen and the ladies were already busy laying out the schedule of work for the day. "We do have a bathtub Jeanne Marie, and I will make sure the boys are heating water by lunch time. If it's OK, you go first, and I will go after you."

"What about the men?" Jeanne Marie asked

"There's a creek," Hattie said. Both of them burst out laughing.

I walked into the kitchen to find the ladies still laughing while they worked to grind the coffee beans. "What can I do?"

"Find Michael, and stay with him," Hattie said, "It will be great to have an extra hand today. But Colonel," Hattie walked up to me and gave me a hug, "Please make sure you take the time to dress your best for the wedding. My poppa will love you as Michael's best man." She hugged me again and then turned back to work. "We will have coffee in about half an hour."

The boys came running into the kitchen with their pails of water.

I skedaddled out of there, back towards the front of the house, and out onto the porch to find Michael, George Washington and Micah all in the front yard talking. I walked out to them, "Morning" I said. Their conversation never stopped by my interruption.

George Washington and Micah turned from Michael when he was through giving instructions and walked briskly, but separately in two directions.

"We have a lot to do Parks. We didn't know the Governor would be here, and now we have twenty-one more guests we didn't know we would have with Major Thomas and his men. So, there's no time to dawdle." Michael said, "We have to get the morning chores done quickly, so we can start the wedding preparations."

"Ok, Michael, I am at your disposal." I said.

He walked down the road towards the creek, and I had to walk quickly to catch up to him. "I am headed down to the encampment to talk with the Colonel, and invite his men to the wedding." Michael said.

The sun was just breaking over the high pine to the east. I don't remember ever being so fully engaged this early in the morning. I guess it was somewhere after six. The sounds of the birds waking up, they were surprised at the amount of human activity this early in the morning. As we walked past the slaves' quarters, and towards the encampment, the smell of coffee and food cooking surrounded us.

Soldiers in various states of dress were rolling their bed roll as we walked up. Colonel Thomas was standing at the camp fire talking to a couple of soldiers as we approached. I noticed two horses fully saddled, though without the girt in their mouths.

"Good morning Colonel," Michael said

"Morning."

"Colonel, I could have some eggs brought down to you this morning if you like."

"That would be much appreciated, Michael, thank you."

"You can imagine we were not expecting twenty-one, well twenty – two if you count the governor more guests, so please be patient with us as we do what we can to offer full hospitality to you, and your men."

"I appreciate that Michael. If you will allow my men to hunt your property, we may be able to get you some fresh meat."

"Thank you, Colonel, that would be really very helpful, but I don't know if we can prepare it in time?"

"We'll take care of that Michael, if it's OK with you?"

"Sure sir, thank you."

"One other thing. We could provide an honor guard for the governor as he arrives, and even provide an arch of sabers for your wedding if like?" The Colonel said as he took the last swig of coffee from his cup.

"That is a very thoughtful offer Colonel Thomas; I don't know how we could repay you for the kindness. If you stay the night, we might be able to have a full breakfast for you and your men." Michael was making an effort to show his gratitude.

"I think that would be more than satisfactory. And I do expect we can stay the night unless the Governor has orders for me to execute immediately."

"Fine, then we have a deal." Michael said.

Just then to our south, a musket shot cracked through the air. "I took the liberty of telling my hunters to find us meat, sounds like they found it," the colonel said. "I believe you will have venison for your wedding." The Major said with a knowing eye.

"Colonel, I notice two mounts saddled, are you going for a ride?" I asked.

"No Colonel, we always keep two mounts saddled, one for an incoming courier to have a fresh mount, and one because." Colonel Thomas said.

"Because?"

"Because this is war, and you never know what can happen." He said, a tinge of the voice of experience in his words.

After some more discussion we parted. "Let's take a walk through the slave quarters on our way back to the house," Michael said. There were only a few women in the village cleaning things up by the time we got there. "Good morning Flora."

"Mornin' Mister Michael," a black woman who appeared older said. "Big day today for Miss Hattie and you." She said with a smile. Some of her teeth were missing.

"Well you sure did get the family out to work early today," Michael said.

"Yes suh, we knows there's much to be done, George Washington gave everyone their jobs last night. We heard the governor's comin' and Masser Taylor, and well we just want to make Masser Tayler and Hattie proud. And you too suh." She said, lowering her head, embarrassed that she put the Taylor's first. "Miss Flora, you always do the Taylor's proud, and me too." Michael said.

Her face rose with warm smile, "It's fixin' to be the Lord's Day to-day, suh."

"We all will have a grand time today, a celebration Flora. See you later." Michael said.

"Yes suh." We continued our walk around the quarters. Past the quarters was a small plowed patch of ground.

"That's their garden, they have others. What they grow there is theirs."

Further down the wood line was a large barn, corral and fenced pasture. "That's where we keep some of the horses and a lot of the equipment."

"Michael, you have some operation here."

"Well it is a large operation, but it takes a lot of people doing a lot of different things. George Washington's people are good people, who do a day's worth of work. He don't allow no Tom Foolery." Michael spoke with a knowing confidence.

"They sure do seem to have real affection for Hattie and her father." I said.

"They sure do. It really is more like a large family then you would think. Last year when Flora's daughter got the fever, Hattie's father had her moved into their house, and brought a doctor from Salem. That doctor stayed for a week 'til the fever was gone. Mr. Taylor spent hours with Ruth, reading to her, and caring for her."

We continued our walk back to the house. "Michael, if we can, I need to try to meet and talk to the governor. The more I know him, the less difficult it will be to gain access to General Jackson. I am hoping to portray myself to Jackson as a liaison from Governor Vance."

"Parks, Mr. Taylor is close to the Governor, I will see what I can do."

All morning the boys were running back and forth to the creek bringing water to the house. George Washington had his people working, cooking, setting up the front yard for the wedding. The weather was clear and comfortable. All the new life on the trees was a lime green, a brighter more vibrant color then would be the case in just a month or so. Small patches of spring flowers had sprung up.

Micah and another man, Cletus, Flora's husband, were working on an arch which was to be used as the place for the pastor, bride and groom. Around 10 o'clock the Pastor arrived from Mt. Airy. He rode a large black steed and looked quite distinguished even for his youth, I don't think he was but forty years old. Hattie told me that not only was he a good pastor, but a singer with a fine voice. He rode up, dismounted and approached me with a smile. "I am Pastor Eitson, Jamie Eitson," his hand outstretched, a smile on his face.

"I am Colonel Walter, Pastor, but please call me Parks. Cletus come over here please."

Cletus came over to us, "Would you please take the Pastor's horse to the line."

The Pastor handed Cletus the reins, "Let me get my Bible?" He reached in to the saddle bags and pulled out a large dark book, leather bound. "Please remove the bridle and put the halter on him so he can enjoy your fine sweet grass."

"Yes, suh pastor," Cletus said. He turned and led the horse away.

"Could you take him to the creek first, let him have a drink?"

"Yes, suh." Cletus yelled back.

"That's a fine mount you have, sir. Let's walk over to the arch so you can see the place where the deed will be done." I said. We walked the short distance across the yard, the Pastor looking in all directions at the activity, the laughter of happy people. The boys ran up to Jamie, barefoot, still not dressed for event. Probably a good thing as active as they were.

"Hello Pastor." Karl David said as he ran into Jamie's leg.

Jimmy Earl, a little more in awe of the Pastor stopped a few feet in front of him. "Hello Pastor." He bowed deeply, then stood back up smiling.

"Well good morning Jimmy Earl, have you learned how to greet a quest today?" Jamie said.

"Mom taught me" Jimmy Earl said.

"She taught me too, Uncle Jamie, but I didn't think you were a guest, I can bow too if you like?" Karl David stepped back, and bowed.

"Very good Karl David, you both seem to have learned well. Don't forget to do it for your grandpa Taylor and the Governor." Jamie placed his hands in his coat pockets, "Now let me see, I am sure I have something for you two."

The two boys rushed to his coat, one on each side. Jamie made a great show of trying to find something in those pockets. "Hummm, where are they now, could some mice have gotten into me pockets? No, I am sure it must be there, I checked before I left me house." Jamie's grim face turned to a smile, as he pulled his two hands from the pockets of his coat. In each hand was a sling shot.

"Wow," Karl David said, a broad grin across his freckled face, "they are beautiful"

"What are they?" Jimmy Earl questioned, a frown on his face.

Karl David turned to Jimmy Earl, "These are special weapons our uncle has brought to us, I will teach you how to use them. Oh, thank you Uncle Jamie, I have always wanted one."

"Me too," Jimmy Earl said, "Me too, I want it too."

Jamie handed a sling shot to each boy, "Now be careful with them, treat them as the weapons they are, just as you treat your rifles." he said.

"We will," said Karl David.

Jimmy Earl stepped up and hugged Jamie's leg, then looked up, "We will, I promise."

"Off with you lads, I have work to do now," Jamie said with the wave of his hand. The two boys took off down to the creek, laughing and screaming a rebel yell.

"Let me go inspect this arch, I have much to do before the Taylor's arrive." Pastor Eitson said, he turned away, and walked towards the arch.

Just then a wagon turned onto the property from the road. On the front bench was a black man and woman, probably in their late thirties I thought. Behind them, in the wagon bed were some small children laughing and waving as they approached. Also, in the bed was a dark tarp which covered quite a large pile of things.

When Micah saw the wagon, he ran towards it, waving "Josh how are ya? Mary, so good to see you." He yelled. A small young boy climbed up on to the front seat and literally dove off the moving wagon in to the arms of Micah.

"We have the chairs and tables, and some food sent over from the Taylor's Micah, can you show us where we should put them?" The woman said.

"Sure can." Micah, lifted the boy on his shoulders, shook Josh's out-stretched hand, and then walked forward, took the bridle of the horse and walked forward to the arch. More of George Washington's family came running from all directions towards the wagon. As they arrived, the laughter and noise of talking rose. The wagon moved the short dis-tance and stopped off to one side of the arch. Micah turned, "This is it."

Josh reined the horses. Micah put the young boy on the ground and crossed in front of the horses to help Mary down. A large group waited to hug and greet her.

About this time, Jeanne Marie appeared walking through the front door onto the porch. She stopped and scanned the front yard. She smiled, seeing how much activity there was, and the joy of GW's people at the arrival of Josh and Mary and their children. Then her eyes came upon me and froze. She waved, then decided to walk down the steps off the porch and towards me.

"Good morning husband," she said loud enough for all to hear.

"Good morning, me lady." I bowed as she came close. Dressed in the clothes of the time the only thing exposed was her head. Her lovely face and blue eyes. And her small hands at the end of the long-sleeved white blouse. Her grayish brown skirt all the way to the ground, her small feet, her shoes did not even appear under the hem as she walked.

She stood smiling before me.

"Would you like to inspect the activities, Jeanne Marie?"

"Yes," she said, placing her arm through and on mine. We made a long broad circle in the front yard. Behind us Micah and his people were unloading the chairs and setting them up in rows facing the arch. The front yard was so beautiful with the new life of spring. The lime green of the new grass, and leaves, and other plant life was brighter, more effervescent than what it would be in just a couple of weeks. For a brief time in the spring the plants are just more alive, more bright. Later the green would get darker. Not ugly, just older.

We finished the circle walking past the fenced area of chicken coup, the corral for the pigs, and then the barn on our right before we started walking down the dirt road that led to the creek and the slave quarters beyond. We moved from the sun, which was now approaching noon high in the sky, into the shade of the trees which bordered the road on both sides. As we approached the creek she said, "Shall we turn around and walk back?"

"No, I think I shall carry you across the creek," I bent down and lifted her in my arms to carry her the fifteen feet to the other side of the stream. She was light, not more than 110 pounds, to be honest she felt like a feather, there was no strain or effort on my part. As I entered the stream the cold rushing water soaked my socks and my brogans, and lower parts of my two pant legs. Cold, somewhat uncomfortable this was the price of chivalry. I would happily do it again, I thought to myself.

I set her down gently on the road while I still stood in the creek. We walked side by side the short distance on the road through the trees, 'til the woods ended on our left opening to a large planted field filled with green sprouts in rows.

Along the tree line were about six small cabins, and past them a large barn and corral where some horses stood in the sunlight. We walked up the tree line towards two women and some small children. The women were stirring two large pots, steam rising from them. The young children played and didn't seem to pay us much attention.

"Hello Colonel Parks," one of the women said with smile, "I am Ruth, George Washington's wife."

"Pleased to meet you ma'am." I said, "And this is my wife ..."

"Miss Jeanne Marie," Ruth said and curtsied. "Very pleased to meet you ma'am. Thelma has told me about you both. So glad you came so we could have this day."

"And who might these be?" I asked

"That is Susannah, my sister," Ruth said, "she doesn't say much."

Jeanne Marie walked up to Ruth, "Hattie is so lucky to have you, and all your family helping her. She is blessed, you are a blessing from God."

Ruth could hear the sincerity in Jeanne Marie's voice, see it in her face. "We be very happy with Miss Hattie, and she will be happy today, we knows it."

"We just wanted to take a walk around and look, we won't be here much longer," I said.

Out in the field, in the middle of green sea of sprouts that swayed in first one direction, then in another depending on the breeze, was a large dark barn. "What is that out there, Ruth?" I asked.

"That's the backy barn Masser, sure'n you knew that?" She said lookin' down into the kettle, the greens in the water rising in the boiling water.

"Of course, "I said hoping the bluff would hold. "We will keep walking on, see you later this afternoon Ruth, and you also Susannah."

We turned back towards the road, "I would like you to see the soldiers camp, if you like?"

As we turned left onto the road a breeze blew up from that direction and the smell of meat roasting filled our nostrils. Jeanne Marie looked at me with a questioning face; "They shot a deer early this morning, Colonel Thomas said his men would help add food to the menu."

The scent only got stronger as the woods on the right fell away, and we came to the meadow which served as the soldiers camp ground. Colonel Thomas was talking to two soldiers some distance away when he saw us approaching. He was not in his blouse, just a pullover white cotton shirt with ruffled sleeves and buttons on the upper half, unbuttoned. He was smoking a cigar. When he finished with his men, he walked towards us.

"Colonel Thomas, this is my wife Jeanne Marie, Jeanne Marie, Colonel Thomas."

Jeanne Marie stretched out her small hand, guess to shake the Colonel's, but he took it raised it to his mouth and kissed it. "Charming Mrs. Walter, you are quite beautiful aren't you," he said with smile. But he quickly looked at me, "You are blessed Colonel."

"I know." I said.

"He is," Jeanne Marie said, "But Colonel don't tell him, I am the lucky one, I think."

"A good match, the two of you, I think," Colonel Thomas said. "Beautiful day, don't you think? This is going to be a fine wedding."

"Is there anything you or your men need?" I asked.

"No, Colonel, we are doing fine. The meat shall be done in time for supper tonight. The men are out in the woods seeing what they might find to place on the table. There could be some early onion grass, or maybe they might find a snake or a rabbit."

"Colonel, that's quite nice of you and your men, I hope they feel comfortable and enjoy the ceremony and the dance after?" Jeanne Marie said.

"I am sure we will." He said, "If you will excuse me, I guess I should go and shave and wash up?"

"We will see you later then Colonel," I said, as Jeanne Marie and I turned to walk back up the road towards the creek.

"I wonder if he would carry me across the creek?" She said, tilting her head and giving me a dreamy look.

"Awe, Jeanne Marie that hurts …" I said, my heart nicked.

She laughed, "Oh don't be such a baby Parks, he's nothing to you in my eyes."

I breathed a sigh of relief. I was growing to really like Jeanne Marie. We had been through some excitement on the flight, and that kind of shared experience can be the basis for a relationship. But this was more than that. I liked Jeanne Marie. She cared for people, was sensitive to them. And she was a romantic … something I like in a woman. She was intelligent and bold.

When we came up to the stream, Jeanne Marie turned towards me "OK, I am ready to be picked up now," a look of royalty in her presence.

"You are?" I bent over, but instead of taking her in my arms, I threw her over my shoulder like a sack of potatoes, and started through the stream.

"Hey, what are you doing, this isn't what you are supposed to do!" She was yelling and kicking her feet, which hit me in the stomach and smacking my back with her hands. "This is not the way Parks …"

"Be careful wife, or you will end up in the creek," I warned as I smacked her behind with my hand.

"Ooouu, I will get you Parks Walter when I am put down." But she stopped kicking and slapping, I think she really thought I would drop her in the creek.

I made my way to the far side of the creek and as I was bending over to put her down, she growled, "You think this was funny Parks Walter, well I will get even with you tonight, you'll see." Her voice sounded playful. But when she stood up, she realized George Washington and Micah were walking into the stream and had seen her butt in the air and heard her last threat. She blushed and turned. ...

Well, I guess I got myself in trouble this time, I thought. I could hear Micah and GW laugh as they made their way out of the stream on the other side. I sloshed out of the creek. Guess I will go get my uniform and boots and come down here and bath since I am already wet, I thought to myself.

One thing I learned pretty quickly in the past was, that life was more deliberate then. It took more time to do things, and so you had to have a plan. And there weren't as many hours to correct mistakes as there were in the future. Many of the conveniences of my time were really created to expedite life, to move things along. But back in this time, you really could not do that. Time was time and things happened at a pace more closely associated with God, than with man.

People were working all over the place, and you could see a great deal of progress being made. I stomped my brogans on the porch outside the front door to make sure I would not track anything inside the house and headed up stairs to the bedroom to get my shaving gear, uniform and boots. When I went through the door into the bed room, Jeanne Marie was there, standing looking out the window.

She turned to look at me, anticipating she was mad at me I said, "I am sorry, Jeanne Marie, I was only playing." She started moving towards me even before I finished my sentence.

"I know, and I love it," she threw her arms around me and stood on her toes to kiss me. I wrapped my arms around her waist and kissed back.

When our kiss broke, she looked me in the face, still on her toes, our arms wrapped around each other, "I like you Parks, ... a lot." She eased out of my arms, "But right now, it's my turn for the bathtub.!" She grabbed her stuff and ran out the door and down the stairs.

"Bathtub?" I said ... not too loudly as I did not want to upset Hattie. Jeanne Marie heard me though, and waved her hand as she got to the bottom of the stairs and quickly rushed off.

Back to the creek I thought. I picked up my stuff.

* * * *

I walked back up the road, refreshed from my bath, and changed into my uniform minus my blouse. It was too pleasant in my cotton shirt and I just didn't see the need to put the jacket on 'til the formal ceremonies were about to start.

As I was walking towards the house, Michael was scurrying down the road towards the creek, "Great best man you are, why didn't you tell me it was time to take a bath?" He went by me quickly. I turned, and tried to say sorry, but he was moving fast. Maybe I best ask about the ring the next time I saw him, I thought.

I walked into the house, Hattie saw me, "I am glad to see someone is organized around here. After you take your clothes upstairs, visit the kitchen and get some lunch, things are going to start moving around here. I am expecting dad by 2."

I heard her shoes on the stairs, "Your wife should be about done with her bath."

I followed Hattie up the stairs, dropped the clothes on the bed, "Hattie, where is the bath?"

"Through the parlor and down the hallway," she said.

Ummm, this could be fun I thought. Guys never grow up,

I headed back down the stairs, turned right through the parlor and headed down the hall. There were a few closed doors, "Jeanne Marie." I called out.

"Yes" sounded like the end of the hall. I continued down the hall, put my hand on the knob, wondered if she locked it. I tried to turn it, it turned! I walked in. There she was sitting in the bathtub. Not much covering her, this wasn't like modern times, no soap bubbles.

She reached for a towel, "Why … you …" she grew red as she pulled the towel over her.

"Just stopping in for a kiss, there has to be some bennies for this gig," I said. I bent over and kissed her. And she kissed back. She dropped the towel and put her hands on my head, almost pulled me in with her. But when we broke, she noticed the towel was in the water.

"Oouuuuu, you, here take this towel and go wring it out." She handed me the wet towel.

"Ok," I smiled. "I will get it dry and give it to Hattie to bring it back."

"You'll do no such thing, bring it back yourself!" She demanded.

"OK, ok" I said, I headed out the door. It was wet, but if I wrung it out good, I should be able to get it almost dry I thought.

Walking through the parlor I ran into Hattie coming down the stairs, "Causing troubles Colonel, take it outside and wring it out, and bring it in the kitchen and I will dry it so you can take it back to your wife." Hattie headed for the kitchen.

After I did all I could I brought the towel into the kitchen. "Stretch it out on the table," Hattie said. She took a thick cloth, wrapped around her hand, and lifted an old iron. It was sitting on the stove, and I could only imagine how hot it was. She walked across the room placed the iron on the towel and you could hear the water sizzle and the steam rise. She ran the iron slowly around the towel. "Flip it over," she said. I did, and she repeated the process, less sizzle and less steam.

"OK that should work for now. Take it back to Jeanne Marie, and stay out of trouble," Hattie's stern face turned to a smile, she put the iron back on the stove.

When I picked the towel up it was warm, maybe not completely dry, but warm and pretty dry. I walked quickly back to the last door, knocked. "Yes."

I went in, "OK hun, gotcha a nice warm towel." Jeanne Marie stunned me, when she stood up. Naked as a jay bird, but beautiful. I moved towards her and wrapped the towel around her. She purred like a kitten. "I best be on my way." Now I knew where the word skedaddle came from as I beat a hasty retreat out the door. One of these times Miss Jeanne Marie, it will be the right time, I thought to myself.

I went upstairs. Maybe I should check my weapons, if there is to be an honor guard, maybe wearing the weapons would be appropriate? Never having been to a wedding in 1863 before, I wasn't sure. But I had the time, and actually I probably should load powder and ball into the pistol anyway. Colonel Thompson's comments reminded me that we were at war. Something I had not really considered since our arrival in this time. My experience in Desert Storm as a Cobra pilot kicked in. I never went anywhere without my .45. The Army had switched pistols, but I kept mine. Weird how you grow attached to things, like people, that you are used too and you know what to expect.

I went into the trunk, pulled out my belt, a small cap pouch was attached along with another filled with balls. And there was my brass tool filled with powder. Sure, took a lot more to load a weapon back then. I pulled the navy colt out of its holster. This holster was not the traditional black one you see. It had been hand made for a cross draw so instead of being on my right-hand side as I wore the belt, it was on the left-hand side, and tilted at an angle to make it easier to extract the weapon. Not exactly regulation, but in this war, on the Confederate side regulation wasn't what it was in the Yankee army. And actually, it was made for a rider, more comfortable when you were on a horse.

Each of the six cylinders was individually loaded with powder. Once that was done, a ball was placed above each cylinder and a handle on the pistol is pulled to drive the ball down into the cylinder. The last step was placing a brass cap on the nipple at the rear of each cylinder which when struck by the hammer, would create a spark driven through a small hole to ignite the powder causing a small explosion, and driving the ball down the barrel and out towards its intended target.

The effective range wasn't more than thirty yards or so. But it was the best quick-fire short-range weapon of that time. Each Confederate cavalryman would carry up to six of these, and a shotgun for the close in fighting they did.

Downstairs and outside I heard a commotion. I put the loaded but uncapped pistol in its holster, lay the belt on the bed and quickly moved towards the door and down the stairs. When I got outside on the front porch, I could see a young woman on a large black mount coming in from the road at a gallop. She was a good horseman and pulled hard on the reins as she flew into the front yard, her long red hair blown back and out.

Michael was the first to her, followed by a number of the slaves. I quickly ran to them when she fell off the horse. Micah had grabbed the reins, Michael caught her in his arms as she fell. She was out of breath and I only heard some of what she was saying; "… they have 'em pinned down at the old fort on the creek about three miles from here." She said.

Michael looked up at me, "some bushwhackers ambushed the Taylors on the way here."

"Cletus, go up in the house, first room on the second floor, get my gun belt," I said, taking the reins from Micah. "Micah, go tell Colonel Thompson what you heard, and George Washington, but tell the Colonel first."

Micah took off at a run towards the creek. "I will head towards them, send help as fast as you can Michael." I mounted the horse, about that time Jeanne Marie came out on the porch.

I looked down at the woman there was a carbine in the rifle holster on the horse, I placed my hand on the stock of the rifle; "Is this loaded and capped?" She nodded yes.

Cletus came through the door at a full run with my weapon, almost running Jeanne Marie over. He got to me in just a few steps and handed the belt up to me. I spurred the mount pulling to the left. The horse took off with a powerful thrust of his hind legs. In just a couple of strides the horse was at a full gallop and the acceleration almost threw me off his back. I recovered quickly though and we were out of the yard and on the road in seconds. This horse was big and strong, I could hear the horse breath and feel each time its hind legs pushed back driving us forward.

I had never been down this road before, was holding my weapon's belt in one hand, the reins in the other. We covered ground rapidly, but it still took ten minutes before the quiet of the woods and the sound of my horse's hooves were interrupted by the crack of weapons firing in front of me, and to my right in the woods.

I pulled on the reins of the horse, to slow him down. I had to try to get an eye on what was happening and get my belt on. There were definitely two sets of shots. One group was closer to me, maybe one hundred yards in front of me and spreading out to my right in the woods. They seemed to fire almost in volley. Sounded like maybe a dozen of them.

My mount started moving forward cautiously, without me making any move to guide him. He seemed to have been in this type situation before and knew instinctively what to do. Without thinking I drew my pistol and started capping the individual nipples, good thing since the weapon would not fire without the brass caps affixed to the pistol's rotating cylinder.

Another set of three or four shots was less audible, further in the distance and down the hill. I guessed maybe only three or four individuals were shooting, and not in unison. I could not see down the hill in front of me, I had not reached the crest yet.

"Stop firing men," I heard a husky voice growl loudly; "If'n you will give up Governor Vance, we will let you all live." He said. I could hear the guns around me being loaded, and I heard the leader say in a more quiet voice, you men be fixin' to rush down on them when I say. "OK," and other muted comments came back towards the leader and me. This guy was buying time to get ready to overwhelm the folks down at the bottom of the hill.

"No deal you Tory," I heard an older man shout up the hill. But I could also hear the whimper of women and children ... very slight, hard to make out, but they were there.

Mark K. Vogl

145

The leader's voice boomed "Taylor you ain't who you used to be, and if you don't quit now, we will sure have some fun with your women folk when you are gone. Or maybe we will keep you alive long enough to watch! Whatcha' think Mrs. Taylor?" The animal yelled down with a snarling laugh. A lot of men's voices in front of me echoed the gruesome sentiments. I thought to myself, I had never seen demons before, but here were some right in front of me.

I had only one chance. I had to do something to buy some time. My belt was on and I had drawn my pistol. I thought of John Wayne in *True Grit*. I decided to pull out the carbine, check it to make sure it was capped and cock its hammer back. I put the reins in my mouth, and when the man gave the order to charge, I was going to spur my horse into the middle of them and try to get off as many shots as possible. If I could just confuse the situation enough, and create violent surprise amongst them, I might be able to stop their charge before it got started.

My horse was breathing heavy and I was kind of surprised the leader had not heard me behind him.

"Who are you?" I heard someone say on the ground to my left. When I looked down, it was a man holding the reins of half a dozen horses. I dropped the barrel of the carbine and fired, hitting him smack in the center of the chest. He fell backward, letting loose the reins. The horses panicked, some running in front of me, some behind, and some scattering into the words.

"Behind us, Jack!" I heard the leader yell. I spurred my mount, dropping the empty carbine, and taking the reins from my mouth. I rushed forward down the road, a hail of bullets from at least half a dozen guns whizzing by me. But they were shooting through the woods at a fast-moving target they could barely see. None of them hit me or my horse.

When I broke over the crest of the hill, I could see something, a part of a stone structure at the bottom of a steep slope, maybe one hundred feet down and off the road on the right. There were two wagons there, though I saw no people in them. I looked into the stone structure and could see a few heads popping up. Another series of gun shots went off, these close enough to whiz by my ears. My mount sprang forward down the slope.

Well it wasn't exactly the plan, but it did cause the bushwhackers to have to reload and regroup. And some of their horses were running loose. My horse went straight for the fort and jumped over the stone wall. As he came down, I lost my balance and fell forward crashing into the dirt floor on my shoulder, but still holding my pistol. The horse took only a couple of steps before it stopped by an elderly, big man with white hair. The horse was glistening with sweat and panting hard.

"Pleased you could join us," the man with white hair said, pointing his pistol at me.

"Sir, I am Colonel Walters, I am not with those men."

"Had to be sure son, I am Andrew Taylor." Turning the barrel of his colt away, he pointed beside him to another man looking over the wall with a musket, "this is Governor Vance."

"Howdy," the Governor said without moving a muscle, or even glancing at me.

"You were riding my horse, so I was hoping my daughter made it to Hattie's." Mr. Taylor said.

"She did, and there's help a comin'" I said, "Colonel Thomas will be here and he has twenty soldiers.

"Ahhh, well now, things are about to get a little interesting around here," Mr. Taylor said with an almost glee. This wasn't this man's first fight. Without looking behind him, Taylor said; "Momma you just keep the girls and kids down, we are gonna get out of this yet. Jacob, how are you doing over there?"

A weak voice came back, "I'ma gonna make it poppa, my guns are loaded, I will hold this corner.

"Colonel, go over with my boy," Taylor ordered

"Yes sir," I scrambled to the far corner where a young man lay. His shirt shinny, crimson soaked in blood. He was pale, sitting with his back to the stone wall in the front corner opposite his father and the Governor.

Behind the boy, in the right rear corner of the house was an older woman with a shot gun. She was crouching, watching their rear and flank, and backing up the boy on his side of the building. I learned later it was Mrs. Taylor. She nodded to me at my arrival and returned to her scanning the area in front of her.

"Howdy sir, they got me with the first shots."

I bent over, opened his shirt. The wound was bloody, but not in the center of his body. It looked like they hit him at, or just below his bottom rib on the left side. "I am Parks Jacob. Help's coming."

"There won't be no more foolin' Taylor, surrender or we are a coming down to skin ya," the leader yelled out from above us.

"I got one for you," said Taylor, "and I am lookin' forward to presenting it to you personal like."

"I warned you Taylor. Let's go men, scalps for the taking men, let's get'em," He said.

I moved to the wall, crouching, and ready to shoot the first demon I saw.

You could hear the woods breaking and snapping as the bushwhackers moved towards us. You could hear them slip and fall as they came down the hill. They held their fire, trying to get close enough to see a head, or some other body part to hit inside the broken down stonewalls. As they moved towards us, I could make out thunder behind them. On the top of the hill a couple of shots rang out, followed by a lot more.

Then all of sudden from our left front we heard rebel yells, and some shots. These boys were in trouble. Behind them was cavalry, in front of them armed men behind a stone wall, and on one flank men moving against them. The predator was now the prey and the trap was closing fast.

But the woods was thick, and the bandits literally melted away as the two forces closed in on them. Coming down the road we could see a large body of men, Confederate, it was Colonel Thomas. And emerging from the woods on our left was George Washington, Micah, Cletus and two other black men armed with an assortment of rifles and pistols.

The fight was over. We did find a couple of their men dead including the one I had hit on the way in.

The ladies rushed to Jacob. Mr. Taylor made his way over to him immediately after he quickly thanked Colonel Thomas. George Washington and Micah came over to the group surrounding Jacob. "Get us a wagon on the road GW, and we'll carry Jacob up there." In the far corner of the remnant of a stone building were some small children, still petrified by what had just occurred. They had seen kin shot, and heard the bullets slapping against stone walls right beside them.

All the women but Mrs. Taylor turned towards the children. I heard one of the younger boys, Isaac, could not have been more than six or seven say; "Pappy showed 'em, ain't nobody can kill pappy Taylor." His little voice was beaming with pride, but trembling at the same time, tears rolling down his face. He was fighting to stay brave, trying to show his grandpappy he was no baby. But, his head dove into his mother's chest when she reached down to pick him up.

Colonel Thomas was busy giving instructions to his men, setting security around the party, and helping get the wagons on the road.

"Colonel Walter, I am Governor Vance," he stuck out his hand to me, "That sure was some show you put on, saved our lives I'll bet ya, don't you think Andrew?"

Mr. Taylor stuck out his big hand, "Been a lot more of our blood spilled here if'n it weren't fer you Colonel Walter. That's fer sure, it is."

I was humbled. These were real men, men who defended their families with their lives, with their fists and guns and wits. Nothing came easy to them. I bowed my head, "I thank God that horse got me here." I looked at the black stallion next to Mr. Taylor.

"Spartacus," Taylor said with a deep sense of friendship, grabbing the head of the horse and pulled it close as if he were hugging a dog. He held its face on one side, talking into its ear. The affection was both sincere and true and the horse did not move, staying trained on its best friend.

George Washington walked up, "We have Jacob on the wagon, suh." Taylor walked over and hugged George Washington like a bear, "I am always glad to see you and yours, Governor this is George Washington Taylor, one of my oldest friends and guardian of Hattie."

"You helped saved us Mr. Taylor, I am obliged." The Governor stuck out his hand and shook George Washington's. GW was overwhelmed; he bowed his head, "Suh, we needs to get Jacob to Miss Hattie's. Micah went for the doctor on Titan."

"OK, let's move," Mr. Taylor ordered with a sense of urgency. The children and women were being loaded in the wagons, helped by some of the Cherokee Confederates. Others were mounted behind and in front of the wagons keeping a look out. Looking at me he said: "You take Spartacus, Colonel, I will ride with Jacob." Mr. Taylor said.

It took only moments before Colonel Thomas had the lead Cherokees moving, followed by the wagon with Jacob, and then the second wagon. George Washington and I, Cletus and the other Taylor people followed, and then the rear guard of the Cherokee. We were only about three miles from the farm, and though not at a gallop we did move at a good pace. The column was longer than you might expect, a couple hundred yards anyway. By the time we pulled into the front yard, they already had Jacob out of the wagon and were carrying him up on to the porch. Micah and the doctor rode in right behind us, rode around us to the front of the house, a worried look on the doctor's face as he went by.

As I dismounted, I heard Colonel Thompson say to his sergeant: "I want two sentries at the turn off from the road. Tell them I don't want to be surprised."

Once off Spartacus, I turned towards the house and saw Jeanne Marie coming towards me. She was in a royal blue hoop skirt, white under sleeves and a white collar, though I barely saw them as she seemed to fly to me and straight in to my chest. She wrapped her arms around me, her head pressed hard against me. "Parks, I am so glad. ..."

Michael walked up, "Good to see you," he was quiet, reflective. Hattie was on the porch issuing orders to anyone nearby. The two boys, Karl David and Jimmy Earl were running pails of water to the house. Isaac, the little boy I had seen at the stone house joined them and was trying to help, though he was still small and unable to carry a full pail. But he was in there trying, making an effort to contribute.

Things started to get back to some sense of peace, but everyone kept glancing at the house waiting on news of Jacob. After some time, the doctor came out on the porch and spoke to Hattie and her sister Catherine about her younger brother. Jacob. Hattie almost seemed to collapse, the doctor grabbing her. A ripple of fear went through all of us who watched the silent scene before us. In a moment, Hattie turned towards us, wiping away tears she proclaimed loudly, "Jacob will not be at the wedding, but we will bring him some supper in the room, he will be fine with rest."

A cool breeze picked up coincident to Hattie's words, and the great sense of relief felt by so many, the woods rustling as almost an announcement of God's peace. A moment later, Mr. Taylor appeared through the doorway with a smile on his face. Pastor Eitson was on the porch and as the two men talked, I thought I heard Mr. Taylor say "Looks like I will be giving my daughter Hattie away again."

Pastor Eitson responded, "To a good man, this time."

"Yes, yes, I think so," Mr. Taylor said nodding his head, the smile never leaving his presence.

* * * *

Despite the excitement and the serious condition of Jacob, activities in preparation for the wedding started back up immediately. Colonel Thompson's escorts went back to their camp ground to water and groom their horses, and maintain their weapons. Colonel Thompson and his sergeant came up to the front yard to look over the seating area and determine where the honor guard would be posted. They decided to use six men with sabers.

After a warm greeting by the women and children of his family, George Washington and all the servants went back to taking care of the afternoon chores, cooking for the evening meal, and bathing and preparing for the wedding.

Hattie finally disappeared in to the house. Jeanne Marie spent the afternoon with her, helping her in every way possible. Mrs. Taylor and Catherine joined them. The smells of food cooking in many places all over the property and in the house permeated the yards. A light breeze from the east carried the smells from the slave quarters and the camp where the dear was roasting. But there were also meats cooking in an outside stove behind the house, and in the kitchen, including bread which was made in the early afternoon.

Meanwhile Michael was using the barn as his headquarters. He did bath down at creek after me. He had gone into Mount Airy even before Jeanne Marie and I arrived and had ordered a new suit. This would be his first time wearing it. He also had bought a vest, and a red tie and even some new shoes all the way from New York. No one asked how he had gotten them here.

At about three thirty friends started to arrive, and several musicians who played the fiddle, harmonica, and a larger fiddle I believe was a viola. The last musician to arrive was wearing a kilt and played a bagpipe.

Pastor Eitson seemed to get larger, more dynamic and more central to all that was happening, as people started to congregate towards the arch, folks taking their seats. Pastor Eitson looked quite distinguished; his black hair combed back, a Bible in his right hand. Dressed in a black robe with a white high collar, Pastor Eitson's soft Southern voice made him easy to like, and easy to listen to.

At about five minutes to four the six cavalrymen, marching in columns of two, marched up to the center row between the chairs, and stopped short of the seats, creating a kind of human hallway up to the chairs, three men on each side. "Rest" the senior man sounded, and the six men relaxed, but did not move from their respective spot.

The rest of the Cherokee and the Colonel came up fully dressed and found places to stand behind the rows of chairs. After a short time, Karl David appeared before the Colonel and signaled for the Colonel to bend over. Karl David whispered in his ear, and pointed down to the front. When the Colonel stood, Karl David led him down to the front row of seats, and took him all the way to end. The Colonel sat, comfortable in the shade.

Mr. and Mrs. Taylor and the Governor stood some distance away between the house and the honor guard. Michael and I stood near the barn. I had decided not to wear my arms, but did wear my red vest under my grayish blue Lt. Colonel's blouse. I wore a gray kepi, the type hat most known to be on Jackson's head.

George Washington and all his people walked up the road together and worked their way towards the back of the chairs, expecting to stand. Mr. Taylor walked up to George Washington and pointed to a large section of vacant chairs. Gorge Washington shook his head no, but Mr. Taylor's face changed, he seemed to be insisting. And so, GW led his folks to the chairs meant for them. Once they were seated, Mr. Taylor walked over to the servants from his plantation and pointed to the vacant seats in George Washington's section.

The string musicians and harmonica had started playing some music, and went through several melodies while everyone moved in to their seats. Finally, Jeanne Marie and Catherine came out on to the porch. Jeanne Marie looking really beautiful in her blue dress, her hair up.

Pastor Eitson took his place in the center, under the arch. Michael stepped from under the shade of a large tree and joined him.

"Attennnnnn shunnn" was heard and six cavalrymen snapped to attention. Karl David came and looked up at the governor. His mouth moved, but I could not hear him, he turned and walked through the soldiers, the governor following. Then Jimmie Earle came up to Mrs. Taylor, offered his arm, and she reached down to take it. Bent over in an odd way, Mrs. Taylor and Jimmie Earl walked through the soldiers and to seats next to the Governor and Karl David.

The string music softly ended and the harsh singing bag pipe began its lonely dissonant melody. Catherine, Hattie's sister walked down through the soldiers and took a spot to one side Pastor Eitson. You could almost see the ghosts, in their kilts, walk with her.

Then it was our turn, Jeanne Marie took my arm and we walked between the soldiers, down through the rows of chairs, and we divided at Pastor Eitson. Jeanne Marie joined Catherine, and I went to Michael's The side.

Just then, I remembered I had never been given the ring! Panic struck, my heart raced. How could I do this, how could I blow their wedding? Everything seemed to be working so well. What could I do? Talk about feeling the pressure, I did.

Mr. Taylor started walking Hattie towards us, slowly. They looked dignified. He looked like an Arthurian king, his white locks and broad shoulders. He was a man who was confident in himself, and you knew it when you spoke with him. There was no conceit, no brag, just a man who was comfortable with who he was, and calmed by his surety in God. Hattie beamed, never taking her eyes off Michael.

Hattie looked beautiful, a princess in a cream white dress. She told Jeanne Marie that it took her years to make this dress. Hattie told Jeanne Marie, "I almost knew from the night I first pointed a shot gun at Michael that I would marry him. It didn't take long after he arrived before I started making this dress. But it would be a long time before he would ask me." The dress Hattie made did show off her form, with a tight waste and a low neckline. Hattie was a fine-looking woman, though most of the time she wore the work dresses of a lady working a farm. Her hands were rough from the chores she did daily. But she was also physically strong from those chores.

When the two came up in front of Pastor Eitson, they embraced, Mr. Taylor kissing Hattie on the forehead. He then did something I did not expect, he turned towards me, reached into his coat pocket and pulled out the ring, and handed it to me just as if that is what was supposed to happen. I took it. He then hugged Hattie again, took Hattie's hand and placed it in Michael's and turned and walked towards Mrs. Taylor, and sat down just as the piper ended.

The wind picked up and blew through the trees. The sky blue, a few white clouds sparsely spread in the sky, the fur pine seemed to sway like tall guests, somehow wanting to participate in the wedding. The rich, thick smells of food cooking, and the scent of the pines and other plants just one more part of the environment created by God for this day.

Pastor Eitson's voice woke me from the trance that had overwhelmed me. Things moved very quickly — next thing I knew Michael was kissing Hattie.

* * * *

Later in the evening Mr. Taylor, Colonel Thomas and the Governor were sitting at a table, on the ground in front of the porch. They had an excellent view of the dancing. Smoking cigars and sipping some bourbon, their conversation was wandering when I walked up.

"Have a seat Colonel," the Governor placed his hand on the back of chair next to him.

"Thank you, sir, I believe I will. Wonderful event, don't you think sir?"

"I sure do, considering the excitement of the afternoon. I have been giving some thought to the deserter problem. I am thinking we are going to have to do something about this, something harsh, to make men think twice about deserting the army. We simply can't tolerate the violence and lawlessness they bring."

"You sure do have that right, Zebulon."

"Well thank you Andrew, I do appreciate your support, as I always have in the past."

Mr. Taylor took the opportunity offered, "Zebulon, your career isn't over yet, maybe you will serve in the Senate in Richmond, or maybe you could be the first post war president of the Confederacy?"

The governor nodded his head, "President Vance, I like that," he smiled and took a good sip.

"Yes, it does have a nice sound to it, don't it. Now, Zebulon you know there are a lot of our boys serving up in Virginia with General Lee, a lot of the regiments with General Jackson."

"Yes, that is true," exhaling a thick cloud of smoke, "We have five and half brigades of North Carolinians up there with General Lee, all of them with General Jackson right now. And, then there's the two regiments of cavalry with Stuart. 27 regiments altogether." The Governor turned his head slowly and looked at Mr. Taylor. "I have heard that tone in your voice before Taylor, what are you thinking?"

"Well Governor, don't you think it would be a good idea to make a special effort to the let our boys know the old North state was thinking about them, worried about them and their needs?"

"Go on," Mr. Taylor had gotten the governor's attention. He pulled the cigar to his mouth and in the evening light its cinders went bright red as he inhaled. "Well, Colonel Walter might just be the man to be your liaison to General Jackson, kind of like an Assistant Inspector General, sent by you, to visit with the soldiers and identify needs we here in North Carolina might be able to fill?" Mr. Taylor's words hung in the air. Each man at the table took a drink, brought a cigar to their mouth, taking the time to think on what had just been said.

"He could even stop in to the 21st North Carolina and tell the boys from around here about Hattie's wedding, and you being here!" Mr.

Taylor had made a strong presentation. I didn't know then that three companies of the 21st had been raised in Surry County.

"Why Taylor, do you read minds? I was just thinking about that very thing this morning. But, was unsure who I should send? And then Providence provides us with Colonel Walter, a sign that God likes the idea." The Governor looked to me, "What do you think Parks? Do you have orders yet? Never mind that, I will supersede them, this is state business. Is there any paper around here?"

Mr. Taylor looked back behind him on the porch, "Flora bring out some paper, ink and a pen and an envelope for the Governor please."

"Yes suh," Flora went in and in a few moments came out. She placed a bottle of ink to the right front of the governor, a few sheets of paper, a quilled pen and an envelope in the space immediately in front of the Governor Vance.

"Thank you," the Governor looked up at Flora. She smiled, curtsied and left. The Governor dipped the pen into the bottle and started to write:

General T. J. Jackson,   April 11th, 1863
    Sir,

It is my great honour to write a field commander of your renown and success. As the governor of the great North State, I knew that the men of this fine state would acquit themselves well in battle if given good military leadership. On behalf of the people of North Carolina I gratefully commend you for the skilled leadership you have provided, and for your relationship with our Almighty Father. Only the beneficence of Providence can explain your miraculous victories.

Sir, with this letter I present to you Lt. Colonel Parks Walter who I am sending to you as a liaison between myself and you to insure that the soldiers of this great state are provided with every possible convenience and supply. Please allow Colonel Walter to fulfill this small duty so that we in Caroline can be assured we know the needs of our men. And feel free to utilize Colonel Walter as you see fit when he is unencumbered by his duties on my behalf.

May I add my congratulations on the birth of Julia, and allow me to pray for you, your wife and child that this tragic event should soon end in the favor of the right. I am, sir,

                    Zebulon Vance, Governor
                    North Carolina

"There Colonel, I do believe this should be sufficient. I want you to visit with all the North Carolina regiments serving with General Jackson, and do the best you can to express our concern here in North Carolina for them, and try to identify one or more needs of the men that we may be able to address from home. Can you do that sir?" he handed me the letter.

I stood up, partially to hide my amazement at the recreation of the letter. "Yes, sir, I will do what I can."

"Sit down Colonel, I saw what kind of man you are this afternoon, I know you will do fine." The Governor said, nodding at Mr. Taylor and taking another drink from his glass.

Jeanne Marie walked up to the table about this time, "Have you men come to an agreement on a strategy to win the war?" She smiled.

I was folding the letter without looking up I said, "We may have."

"Governor Vance, I don't believe we have danced tonight?" Jeanne Marie said. "As the Maid of Honor, I claim my dance, sir?"

Vance looked at me, "The things I have to do …" he got up and walked Jeanne Marie out into the dance area in the yard, he looked back and smiled! The music began and Jeanne Marie's skirt swirled as she and the governor danced. They looked really fine, it was obvious Jeanne Marie had learned at least one of the dances of era. When the music was through the leader of the band announced: "We are going to take a short break, and when we return we will commence with the Virginia reel, wives get your husband ready!"

A gallant Southern gentleman, the governor seated Jeanne Marie next to me, before he took his own seat.

"You are quite a dancer, Governor Vance, very graceful," Jeanne Marie said, "Parks, it's your turn next!"

I bet I turned pale white. The governor laughed; Mr. Taylor joined in. "Ah Parks, you'll do fine." Jeanne Marie placed her hand on my arm, looking at me with a gentle smile, she was gorgeous I thought. When the band returned, I didn't wait, I rose to pull Jeanne Marie's chair out. We walked out together arm in arm and Jeanne Marie whispered, "It's long, but there's nothing to it! So, enjoy it and we'll see what kind of shape you are in!" She laughed.

The reel is a long dance, it's length really depends on how many people are dancing. The entire yard filled with people, black and white for this dance, not two groups but all together. But it was fun and really the first time in the whole day and night I could relax. The sky was black, stars, … cooled as time passed.

* * * *

The night was getting late when Colonel Thomas walked up to the Governor. His men had ridden up in column of twos and were mounted on the road that came up from the creek. "Sir, it's getting late, and we have to get moving. I think we can have you at The Hollows Inn in less than an hour."

"The Hollows Inn?" I asked.

The Governor turned to me, "Yes Parks, it was the original name for Mt. Airy. When the community changed its name from The Hallows, the founding family kept it for the Inn. I have to get down there tonight to catch the stage in the morning for Greensboro, to catch the train the next day."

"Colonel Walter, I would like you to take charge of a wagon supply train coming in this direction for General Lee's Army. I expect it will be here in two days. Major Hill is presently in charge, and he is good man, but maybe not quite as bold as you. So please take charge of the train and get it to Richmond, OK?"

"Yes sir," I said.

"Fine, that's good. The men from Surry County on furlough home can catch a ride back with the train. The weather's changing, 'bout time for operations to commence up in Virginia. Andrew, can you get that word out in Surry County?"

"I will, Zebulon."

"Well Andrew, it has been a wonderful wedding, I am glad I could be here to be with you and your family for your daughter's wedding."

"Zebulon, it was a great honor, and I certainly do appreciate it. And who knew we would get into one more fight together?" Mr. Taylor stood tall, smiling. Hattie must have seen the commotion at the table, because she came over with Michael.

"Governor, sir, please take these sandwiches with you for your trip." Hattie signaled Flora who came up with a sack and handed it to the governor.

"Thank you, Flora, come here Miss Hattie and give me a hug." She did and they embraced. "Michael, I know from what I have heard of you from Mr. Taylor that Hattie is in the best of hands. I look forward to seeing you when a future grandchild arrives?" The governor extended his hand.

They shook hands, "Thank you sir."

"Parks, I am also looking forward to your report on the needs of the men, don't dawdle or be distracted by combat operations to drive the invaders from Virginia!" He winked and smiled. "Let's go Colonel." Just then Jeanne Marie walked up. "Oops, wait," the governor turned to Jeanne Marie, "it was a fine dance my fair maid." He bowed, Jeanne Marie curtsied. "Now we can be off Colonel." Jeanne Marie handed him a flower.

The two men walked away towards the column. The Cherokee Cavalry were not as frightening as when they first appeared. Their hair was long, and there were sufficient Indian items to demonstrate their creed. But they had been noble fighters, and polite guests. Their participation in the wedding as an honor guard had really made an impression on all who had been in attendance.

I was surprised by the grace of the governor, an older man, and not exactly a thin one, he mounted his steed seemingly effortlessly. The two leaders both looked at us, waved, and the column began to move off.

The Virginia Reel did me in. I was exhausted and even Jeanne Marie was tired. We retired shortly after that dance. The music played on after we had said our good nights. We walked up the stairs onto the porch together. We turned around to see a picture I will never forget. The entire front yard filled with people white and black, not integrated, but within their respective groups, standing around in the yard, but still sharing the enjoyment of the evening. Lanterns blew in the light breeze, people laughing and talking; the war a long, long way off. A haze was settling in and the whole affair appeared as a dream.

A Stolen Day
Heading to Mt. Airy, North Carolina for a day
April 12, 1863

The light burst through the window onto my face. I woke and reached over for Jeanne Marie, but she wasn't there. The bed sure was comfortable enough, but small. I stretched, stood up and put some pants on. I hadn't quite figured out a routine. There was no bathroom in the house, except for the room with the tub downstairs. But there was a pitcher of water, a wash bowl, soap and towels on a chest in the room. I figured I would do the best I could to clean myself up, before I headed downstairs. It didn't take long.

As I made my way down the stairs I could smell and hear bacon cooking. It reminded me of the smell of mother's cooking on the weekends when I was just a boy. A common smell in this time, it was not one in the twenty–first century in most homes after the women had decided work should be at a work place and not at home every day.

I walked into the kitchen to find Jeanne Marie at the stove, flipping bacon. "There's the coffee." She pointed to a pot on the stove.

"Cups?"

"In the cupboard, where else?"

I got myself a cup, poured some coffee, "Where's Hattie?"

"Oh, they won't be back 'til sometime this afternoon."

"Huh?"

"Sure, they had a wagon packed and took off for a pond somewhere on their property. But she told me they would be back today before evening chores."

I shook my head, "A honeymoon," smiling.

"Yes, I like the ingenuity of it. They couldn't be away long, but they wanted the time together to make a memory, and maybe a baby." Jeanne Marie said.

About that time Mrs. Taylor walked in.

"Morning ma'am," Jeanne Marie said, I echoed.

"Oh, Mrs. Walter you should have woken me, I will help you."

"Well, you deserved some rest."

"About that time Karl David, Jimmy Earl and Isaac, the small boy, all came into the kitchen through the back door carrying pails of water. The room was getting a little crowded so I decided to go out on the porch, had to squeeze by Mr. Taylor who was headed for the kitchen and coffee.

"Mornin'"

"Mornin'"

Stepping out on to the porch was like walking into an opera already in full orchestra, with God as the conductor each morning; the chickens clucking, pigs squealing and grunting, gates opening and closing and horses being moved around. A dozen people moving around engaged in the morning routine. The various and unique sounds of the different animals, were like instruments competing for the attention of whoever would take the time to listen to them.

Some of the Taylor clan had slept in the front yard, on the ground, or in the wagons, after the guests left. They were up in different stages of dress, rolling up their bed rolls, or brushing their hair. Catherine's children, except Isaac, were busy offering to help with the chores.

George Washington's people were at work, milking cows, cleaning out stables and doing any number of morning chores that have to be done every time the sunrises.

Maybe I should have felt guilty because all these people were working and I had sat down at the table on the porch, and was drinking my coffee. After a few minutes Mr. Taylor came out and came over to the table to join me.

"Hi ya father," Catherine walked up on the porch to Mr. Taylor, bent over and gave him a hug.

"Morning Kitty," Mr Taylor hugged her back, "mother's in the kitchen."

"Parks," Catherine's eyes glistened, "can I give you a hug for what you did yesterday." She stepped around her father and gave me a big hug. With enthusiasm she added: "I guess we are related now!"

"Catherine, I think you were the hero yesterday, because you got through to us so we could rally to help."

"That's my girl Kitty, she has always been something of a Tom boy. I knew she could get through riding Spartacus." Taylor reached his arm around her slender waste. "You best go help the woman before they start saying you are my favorite."

Kitty hugged her dad again and then spun around and walked away. Her long red hair running halfway down her back looked even redder against the yellow of her blouse. She quickly strode towards the door where she disappeared.

"You may run into Kitty's husband commanding one of the Surry County companies," Mr. Taylor said.

"I hope I do," I said, "what is his name?"

"His name is Captain Buford Maxwell, he commands A Company of the 28th North Carolina Volunteers. We got a letter from him just before we left for the wedding, they have been assigned to Ambrose Hill's division."

"I will have to remember that," I said, I stood up, reaching for my pocket, wishing I had a piece of paper and pencil to write it down. "Well, I guess I had best spend the day with Jeanne Marie and get prepared for the arrival of the wagon train, and my departure."

"That reminds me," Mr. Taylor said, he looked across the front yard and Micah walking across, "Micah come here please."

Micah came up to the porch, "Please get your father, and tell him I need to see him."

"Yes, suh." Micah took off at a run towards the creek. In a few minutes George Washington turned the corner around the house, "You wanted to see me Mr. Taylor?"

"GW the Governor wants me to get the word out across Surry County to men home on furlough. They can hitch a ride with the wagon train coming through here tomorrow. Do you think you can get the word out? Maybe send someone to Mt. Airy?"

"Mr. Taylor, I would like to go to Mt. Airy with Jeanne Marie today. George Washington, whoever you might send that way could ride with us."

"Yes, suh," George Washington nodded at me, "Is there anything else Mr. Taylor?"

"No, GW, but please tell my people we will be fixin' to leave about mid-afternoon to go home."

"Yes, suh. Good morning suh."

"Good morning George."

"He is one terrific man," I said of GW as he walked away.

"He sure is," Mr. Taylor said, "we practically grew up together, went fishing together as boys. I have known him all of my life." The connection between white and black in this time was not understood in the time I came from. I know I never realized how close the two groups of people were, how interdependent they were. And there was respect, and love between the two groups. No there was no equality, either in material terms or in terms of authority. But there was a bond, ever present. I realized this family could be the exception to the rule, but I doubted it.

The ladies started coming out with the food, and a coffee pot, activity around us rose pretty quick. The boys rushed to the table.

"Karl David, will you say the grace?" Mr. Taylor said to his grandson sitting beside him.

Karl David looked up, and nodded, "Almighty father, thanks for the food, I am hungry, Amen."

Mr. Taylor chuckled, "think we are gonna have to work on that boy." The clatter of silverware striking plates were an appropriate sound at the end of the prayer.

Finally, Jeanne Marie sat down beside me and reached under the table to hold my hand.

"Jeanne Marie, I would like for us to take a wagon into Mt. Airy today. We have some things to do before I leave."

"That sounds fun," Jeanne Marie said, "I want to see the shops in town."

"Hold on to your wallet, Colonel." Mr. Taylor smiling, chided Jeanne Marie.

"I want to go to town." Little Jimmy Earl said, without raising his head from his plate.

"OK, Jimmy Earl, you can go with us!" Jeanne Marie said. "Next time Karl David, we'll take you."

"Jimmy Earl looked up, smiled, his freckles bright, and then looked at his brother with a smug look.

After breakfast George Washington had a wagon fixed to take us to town. Micah was chosen to go with us. I dressed in civilian clothes, Jean Marie in a long wool dress with light blouse, short jacket and straw hat. The seat for the wagon was wide enough for three, little Jimmy Earl was in the back. Micah had put a couple thick blankets down, to absorb the shock of the bumps in the road. We also had two loaded carbines on the floor in front of us. We didn't expect trouble, but the fight with the Tories the other day proved that it was smarter to be "better safe than sorry."

"Michael, can I speak with you a moment?" I asked. We stepped away from the crowd. "Michael, I don't have any of the period currency, and there are a few things, like a rain coat, a bag, underwear, etc., I would like to get. Can you give me some currency?" I sure did not like asking that.

"No," he said.

"No?"

"No," he said sterner, than smiled, "Tell George, the owner of the store to put all your item's on Hattie's account."

Relieved I said, "Thanks, and if Jeanne Marie needs something?"

"Same, if he gives a look, Micah will vouch for you, have a safe and fun trip," Michael said.

"Mt. Airy is not far, less than an hour," George Washington said to all of us, "We won't get much done here today, with my people out on the roads spreading the word for Mr. Taylor. We will look for you before supper."

With that Micah snapped the reins and the horses jerked us into motion.

April is a great month in Carolina. Not too hot, bright with sunshine, or sometimes cloudy and rainy, bringing the rain which is so important to the crops. The air is fresh, crisp and often filled with the sweet scents of flowers blooming.

The wagon rolled along, Jimmy Earl was in the back with his sling shot and a pile of small stones he had put in the wagon before we left. He wasn't hitting anything, but he kept trying.

Micah was just enjoying the day, and a break from the really tough physical labor required in the fields. Sun up to sun down was the normal work day on the farm, except for Sunday. And in this case, the farm had shut down except for basic chores for two days. One for the wedding, and one to get the word out to the soldiers who were home.

"Jeanne Marie, I was looking at the map this morning. I am thinking if I can get thirty miles a day out of the wagon train, I can get up to Fredericksburg in about ten days; unless we run into some unexpected troubles."

"I am hoping to join General Jackson on the 24th," I said. "Now I understand why we had to get here when we did."

"Father had put a lot of thought into the timing of everything. Remember he had a long time to plan this, and he had a lot of people helping him, including historians, and military people. Back planning was a key word I learned twenty years ago." Jeanne said.

I shook my head. "You guys actually really did do a superb job."

"Don't say that, we haven't finished our job yet, and we aren't home yet." Jeanne Marie could flip into a serious deliberative mood very quickly. "I am thinking I will have to leave Michael's farm on the 15th, to catch the stage coach to Greensboro in Mt. Airy on the 16th so that I can be at the railroad station in Greensboro on the morning of the 17th."

"Ummm. That sounds right Miss Walter," Micah said unexpectedly.

"Jeanne Marie turned to Micah, "You think I am right Micah? Have you made that trip before?"

"Yes Ma'am."

"You have?" I asked.

"Yes ma'am, when Masser. Taylor went to Washington, D.C. to meet with Senator Jefferson Davis back in 1859, I got to go with him." Micah said.

"Four years ago!" Jeanne Marie said

"Just about, but Masser Taylor wanted to take someone along as a man servant, and George Washington talked him in to taking me." Micah smiled.

"So, you rode on a train before Micah?" I asked.

"Yes, but I was a boy then, not a man." Micah said.

"Jeanne Marie, we seem to have a plan to get where we need to go, but how will we organize our exit?"

"Well, we have to be gone by … "that was a talk for another time.

Jimmie Earl had over heard the conversation, he popped up between us, "Can I go with you Miss Jeanne Marie, please!!"

"Jimmie Earl, I don't know about that."

"Come on, I am big enough, I can help Micah carry your bags." he said.

"Let me think on this awhile," Jeanne Marie said.

Riding in the wagon on a dirt road took a degree of patience and endurance, as bumps and shocks came more than occasionally and jarred the body. Micah tried to avoid the obvious ruts and holes, but a wagon pulled by horses is not the most nimble vehicle. The road cleared the woods on both sides as they entered what was Mt. Airy.

Micah said, "We will need to go to the Post Office, and the General Store for Miss Hattie."

"Great, I want to look in the store," Jeanne Marie said.

When in the center of town Micah stopped the wagon, pointed to the general store, and said; "Miss Jeanne Marie, there you are, ma'am."

Unexpectedly, the smells of the town rose up quickly. Between horse urine and manure in the streets, mixed with whatever else people threw out into street, the smells were definite, if not overwhelming.

I dismounted the wagon, and helped Jeanne Marie get down.

Micah said, "Suh, I will go find a place for the wagon."

I looked up at Micah, "That's fine." By the time I turned back around, Jeanne Marie had gone up the stairs to the raised wooden walkway in front of the buildings and was headed towards the general store. She disappeared inside.

I decided to do a general reconnaissance of main street.

* * * *

The store was busy inside, maybe a half dozen ladies, shopping, but always returning around one woman who seemed to be the center of their group. As Jeanne Marie looked at the materials, she heard one of the women say, "Mrs. Stuart, do you think James would like this for his wife?"

The woman had laid on her arm a very lovely lace doily.

"Oh, that is beautiful," she said.

"Elizabeth, have you heard from the General, recently?" Another woman said.

"Yes, I just received a letter from him today," Mrs. Stuart said. "He is in very good spirits, though he writes he can't wait until the war is over, so that he can return to Laurel Hill. I don't think he was happy that I sold the farm in '59."

"Well, surely they would sell it back to the South's most heroic cavalry commander," yet another lady said.

Jeanne Marie stood there; her mouth open. She was actually in the same room, not feet away from Mrs. Elizabeth Stuart, mother of the South's renown cavalry commander, Major General J. E. B. Stuart.

Mrs. Stuart stood a little taller, and announced to the other ladies in the store, "I am looking for a small gift to send to James, so if you see anything you think he might like, let me know."

The clerk had heard Mrs. Stuart, and he knew he had just received some items that she might be interested in. Jeanne Marie was at the counter, just across from the clerk when he called Mrs. Stuart over to him.

"The runners brought some items into Wilmington back about a month ago. I was able to get them at the auction. I even thought of your son when I bid on these," the clerk pulled from under the counter two small packages, still wrapped in brown paper. As he carefully undid the paper, he revealed two small red books, gilded in gold. Shakespeare was easily discernible.

Mrs. Stuart moved her hands slowly and carefully to the counter, and lightly touched one of the two books. They were so new they shined, a very smooth red leather, with engraved gold lettering. "I know James liked Shakespeare. When he came home from the military academy and came in here, I heard him talking to his cousin Bettie about Shakespeare. I know there was something between them, but he certainly was talking authoritatively about this fella," the clerk seemed to swell with pride because of his personal knowledge of one of the South's most celebrated heroes.

A few of the women quickly rushed towards Mrs. Stuart, jostling Jeanne Marie, pushing her aside to see the books.

Mrs. Stuart lifted one of the books to the "oohs" and "ahs" of the women. She gently opened the book, sliding a couple of the pages with her fingers. "These are truly marvelous, and I know James would dearly love them ..." her voice trailed off.

She simply stood there, looking down ... lost in thought.

As the women moved away, Mrs. Stuart said, "I know he would enjoy these, but they are so nice, I just don't think I would want to send them through the Post Office."

After a moment, Mrs. Stuart said, "Let me think about this, George, maybe pray on it."

"Yes, ma'am," the clerk responded.

Jeanne Marie saw her opening, "Mrs. Stuart, maybe I could be of some assistance."

Mrs. Stuart turned and looked at Jeanne Marie. "I am sorry, did you say something?"

"I did, Mrs. Stuart I am Mrs. Walters and my husband, Colonel Walters is leaving for Richmond, and the Army tomorrow. I am sure he could carry them to General Stuart for you."

"Hmm." Mrs. Stuart moaned slightly.

"I could go fetch him, and introduce you to him so that you might gain confidence in the idea of allowing him to be your messenger?" Without, waiting for a reply, Jeanne Marie, turned and walked briskly out the door. It was only then that she realized, she had no idea where he was!

Saving the day, she saw Micah walking towards her out in the road. She headed directly towards him, but staying on the elevated walkway and out of the street.

"Micah, have you seen Colonel Walters?"

"No, ma'am, he said he was doing a general something. ..." Micah replied.

"OK, you take that side of the street, and I will take this side. If you find him, tell him I need to see him at the general store as soon as possible." Jeanne Marie said.

"Yes, ma'am." They split apart, each headed in their own direction.

Jeanne Marie began her walk down the street. There was a wood working shop, lawyer's office, then an apothecary shop, and doctor's office and then she came upon the Blue Ridge Inn, the smell of food coming through the door. Jeanne Marie decided to go in there and see if Parks might be there.

The lobby was open, well lit, clean, and vacant but for the clerk behind the counter. On one side was a large open doorway leading into a dining room. Jeanne Marie moved towards the door, and looked in. She saw what she thought was Parks, from behind, sitting at a table with two men. The men seemed huddled, very close together. Jeanne Marie stepped off directly towards the table, moving quickly until she arrived beside Parks, from behind.

Parks, rose kissing Jeanne Marie on the cheek. When she turned to face the two men, she was astonished. The two men were ... one. Asian in appearance, two heads and separate upper bodies, they were connected to one another at the mid-section, but with separate abdomens and each with a pair of legs. Jeanne Marie lost her breath, and when she finally gathered herself, she curtsied.

The two men bowed as Parks said; "Jeanne Marie, this is Eng and Chang Bunker.

At that moment, another man, John Prather, walked up to the table with two drinks in his hand, he handed one to Parks.

"John, this is my wife, Jeanne Marie."

Jeanne Marie offered her hand, and John took it gently. "George is the owner of the local tobacco warehouse here in Mt. Airy," Parks said.

"Pleased to meet you, ma'am." John said.

"Pleased to meet you sirs," Jeanne Marie still not at ease, spoke quietly to Parks' ear, though not in a whisper, "Come Parks, Mrs. Stuart would like to meet you."

"Mrs. Stuart, the general's wife ...?"

"Mother," Jeanne Marie said turning to the gentlemen, "I beg your pardon sirs, but this really is important business." She grabbed Park's arm and attempted to pull him away.

"Gentlemen, it was a pleasure, and I wish you the very best. But as you see, the master calls," he said, bowing slightly and turning. The men smiled, and the three sat back down at the table. Parks took a large swallow of the whiskey before he placed the glass on the table.

The two walked through the lobby, out the door, and onto the walkway and back towards the general store.

"Mrs. Stuart wants you to carry a gift to her son, General Stuart," Jeanne Marie said.

"Really," I said.

"Well, she will once she meets you."

The two walked into the store, and both immediately spotted Micah standing by Mrs. Stuart.

"I understand you saved the governor's life yesterday, Colonel Walter." Mrs. Stuart said.

The two walked directly towards Mrs. Stuart, "May I present Mrs. Stuart Parks, this is my husband ma'am." Jeanne Marie said in a confident voice.

Parks, bowed, "I am not sure I did, Mrs. Stuart, there were a lot of men at that incident," looking at Micah, "Micah was one of them."

Micah grinned.

"I have known Micah his whole life," Mrs. Stuart said, "and, I know him to be both truthful and brave."

Micah, kind of bowed his head sheepishly, everyone seemed to be making a fuss over him.

"I have only known him and his father a short time, ma'am," said Parks, "and I feel blessed to have been so fortunate."

"So, will you allow Parks to carry a present to your son, Mrs. Stuart," Jeanne Marie asked.

"Sir, would it be an imposition?" Mrs. Stuart tilted her head slightly as women often do, when they ask a man's attention.

"It would be an honor ma'am, what soldier would not want the opportunity to meet your son?"

Turning to the clerk, "George, I will take them both, please make sure you wrap them well for the journey," she said.

"Of course, ma'am." George took the books from the counter and headed towards the end of the counter, a place that appeared to be where he prepared items that had been purchased, for their destination.

"You leave tomorrow then," Mrs. Stuart queried

"I believe so ma'am, I am to take charge of a wagon train passing through this way." Parks replied.

The clerk returned, he handed the package to Mrs. Stuart, "Thank you George," she turned and handed it to me, "I trust you will care for this until you are able to deliver it, and please tell James his proud mother is always thinking of him.

"I will do that."

"Seems God had decided I should purchase these gifts for James, by providing you as means of insuring it's safe passage."

Parks was thinking, you have no idea how right you are. "I will be taking my leave of you both," she looked at Jeanne Marie extending her hand, "I must be on my way home."

Jeanne Marie took her hand while she curtsied, then Parks bowed, and shook her hand gently. "Safe travels," Parks said. With that, Mrs. Stuart left the store, most of the women following her out.

"Micah, did you give George that list of things Hattie wanted," Jeanne Marie asked.

"Yes, ma'am."

"I am collecting the items now," George yelled out from the back of the store.

"George, when you are finished with Hattie's list, I will need your help." I said.

"Yes sir, Colonel Walter, it would be an honor sir."

Parks had prepared himself for many military missions in life. He realized this was his only chance to gather items for the journey ahead. He took his time looking at every item available in the store. For once, it would be the woman waiting … he smiled when that thought came to his mind.

The trip to Mt. Airy ended without any other remarkable events, and the three made their way back to the farm.

Looking towards Mt. Airy from Pilot Mountain.

Hattie's farm, near Mt. Airy, North Carolina
Evening of April 12, 1863

That evening, after dinner, sitting at the table, Michael said to Hattie, "I am gonna take Jeanne Marie and Parks for a ride on the wagon to see the rest of the property and talk. We won't be too long, OK?"

"Sure," Hattie replied, "Y'all haven't really had any time to visit."

"Jeanne Marie, make sure you take a shawl dear, it can get kinda cool once the sun drops," Hattie advised, almost like an older sister.

"I am glad you said something, I would have been a darn fool and just run straight out that door without thinking." Jeanne Marie reached and gave Hattie's arm a squeeze."

"It was a wonderful meal Hattie, I can see why Michael is so stocky and healthy," Parks said.

"Plenty of left-overs from the wedding to work with," Hattie said, her voice rising, she went on, "Ruth, will you help me clear the table?"

"Yes, ma'am," Ruth said from the kitchen.

Everyone rose, almost simultaneously, the two men moving towards the front door and porch, Jeanne Marie heading upstairs to get a shawl, and Hattie working with Ruth to clear the table.

"I think we need to talk tonight, our last chance as a threesome, to sort out how we proceed," Michael said to Parks.

"Yes, that sure would make sense, this entire adventure has moved so fast, almost like an avalanche where gravity is the constant force, and we just keep tumbling forward. I have to admit, it has been amazing," said Parks.

"I am headed out with the men, see you later Hattie," said Jeanne Marie.

"Bye, honey."

Just then, Micah walked a duo of horses and a wagon up to the front of the house, "Here we is, Masser Michael, ready to go?"

"Yes, Micah, thank you, you can call it a day Micah." Said Michael, "I will take care of the horse and wagon when we return."

"Are you sure, suh, I thought I would drive for y'all?" Micah said.

"No Micah, you are done for the evening, see you in the morning." Michael said.

I helped Jeanne Marie up on to the wagon, as Michael went around and climbed up. He sure was in a rush, as the wagon started moving before I was seated. "We'll head to the barn, we have a lot to discuss tonight," Michael sounded very serious. We didn't really talk on the ten-minute ride over there, Micheal was in thought, and Jeanne Marie and I in wonder at the beauty around us. The sun was setting, bright colors filled the sky, reds, yellows, whites and blues. The peace was often disturbed by a bump, or loud noise as the wheels of the wagon moved over the less than flat dirt road. As we passed into the wood line, most of the light was lost. It was kinda weird, the sky that we could see atop the trees was still bright blue, but we were in a darkness of shadow caused by the height and fullness of the trees.

To our left, the wood line broke, and there was the field, and the barn on the other side and across the field. Just then I realized how slow time moved back then. It took five minutes or more to get to the barn, all that time we were looking at it. "OK, folks, here we are. Let's get inside, and get a lamp lit." Michael said.

He must have visualized this meeting many times in the months before we got there. He seemed deliberate, rehearsed in everything he did, from finding and lighting a lamp, to pointing to a dark, old wooden table and chairs. It was getting cooler as the sun went down, he placed the lamp in the center of the table, promising some heat from it.

He pulled some notes from his pants pocket as we sat down.

"First let's talk time line," he said with a clear sense of urgency. Today is April 12th, tomorrow Parks you leave with the wagon train, April 13th." He went on: "That was a kind of fortuitous event, I didn't know how …"

"We knew that would happen," Jean Marie said with a smile.

"You did, how?" He said, with a twisted look on his face.

"You know the letter the Governor wrote," she continued and he nodded, "we found that letter in Parks" Confederate blouse, with dad in the kitchen, the day we left."

"Really, so you have two letters?" He asked.

"No, and we don't need to go into that right now." I said.

"Well, I figure it will be at least ten days with the wagon train before you are in Richmond, and maybe another two until you are caught up to the Army, so let's say you reach the Army by April 26th, that gives you almost a week to meet General Jackson, gain his confidence, and do whatever your plan is to save his life on May 2nd." Michael said, looking at me with questioning eyes.

"Yes," I said.

"Yes, are you kidding? So, what's your plan Parks?"

"OH … now you want to get to the hard part!" I responded.

I scratched my cheek, "Let's say I am still working on that."

"Wait, you mean there is no plan? Dad didn't give you a plan?" Michael said.

Jeanne Marie interrupted, "Michael, Parks was kind of a late addition. …"

"Like last second," I grunted.

"I can't believe this, half a century in the making, millions of dollars invested, an organization of more than a thousand, and we don't have a rock-solid way to ensure that General Jackson survives Chancellorsville?" Michael said.

Michael was obviously upset. "We are here, aren't we?" Jeanne Marie said. "Michael, don't go getting all negative on us, we are here, we all made an unbelievable trip through who knows what, and you have spent three years doing your path finder stuff … so, let's talk about what we do know."

Jeanne Marie was my kind of girl. Don't get confused by the facts, don't let the impossible get in the way, just do it. I liked that.

"Do you have the charts of central Virginia in the *Alabama*?" Michael said

"Charts?" I asked, Michael got that look again.

"Yes, we do, let me get them …" Jeanne Marie said. She got up and started to walk over to the Alabama.

I jumped up awkwardly, "You think you can climb up in that bird in that outfit, Jeanne Marie?" I said, as I rushed to follow her.

We walked over to the bird, opened the side door, "They are either over at my station in a pocket against the wall of ship, or they are up in the cockpit," she pointed to her area, "I don't remember where I left them."

"Geez," Michael moaned, making a face.

"Ah hush Michael," Jeanne Marie said looking over her shoulder towards her brother, "he was always the whiner when we were kids." She patted my butt as I climbed into the bird. I got over to her station, and looked for a light switch. "It's the first toggle on the left," her voice was comfortable, she probably knew her instrument panels by heart. I clicked the toggle and the overhead light came on. "Now look down, on the other side of the chair, against the wall."

She was right, there were charts in a leather folder. "Here, they are," holding them up in the air.

"Great, shut down the light." She turned to face Michael and smiled … "told ya." I chuckled, boy I bet they had some fights as a brother and sister I thought. We walked back over to the table, her grabbing at the charts with each step.

We sat back down. "So why do you need the charts of central Virginia?" I asked.

Here's the hard part Parks, you all have to depart this time on May 4th to make the window that will get you back to Mayberry in July, 2012. If we don't make that window, you can't get back until 2015.

"What?!" For the first time during this adventure, I felt anger welling up inside me. "How the heck would I explain that to NASA? Your dad never told me that. And you Jeanne Marie, did you know this?" I looked at her mean … let's say.

"Parks, …" Jeanne Marie started to speak.

"If it takes me two weeks to get up there from here, how the heck am I gonna get back here in two days?" I slammed the table with my fist, and stood up.

"Parks," Jeanne said, "Hold on,"

"What? You knew didn't you, and you never told me." I walked away.

"Hold on Superman," Michael said, "we have this taken care of, if you will cool down, and come back here and listen." He said that as he handed the lamp to Jeanne Marie, and laid out the Virginia charts on the table.

"Parks, if you knew all the obstacles and adversity, we, dad and us, and so many others have worked through, you would know that working the problem is a family characteristic." Jeanne Marie went on, "When we got here, Michael and I realized immediately the problem. The answer is really quite simple."

"OK, lay it on me."

"I will fly the chopper up there and get you," she said.

I wanted to say "what" at the top of my lungs, but I knew drama wasn't a winner here. I took a breath, "OK, what's the plan you cooked up?"

Jeanne Marie looked at Michael.

"He pointed to a mark on the map, a mark that was west of Chancellorsville. This is the LZ, landing zone Jeanne Marie, this is where we will pick you up. I have reconned that area when I was up there, and there should not be any major formations of soldiers in that area. There is a clear field for a safe landing area. All you will need to do is take a beacon with you when you leave here, and make it to this point by the night of May 3rd."

"So, you planned this before you left, Michael?"

"No, but there was always a contingency for this. If dad had come instead of you, the return to our time was not as critical. But getting someone like you had always been a possibility. So, we planned for that possibility."

"So how do you expect Jeanne Marie with ten hours flight experience to fly up there and get me? And how are you going to do this without alerting the entire Confederacy to a HIND helicopter?"

"Good questions," Jeanne Marie said.

"First, I will fly as her engineer, that should help with navigation, and second, we will fly after midnight, and should be back here before 4 am. Most folks in our flight path will be asleep, and probably won't even know we were over them, and those that do … well, UFO sightings go all the way back to the Bible! We will fly above 5,000 feet with no lights."

Michael went on: "If you are where you are supposed to be, if the beacon works as it should, this should be a piece of cake."

Michael said two things I needed to remember. First, check the beacon tonight, to make sure it's working, and make sure you memorize the pickup point."

"So, you will be staying here, while I am away, Jeanne Marie?" I asked.

"No, I have a secondary objective," she said

"A secondary objective?"

Michael cut in, "Hold on, before we start on the secondary objective, we need to make Park's kit for the LZ; you will need a beacon, and a radio, and maybe we should give him a smoke grenade."

"A smoke grenade?" Parks said.

"Let's go back over to the *Alabama* and get your stuff. We can put it in the bag I used for my crash here." Michael said, "Sure, a smoke grenade, you might need to create some cover at the last moment to get us out, and help confuse the situation."

"Good thinking," these folks had nimble operational minds.

Michael opened the door, jumped up in the ship, switched on the light, and threw me his bag. He opened a small hatch and grabbed a small black box, closed the hatch, and went into another. He grabbed a small radio, and closed that hatch, and then went to a lower hatch along the deck, and pulled out an OD green canister, the smoke grenade.

He handed me the items and jumped out of the bird, slammed the door and we walked back to the table and rejoined Jeanne Marie.

"Take it away Jeanne Marie." Michal said.

"Yes, I intend to meet Mrs. Jackson, and attempt to do two things. First to warn her about the coming events, and second to give her medicine, aspirin and antibiotics for pneumonia, in case you can't prevent General Jackson from being shot." Jeanne Marie said.

My look must have shown my concern.

"Don't worry, I understand our limits, and it may not be possible to address the issue. However, if an opportunity presents itself. ..."

Jeanne Marie has a wisdom past her age — and understands nuance.

"But the most important aspect of Jeanne Marie's mission is getting back here in time to be able to fly the *Alabama* up to Virginia to pick you up." Michael said. "She is leaving here on the 17th, to catch the train from Salem on the 18th."

"My research says Mrs. Jackson will most likely be traveling up from Charlotte on the 18th. If she is on the train, I hope to be able to meet her." Jeanne Marie went on, "But no matter what, I should be in Richmond on the night of the 18th, morning of the 19th. And from there I can start my hunt for Mrs. Jackson and hopefully work on another part of the plan."

I looked at, "What?"

She raised her hand and went on: "I plan to leave Richmond on the 23rd, I am playing it safe, that should be more than enough time.", Jeanne Marie crossed her arms, nodding her head with finality.

So, for the first time in this adventure I finally had some idea what we were all doing. I knew the plan was to save Jackson's life, but I didn't know how that was supposed to be done. And now, I at least had some idea what Michael and Jeanne Marie were doing.

They both looked at me, waiting.

They waited.

"Do you have any ideas, Parks?" Michael asked.

"Not at the moment. I will take the wagon train up, will deliver

Stuart's present and look for an opportunity to get near Stonewall. But right now, I don't have any more of a plan than that."

"I guess it's time to return to the house," said Michael. And with that, he blew out the lamp, and we got up and headed to the wagon. It was pretty late when we got home, there was no sign of Hattie. We all said good night, and the two of us headed upstairs to bed.

"Parks, I just wanted to tell you how well I think you have done in an unbelievable situation. I don't know anyone who could have jumped in to this like you did, and with almost no preparation, quickly acclimatize to the situation, and maintain your poise in so many unexpected situations. I really just want to say … wow. And also say, be careful, please." Half dressed, or half undressed, she moved towards me and gave me a hug. The scent of her hair was nice, and she held on for a long time. Her bare shoulders so soft.

"Jeanne Marie, we still have so much to do, and the fun starts tomorrow." I said holding her. She looked up into my eyes, and pushed up to kiss me. It was a deep long kiss, one that was strong and freely given, and one that could have led to much more. "I wish we could follow our feelings Jeanne Marie, but that is going to have to wait. Let's get ready for bed. Will be a long day tomorrow."

Hattie's farm, near Mt. Airy, North Carolina
Morning of April 13th, 1863

I was sitting on the porch, in a white blouse and pants, drinking a cup of coffee. The smell of biscuits and bacon filled the air. Jeanne Marie said she was going to bring my breakfast out to me. At that moment a half dozen Confederate cavalry, in column of twos, came riding up. This time, I was more comfortable as I recognized they were Cherokees, part of Thomas' Legion. They stopped abruptly in front of the porch, the sergeant asked: "Are you Colonel Walters?"

"Walter, yes" I said.

"Sergeant Woodpecker," he announced, and saluted, "Major Hill's compliments, sir."

I stood and returned the salute.

"Sir, the train is not going up this road, so my detachment and I are here to fetch you."

"Well, dismount Sergeant, I have not had my breakfast yet," the words were barely out of my mouth when Jeanne Marie walked out onto the porch with my breakfast. She was a bit surprised, the sergeant bowed some, a few of the horses whinnied.

"Good morning gentlemen, would you like some breakfast." She asked. Those words seemed to activate the order I had given about dismounting, the men almost in unison, swung out of their saddles.

"Hattie," Jeanne Marie, was loud, "We have some surprises." About that time, activity increased, as Ruth and others quickly joined Hattie and Jeanne Marie. They decided to invite the soldiers into the house, and feed them in the dining room. I stayed outside, enjoying what I thought might be my last breakfast at Hattie's farm.

Meanwhile Michael and Micah walked up with a beautiful tan and white horse, saddled. "Morning Parks." Michael said.

"Morning."

"Masser Parks, here's your ride, suh." Micah said beaming.

"My ride," I said.

"Yes, Parks," this is the horse I would have taken, had it been me that had to do what you are doing. He is bred for this mission, a three-year-old named Phoenix."

I gave Michael a knowing glance as he said his name. I got up, stepped down the stairs, "Michael, he is beautiful, look at that horse."

"He is fast, alert, powerful and doesn't scare easy." Micah said holding the reins close to the bridle while he rubbed his head.

Jeanne Marie walked out onto the porch, "morning boys. What a beautiful mount."

"He's for me, Jeanne Marie," I said with an almost childish pride, like a kid surprised at Christmas.

"You don't say," she came down the stairs. "Your escort is chowing down; you best get your kit." She patted me on my butt as she walked around Phoenix.

Micah whispered in my ear as I went by him, "This is the best horse I ever seen, suh, he will serve you well."

"Thank you, Micah," I said as I walked up onto the porch and into the house. I was going to have to make a couple of trips to carry down my bag, sleeping roll, guns, and all. For traveling light, I had more than I realized any man and horse would carry.

I put on the blouse, realizing the moment I did I was now an enemy of the United States of America and a soldier in the Confederate States Army. That thought took my breath away. I had never, at any time, realized the consequence of my decision to travel back in time. It was a shock. After I regained my composure, I brought my pistol belt up around my waist and locked the belt buckle, a buckle that featured a raised NC inside the brass circle.

By the time I got back down with the second load, George Washington, and many of his family were there, and the Cherokees were back outside, fussing with their mounts, saddles and stirrups.

"Colonel Walter, I spoke to Michael about sending someone with you, but he told me he didn't think that was a good idea, suh." George Washington went on, "Cletus can be ready in five minutes if you want him to go with you?"

I turned and looked at George Washington in the face, "George, I appreciate that offer very much, I understand what that would mean to you. But I believe Michael is correct. Thank you so much, I trust all will be well here in your care." We shook hands.

I was just about finished packing my horse, arranging things around the saddle, when Jeanne Marie walked up to me. She reached with her hand to my arm. "Let's take a short walk," she said. We walked off away from everyone from.

"Parks, please be careful darling, this is all real, and we are in a war. I need a pilot to get me home." We stopped, turned towards each other, and kissed. I had never felt like this for a woman before. She held me tight.

"OK, Jeanne Marie, its time I go," we turned back towards the group, "I look forward to seeing you again soon."

My escort was mounted, I followed suit and mounted Phoenix, I waved to the small crowd around and saw many sad smiles and waves. "Sergeant Woodpecker, at your convenience." With that his horse turned, I followed with the rest of the escort behind us. We trotted down the path to the gate and out on to the road. The clatter of the escort was a sound I would get used to over the next couple of days.

We would ride most of the morning before we finally caught up with the tail of the wagon train on the road to Danville, Virginia. During the ride, Sergeant Woodpecker informed me that they were a section of A Troop, from the Cherokee Battalion of the 69th North Carolina Cavalry. He said the battalion was about 400 braves. And that the 69th was also known as the Thomas Legion. He also told me he was the nephew of a Cherokee Chief

It took most of the afternoon, at an easy pace, to move up the train, through 100 wagons, while it was on the move. We finally reached the command section at the front of the train around mid-afternoon.

When we finally caught up to Major Hill, it had been a long day's ride, and we still had some distance to travel. "I am trying to make thirty miles a day, Colonel." He reported.

"You know your equipment and mounts," I responded, "if you feel good about that distance, I endorse your decision."

* * * *

The ride during the day went by without incident. Major Hill explained that the Thomas Legion was only a portion of 69th North Carolina, which had been originally formed in Tennessee. But had been active in the east, and the Legion had done a lot of work protecting rail lines, supply depots, etc. It wasn't only the Yankees that were troublesome. Small groups of deserters and other ne'er-do-wells were constantly harassing small detachments and towns. They seemed impressed by the incident we had experienced on Hattie's wedding day.

Andrew Taylor seemed to be a kind of legend in central western North Carolina, men spoke of him in awe, but also with fondness. He and Governor Vance were known to be almost brothers for the past half century. Apparently, they were in quite a few fights, which explains their cool when outnumbered and about to be overwhelmed

Hill explained that we had 28 troopers with us. There was another officer, a captain, who joined us. The captain was in charge of the troops, Major Hill had been in charge of the entire operation. He advised we did march with an advanced guard of four troopers, a detail upfront by the command section, and a larger detail at the rear of the train, whose responsibility was to cover both the rear and flanks.

Major Hill reported that soldiers had been found standing on the road waiting to catch the train to Lee's Army. These men were sprinkled throughout the train in the wagons, one or two here and there.

As we would every night, we camped by the side of the road. After pulling my gear off Phoenix, and hanging the empty feed bag on the saddle horn one of the troopers came and took our horses, to unsaddle and feed and line them. The lead group of wagons would be our source of dinner and breakfast. The wagons were driven by slaves. Tens of thousands of African Americans, slave and free man, served the Confederate States as soldiers, sailors, teamsters, cooks, laborers, and in other ways.

Greensboro, North Carolina
Railroad Station
April 18th, 1863

If distance were the only consideration, it would have been shorter for Jeanne Marie and Micah to travel to Burkeville to catch the train. But Jeanne Marie wanted as much time as possible with Mrs. Jackson, if she was on the train. So, she decided to go to Greensboro to catch the train. But she told Michael and George Washington that they would be coming back through Danville, and get off at Burkeville, and for him to send folks to meet them there on April 25th.

Hattie and Michael had decided it would be OK if Jimmie Earl traveled with Jeanne Marie to Richmond. At first, Jeanne Marie was hesitant, but then she softened to the idea when reminded it was she who had first mentioned it. Sometimes, I speak too fast, she thought to herself, but she remembered her father taking her to Atlanta when she was young, and how excited she was to go, so she agreed.

They left on the 17th, planning to stay overnight in Greensboro. On the wagon ride Jeanne Marie was stern with both Micah and Jimmie Earl about watching for each other. They were almost like brothers, though Micah was more than ten years older.

The next morning Jeanne Marie and Micah sat on the bench at the train station. Jimmie Earle was busy with his sling shot. For Jeanne Marie, it would be her first ride on a steam engine drawn train. Micah was more open in his anticipation of the great adventure. He kept getting up from his seat, walking to the edge of the platform and looking in both directions for the train he knew was coming.

"Come sit down Micah, you won't miss it, it has to come right here on that track in front of you." Jeanne Marie said, almost as if she were talking to a child.

"I know Miss Jeanne, but I juss can't believe we be gonna ride the iron horse. I remember how fast the land can move." Micah strained to look again in both directions.

"Micah, come here I want to talk to you."

"Yes, ma'am," he withdrew slowly from the edge of the platform, always looking back and forth. He made his way over to the bench.

"Micah, when the train comes, I want you to make sure our trunk and bags get in the freight car. Help the train master, or whoever is moving the trunks and other items. Get his name, and make sure you see our luggage on the car, OK?"

"Yes, ma'am."

"Micah, it's all we have for this trip, so we have to make sure where it is and that it is on the train."

"Yes ma'am," even from the bench Micah stayed focused on the track.

"Micah, you will hear it when it is coming, please listen to me." Jeanne Marie pleaded.

"Yes, ma'am, I am listening." Micah looked at Jeanne Marie.

"When the train comes, I will go into the passenger cars and I will look for a seat, when you are sure our baggage is loaded and have finished helping the men load the other freight, come look for me in the passenger cars, OK?"

"Yes, Miss Jeanne."

Just then a whistle far off in the distance sounded. Micah jumped, got off the bench and ran the short distance to the edge of the platform. Jimmie Earle joined him a second later, Micah pulling him close. When they got there, they could see the smoke tail of the engine rising above the trees in the distance; "Here it comes ma'am, here it comes." When just a few moments passed, the puff of the engine could be heard, and in a few more moments the sounds of metal against metal, the wheels churning could be heard, and grew louder rapidly. Finally, the nose of the engine turned a shallow corner and appeared out of the trees about half a mile down the track.

Whistles, and the sound of steam escaping, the bumping of the cars as they traveled behind the engine filled the scene. Activity started on the platform as various people at the station, with different purposes, began to move. Micah stood motionless; his eyes fixed on the train as it approached. He seemed totally unaware of all the activities occurring feet, sometimes, just inches from him.

Jeanne Marie sat, primping and looking at a hand-held mirror given to her by Hattie. Jeanne Marie wanted to look her best as she moved through the passenger cars looking for Mrs. Jackson. They had no specific evidence she was on this train. But it seemed likely. If she wasn't, Jeanne Marie's plan was to get off at Petersburg and wait in hopes of finding her in trains that followed.

Micah and Jimmie Earle were almost too close to the train when the engine rolled into the station, but they didn't back up until the approaching cab, that extended further out almost hit them. The engine rolled by slowing, the engineers' intent to bring the passenger cars to the platform to facilitate the boarding and debarking of passengers. The conductors hung out the front door of the passenger cars, dressed in dark blue jackets with hats.

"Micah, go help with the luggage," Jeanne Marie yelled in competition with the loud sounds of the train as it finally came to a stop; steam rushing out, the cars colliding into one another and other extraneous sounds. Micah sent Jimmie Earle towards Jeanne Marie. He was going to need help getting up on the stairs of the train car.

The cars were a burnt red, Piedmont Rail Road stenciled in white above the windows. A conductor was hanging out the door; his hand wrapped around a thin, iron rod running vertically up the car. Once the train had come to a complete halt, the conductor jumped out and down and reached for wooden steps. He placed them on the ground in front of the stairs so the debarking passengers could descend without falling. Only a few passengers came down, then the conductor yelled out in a strong baritone voice "boooard."

The sound of the train was deafening, whistles blowing, something clanking, though Jeanne Marie could not tell where or what that sound was. Activity buzzed along the platform.

Jeanne Marie had gotten her tickets out of the bag, and holding Jimmie Earle by the hand, waved them as she approached the conductor.

The conductor reached down to pick up Jimmie Earle and place him on the steps on the car. He extended his hand to Jeanne Marie, "Step up now, ma'am, I will take your tickets inside." The conductor said as he offered a hand and tipped his hat with the other.

"Micah, my escort went to help load the bags, there, ... see him." She pointed down the train to the baggage car, "do you see him?"

"Yes, ma'am."

"I have his ticket, please let him board." she said standing on the bottom step.

'Yes, ma'am, move along now, please."

Jimmie Earle disappeared up the steps and into the car.

Jeanne Marie, a little distraught, made her way up the steps and turned left into the main cabin, the strong smell of cigar smoke almost knocking her down, and burned her eyes. She looked to find Jimmie Earle. She found him in the car, looking at a baby in a woman's lap. The woman smiling, the baby laughing at Jimmie Earle's antics.

Jeanne Marie rushed down the aisle, "Jimmie Earle don't …"

The woman waved her off, "he's fine, Julia loves him … instant love."

Jeanne Marie looked at the woman, could it be Mrs. Jackson?

It was a long car, and she continued down the aisle. Meanwhile from the other end of a car, a conductor was headed rapidly towards the lady. There were no passengers but the woman and child in this part of the car. The seats in the train could be reversed and many were allowing four to six people to sit across from each other. The woman sat in the second seat facing forward, with the first seat facing to the rear and empty. Across the aisle the two seats there were set up the same way, so Jeanne Marie went to the seat at the wall so that she could see the woman's face.

Jeanne Marie sat down placing her bag on the bench beside her, closer to the window. The woman, playing with her child and speaking to Jimmie Earle, looked up, smiled but said nothing. Julia was in her lap, five months old.

'Madame, Madame," Jeanne Marie heard a voice getting louder as the conductor's steps sounded heavy on the car floor, "Madame, you will have to move back this a way …" the conductor said excitedly, " … this space must be reserved for Mrs. Ja… for special concerns." He said. By that time, he had made it to the front of the car and had taken Jeanne Marie's upper left arm rather forcefully.

"Now Robert, tut tut," Mrs. Jackson said, waving him off, "it's been lonely here sitting by myself, and she will be fine company for me, and look Julia is smiling, she likes her boy. Now be off, unless you need to get her tickets?"

"But ma'am the president of the company was very firm about your safety, and I can't…"

"My servant will be here shortly, "Jeanne Marie said, "he can look after our safety."

The conductor looked even more upset. "No, I …"

"Robert, I should not be in solitary confinement. Please now, just do what you have to do, and we will be fine. If you have worries, allow this woman's servant …"

"Mrs. Jackson, my name is Mrs. Walter." Jeanne Marie interjected, "this is Jimmie Earle my nephew and Micah is our companion."

"Yes, let Mrs. Walter and her crew sit with me and Julia."

"Alright, alright, I was just trying to do my job…"

"I know you were Robert, and believe me, I will tell my husband all about it when I get to Guinea Station."

The conductor braced up knowing that the famed General Jackson would hear of him and his valor in protecting the general's wife. "Tickets please," he said with a renewed confidence. The train jumped, rolling forward, jarring the conductor who had to grab the top of a seat to steady himself. Jeanne Marie looked to the back quickly to see if Micah had appeared up the steps, he was not there.

'Mr. Conductor, you must stop the train, my servant has not made it aboard. I can't leave without him." Mrs. Jackson got a concerned look on her face, but the conductor never saw it, "Ma'am we are on a schedule, we can't dilly dally for a negro servant, I am sorry." About that time Micah showed up coming through the rear door of the car. He was smiling, and looking, searching for Jeanne Marie.

The train was starting to pick up speed, which sharpened the bumps and added a g force which, though not terribly strong, was enough to throw Micah off balance. But he continued to move forward, enjoying the challenge as a kind of ride at an amusement park. He saw Jeanne Marie, waved, and kept on moving towards her.

"Your servant?" The conductor asked.

"Yes."

"Very well, come here son," he shouted at Micah, come and sit here. The conductor pointed to the grouping of seats behind Mrs. Jackson, but across the aisle and opposite of Jeanne Marie. Micah went to sit with Jeanne Marie, but the conductor stood blocking the aisle, "No, boy, sit there!" he said pointing his finger to the seats he had first indicated.

Micah had never been spoken to like that, and his face grew iron like, he looked directly into the eye of the conductor, the car jarred and bounced and the two men fell into each other, though neither completely lost his balance.

"Micah, please do as he asks, it's their train and their rules," Jeanne Marie asked.

"Yes, ma'am," Micah stepped back, moved into the seats and sat down facing Jeanne Marie.

"Thank you," the conductor said to Micah, the tension reduced a lot on both sides. "I could be fired for letting you sit here, but Mrs. Ja… ah, I am trying to be agreeable with your mistress." The conductor looked down the aisle and started to walk.

Jeanne Marie wasted no time, "Hello, I am Jeanne Marie Walter." She reached out her gloved hand. Mrs. Jackson reached to shake, but Julia restricted her movement and Jeanne Marie had to stand and move towards her in order for their hands to meet.

"I am Anna, Anna Jackson."

Jeanne Marie pretended not to know who Anna Jackson was. "Pleased to meet you, and who might this be? Did you say Julia?" Jeanne Marie touched Julia's face softly and the baby cooed and smiled.

"Yes, … a gift from God. We are going to see her father for the first time. "

"That must be so exciting. My husband and I have no babies yet. I just left him at my brother's farm. My husband is to command a wagon train headed north to supply North Carolina troops assigned to General Lee's Army."

"Really?" Anna said looking down on Julia.

"Yes, Governor Vance just asked him to do it, and he then gave him orders to report to General Jackson."

"Interesting."

"Well, of course you know who he is, you know the one they write about all the time?" Jeanne Marie played it for all it was worth. "Can you imagine, my husband will be on his staff. "

"Governor Vance? Do you know the Governor?" Mrs. Jackson asked.

"Well we just met him. We were at a wedding and Mr. Taylor brought the Governor."

"So, you know Mr. Taylor?" Mrs. Jackson's eye brow rose.

"Yes, you see he is my brother's father-in-law." Jeanne Marie sat with an inflated aire of pride. 'Do you know Mr. Taylor?"

"He comes to Charlotte occasionally. I am sure my parents know him," Mrs. Jackson said.

"Are you from Charlotte?"

"For the moment, we did live in Lexington."

"You did, well did you know the Jackson's? I mean … oh my, did you say your name was Jackson?" Jeanne Marie said, fussing as if extremely embarrassed, hiding her face in her kerchief.

"Yes, I am that Mrs. Jackson, and don't worry, nothing is wrong." Anna said smiling. We will probably get to know each other very well over a lifetime, and laugh about this first meeting years from now in our future. May be at Julia's wedding?"

"When this dreadful war is over, and we are at peace." Jeanne Marie said, a heartfelt tone in her voice.

The clickety clack of the train was consistent, its rhythm seldom changing. A strong breeze, sometimes with the scent of honey suckle blew in through the front windows that were open and pushed the smoke from a few men at the head of the car, to the back of the car where it escaped out open windows and the open doorway. The trees decorated with green leaves and pine needles passed by quickly, and when the woods broke the view from the train could be breathtaking or peaceful and bursting with the colors of spring.

Jimmie Earle had been surprisingly good, he climbed into the seat beside Mrs. Jackson and was looking out the window.

The two women talked more and more, and started to form a friendship as time passed. Jeanne Marie told Anna about the gun fight and Park's actions to save the Governor. Anna told Jeanne Marie about their brief years in Lexington, and about the last time she saw her husband in Winchester.

"I had taken the train from Richmond out to Strasburg in the Valley, and from there caught a stagecoach to Winchester. While on the trip an old clergyman volunteered to be my escort and look after me. He was a kindly old gent, and he tried very hard to make sure I was comfortable. But alas, he was not a great steward of our luggage and I lost a piece of my baggage." Anna said as she held Julia against her chest.

"Umm, that could be troublesome, and now you with the baby," Jeanne Marie volunteered, "Well, I have Micah with me, and he is a good servant and loyal, and he could help me watch after you and your luggage so you would not have to worry about that."

"That's mighty kind of you Jeanne Marie. I accept your offer. Though we will be disembarking in Richmond for a night with the governor, how would that suit you?"

"Governor Letcher? Are you sure the three of us will be no imposition?"

"He's the governor! He will have to make accommodations. I will tell him you three are my staff." The ladies burst into laughter.

"But the last time someone offered to escort me, he forgot my baggage. Fortunately, it was when I was headed to Charlotte." Anna Jackson said.

"Micah is a good man, we won't lose your luggage," Jeanne Marie assured her.

"Here, could you hold her," Anna handed Julia to Jeanne Marie," I need to use the facility."

"The facility?" Jeanne Marie asked.

"Yes, it's in a closet, behind you, at the end of the car." With that Julia got up and headed to the end of the car.

Jimmie Earle had laid down on the seat, he was asleep. Micah was looking out the window.

Julia smiled and gurgled as Jeanne Marie played with her. All of a sudden Jeanne Marie felt a pang of fear. The train was rocking, sometimes violently, and Jeanne Marie felt fear for the baby. She brought her up to her chest, and held her close. She could not stop thinking that she might be responsible for hurting Julia, by dropping her, or letting her fall. Each time the car shook, Jeanne Marie closed her eyes.

Finally, her heartbeat slowed and she realized she was overreacting. But she had never had a child, and rarely held one. In this time, life was more at risk, diseases more deadly, accidents more likely, food could be poisoned, or men could act violently without much provocation. For Jeanne Marie, the reality of this new time finally came home, as it had for Parks when Colonel Thomas had explained why he had two horses saddled at all times. But with that realization of the time, also came a new appreciation for life, for its fragility, its special place in the world.

Jeanne Marie held little Julia out and was amazed by her. Amazed at the tininess of her hands, and the seeming wonder in her eyes, Jeanne Marie leaned forward and tenderly kissed her.

"She is adorable; her father will be just as tender as you have just been." Anna Jackson said standing in the aisle. She must have been there and seen at least the last moments between Jeanne Marie and Julia.

Anna stepped in between the seats and took Julia from Jeanne Marie, slowly, with a delicate touch, not wanting to hurt Jeanne Marie's feelings, or rush the exchange. Two women taking a moment to fully recognize and appreciate the special gift their Lord had given them, to give life, to be a mother.

"The general has not seen Julia yet?"

"No, I wanted to come up during the winter, but he was firm in his warning against it. He was really worried about the weather and its effect on Julia while we traveled. He would not have it. I could feel in his letters great sorrow, and a wanting to have us with him. But Thomas is guided by a stern commitment to caution and wisdom. He is not in any way brutal or callous, his caution is always based in love." Anna said as she fidgeted with Julia. "Ummm, I think there is bottoms to change."

"Jeanne Marie, I believe I will have to use your bench, could you reach into the bag beside me, and pull out one of the cloth towels and fold it in a triangle and place it on the bench? Once you have done that you may want to visit with your servant. ..."

"Micah"

"Yes Micah, while I change her bottoms."

Jeanne Marie reached into the bag, pulled out the towel and folded it, placing it where she had been sitting. "Thank you, I think I will take a few minutes with Micah." Jeanne Marie took a few steps into the center of the car, where Micah was seated. He was looking out the window completely amused by the passing of Carolina, even when most of the time it was just a wall of green trees only ten yards away.

Jeanne Marie sat down on the bench opposite to Micah, close to the window, "How are you doing Micah?"

Micah looked at her, "This is a wonder isn't it Miss Jeanne? Look at how fast those trees can run past us! Isn't that something! Theez machines are black magic. I remembered this from four years ago, but I wasn't sure if I dreamed it or not?"

"Micah, we have been invited to escort Mrs. Jackson, and that means a lot of responsible for you."

"Responsibility? How's that ma'am?" Micah said.

"Well, you will not only be responsible for our baggage, but also hers and little Julia's, can you do that?"

"Sure enough, ma'am."

"Now this is important Micah, the last time someone escorted Mrs. Jackson they lost her luggage, you won't do that will you?"

"No ma'am, but she has to show me what's hers, I can't read."

"OK Micah, we will take care of that. And you know what? We will be staying with the Governor of Virginia tonight!"

"Is that so ... you don't say." Micah smiling, "the Governor of Virginny. Ain't that somethin'. Bet we will eat good thar!"

"Micah, Mrs. Jackson has to care for that baby, and we have Jimmie Earle, ..." Jeanne Marie was saying.

"We will be alright ma'am." He was sounding more like George Washington. Micah looked back out the window. Jeanne Marie had done the best she could to tell Micah the future she knew and what they had to be focused on. "I will talk with you later Micah, I am gonna return to my seat."

"Yes Ma'am".

Jeanne Marie made her way back up to Anna Jackson slowly, she was swaying back and forth with the rhythm of the train. Jeanne Marie knew the trains of the 1860s would be less stabilized and smooth than those of her day, but this train seemed more like an amusement park ride, than a means of transport.

About at the time she sat down, Robert the conductor made his way forward to the ladies.

"Mrs. Jackson, ma'am, we have about ten minutes before we will pull into Danville. Once we are there, you will disembark and move to another train for the ride from Danville to Richmond."

"Is this an old line? This train seems a little rougher than most." Jeanne Marie said.

"No ma'am, it's a new line. This section was just built, and is North Carolina gage track, that's why you have to switch at Danville." The conductor reached into a pocket inside his jacket and pulled out a leather wallet. "Look here, we even advertised for help to build this line in the *New York Times*, look here!" Robert, pulled a browned piece of paper out of his wallet, carefully unfolded it and handed it to Jeanne Marie:

From a June 29, 1862 article in the *New York Times*:

> Office of the Piedmont Railroad Company June 17, 1862 — Mules and Carts Wanted. Five hundred mules, and a proportionate number of carts, are wanted immediately, for the construction of the Piedmont Railroad from Danville, VA, to Greensborough, NC. The highest market rates will be paid for those which pass our inspection, if delivered at an early day. Apply at the office of the Richmond and Danville Railroad Company, either at Richmond or at the town of Danville.

Jeanne Marie had to read it twice, this was an advertisement to help build a railroad in the Confederacy in the *New York Times* just a year ago!

"The ride from Danville to Richmond should be smoother." Robert said. "This was just a short fifty-mile trip!"

"Robert, Micah needs to help with the transfer of Mrs. Jackson's luggage and mine, so he knows how many pieces we have and what they look like, can you arrange that before we reach Danville?"

"Yes, ma'am," Robert said.

"How long is the ride from Danville to Richmond?" Jeanne Marie asked.

"Hmmmm, I am not sure. The line is one hundred and forty miles. It's about three hours to Burkeville, and that's about sixty miles southwest of Richmond." Robert said. "You can get some lunch in Danville, before the train leaves. But be quick."

"Thank you, Robert. Please make sure you show Micah Mrs. Jackson's luggage." "Micah," Jeanne Marie called. When Micah looked, Jeanne Marie said, "Please go with Robert when he calls you and take care of our luggage and that of Mrs. Jackson too."

"Yes, ma'am," Micah answered.

"Micah, we best go now, I have things to do once we get into the station," said Robert.

Micah moved to get up, "Yes suh."

Thomas J. "Stonewall" Jackson

Danville, Virginia[1]
Railroad Station
April 18th, 1863

As the two women, with Julia, and then little Jimmie Earle dismounted from the train in Danville, Mrs. Jackson did not know her husband, Thomas would write a letter to her that night:

"Last night I dreamed that my little wife and I were on opposite sides of a room, in the centre of which was a table, and the little baby started from her mother, making her way along under the table, and finally reached her father. And what do you think she did when she arrived at her destination? She just climbed up on her father and kissed him! And don't you think he was a happy man! But when he awoke, he found it all a delusion."

The "Stonewall" who could be a terror on the field of battle, had a deep love for the child he had not yet seen.

Danville emerged from the woods, a growing and prosperous rail connection to Richmond. With 1,000 residents, the town included 115 houses, three groceries, two commission houses, two tobacco warehouses, two branch banks, a Masonic Hall, a female academy, a male academy, and a seminary for young ladies! But that's not all. Danville also had one apothecary shop, two tobacco factories, one oil mill, two flour mills, three sawmills, one iron foundry, two taverns, one printing office, two tanyards, one saddler, two boot and shoe factories, four tailors, three cabinet makers, one chair maker, two milliners, one plow factory, and three blacksmiths, as well as three lawyers and seven doctors.[2]

"Right this way Mrs. Jackson," a conductor led to the opposite side of the station. He pointed to a tavern where they might eat. The two ladies, followed, Anna carrying Julie. Jeanne Marie glanced down the train, seeing Micah moving trunks from the baggage car to the siding. He looked up and waved to her. She waved back and pointed to the building they were headed to.

---

1 The connection between Greensborough and Danville did not occur until 1864, so "creative license" has been applied for the sake of the story time line. In 1863 the line ran southeast to Raleigh and then north to Petersburg.
2 Danville Historical Organization — provided is the length of the line, and the size of Danville.

It was still early spring, the air cool, clouds overheard. The ladies crossed the street and walked quickly to the tavern, where a stranger coming out, tipped his cap to them and held the door, "good day ladies." The tavern was full, but in the corner was a table with a young woman sitting alone. Candles, flickered along with a few lamps that lit the dining room. It was mid-day, but there were few windows, and the door way let in only limited light, so the interior was certainly not bright, though not dark either. The two made their way over to the table, where Mrs. Jackson inquired, "Are these seats taken, dear?"

Looking up, the young woman hurriedly chewed her food so as to answer; "No ma'am, please have a seat. My husband stepped away, but there's plenty of room for you three." At that moment Jeanne Marie realized there might be a problem getting Micah fed. And Jimmie Earle was with him. She excused herself to find the owner.

When she found him, she asked him directly, "Sir, would Micah, our traveling servant be able to eat in this establishment?"

"Ma'am we have another area for servants, but he will be taken care of."

"My nephew, a small boy named Jimmie Earle will be with him. ..."

"I'll send him over to you," the tavern owner said. For Jeanne Marie, it was an awakening moment, this is how they lived, she thought. The issue of slavery was a constant element of life affecting everyone, all the time.

By the time Jeanne Marie got back to the table, Anna Jackson and the woman were talking. "Jeanne Marie this is Mrs. Melissa Scharf, we expect her husband any moment."

Jeanne Marie extended her hand, "Nice to meet you Melissa, I am Jeanne Marie Walter."

"Yes, Mrs. Jackson was telling me about you. ..."

"That's Julia, Melissa," Anna interrupted. Julia was asleep in Anna's arms.

Just then a young man walked up to the table, Melissa stood, "John Thomas, this is Mrs. Thomas Jackson." John Thomas tipped his cap, bowed slightly, and sat down. Timing was perfect as the food was brought to the table. No one was paying attention; time was passing and the train would be leaving soon.

Jimmie Earle came running up, "Jeanne Marie," he grabbed her, "I thought we lost you, I was so worried." He pulled as close as he could to her.

"Everything is fine Jimmie Earle, where's Micah?" Jeanne Marie said.

"He's round back, that's where they took us to eat."

"So, did you eat?" Jeanne Marie asked.

"Yes, ma'am, I am full." He smiled.

John Thomas was eating at a rapid pace, Anna and Melissa were wasting little time, not talking, though trying to maintain delicacy and remain poised. Jeanne Marie joined, eating what looked like a stew. The bread smelled delicious. Once she took a bite, she realized how hungry she was. There wasn't any food on the train, and she did not know when the train would get to Richmond.

"Board in five minutes," a conductor yelled loudly within the tavern. The folks who had already finished, immediately started moving. The owner was at the door to collect the money, 50 cents Federal, or three dollars Confederate a meal, from the people as they left.

Jeanne Marie picked up a piece of bread and placed it in her bag, as she rose. Micah was outside the door when Jean Marie and Jimmie Earle came out. Anna, Melissa and John Thomas were ahead of them as they all walked to the station. There was quite a crowd gathering. Much of the crowd were soldiers, clad in gray, men who had been home on furlough, but had been called back. Some wounded, not seriously, but obviously still not fully recovered, yet they were headed back to war.

Mrs. Jackson had a lot of questions for Private John Thomas Scharf who served with the Maryland Line. He had been wounded twice but had been in many of the major engagements, including Sharpsburg.

Scharf told them much about the fighting, and about General Jackson, himself. Ole "Blue Light" as many of his men called him, was something to behold on the battlefield. He was fearless. Thomas had seen cannon ball rounds land near the General, and while others lost control of their horses, or seemed very scared, he said the General and Little Sorrel were the picture of calm.

John Thomas told the ladies about Rocketts, a naval facility in Richmond that had been used the first two years to work on Confederate naval vessels. He said a second facility had been built across the river from Rocketts. We could see them from the bridge that crossed the river into Richmond, but it would be too dark by the time we got there.

He turned to look at Jimmie Earle for a special story: "But the really magical thing I saw on the James River was the C.S.S. *Teaser*, a converted tug, now used as an a gunboat. But, in '62, when the Yankees were at the gates of Richmond, the *Teaser* had been used to carry an aerial balloon and launched it into the air. The balloon was held to the *Teaser* by ropes, when it went several hundred feet into the air, and carried two men who could observe the Yankee Army, and its formations and movements. The *Teaser* would change positions in the River to give the men better or different views."

"A balloon," Jimmie Earle said excitedly.

"Yes, way up in the air with two men in it. It was something to see." John Thomas used his hands to try to explain the image.

Melissa said, "John Thomas had been wounded several times, and that he was trying to secure an appointment to the Naval Academy. And, that he had been encouraged by his officers."

"My appointment may already be there when we get back," John Thomas said.

Throughout all the talks, Micah and Jimmie Earle sat spell bound listening to the war stories. Although later in the afternoon, when the talk swung to the women both feel asleep.

For much of the afternoon, Jeanne Marie held Julia, awake and asleep. She listened to the stories, but at times, the mother instinct within Jeanne Marie stirred. She was fascinated by this young, new life. She had never spent any time around babies and it was a new experience. A couple of times Julia cried, and Anna had to quiet the little girl, but most of the ride she was content and would, from time to time, smile.

When things had calmed down, the men dozing and Anna feeding Julia, Melissa and Jeanne Marie had a chance to talk.

"We will be off to the Governor's mansion when we arrive in Richmond tonight, where will you two be going." Jeanne Marie asked.

"John Thomas has to report to his unit, so he will continue to the Army." Melissa said. Jeanne Marie got a look of concern on her face.

"No, don't worry about me," said Melissa, "When you are the cousin of the president you always have a place to stay in Richmond." A small smile came across her face, as she looked down.

"You are a cousin of President Davis?" Jeanne Marie asked in astonishment.

"Well not exactly, my mother is." Melissa said. "So that makes me kin somehow …" she said looking out the window. The sun was setting, and off in the distance, there a large gathering of buildings was silhouetted. "Look that must be Petersburg."

Three Pines
Rebel Mountain, Texas
July 19th, 2012
The velocity of Time

The chimes of the doorbell rang at Three Pines. Nash always heard a slight echo inside his home when he was there alone. He went to the door to find four men, friends waiting.

"Come in, come in," he said with a big smile on his face. Seeing these men, he knew they must be carrying news from Michael. King had called the night before, though he did not say much on the phone.

"Frank, how are you?" Nash said as he extended his hand. Frank had been one of the first men Nash talked to, almost a half a century ago, about the idea of going back in time with the intent of changing the outcome of the war. Frank had been the sower of seed, he had gathered thousands, quietly, discreetly, to the Cause. He had come up with the marketing monica, the "Alabama Project."

"And King, how are you sir?" Again the two smiled in the greeting and shook hands warmly. The shortest of the four, King also had aged the least, looking much as he did when he met Nash almost forty years ago. King had been one of the long-time central financiers of the Alabama Project as the time travel initiative had come to be called.

"And, you Reece, how have you been sir? And how is Vera and the children?" The two revealed a deep long friendship of many score years. Reece was a Citadel man, and an engineer who led much of the work in transforming the Soviet HIND into the *Alabama*. Though all the men were unaware of it now, the work Reece had done to extend the operating of the HIND from 280 miles to almost five hundred miles was making all the difference to recovering Parks near Charlottesville, VA.

Last but equal to the rest, was Charles, the oldest of the four by a considerable amount, was the man who engineered the time propulsion system for the *Alabama*. The two embraced warmly. "Hello friend," each said to the other.

"Let's go into the Parlor." Nash said.

"Where's Mark?" King asked

"He's in the barn," Nash said.

These six men were the core intellect of the Alabama Project. They knew each other intimately, their families had often come to Rebel Mountain for meetings, planning, and just to celebrate holidays. All had long lineages back through two centuries of the South. All were highly successful in their own way. All were Christians.

As they walked into the Parlor, Frank reached in to a thin leather brief case and pulled out a piece of paper. "We have a report from Michael, I thought you would like to see."

> Dad,
>
> Jeanne Marie and Parks have arrived safely. All is well. They have both departed on their separate missions. Parks earned his hero spurs rapidly and has been placed in charge of supply train by the Governor. The train is headed towards our object.
>
> One other thing dad, I married a woman named Hattie, with two children Karl David and Jimmie Earle and I do not intend to return with Jeanne Marie and Parks. Jeanne Marie will explain when they return.
>
> Love your son, Michael.

The men had sat down, as Nash stood and read the note. When he looked up, he had both a smile on his face, and a tear in his eye.

"This came in with Reece, last night," King said, "I knew you would want to see it." King was Texan with deep roots. His family was of consequence in East Texas, both in wealth and in the politics of the state.

"Have some coffee, gentlemen." He waved towards the table. Nash had prepared for the visit. The gathering had been planned months ago. The men had joined in Ft. Worth the day before. Nash had a large silver coffee dispenser, with silver cups, and silverware on the table. Peach cobbler cut into pieces was on plates. Nash had been a busy fella that morning.

"It seems I am a father-in-law, and grandfather." Nash said. As always, dressed in his white shirt, slacks and shoes, with red suspenders, Nash looked the part.

"Yes, it does," Reece said. Reece was tall, thin and wiry. Always quick to smile, his mind was incisive. He wasted few words.

"Not something we anticipated I am afraid," Frank said. "It raises unexpected questions we had not ever considered."

"True," said Reece, "but we are already learning from this exercise, it appears our conjecture about the velocity of time, about its compression is true."

King said, "I never quite understood what you guys were talking about, the velocity of time? Strange idea."

Nash got his cup of coffee last, "Actually, I don't think we ever knew for sure, but this clearly seems to indicate, that time is compressed, like the pressure of deep water in the ocean. The more time that passes, the faster the day and year move in the past, relative to this time."

"That's about the size of it," Reece said. "Einstein indicated there would be different rates of time, or its speed of passage, depending on where you were in the universe."

"Well, from my perspective," Charles entered the discussion, "this boy Parks and your daughter are following the plan we laid out. When you think of what we have accomplished over the past half century Nash, it is … immeasurable, unfathomable." Charles was also a man of science, but more blunt and to the point than any of the rest. "It's fresh in my memory how doubtful, how skeptical I was of this whole thing when you approached me Nash, in the early 1970s." Charles said.

The minds of these men were all operating, and considering the mission, but from very different perspectives simultaneously. It has been their modus operandi as a project group. Nash had proven to be a gifted gatherer of diverse talent that could focus their respective skills towards a single purpose.

"I know," said Nash, "since they left, I have had time to just sit and think here in peace. So different from the urgency and pressure of the last decades. And each of you has made such a large contribution."

Frank spoke with a sense of fear, "Nash we do not know how Michael's decision will affect the time line! It could be disastrous."

"Frank, the unknown, the repercussions of our actions and this mission have always been unknown. We did this with the intention of changing history, so we bear that responsibility however this all plays out." Reece said.

"I am not as worried as some of you," said King. "Don't forget God. Providence is not a myth, or wishful conjecture. All that has happened was God's plan, and I am not sure God's Will is as malleable, as we may have thought when we started this dream long ago."

"Gentlemen, when we finish with coffee, you are free to move into the bunkhouse, and then we can get to work … though much of that will just be waiting. …" Nash said, his voice quieting with his last words.

Richmond, Virginia
Train Station
April 19th, 1863

It was after midnight when the train pulled into the station at Richmond. Everyone was sound asleep when the conductor came through. The car was dimly lit, bodies were in all shapes and configurations as they began to stir in response the to the conductor's call; "Richmond, Richmond, all passengers, Richmond."

By the sound of it, Julia was the most disturbed, her cry was loud. And it woke everybody else up. Micah stretched; Jimmie Earle did not want to wake up. Melissa was laying on John Thomas' arm and chest. The noises of movement were quiet and tepid at first, but before long, activity was buzzing. The light from outside the train, coming in through windows helped, first to see, and second bringing excitement of arrival to the full car.

John Thomas and Melissa bid their ado. "Maybe we will see each other," Melissa said to Jeanne Marie as they touched. "I hope so." Jeanne Marie replied. Now she had a reason to go to the White House, and with luck, see the president and complete the deepest held secret of the mission.

"I believe the Governor's people will be outside to meet us," Mrs. Jackson said to Jeanne Marie.

"Micah, remember, we have to get Mrs. Jackson's bags, along with ours." Jeanne Marie said, looking at Jimmie Earle still asleep on the seat.

"I will get him, ma'am." Micah said as he reached down to Jimmie Earle.

"Micah, you are a saint, but you can't do it all. I will get him, you make sure we have all our bags." Jeanne Marie touched Micah on the shoulder.

"Yes, ma'am," and with that Micah joined the other passengers as they stood in line to get off the car.

It didn't take long for the car to clear, all that was left was Anna, Julia and Jeanne Marie. A conductor rushed into the car, accompanied by a man dressed in a suit. The conductor looked frazzled at first, then relieved when he saw Mrs. Jackson.

"Mrs. Jackson, this is Mr. Stewart from the Governor's office. He is here to take you to the Governor's mansion."

Anna was still sitting rocking Julia, she extended a hand to Mr. Stewart. "Mr. Stewart, how nice of you to meet us. Mr. Stewart, this is Mrs. Walter and Jimmie Earle, they are my traveling companions, as is their servant Micah, who has gone to retrieve our bags."

Stewart seemed annoyed by the surprise of unaccounted for strap hangars, but quickly removed the look, smiled, and bowed slightly to Jeanne Marie. "I am sure the Governor and Mrs. Letcher will be happy to make your acquaintance, Mrs. Walter." Mr. Stewart said, "Let's get you all to the carriage. It's chilled outside, Mrs. Jackson," he warned. Stewart picked up Jimmie Earle, to carry him to the carriage.

"Thank you sir," Jeanne Marie said in surprise, "that is kind of you." And the party moved off to leave the car. The conductor was at the steps to help Mrs. Jackson, and then Jeanne Marie descend safely to the platform. It was late, but there were still many lights flickering all around. A fog encased the area, it was a surreal scene Jeanne Marie thought.

In the countryside, southwest of Petersburg, Virginia
April 19th, 1863

We were about half way to Lee's Army. The weather was cool, cloudy, and sometimes wet. My butt hurt, and so did my back. I had been riding Phoenix for almost a week. I never knew how tough it could be to live in another time. My clothes were wet, I didn't smell too good. And shaving is no fun with a straight razor, cold water, and a soap that doesn't seem to make the blade glide over your face.

"Tough night, sir?" Sergeant Woodpecker asked as he handed me a cup of coffee.

"You could say that," I responded, "thanks for the coffee."

"Sir, Phoenix is without a shoe, I suggest you ride in one of the wagons today, 'til we can get that mended. I believe we could have him back to you tomorrow morning."

Relief I thought, thank you God. But my face remained blank, "Really Sergeant, thank you, I appreciate your observation and recommendation." I couldn't help but wonder how long that shoe had been off, and what the men thought, did they question my equestrian skills?

"Sir, no problem." He turned to leave.

"Sergeant, would you ask Major Hill to come over to see me."

"Yes sir."

"And could I ask you for a recommendation of who I should ride with, which wagon, I mean."

Sergeant Woodpecker thought a moment. "Well if you want a musician, who sings nice, there is Isiah, if you want silence, there is Deek, or if you want to ride with a man who knows all the drivers, is a kind of leader of the drivers and also a pastor for his plantation, there is Joshua.

"Sergeant, would you ask Joshua to come and see me."

"Yes sir."

"And Sergeant Woodpecker, thank you for your performance of duty and advice to me." I said. Sergeant Woodpecker, saluted, turned and walked away.

The coffee was good. When a person is outside for days at time, the small things become very important, like hot coffee in the morning. It doesn't stay hot long, so you can't dawdle, no microwave to heat it back up.

After a few moments Joshua walked up. He was an older man, with white hair. Tall, strong, he removed his hat, "You wanted to see me, suh?"

"Joshua, I was wondering if it would be alright to ride with you today, it seems Phoenix is missing a shoe." Joshua seemed to stand taller when I finished my question. "Yes, suh, it would be an honor."

"Where is your wagon, Joshua?"

He pointed to a group of wagons some distance away. He reached down, picked up my saddle, "I can send some men over to get the rest of your things, sir." He said. His diction was better than most I thought.

"That's alright Joshua, I will carry it myself. Thank you, that will be all." I said. Joshua, turned, put his hat on, and walked towards the wagons he had pointed to.

Moments passed, and Major Hill rode up. He saluted, and I returned the salute. He dismounted.

"Are the scouts out, Red?" I asked.

"Just about, they were leaving when I got word you wanted to see me." He replied.

"Phoenix is down for today, so I will be riding with Joshua, on his wagon. You will have to be more active today, in terms of controlling the train." I said.

"Taking a day off?" He said with smile.

"Hey," I said. Hadn't expected his comment.

"Sorry sir," he said sheepishly.

"No, it's OK Red, fair question. I guess I haven't been in the saddle in quite a while, my body can use the rest." I said packing up my gear in the saddle bags. "When you are ready, you can commence the movement of the train, Red. You know where I will be."

He saluted, and again I returned the salute. He turned, mounted, and was off.

I picked up my gear, and headed in the direction of the wagons Joshua had pointed to. As I got closer one of the younger men ran out towards me, "I will take that suh, I am Jackson," he said with a smile, some teeth missing. He took my saddle bags.

"Thank you, Jackson."

"I suppose to take you to Joshua, he said you'd be ridin' with us today."

"Yes, I am riding with Joshua today. Do you ride with him every day?" I asked.

"Yes, suh, I am his fetcher, suh." Jackson said, looking straight ahead, but with an apparent bit of pride.

"His fetcher, what is that?"

"Well suh, I's fetches things, you know. He may want one of the drivers to comes see 'em, or he may want something from the back of the train or the front of the train, whilst we are moving, and so's I fetches it. See?"

"Yes, Jackson I see." I liked this guy, he was content, knew his job. About that time, we came up on a wagon. "This is it, suh." He said.

"And where is Joshua," I asked.

"He off prayin', see him thar suh?" Off in the woods maybe fifty yards, there was Joshua, hat off, … and it looked like he was reading a book, I presumed the Bible. Jackson walked to the back of the wagon, and I could hear him throw my gear in the back. I looked around, the wagons seemed ready to go, men were standing in groups talking, smoking pipes.

Joshua walked up, "Welcome to my humble wagon, sir. Jackson has taken care of you, I see." He reached up and put the Bible under the seat of the wagon.

"Yes, quite a fetcher you have there, Joshua."

"He's my sister's boy, fine boy."

All of a sudden, at the sound of a trumpet barely heard, men started to move quickly to their wagons. "Time to go," Joshua said. A group of wagons in front of us, pulled out of the woods and started down the road.

I climbed aboard quickly, not wanting to be the cause for delay of this group of wagons. I had barely sat down when Joshua said "Giddy up thar," and pulled the reins so they snapped loudly and slapped the backs of the horses. There was a jerk, and a second jar, and we were moving.

We rode on for a while, not talking.

"Sir, we heard about your bravery saving the Governor and Mr. Taylor." Joshua finally said.

"You did?" I said.

"Yes sir, some of the drivers are from Miss Hattie's. Boy, you should hear them tell the tale. You get bigger every time they tell it," he said with a smile getting larger on his face. I laughed myself.

"That's how legends start, I suppose," Joshua said.

"It wasn't that much, Joshua." I said.

"Maybe not to you sir, but to those kids, and Mrs. Taylor, when you came bursting through the woods and leaped that stonewall into their makeshift fortress, it was like the god of war showing up." Joshua said in a solemn voice. "Those men are evil, and nothing good was going to happen there, 'til you showed up."

"Thank you Joshua, but I still think any man here would have done the same." I meant what I said. The men I had met in this time, black or white, were men of action. They were used to danger, used to threats, real threats that could kill, and they acted to defend what they loved. They were quick, decisive, and not real interested in worrying about what people might think of them.

"Maybe so," Joshua almost whispered.

"So, what were you reading in the Bible, Joshua?" I asked.

I must have caught him in thought, "What's that?" He replied, "Pardon sir, was thinkin' of something. What did you ask?"

"What were you reading in the Bible this morning?"

"Chapter twelve in Job, verses five through eight," he said, and then he quoted it word for word, " I would seek unto God, and unto God would I commit my cause: Which doeth great things and unsearchable; marvelous things, without number: Who giveth rain upon the earth, and sendeth waters upon the fields: To set up on high those that be low; that those which mourn may be exalted to safety. He disappointeth the devices of the crafty, so that their hands cannot perform their enterprise."

"I am not sure I have heard those verses before," I said.

"You are a church-going man, sir?" He inquired.

"Umm, well, maybe I can't claim that," I said.

"Well sir, God's Word is comforting in these times of uncertainty. It is of great peace to know that God has a plan, and all things work for the good of those who believe," Joshua almost radiated when he said that.

"You believe in God's plan Joshua," I asked in all sincerity to a man who was a slave.

"I do sir," Joshua said.

"I don't know, I see a lot I just can't accept as God's plan," I said.

"We are not God sir, we don't have His Sight, or His Wisdom, all we have is His Word. And, that is as He would have it."

Joshua was so wise. I was sitting next to a man so sure, so peaceful, so confident.

"How did you first learn of God's Plan Joshua?" I asked.

'Since I was a boy, I heard of it, but about eight years ago I was in the Shenandoah and I heard about Providence from a man who was a teacher of cadets. He was just a simple man, no one had ever heard of." Joshua said. "But he was not just a teacher of cadets, but a teacher of slaves, like myself."

"Who was this man, Joshua?"

"You are doing his work, sir, it was Major Jackson then." He said.

"You mean General Jackson, Joshua?"

"I do," he said.

"General Jackson taught you about Providence. ..."

"Among many things, Colonel Walter. The General is devout and teaches the writings of the Word."

"But, he is a general..." I said.

"He is, some say the sword of God," Joshua said, "But many many of the generals of Marse Robert are Christian men sir. You will see, when you get there, I bet."

"So, you are a slave because of Providence?" I asked.

"I am what God made me," Joshua said.

"I don't understand," I said.

"We are not God sir, we can't understand why God has arranged things as He has. But we can have faith, and it is the answer to all things." Joshua said. This man was a preacher; he was a man of faith. His arguments were steady, constant and centered. The Bible spoke to him, and it was projected by him in his words.

I didn't feel the bumps and jars as much, my mind was deep in thought. This was not the twentieth century with all its conveniences, all its easy ways, this was a world where God was still dominant, pervasive. This is where America came from.

Joshua was a good teacher, once he had made his point, he did not speak. Rather he allowed time for God to speak to the student. And because things moved so slow here, nothing to distract, there was time to consider questions that were not even asked in the time I came from.

The Governor's Mansion
Richmond, Virginia
Noon, April 20th, 1863

Jeanne Marie awoke, sensing someone close by, looking at her. When she opened her eyes, there was someone so close it startled her, … Jimmie Earle.

"Jimmie Earle, what are you doing?" she said. His response was an immediate jumping into her bed. It was clear Jimmie Earle had grown very fond of Jeanne Marie, like a big sister, or aunt.

"Time for you to get up sleepy head," he said. Jeanne Marie stretched, and yawned. She had not slept so well since she had been back in this time. I guess the beds in a Governor's mansion are more comfortable than any others she thought.

"Come on, come on" Jimmie Earle said as he backs off her bed.

"OK, OK boy." But she didn't move.

"Mrs. Jackson is waiting for you," he said.

That got her attention. She still had things to do with Mrs. Jackson, and she could leave any moment for the army. Jeanne Marie rose quickly. She looked around.

"They have a room here," Jimmie Earle said, "a room where you can do things," he said with a smile. Without being specific, Jimmie Earle had sent a message.

Jeanne Marie grabbed her robe and put it on, "Where is this room Jimmie Earle?" He took her hand, led her out into the hall, and to a room. "Thank you," she said, and closed the door.

Jeanne Marie dressed quickly and went down stairs to find Mrs. Jackson. Half the day was already gone, and she still had to talk to Anna about the threats to General Jackson's life, and to give her the medicine she had brought to treat the pneumonia Jackson would get if he were wounded on May 2nd.

Anna and Julia were surrounded by admirers. Mrs. Letcher seemed to be a traffic cop, directing people to Mrs. Jackson, and after a time, moving them on so others could spend time with the wife of the South's most successful general. "Folks, we have to give everyone a chance to meet Anna, but she will be leaving soon for the mail train. Today, she will be with her husband, God Willing." Mrs. Letcher said.

Anna, saw Jeanne Marie and waved. Jeanne Marie waved back.

After some time passed, the Governor came into the room, his wife leading him around the women to shake hands, chat briefly with each, and move on. They were practiced at this. After he made the rounds, he went to the center of the room and made some comments to all about Mrs. Jackson, and closed by saying that it was time for the folks to leave, so the Mrs. Jackson could have a bite to eat before she had to leave for the train.

As the folks cleared the room, Jeanne Marie made her way over to Anna and sat down. "You are some celebrity," Jeanne Marie observed.

"Not I," Anna pleaded, "But my Stonewall certainly is. I don't know why I called him Stonewall, I have never done that before. He is my Thomas."

"Anna, I have brought something, I want to give you." Jeanne Marie reached into her bag and pulled out two small glass bottles. "These are medicines I brought especially for your Thomas."

"But he is not sick, I would have heard." Anna said. Anna's face quickly went to a frown, and one of concern.

"No, he is not, but these are medicines should he be wounded, God forbid." Jeanne Marie said. "They will help him recover. He should take one each, every six hours if after being wounded he gets a fever."

Jeanne Marie handed them to Anna, she didn't want to take them. She shuttered coldly. "No, I don't want. …"

"Anna, no one wants your husband hurt, much hope is placed in him. I ask you to take these as a safeguard." Jeanne Marie tried again to give her the medicines. Anna was not happy by this. The two had known each other just a few days, and Anna was so happy to be taking Julia to her father. Any mention of bad fortune could be a jinx.

Jeanne Marie had not anticipated Anna's reaction. "I have come a long way to give you these Anna, please take them."

Anna took the bottles and rose. Almost like a queen who was not pleased, "I have to go get something to eat now." She turned and left Jeanne Marie alone in the large room.

After a few moments, Jeanne Marie got up and decided to go upstairs and pack her bag and find Micah and Jimmie Earle. She could not presume she would be welcome in the Governor's mansion once Mrs. Jackson left. And she might even find herself removed without even seeing Mrs. Jackson again.

With a little bit of hunting, Micah and Jimmie Earle were collected, and told to pack their things and ready themselves. While she was packing, a female servant came into the room; "I have a note for you ma'am." Jeanne Marie turned and the woman held a small silver plate with an envelope on it. "Thank you," Jeanne Marie said as she took the envelop.

"Will there be anything else ma'am?"

"Could you wait one minute please." Jeanne Marie saw her name written on the envelop, and opened it and took out the note. As she unfolded it she could see that it was WHITE HOUSE stationary.

> April 20th, 1863
> Jeanne Marie,
>
> I hope this note finds you well. I know Mrs. Jackson was leaving today, and have asked Mrs. Davis if it would be convenient if you joined us. She was quite pleased at the idea, and said it would be fine. A carriage can be sent for you, at your convenience.
>
> Hope you will accept this offer,
> Melissa Scharf

Jeanne Marie looked to the servant, "Is there a writing desk and stationery available?'

"Of course ma'am, right this way," The woman went out the door, down the hallway two doors, "… right in here ma'am." Before she could say anything, the servant was gone. It was a small room with a window out the front. There was quite a commotion which caught her eye, it was Mrs. Jackson and Julia leaving for the train to meet her husband.

It was raining and clearly breezy outside as people's coats and dresses were rustling in the wind. Mrs. Jackson, and then Hattie, after handing Julie up to Anna, disappeared into the coach and the driver moved off briskly. Hattie was Anna's servant who had been waiting for her in Richmond.

Jeanne Marie sat down, pulled a piece of the Governor's stationery to her, dipped the pen in ink and wrote:

April 20th, inst.

Melissa,

Thank you so much for remembering me and my party. I could not appreciate your invitation more, and ask that you send a carriage at your earliest convenience.

Regards,

Jeanne Marie Walter

She gently blew on the script to dry the ink. Once dried, she pulled an envelope, folded the paper and placed it inside. On the outside of the envelop she wrote WHITE HOUSE and below that Mrs. Melissa Scharf. She rose, and went out into the hallway, called for Micah and Jimmie Earle and proceeded down stairs, where she spoke to the first male servant available. "Please have this taken to the WHITE HOUSE as soon as possible. And could you tell me where I might wait until a carriage comes for us?" The servant said "Follow me" and led her to a small parlor. "Could you have our luggage brought down when convenient," she said.

"Of course, ma'am." And he was gone.

Guiney Station, Virginia
April 20, 1863

The rain was constant, but not a downpour, just steady. The sky dark, the temperature cool, but not cold, with only an occasional gust of wind. General Jackson put on his rubber raincoat, grabbed his kepi and gloves and walked out the door towards the orderly holding the reins to Little Sorrel, a small red horse. Today was a special day, Jackson looked up to Heaven to thank God for the rain which brings life, and for the train coming on the Richmond, Fredericksburg and Potomac Railroad, that was bringing Anna and Julia to him.

Thomas Jackson had waited a long time to see his wife. His own self-discipline and self-denial had kept Anna away. But now, she was coming. He decided it was a great day to wear a brand-new uniform given to him by his friend General J. E. B. Stuart.

As he dressed, he thought of the last time he had seen Anna. It had been in the Valley, at Winchester over the Christmas season, 1861. His anticipation of his ladies, Anna and 4-month-old Julia, was strong, and he left the house a little early, he simply could not wait. What if the train got in early?

General Jackson pulled on his heavy raincoat and stepped outside the Yerby home to find Jim standing in the rain with Little Sorrel. "Morning sir," a large smile on his face.

"Jim, you shouldn't be standing out here in the rain," the General said, as he took the reins from Jim. "Go find a warm dry place." The general put a hand on Jim's shoulder.

"Sir, I have an ambulance to carry the Mrs. and Julia."

"Jim, that's kind of you sir, then follow me."

"Yes, sir."

The general mounted and touched Sorrel's flanks.

As he rode slowly towards Guinea Station, he had time to remember those days in Winchester. He remembered that he was not there to meet the stage from Strasburg when his wife arrived, and that Anna had to walk up to the Taylor hotel at midnight on a dreary cold night. He remembered her walking in the mud up the dark street and looking back, seeing him wrapped in an overcoat and hat but not recognizing him. He was puzzled when she worked hard to create distance between herself and him.

He remembered how surprised she was when he grabbed her as she made it to the top step. He had wrapped her in his arm and kissed her several times ... before she realized it was him! She wasn't happy with the surprise. He didn't want to do that again.

Sorrel had taken Stonewall to the train station while Jackson's mind had wandered. When Thomas came back to reality and saw the tracks and station house, he shook his head. Sorrel had done what he did so many times, he had taken him to the precise spot he wanted to go without guiding him at all. Or so it seemed.

Officers and soldiers, and others gathered at the small, single building station to meet the mail train from Richmond that was part of the Richmond, Fredericksburg and Potomac Railroad. It was a daily occurrence and always drew a crowd. But today, the gathering would have an anticipated member. Every man in Jackson's Corps had heard the news, Anna and Julia were coming to visit the general.

General Jackson and the ambulance arrived. Jackson decided to remain mounted. The rain continued. The gray clouds obscured the normal long-distance sign of smoke rising from the engine. But after some time had passed, Jackson could hear off in the distance the sounds of a coming train. He dismounted and tied Sorrell to the right front wheel of the ambulance. He moved forward, and then through the crowd. Soldiers made way for their commander.

For the General it seemed to take forever for the train to make the mile from first sight, until it loudly pulled up to the station house. Steam and smoke pouring out, the screeching of the breaks on the wheels. Normally a reserved man, not one to show too much emotion, except in battle, Thomas Jackson was as anxious as a school boy on his first date. He simply couldn't wait the moments it would take for the train car to empty, and for Anna to gather all she had and step down off the car into the rain. When the train stopped, Jackson bolted to and up the stairs into the car. His coat was drenched and water was running off of him in rivulets as he stepped into the car where the passengers were standing, putting on their coats and gathering their things. Thomas moved into the car, bumping into people, who were not happy at the soaking he gave them. He searched the car for Anna, and finally there she was, smiling, looking at him.

But where was Julia?

Ah, there she was, with Hattie, Anna's traveling help, holding Julia. The young four-month-old had been activated by the all the goings on in the car.

As passengers recognized who this large bearded, wet, soldier was, or heard from others in the car, who he was, they moved away from him, making room between him and Anna. Like the force of newly established vacuum, Jackson was pulled towards Anna. He was aware of being wet, and resisted the strong urge to sweep her in his arms. Their eyes met, he was close enough to smell her perfume.

Jackson said almost in a whisper: "My esposita ..."

Julia had noticed the movement towards her mother and looked at the General. When he turned towards her, small hands reached for him, ... and smiled. The connection was immediate.

A few of the passengers watched the moments, then most hurriedly made their way out. They didn't want a second soaking.

"I shan't touch you now my esposita, follow me, Jim has an ambulance waiting." General Jackson smiled.

Jackson helped Anna put her coat on. Anna took Julia so that Hattie could get ready to disembark.

The conductors waited at the end of the car, "I don't want to get my family wet, would you help them down the stairs. ..." Jackson said to the men as he walked up. At first, they were stunned, the legend had spoken to them ... then confusion as who would go down the steps and who would remain in the car ... it was almost comic to watch them scramble after the General passed them. But the exit for Anna, Julia and Hattie went smoothly enough.

By the time they made it to the steps at car door, Jim had moved the ambulance parallel to the tracks, and close by. The back gate to the ambulance was near the steps so that the women would not be in the rain long. Still it was a challenge to relay the three of them up into the ambulance. Nearby soldiers sheepishly stepped up to help.

Once the women were seated, Jackson mounted Little Sorrell and the party was off for the Yerby home.

The White House of the Confederacy, Richmond, Virginia.

The Confederate White House
Richmond, Virginia
April 21, 1863

Jeanne Marie had paid her respects to Mrs. Letcher. They left the Governor's mansion in a carriage to the White House not long after she, Micah and Jimmie Earle had gotten comfortable in the parlor.

It took almost no time for the ride to the White House, which was good given the cold wet weather. The White House did have a portico so they were covered when they stepped out of the carriage.

At the door to meet them when they arrived was Melissa, with a small African American boy standing beside her. Melissa was very happy to see them, and after a brief exchange with Jeanne Marie, she presented the boy, Jim to Jimmie Earle. Within moments the boys were off, not to be seen for hours.

"That's Jim Limber," Melissa said to Jeanne Marie.

"How cute," Jeanne Marie said. In her research for this mission, she had learned of the black boy adopted by the Davis' who would be a part of their family until the Yankees captured President Davis in late spring of '65. Jim would be separated from them in the woods in Georgia and never see them again.

Jim and Jimmie Earle instantly joined and within seconds were off on adventures.

The two women watched the boys run off. " I knew he would be excited about Jimmie Earle coming. We won't see them for a while." Melissa assured Jeanne Marie. "Let's get you settled in your room, and have some nice hot tea brought up, and talk."

The two ladies spent the afternoon until dinner, chatting, laughing, and just enjoying each other's company. "Jeanne Marie, tonight you will dine with us, Postmaster General Reagan, of Texas, should be joining us tonight. He is a delightful man, and has done an excellent job forming and running our mail service."

Jeanne Marie perked up at that comment. As a Texan she knew of John Reagan and now could look forward to meeting a man most Texans had only read about.

Meanwhile, Micah was thoroughly enjoying the treatment, servants at both mansions insisted on carrying the baggage, and in each place, Micah was given a clean, warm place to sleep. The meals were great, and there was plenty of company with the women servants flirting with the new man in the house.

The evening came, and Melissa and Jeanne Marie were expected for dinner with the Davis'. It was a good thing Melissa had brought a trunk full of dresses and the necessary undergarments. She dressed that afternoon to meet a president.

As she entered the room, Jeanne Marie got her first glance at the president standing next to Varina, his wife. He was tall, thin, erect, with a slight beard, well-trimmed hair and a sharp nose. His hair was dark but with clear shades of gray inserting themselves here and there; they gave him a distinguished look.

"Good evening Melissa," the President said, as he kissed her on the cheek. "And you must be Jeanne Marie," a glint in the President's eye. "Ladies may I present Postmaster General John Reagan." Reagan bowed slightly, and then took the hand of each lady in turn, saying "good evening."

John Reagan was in his mid-forties, a good-looking man with a mustache, beard and full head of brown hair. He was from Palestine in East Texas, and spoke with a heavy accent. He had fought the Cherokee in Texas, and participated in the secession convention. He had served as both a representative and senator from the Lone Star state. He was smart, and ran a tight shop in the Post Office where they were actually making money. Among his reforms, he had cut losing routes to help make that happen.

Reagan pulled out the chair for Varina a well-dressed, tall servant did the same for Melissa and the President did the honors for Jeanne Marie. The table was beautiful decorated with a fine table clothe, polished silver ware, and sparkling glassware. The chandelier above was lovely, Jeanne Marie had never seen so many candles.

"Before we commence, I should like to offer thanksgiving, let us bow," Jefferson said. "Almighty God, we humbly thank you for what we are about to receive. We ask your protection for the noble men in the field, and a quick end to the unpleasantness that has befallen our people. Thank you for our Savior, and may we be safe within the palm of your majestic hand, Amen." The others echoed, amen.

"So what do you think of our fair city, Maid Jeanne Marie?" The President asked with a smile on his face. The serving staff began working around the table filling water glasses, bringing in salads. A tall man brought an unopened bottle of wine to John Reagan.

"Very busy," she said returning the smile.

Reagan looked at the man, take it to the President please, Reagan turned towards the President, "A special bottle of French wine, given to me by Rafael the last time I saw him, sir."

Davis took the bottle from the servant's hand to inspect the label, "When did you last see Captain Semmes, John?"

"Oh, let's see, I think it was in Mobile, after we re-took Galveston, in January, sir. He was in fine spirits, and told me how had baited the Yankee ship *Hatteras* out into the Gulf for its final moments."

"Yes, the commerce raiders have surprised many with their effectiveness, but sinking a ship of war I believe, startled the Yankees!" The President joked. There was a round of laughter at that. "And Galveston, that was a neat a trick, John."

"Mr. President, John Magruder is a more ingenious and skillful commander than General Lee knew, I think," said the Post Master with a tinge of criticism.

"John, John was not sent west because of his failings on the field," the President said without looking up from his salad, "But because General Lee is quite committed to a moral code that does not tolerate dalliance."

"Hmmm." Reagan said quietly.

Varina was quick to jump in, "How was Mobile, John?"

"Fun," he said. "The people are in good spirits, work has progressed on the fortifications at the lower end of the bay, and torpedoes have been strung across its mouth. But they are easily moved when Runners, come and go."

"Runners?" Jeanne Marie asked. She knew precisely what they were, but this provided an opportunity to enter the conversation as a no nothing woman who was no threat to anyone at the table.

"Yes, Mrs. Walters, Runners, they are the ships which bring in the goods, whether they be the dress you are wearing, or the morphine given to our wounded in the hospitals," Reagan pronounced.

There was something of an arrogance about this man Jeanne Marie thought.

"Tell us about yourself, Jeanne Marie," the President asked.

Oh, I knew we would get to this … now what do I say, Jeanne Marie thought to herself: "Well there isn't much to tell sir, I am a soldier's wife."

"And where might you be from?" Reagan asked.

If you only knew, she thought, "Most recently I am come from Mt. Airy, North Carolina, sir," she said.

"Her husband just saved Governor Vance and Mr. Taylor from a perilous situation," Mrs. Davis offered, "a story worth hearing I think, my dear." The servants were removing the salad plates and silverware. The President's eyebrow had risen when he heard the word perilous.

"Pray do tell, Mrs. Walter." Davis looked into her eyes as he said that.

Slyly Jeanne Marie opened with "We were on the farm, when a rider, a woman rider we had never seen before, came bursting down to the home and told us of the Governor, and Mr. Taylor and his family were under attack by outlaws and deserters at an old broken down home not far from us." By saying it that way, a listener could easily presume the farm was theirs.

"And," John Reagan pressed.

"My husband, mounted the horse, his guns were handed him and he bolted off, commanding others to follow as they could. He singly handedly rode through a dozen of the devils, killing one … (her voice rising) shot him right through the head!" Jeanne Marie, covered her face with her napkin, acting embarrassed at her enthusiasm.

Davis reached a hand out towards her, "It's alright Jeanne Marie, go on."

"They held off the bad men 'til our people, and troopers from Thomas' Legion reached them and drove them off." Jeanne Marie said.

"She tells that story so quickly, and cleanly," said Melissa. "But Micah, who was there, said the Colonel was something to behold on that horse, with guns in both hands, firing."

"And who is Micah, Melissa?" the President asked.

"Micah is one of their slaves sir, he is traveling with Jeanne Marie." Melissa replied.

"I may want to hear more from Micah," the President said as the main course was placed on the table."

The rest of evening passed easily enough. Jeanne Marie had handled the toughest aspect, establishing a residence in their minds, without directly lying. She would have to lie the next night.

* * * *

The next evening was young, the sun still up, when the guests began arriving at the White House. Cabinet Secretaries, naval and army officers, the most important bankers and businessmen of Richmond all gathering at the request of the President. Young cadets from the Confederate Naval Academy were in attendance as escorts to this year's group of Richmond's débutantes.

A band played music as the guests were announced.

The atmosphere festive, the mood good. Things were going well for the Confederacy, and there were high expectations for the coming summer. Women could still find beautiful dresses and accessories. The blockade runners were still coming into Wilmington, and Charleston, and along ports on the Gulf coast. General Lee's Army was resting near Fredericksburg.

Jeanne Marie and Melissa had been on a shopping trip all day with Varina Davis in Richmond. Jeanne Marie wanted a gown for the evening. It was a girl's day out, something Mrs. Davis truly enjoyed. She had not had such fun since before the war. Melissa had a great personality, she never met a stranger, and was always laughing and making her companions laugh.

Richmond was a buzz with activity, and people were generally optimistic. They had known great fear a year ago when McClellan's army had been at the gates of the city. But Robert E. Lee had changed all that. He and his right arm, Stonewall Jackson, had given the Yankees all they could handle at Bull Run, Sharpsburg and Fredericksburg last December. There was hope.

Jeanne Marie noticed the streets, they were filled with people, including women and children rushing here and there. The weather remained a problem, wet and chilly. Varina said that was normal for this time of year.

When the ladies went into a restaurant for lunch, it was clear the presence of the First Lady was noticed by all.

In the afternoon they settled down to some serious shopping. Jeanne Marie wanted a gown that revealed her bosom, and was tight around the waist. She had the figure for both. But, it just took so long trying a dress on, not an easy task.

Finally, she found what she wanted. A beautiful yellow gown with a white frilly collar made of a very light material. As she got the Confederate money out of her purse, she thought to herself, this was my only dream for this mission. I had wanted this since childhood. She smiled as she passed the money over to the clerk. Varina was direct with the saleslady, "You will have this brought to the White House immediately, correct?" The woman nodded. "This woman will be sitting next to the president tonight … all must be ship shape!"

It wasn't until the ladies were headed back to the White House that Jeanne Marie realized, there were no security people around Varina. When she thought a moment, there weren't any at the White House either. Presidents and First Ladies just walked among the people like they were Tom, Dick and Jane — nothing special. And no one bothered them. Oh, yes, people looked and pointed, and talked amongst themselves, but no one came up asking for autographs or complaining about life or government.

The late afternoon passed, the ladies resting for the gala in the evening. Jeanne Marie was able to spend some time with Jimmie Earle and his new friend Jim. Jim had his own room on the second floor, and the two spent a lot of time in their playing.

Micah had joined the White House staff on their food shopping for tonight.

When the first guests began arriving, Jeanne Marie was still getting her dress pulled tight by the servant assigned to help her dress. Melissa came into the room, saw the situation, and jumped in to help finish off the dressing of Jeanne Marie!

"Let's go," Melissa said with a regal air, "the President awaits." The pomp made both women burst into laughter.

Coming down the steps into a crowd, two beautiful young Southern belles always took the room, men looked … married men, engaged men, all men. It was only moments, but moments neither Jeanne Marie or Melissa would ever forget — for those seconds the universe revolved around them.

The dusk time of day was always special to Jeanne Marie. Inside the White House, there was excitement, glitter, the music, and the constant contact of people bouncing off one another, making their way through a crowded room. The smells were interesting, sometimes downright repugnant; some folks obviously had not bathed in some time. And deodorant wasn't a thing in this time.

After some time, the President and Mrs. Davis were introduced. A small applause, but not long, and then everyone back to their conversations and hors d'ourves.

Jeanne Marie and Melissa were talking with some folks when a servant came up and whispered in her ear, "The President would like you two to join him." She looked at the servant, he nodded, she touched

Melissa, "We are beckoned." The two followed the servant to the President and Varina sitting on a coach, facing the room. There were open spaces on both sides. The President patted the couch looking at Jeanne Marie. She sat down, Melissa sat next to Varina.

For hours, it seemed, people came up to speak briefly with the president. The noise of the crowd made it difficult, at times, to hear the person standing directly in front of the president. Finally, when a break came, Jeanne Marie sensed it was her moment.

"Mr. President, might I speak to you privately, to share something told to me when I was overseas, earlier this year." Jeanne Marie said to President Davis.

"Mrs. Walter, my plate is very full tonight, maybe another time." President Davis said, he started to rise to leave.

"Mr. President, your ear please," she said in a whisper. He stopped and leaned towards her. "I have a message from Otto von Bismarck."

He backed away, and looked at her sharply. She nodded.

"I can give you a few minutes," he said, "Come with me please. He turned to Varina, "We will just be a short time, darling." The two walked quickly to his office.

This was the ultra-secret mission only Nash and Jeanne Marie, and two other men knew. Michael didn't even know. It had been developed by a couple of men working inside the Alabama Project, intelligence and strategist professionals who had earned their covert operations pedigrees in the Central Intelligence Agency. Together they conceived Jeanne Marie's role in this trip. This plan was devised as an alternative to saving Jackson's life. It wasn't possible to know if that could actually be done when the Alabama Project was developed. A second idea had been kicked around, and this was its result.

The plan took advantage of the slow cross ocean communications of the time, and the lack of a practiced, formal state department within the Confederacy. The plan relied on Jeanne Marie's knowledge of the history of the period, and her ability to tell a convincing tale to a head of state.

Jeanne Marie felt like she was about to go on stage, with all the lights and audience looking, focused totally on her. Jefferson Davis opened the door to his office and allowed Jeanne Marie to walk in first. He closed the door and offered a seat on a settee. "Now tell me, Mrs. Walter, what is that Otto has to say?"

Jeanne Marie was taken aback by the informality of Jefferson Davis towards von Bismarck. He seemed to know him, but her investigation of history never indicated Davis had met Bismarck.

"Mr. President, the Chancellor expressed his disappointment in your decision to launch a unilateral invasion of the American southwest. He believes if you had waited just a year, you could have approached the Emperor Maximillian of Mexico and proposed a joint invasion, promising Mexico it could have California, if the two allies were successful in the effort. He believes that could have changed the conditions of the war."

Jefferson Davis was outwardly disturbed by Jeanne Marie's comment. Matters of high state national security were not normally known by the common people, and how would a woman of unknown pedigree know so much, no less be on speaking terms with Otto von Bismarck, Chancellor of the German Confederation?

After he composed himself, the President said, "Mrs. Walter, why should I believe you are properly relaying information from the Chancellor?"

"Sir, my mother's family are the Trenholm's of Charleston. As you know, they have extensive holdings and dealings with much of Europe. I first met Otto as a child, twenty years ago, he is almost an uncle to me." Jeanne Marie said with no change of tone in her voice.

The President, who had been pacing, sat down. If Jeanne Marie was who she said she was, her information was pertinent and important. "Does the Chancellor think Mexico might still be open to such an endeavor?"

"Mr. President, I have no knowledge of that. But, he told me to tell you that in his opinion, the key to winning the South's war, is similar to that of the key to Washington's victory." Jeanne Marie said.

"And that key would be?" Davis asked.

"Keeping your armies in the field, at the best possible strength, for as long as possible, at least until November, 1864. He thinks Lincoln can be defeated in the next election, if the Yankee people believe the war is endless, with no sight of victory." Jeanne Marie said, emphasizing by lifting and dropping her hands to her legs with the last word.

Davis sat back. He thought, she cannot know this, but we are struggling to come up with a plan for this summer's campaign. General Lee has offered an extremely aggressive proposal, one that certainly does not place preservation of the force as the essential element.

"Thank you, Mrs. Walter, is there anything else?"

She could see her words had weight with the president. It was best not to over play the hand. "No sir, that is what I was told to say to you."

Davis rose, offering his hand to Jeanne Marie. "Well this was a very worthwhile moment for me, Mrs. Walter. I thank you for being so forthright, let's get back to the party."

This part of the Alabama Project could be said to be completed. The idea being, to offer to President Davis the best strategy to win the war, if Jackson did or did not survive Chancellorsville; preserve the force and look strong through November, 1864.

As they walked back towards the party, Jeanne Marie felt both fulfilled, and anxious to leave Richmond to return to Mt. Airy. She had accomplished both her assigned missions concerning the outcome of the war. Her next vital mission was getting Parks back to North Carolina in time to meet the window to return to Rebel Mountain.

John Yerby's Home, Virginia
April 23, 1863
The Baptism

Thomas Jackson sat on a chair, underneath a large oak, with tiny Julia sitting on his leg, smiling. Though some distance off, his staff could hear Julia's giggles.

It was a scene no one on his staff, not young Sandie Pendleton, not Henry Kyd Douglas, not Robert Dabney ever thought they would see. The great Stonewall Jackson, the man who shattered armies with a mere look, was sitting there smitten by less than 20 pounds of female.

No one wanted to disturb the general. It was too much pleasure for those who knew him best. Stonewall was not a mean man, not someone who was normally in a bad mood. But he only glowed in battle. He was not someone who was easily moved to delight. In fact, the last time anyone saw delight in his eyes was in the Shenandoah, at Winchester, the last time Anna visited a year and half ago. Turner Ashby was still alive then.

And they knew it was a special day. The Reverend Beverly Tucker Lacy was going to baptize little Julia today. For her father, life doesn't get much better than this.

Thomas Jackson was a man of faith. His entire life, including what he did on the battlefield, rested on his faith in God and his understanding of the Bible. He was known to pray in the midst of battle, and yet, not for his life. In fact, Stonewall had said he felt as safe on the battlefield as he did in his bed! Stonewall was praying God's Will be done.

But now at this moment, Stonewall was Thomas, a married man with a daughter he cherished. He had lost a wife, and two other infants at birth, or nearly. And none of those losses, and earlier ones, his parents and a sibling, had not turned him sour to God. He had a difficult life since early childhood, but that only created a need God would fill with God.

Anna and Julia had arrived on the mail train on the 20th. For the past couple of days, it had been a whirlwind of catch up, and staff members re-acquainting themselves with the Mrs. and with the newest Jackson.

Whenever possible, the staff set up a quarantine around the Jacksons. It wasn't driven by jealousy, or some need to feel special, but rather to give their beloved commander time. Jackson had been rigid in terms of self-control when it came to leaving his men. He would not do it. Though he had the same needs and feelings as every man, he saw duty as the commander his most sacred obligation. He had ordered countless thousands to the hell fire of battle, and the savagery and butchery had been burned into, embedded in his soul.

In this time, here near Fredericksburg, Jackson and his commander, Robert E. Lee had seen fit to give men furloughs, to visit home and family. After the awful victory in December, when they butchered a Yankee Army that marched into sheets and sheets of fire, for two days, the Yankees were simply too damaged to do anything but pull back across the narrow Rappahannock River and rest. They had done the fool's mission, and bashed themselves against an impregnable position, where all the soldiers of the Confederate battalions had to do was keep passing loaded muskets to the front ranks.

The carnage was so terrific, the slaughter of the Yankee battalions so horrific, that General Lee himself said: "It is well that war is so terrible, lest we should grow too fond of it."

And so, the Army of Northern Virginia had earned a repose. For a few cold months they could relax, though two divisions, and Lt. General James Longstreet were sent southeast into North Carolina to contest a Yankee foraging raid. Those divisions were out of reach, and would not be back for the Yankees next move.

It was in this brief moment, that Jackson allowed himself just a few days to enjoy the love of his wife, and the splendor of a daughter much loved and hoped for.

Anna had told Thomas about her train trip, and meeting Jeanne Marie, and the wagon train coming from North Carolina with things for men of that state assigned to Stonewall Jackson. But it was just a fragment of information, not pressing or important.

Anna appeared at the doorway, and Sandie strode towards her, "Good morning Mrs. Jackson," he offered with a smile, taking off his hat. "Could we fetch you a cup of coffee?"

The sun was bright, the air crisp but warming. "No, … well maybe, … ah sure Sandy," she laughed as she finished her contortions. Her eyes never left the two under the tree. "Having fun is he?"

"A show we would pay to see," Sandie handed her a cup of steaming hot coffee.

Reverend Lacy rode up at that moment from the back side of the house, he saw Sandie first, "Hello Pendleton, how are you?" As he turned the corner of the house, he got his first glimpse of Anna. He gasped, and unexpectedly reined his mount which made the horse rear and kick up. When the horse settled, he said, "Anna you are quite a sight for this old man."

She blushed. "Reverend, … I never, … bless your heart."

As he dismounted, facing the house, "And where is my compadre?" Lacy had a familiarity with Jackson few men had.

Anna pointed with her cup, and Lacy spun around. Another gasp, "Well I'll be." He stepped off, almost at a run, towards Thomas and Julia.

When he was about halfway to Thomas he shouted out, "Well, hello papa."

Jackson looked up at him with a huge smile, and then back to his daughter who he was bouncing on his knee. She was blowing tiny bubbles out her mouth. He slowly rose, bringing Julia to his chest oh so gently. As Lacy closed on them, he gave Jackson a bear hug, his beard falling on Julia's face. Julia laughed at the tickling feeling, and reached for it with her hand.

"I am so glad to see you Thomas," Lacy said.

"And I you, Reverend. Can you believe this bundle from God?" Lacy had never in all his years with Jackson, heard glee in his voice.

At that moment Jackson saw Anna in the doorway, he waved, and then held Julia in both hands, raised her up, and in front of him, towards Anna. Who would believe this man was a three-star general?!

The two men started walking back to the house to prepare for the baptism of Julia.

"How goes it with our plans to bring the Church to those regiments without Chaplains," Jackson inquired of Lacy. Lacy and Jackson had decided to make that effort and began it on March 1st of this year. The Confederate Congress had gone so far as to appoint Lacy Chaplain, without a sponsoring regiment in deference to General Jackson. Of course, General Lee endorsed the idea completely.

The baptism would occur in the parlor with the Yerbys and members of the staff. Several members of the staff had gotten together to have a silver mug engraved with a special message on it:

Julia Jackson
from the
General Staff Officers of
Her Father
Maj. Harmon Maj. Hawks
Col. Allen Col. Pendleton
Dr. McGuire

Jackson was humbled by the gesture, great emotions welled within him. Of course, Anna was touched, for Julia, but mostly for her husband Thomas who was clearly loved by his subordinates. It was apparent everywhere they went.

The event exemplified the family nature of military service. There can always be strong emotional bonds between the men who work together in war, but in the case of Jackson's headquarters it was exceptionally strong for two reasons. First, because of the devout Christian faith of each man, and secondly because of the quality of men Jackson had on his staff. Each of the men was devoted to Jackson and to the Cause. There were no exceptional egos amongst the staff.

The incident in the Yerby Parlor was a significant occasion in a brief period of days seemingly crafted by God. This short period seemed to be a bubble of peace, tranquility, safety, joy and love. It was a rare moment for the general and his headquarters.

Three Pines
Rebel Mountain, Texas
Afternoon, July 19th, 2012
The Wait

Mark Patton was sitting at the table in the barn used for conference. On other tables against the wall were computers, maps on the walls. This was the operational headquarters for the Alabama Project. There was a telephone with speaker on the conference table, and a telephone near one of the computer stations.

Mark was younger than the other men, maybe late forties. He had been an Army officer, and in Project Alabama he was the Operations Officer, the man responsible for the details of the operation. He had been an infantry officer, and knew by rote the mechanics of a raid, which is essentially what the Alabama Project was.

Mark stood as the men came in, a look of worry was on Mark's face.

The men all walked up to Mark, in line, shaking his hand, and offering a greeting. Each smiled at first, but then got more somber as they looked into his eyes. "What's the dour look," Reece asked.

"Oh, you know Mark, he's always seeing goblins," Nash said.

"Worry is a constant companion of an operations officer," Frank said.

"The extraction elements of this operation have always been uniquely problematic for me." Mark said. "Leaving the extraction of Parks from the vicinity of the Army back to Mt. Airy to the team on the ground was a real gamble."

The men had made their way around the table and sat down in a seat that had become theirs over the years of planning this operation.

Nash, who normally was an easy going, happy man, had a look of distress on his face. "Mark, we have been through this a dozen times. If the mission is to save Jackson's life, and the time and location of the window for return to this time is fixed, we all agreed we had to give the operators the most flexibility possible. If we had set a strict end time for the operator with Jackson, we would have tied his or her hands to the point that the chance for success was almost zero."

"Nash is right," Charles said. "And there isn't squat we can do about it now."

"Let's move on to what we can do." King offered quietly.

There were folders at each man's place. With King's word, they all reached for the folder and opened it, in sync, an event that happened at every meeting.

"Before we start, let us go to the Lord." King offered, "Almighty Father, we gather here to do your work. We each know we could not be here, at this point, without your Will and Blessing. Almighty God please be with Michael, Jeanne Marie and Parks; watch over them, and protect them, and bring them home safely to us. Amen."

"Amen," they all echoed.

"OK," said Nash, taking charge of the meeting, "Frank is the Medical team taken care of.?"

Frank answered, "Yes, they will gather at La Quinta today in El Paso. The team lead will call me tonight to give an up on everyone arriving. They will fly in tomorrow, land here at Three Pines. Does the medical staff at the hospital know about this group?"

Nash responded, "The right people know."

Reece asked: "Who are the right people, Nash?"

"Staying faithful to our "need to know" security protocol, the head of the hospital knows we may have patients for them tomorrow night and that they have to be treated in an expeditious way. And also, that we will be bringing in special staff, and will need access to their labs on a priority basis." Nash said. "In addition, I have had the doctor who will be on duty in the ER tomorrow night out here to Three Pines, and have explained to him that we could have patients with radiation concerns, and issues concerning age that we simply can't know in advance."

"Age?" King asked.

"King, we have no idea how human cells and the nervous system will react as a result of moving in and through the Space–Time environment, and also Michael's extended time, three years, in the past." Nash said.

"Who else is on the team?" Charles asked.

"We have a dietitian on the team," Nash replied. "Again, it comes down to what we do not know. How will the food in the stomachs of our people, react to coming to this time?"

King, "I cannot believe how complex the return is? I mean what you are saying Nash, is all this relevant, it's just so … mind boggling."

"King, now you know why I pestered and bothered you for decades for more and more money. The goal has always been to try to think of every contingency, and game out what could happen. We have worked with a lot of groups, from Texas A&M and Baylor, to M. I. T. and select folks inside NASA."

Reece, leaned forward to the table with Nash's last words. Is there a record of all this Nash?

Mark replied quickly, "Reece, there has been a real effort to keep records, and organize it for an After-Action Report. Nash was always worried that King and the other fund raisers and financiers would want a strict accounting of the money."

At that point the phone on the Conference table rang. Nash hit a button on the phone which answered the phone with the speaker. "Hello"

"Nash, this is Kelly at the Library."

"Yes Kelly."

"Sir, there has been a change to the Mt. Airy newspaper, I thought you would want to know."

"Really, what changed Kelly."

"I think you will want to see it, there is a picture, actually a drawing on the front page."

"A drawing?" Reece said.

"Yes Reece," Kelly said, "And I think it's Jeanne Marie and Parks. And there is a headline, Governor ambushed by outlaws."

"OK, Kelly, make sure the paper remains in its protective case, we will be there shortly." Nash said.

"I can't believe your idea worked Mark," Charles said.

Mark smiled, he had been the guy who found an original copy of the *Mt. Airy Gazette* at a flea market in North Carolina. And the date was April 19th, 1863.

"Finding the paper was luck on my part," Mark said, "It was Nash who saw it as a possible communications link between whoever we sent back in time, and us here."

"OK, I guess we should adjourn and head over to the Library," Nash said.

"I will remain here," said Mark. "I think we are going to have to keep the headquarters manned now, until they are back."

"Good point," said Frank. "If we are going to keep it open all night, I guess I will head to the bunk house and get some sleep to take the night shift."

"OK, that leaves four of us to head over the library. Mark you need to set up a roster to keep this place manned."

With that the group broke up, each going to their assigned place. For Reece, King and Charles it would be an opportunity to visit the library.

On the way to Jackson's Camp
April 25th, 1863

Parts of my body felt like they had been beaten up over the past ten days, and I couldn't help but wonder if Jeanne Marie had a similar rough experience in her travels with Mrs. Jackson. Flying a helicopter takes something out of a pilot, the beating of the rotor, but riding a horse over long distances for weeks is even more strenuous. You don't just sit on a horse, you ride it, and that requires the constant use of muscles. Muscles I never knew I had, and not just in your rump, but in your lower back and thighs.

Spring was in full bloom, now. The year's new growth, the electric lime green color was everywhere. The smells of God's green earth, the flowers and the manure along the dirt road were almost strong enough to intoxicate you. As I rode up Telegraph Road closer towards the Army of Northern Virginia encamped near Fredericksburg, the traffic along the road had picked up quite a bit.

The plan to get into the presence of General Jackson was simple. The travel time from Michael's farm to here, about ten days, had given me the days necessary to acclimatize to the soldier's life of 1863. I had learned how to care for my horse, Phoenix, and had gotten used to rolling my bed roll. It took a little more pain to get used to the sparse and coarse food. Last fall's corn was good for Phoenix, but for me, I was hungry most of the time. The spring berries had not come in yet. I had shot a few rabbits, learned to skin 'em and gut 'em, and roast 'em. But, I just wasn't used to the taste of greasy meat sustained by the wild.

I had done some shooting with both my carbine and my navy colt to ensure that I was at least respectable, could handle the weapons with ease, and clean them. My years in the army really had not been worth too much in this regard. These weapons were generations earlier than the ones I was familiar with. Shooting black powder, cap and ball is completely different, much dirtier, than the weapons I had used at ranges at Fort Bragg and Fort Hood. I couldn't help but think that when I was at those forts named after Confederate generals, I never imagined that I might one day meet one or more of them. General Hood was with Lee's Army. Then I remembered, Hood was off with Longstreet in North Carolina.

Along the way, folks along the road might invite us in for a meal, always quickly accepted no matter what time of day it was. The food made by the women in southern Virginia was truly fine compared to my own efforts. Though I must admit, the taste of warm, fresh, raw milk took some getting used too. More than once I had found myself in the woods with my jacket off, and my trousers down enjoying the diarrhea which comes when you change your food intake.

"Morning Colonel" I heard as some dismounted soldiers passing in the opposite direction, say.

I reigned in Phoenix, "Could you men tell me the whereabouts of General Jackson's camp?" I was a little nervous as I spoke, though Southern by birth and upraising my 21st century, drawl was not that of 1863.

"Sir, it ain't fer." A sergeant broke from the group. He pointed up the road, "just continue a couple leagues and after a while u'll come upon the road to Fredericksburg. I am sure you can get directed from there, sir" The soldier was a sight. His clothes were tattered, though still serviceable. He hadn't shaved in a while, and his hair stuck out in all direction underneath his kepi. His eyes were clear and he had a smile on his face which revealed some teeth missing.

"What's the condition of the army, sergeant?" I surprised myself with the question.

"Sir, we getting' stronger every day. Ceptin' Longstreet and his fellas are off down in Caroline hunting fer some grub. But them Yanks are in for it if they come a messin' with us. Marse Robert is no man to fool with. As long as we have him and Stonewall we can whip 'em sir."

"Thank you, sergeant, carry on." I said, and I saluted him. He was exactly what I had read about. But, my salute to him took him off guard, and he thought it was a rebuke. He quickly jumped to attention and saluted. "Sergeant I appreciate your report, God's speed." With that, I spurred Phoenix gently and headed down the road. I should reach Jackson today.

The slower times provided a lot more time for reflection. Things had moved so fast back in Mayberry, Texas that there hadn't been really any time to consider what we were doing. Nash, Jeanne Marie, Michael and who knows how many people had been involved in making this trip possible for a lifetime. It had taken decades to make this a reality. How many of those folks wished they were in my shoes right now?

I still could not believe what we were attempting to do. We were trying to change history. If this mission was successful, we could not know what we would be returning too. If the South did win the war would there be a Mayberry, Texas? A Nash Laurent? Hell, would I even exist? There just was no way to know.

But for the question, it was much bigger then whether I would be alive, or Jeanne Marie would exist. For me, as a man, I had always believed God had a plan, that history unfolded as God intended. For a soldier that belief can be the difference between uncontrollable fright, and the ability to do a job while the entire world explodes around you. If you truly believe in God, you know all is in His Hands. For most people this sounds trite. But for someone on the cutting edge of history, whose very life could be gone in a moment, God is more than a decoration of life. He is life's cornerstone, and a constant companion.

During this war that I was now a part of, the reality of Christian faith spread through the Southern armies like wildfire. Religious revivals were very much a part of non-combat time for the Confederates. Groups across the South worked to have Bibles, and other religious books brought through the blockade to be distributed to men in the field. Some of those books came from New England! Hard to believe, but true.

And the commanders of the Army of Northern Virginia were devout men. Even the young and dashing J. E. B. Stuart was a devout Christian.

Nash read my book *Ten Moments of God in the Civil War*, to help decide when to make the trip back to change history. In my book I offered two independent observations of God's Hand in the war. First, I offered the concept that it was God's Will that the South should lose the war. The fact there were so many instances where only the smallest change could have made significant difference in the course of the war, indicated to me a Divine Providence.

Secondly, the deep Christian faith of the Southern men gave them the strength to fight this horrible war; to stand in ranks and be blasted apart by the superior firepower of the Yankees, to starve, to make the marches they made with no shoes. To face the fever, the bugs and lice, and the harsh weather without the necessities and comforts provided to the invading Yankees. And, to fight the odds and win, to do what seemed impossible, only a faith in God could make those things real.

So, for me to participate in a mission to change history meant intentionally and purposefully trifling with God's will. The talk with Joshua had reminded me of Providence and God's Will. And the more I thought of that, as the time passed in this new reality, the more concerned I became with the future of my own soul. God had to know what we were doing. Was He going allow to it? Up to this point in my life, I had never been afraid. Never. Not even when we dove that "souped-up" Hind helicopter into the side of Rebel Mountain looking for the space-time window I wasn't sure existed. But now, I was scared. I was messing with things way above my pay grade.

I did what I always did in tough situations, I prayed. "God, I am yours, I am so sorry for what I am doing. Please guide me, tell me what to do. Put me on the wrong road, or give me the fever to stop me from wandering off your path. Please God, I want to do your will."

"God, you know Nash and Jeanne Marie, and Michael are good people, Lord. They believe in you God. There must be something you want, or they would not have gotten this far. Please Lord help me find Your Will."

Just as I came out of my prayer, I heard some riders behind approaching at a slightly faster pace than that of Phoenix. Just as I turned to look back, they closed up beside me.

"Morning Colonel, I don't think I have met you before. I am Colonel Dabney."

"Sir, you are correct, we have never met. But I have certainly heard of you, I am Lieutenant Colonel Walter." I reached across my body with my right hand to shake his hand.

"And this is Captain Douglas." The Captain saluted.

"Pleased to meet you captain." I said. "This is fortunate for me sir, if you are headed to General Jackson's camp, I would like to ride along with you both."

"You are to see the General?" Colonel Dabney asked.

"Yes, sir, I carry a letter of introduction from Governor Vance. I am leading a wagon supply train from North Carolina to our men in the General's command. I rode ahead to find out where I should direct the train? And the Governor expressed a hope that I may serve as a liaison between the governor and General Jackson."

"Ah, a new staff member," Dabney said with a chuckle to Captain Douglas. "Well, I told you it would be a good day, that something good was to happen, didn't I Henry?"

"Yes, sir you did." Said the young captain. I knew of Henry Kyd Douglas by the book he would write titled *I Rode with Stonewall*, but of course I had to act like I had never heard of him.

"Captain, you are on the General's staff too?"

"In a minor way ..."

"Nonsense," interrupted Dabney, "he practically runs the staff!"

"Sir ..." an embarrassed Douglas bowed his head.

"I am only kiddin' Henry, but you are quite a valuable officer, and a very important member of the general's entourage." Dabney turned towards me, but spoke a little louder as the noise of the horses' trot, the sound of swords and harnesses jingling and clanking, and the mutual whinnies of the three horses getting to know one another, competed with the colonel's words.

"Thank you, sir," Douglas lifted his head with a smile.

"I must admit I find it hard to believe I will join the living legends whose exploits are retold across the many towns and villages in the old North State. It will be a true privilege if General Jackson will allow it." I said.

"If you want to know how to get a job on our general's staff, ask Jim Lewis, his cook," offered Captain Douglas offered.

"So how is Zebulon, ah Governor Vance, Colonel Walter?"

"Well, it's been several weeks since I have seen I him," I replied, "but his humor is the same. We were honored to have him at my brother-in-law's wedding!"

Just at that moment, a large force of horsemen came up on the road in front of us. They approached at trot and for the first time I saw the crimson banner, the Confederate Battle Flag rippling in the wind. The lead horseman was large, a cape flying behind him, a long brown beard. It took no time to recognize that this was J. E. B. Stuart, commander of Lee's cavalry. They approached quickly, and almost in unison we all raised our hands in salute as the general passed.

I had never heard that sound before. The rhythmic pounding of the hooves of even twenty horses at a trot moving in one direction is thunderous. The clanking and tinkling of their weapons, and the other noises that always accompany a body of mounted men on horse moving. What must it sound like when a thousand horse, or more, move in unison on the enemy? They were by us in just moments. And then there was silence.

Bouncing along on Phoenix, I asked; "I have a gift for General Stuart, from his mother. Does he visit General Jackson often?"

"Yes, they are good friends," Captain Douglas said.

"Captain Douglas, I want you to take care of Colonel Walter when we get to Belvoir." Dabney's tone had changed from one of banter to a more official one.

"Yes sir."

"I want to get him to Sandy, and then help him find the horse line and a place to sleep, and let him know where we meet for meals, and the daily routine." Dabney sounded like he had done this before.

"Yes sir, I will take care of Colonel Walter, sir."

"And if you see Lt. Morrison, please tell him I would like to talk to him, and Jed Hotchkiss too."

The ride was long, we had to turn right onto another road.

We passed a company sized group of cavalry bivouacked along the road, and Colonel Dabney said: "This company is Captain Randolf's, and came to Jackson's headquarters in the past couple of weeks. They were formed by General Early for his headquarters and General Jackson stole them," a smile came across his face. "They act as our scouts, and as guides, guards, orderlies and messengers for our headquarters."

Finally, we came upon a two-story house, with a small porch and maybe eight or ten steps up to the front door. They either had a raised basement, or vented the ground beneath the first story. One larger tent, and some other smaller tents were set up in the front yard. A wagon, rested nearby, with a black man sitting, smoking a pipe. His area appeared to be the cooking area.

Dismounting, we walked our horses over to a rope line where other saddled horses were quietly munching on grass, or bags of meal under the shade of the trees. Douglas had taken Dabney's horse when he dismounted. The Colonel headed towards a large white officer's tent that seemed to have a lot of officers in its' vicinity.

"Sir, you should leave your gear here, we can come back to get your bed roll and other things later."

"OK captain."

"But make sure you have your orders, or whatever documents you need to present to the Major Pendleton, the Adjutant. He will need them to bring you into the General."

"Is the general here?" I asked weakly.

"Sure looks like it, I see a couple of the horses for the division commanders over there by Little Sorrel, the red, on the senior officer's line near that tent." Even back then, they had designated parking I thought to myself!

Little Sorrel. I had actually seen this horse in the museum at Virginia Military Institute, it had been stuffed and mounted by a taxidermist. I remember thinking how life-like it was. And now I might see many of legends of history I had read about since I was a boy of eight or nine. For the first time since Little League, I had butterflies in my stomach.

"Follow me sir." Douglas was really trying to be a good escort. We walked across the front of the home and towards a smaller tent in front of the General's tent. "Why don't you have a seat here Colonel while I find Major Pendleton."

I took a seat on a small wooden chair. It has a deep seat, and I almost fell into it when I sat, but once in the chair I realized its configuration was very comfortable on my back; especially after this morning's five-hour ride. As I got comfortable, I could hear voices in discussion. One officer said they thought this campaign season would be very important. With that another voice replied:

"Gentlemen, we must make it an exceedingly active one. Only thus can a weaker country cope with a stronger; it must make up in activity what it lacks in strength. A defensive campaign can only be made successful by taking the aggressive at the appropriate time. Napoleon never waited for his adversary to become fully prepared; but struck him the first blow, by virtue of his superior activity." [3]

I had obviously never heard the voice before, but the words were unmistakably those of Thomas Jackson. A chill went up my back.

"Colonel Walter, I am Major Pendleton."

Lost in the moment I never saw him walk up in front of me, come to attention and salute. I had to make a real effort to rise from the chair, and almost fell into him. Returning the salute, I took his hand; "Colonel Walter at your service, sir."

"Sir, please come into the tent and we can visit awhile, and I can review your orders, while we wait for the meeting to break up."

"Major Pendleton, I was charged with bringing a wagon train of one hundred from North Carolina to Jackson's command for distribution to the Tar Heel troops, the train is presently headed this way, and I need to find out where it should go?"

At that the Major yelled, "I need a runner here ... right now." A moment later a soldier arrived at his tent. Private, I need you to find Major Harmon and ask him to come here as soon as possible."

"Yes, sir." The private turned and moved away briskly.

"Major Harmon is our Quartermaster; your next moves will be

3 A direct Jackson quote from Dabney's book, *Life and Campaigns*.

directed by his guidance." Pendleton told me, "May I see the letter from Governor Vance?"

"Certainly." I reached into my pocket, pulled out the envelop, and handed it to Major Pendleton. He took it, opened it, and quickly scanned the letter. A smile came across his face as he read it; "I am sure this will be well received by the General, and more by the troops."

A few moments later I heard someone approaching the tent, it was Major Harmon. Pendleton looked up from his desk: "John, this is Lt. Colonel Walter, he is bringing in a train for the North Carolina regiments." I stood, we shook hands, and he said, "Hope I can keep some of those wagons." He had caught me off guard, I had no idea how to respond to that; "I will see what I can do, Major."

About that time, Lt. Morrison and Jed Hotchkiss arrived. "Jed, this is Lt. Colonel Walters." We shook hands. Pendleton went on, "Jed, General Colston's Division will do a review for Anna and Julia tomorrow. Pendleton looked at me, but then returned looking at Hotchkiss. "I need you to lay out a parade ground for that event, OK?'

"Sure Sandie, I will get right on it." a smile came across his face, Hotchkiss nodded to me, and left.

"Joe, this is Colonel Walter," we shook hands, "Have you had any time to visit with your sister?"

He smiled, "Some," he said, "though, I know they need alone time, so I have tried not to impose."

"Anna is your sister?" I said.

"Yes sir."

Pendleton retook charge of the discussion, "Joe, I want you to shepherd the Colonel for a few days, when you can. Show him where we have bedded down, and kind of give him the routine of how we operate around here."

"Sure," he said, looking at me.

"Major, …"

"Call me Sandie, sir, if you like."

"Sandie, maybe Joe could ride with me back to the train, I am going to have get back there after I see the general to get them to the right place."

"Maybe, if the General doesn't need him," Sandie said.

Pendleton looked to John Harmon, "John, have you figured out where you want the train to go?"

"I have an idea, but would need a map to show, Colonel Walters."

The Adventure – Stolen Days

"Maybe, if you tell me where sir, I could guide him there." Joe Morrison spoke up.

"Good thinking," Sandie and Harmon said in almost perfect unison.

"Do you fellas do harmony," I quipped.

"You'll see tonight," Sandie said with a smile.

Though Sandie was only in his early twenties, he clearly held sway amongst the staff, and seemed confident to direct activities.

The voices coming from the larger tent, one of them Jackson's I presumed, got louder and it was apparent they were breaking up.

"Well, it's your moment," Sandie said, as he put his kepi on. "Let's go see the general." We got up, went out the tent, and he led around the left side of the tent and towards its rear, where the generals were standing and talking. My God, these were the men I had known my whole life, from countless pages. Each of these men was a giant, my knees got weak.

"General Paxton, I am sure the brigade will look sharp for Anna tomorrow." Jackson said, "And you too, Major Pelham."

Seeing us coming, the group turned in our direction as we walked up. We stopped together about three feet from them, came to attention and saluted. General Jackson, and one or two others returned the salute, the others just looked. "Hi Sandie, how are you?" One moved towards us. "Hello sir," Sandie said, "this is Lt. Colonel Parks Walter, General Hill."

I was frozen. "Don't look so scared man, we won't bite you," he said with a huge smile, extending his hand. Ambrose Powell Hill, his division saved Lee at Sharpsburg.

He stepped aside, Sandie pointed to each as he introduced them, "This is General Early, General Jackson, General Rodes, General Colston, General Paxton." I shook hands with each in turn."

General Rodes said, "Just arriving Colonel Walter?"

"Yes sir, from Carolina, sir."

"He has brought wagons of supplies from Governor Vance for the North Carolina boys." Sandie said, "and he may be joining our staff." General Jackson's eyebrow rose, only he decided who was on staff.

The other officers sensing the General's time was needed, all bid Jackson adieu, and welcomed me as they left. Except General Early who reached for Jackson's arm and said, "Could I have a moment of your time?" The two turned and walked a few steps, but not so far that I could not hear them.

"General, I am concerned that our army has only one of its Corps Commanders, and only six of its eight divisions, and the season is turning. General Hooker will surely be on the move soon." General Early said.

"I have spoken to General Lee on this issue, and he assures me he has contacted Richmond urging them to recall General Longstreet, and the divisions of Pickett and Hood." General Jackson replied.

General Early came to attention and saluted. He then turned and as he was mounting his horse said, "They best hurry them up, I am sure Hooker is fixin' to move against us." With that, Early turned his horse and rode off.

Jackson watched him for a moment and turned towards me; "Come into the tent Colonel Walter, let's visit awhile, he said. Sandie, ask Jim to bring us some coffee, please."

"Yes sir." Sandie handed Jackson my envelop, and turned towards the wagon and moved off, leaving me alone with the General.

Jackson opened the envelop, pulled out the note, and read it as he walked around his desk and sat down. I walked up to his desk, facing him. A slight smile came to his face as he placed the letter on his desk, and looked at me. After a moment a puzzled look came to his face, I could see him scanning his mind. Then a look of relief, "Have a seat Colonel Walter." He pointed to the chair.

As I sat down, Sandie came in with two cups of coffee, handing one to the General and one to me. "You know Sandie, I think Anna told me this man was coming." He tilted his head towards me. I looked at him questioningly.

"Yes, I think your wife met mine on the train coming up from North Carolina." He said as sipped his coffee.

The black man who had been by the wagon stuck his head into the tent. "What is it Jim?" Jackson asked.

"The Mrs. is calling you for lunch, sir." Jim said.

"Yes, … thank you, Jim." He rose quickly

I stood up … fast.

"Colonel, I must go, but we will talk again soon, today, I hope."

"Sir, the Colonel must return to his train to bring them in, I would like to send Joe Morrison with him." Sandie said.

"Sure, sure," Jackson, was walking out the front opening of the tent. He strode off quickly towards the house.

"Colonel, that's the quickest first meeting I have ever seen." He laughed, "That Anna uses the whip."

I took a deep breath, "For me, it will give me time to gather myself before our next meeting. Can you have Joe meet me so we can get on the road?"

"Yes sir, right with you." Pendleton turned and walked away.

Jim was still standing there, "So you are Jim?" I extended my hand, he took it. "Yes suh. Welcome. If you ever need coffee, or something, just come on over sir."

"Thank you, Jim."

"Jim, Captain Douglas advised me that if I wanted a job on the general's staff, I should ask you for advice, can you give me any?

"Well, suh, when I went to him for my job he said: "If you love your country, fear the Lord, and have no trouble getting up at 4 'clock in the morning, the job is yours." Jim said with a broad smile.

I smiled back, "thank you Jim."

Pendleton had found Morrison and was walking towards me. "Ready to go Lt.?" I asked.

"Yes sir."

"See you tonight, Sandie." I said, we turned and headed for the horse line.

＊ ＊ ＊ ＊

We rode off at a quick pace, it would be more than an hour before we connected with the wagon train, and probably almost three more until we got them where they were supposed park.

We had time to talk on the way. Lt. Morrison said the General was the happiest he had ever seen him. He said that Anna told him when they first arrived in the upstairs room they were staying in, he took off his raincoat, then went straight to Julia, lifted her up to his breast, walked over to a mirror in the room, and said to her, "Look how pretty you are, look how pretty you are."

I chuckled.

Then he said, that when the train arrived at Guiney Station from Richmond on the 20th, the General did not have the patience to wait for Anna to disembark. Instead, he charged up the stairs of the car, and pushed through the crowded passengers until he found them. "Now, that story is going to get around," the lieutenant said.

I thought to myself, he sure is ready to talk about this family stuff. I guess after endless months of war, and that's all there is to talk about, to

Mark K. Vogl
247

have an opportunity to think about and enjoy real life, life with family, must seem a Godsend.

"Little Julia was baptized two days ago, in the parlor of Belvoir," Lt. Morrison said.

"Belvoir?" I asked.

"Yes sir, that's the home, the Yerby home right there. The Jacksons are staying with them. Julia was baptized by Chaplain Beverly Tucker Lacy, the General's minister. I was proud to be there, as were many of the staff."

"That must have been a real pleasure." I said.

"It was, and it's good we were able to get this done, because things are about to start warming up around here," Joe said, looking straight ahead as we rode on.

Joe was a bright, energetic young man, who seemed very confident in the coming fight. "The men are returning from furlough, there were plenty coming in on the train this past week. Spirits are high."

We finally met the slow-moving train mid-afternoon, and guided them to their park. I informed Major Hill that Major Harmon would be in contact with him, and that he hoped to peel off some of the wagons to keep with the army here, when the train returned. Hill and I said our good byes, I didn't think we would see each other again. I asked him where Joshua was, he pointed to a group of wagons. Morrison and I rode over to them.

Jackson was first teamster to see me, "Hello Colonel, nice to see ya."

"Hello Jackson, how are you? Is your uncle around?"

"Right here, sir." Joshua said.

I dismounted. We walked towards each other, "Joshua, my time here is finished, and I am not sure I will see you again. I wanted to say thank you for our talks. I learned much from you, sir." I extended my hand.

We shook hands, "Colonel, it was a pleasure, sir. Be safe sir, may God guide you, and I hope we meet again in Caroline."

"Jackson, get the Colonel's gear," Joshua called out.

Jackson's Camp, The Yerby Home Belvoir
Evening of April 25th, 1863
The campfire

The sun had gone down about an hour before. We had gotten the wagon train to its link up with the Jackson supply train, and I turned it over to Major Hill. Now we were on the way back to camp. It had been a long day in the saddle, and I hoped there might be something to eat when we got there.

"Each night, when conditions allow, the staff gathers to talk about home, or the events of the day." Lt. Morrison offered a preview of the evening's festivities.

When we turned south off Plank Road I knew where we were. Riding through the dark woods there were camp fires on both sides of us, soldiers moving about leisurely. After traveling a few miles down the road, I saw dim lights, and as we continued a second set of lights below the first ones. Finally, we were at Belvoir, and down in front of the house some distance was a camp fire with some men sitting on logs around it, and the shadows of a wagon and tents.

A soldier detailed to take care of the horses met us at the line. "I will take care of these sir." He took the reins of both our horses. I grabbed the saddle bags, my bag and the canteen off my horse. I was out of water, and had been for hours.

"Let's see if Jim has anything for us." Lt. Morrison said. We headed directly to the chuck wagon; a small fire could be seen.

A good smell filled my nostrils as we got closer to the wagon." Evening, suhs, got some stew in the pot for ya." Jim was sitting on a chair near the rear of the wagon smoking a pipe, "and a biscuit for each there on the board." He pointed with the pipe.

"Do you have any water, Jim?" I asked.

"There's a creek over that way about 50 feet, suh" he said pointing in the opposite direction of the house, away from the wagon. I headed that way, and came upon a line of trees, which indicated proximity to a creek. I could hear the water running, and as I looked down, and to the right and left, I could see light reflecting off the water. I would have to be careful, as I could not see the ground as it dropped sharply to the water.

I held on to a tree, and dropped myself hoping to find a rock or plateau of ground … instead my right boot went right into the water. I could feel my boot filling with cold water. I bent over, pulled the cork from the canteen and dipped it below the water. It filled, I corked it, and pulled myself up, making a splashing sound and then water ran out of my boot. A squishy sound accompanied each step back to the wagon, one wet cold pant leg clung to my calf — yuck.

I picked up a metal plate, got some stew, and my biscuit, and headed to the camp fire. Sandie Pendleton, Henry Kyd Douglas, and Jed Hotchkiss were already there with Lt. Morrison.

A chorus of different welcomes were offered to me as I sat down.

Two riders rode behind us and up to Belvoir. One rider with a cape, and a hat with a large plume, was the image of General J. E. B. Stuart I knew from my readings. The general dismounted, handed the reins to the other rider, and bounded up the stairs into the house. The other rider headed towards the wagon and Jim.

Sandie Pendleton asked: "Jed, how was your day with General Colston, laying out the parade field for Monday." When Jed answered I was a little startled, he did not speak with a Southern accent.

"Fine I guess, it was easier than working with the general to position abatis." The small group chuckled. Sandie warned, "Remember General Colston was with General Jackson and Anna at Virginia Military Institute. He was an instructor with then Major Jackson, and they are friends."

"I hope he is better in a fight than he was today on a parade field," Jed said.

I finished my stew and headed with the plate over to Jim to see what to do with it. The rider who had come in with General Stuart was eating and talking to Jim. He was wearing sergeant's stripes.

"Sergeant, was that General Stuart who went in?" I asked.

"It was sir."

"Are you …"

"I am his Color Sergeant, sir."

"Wait here a moment please," I asked. I put the plate down on a board extending from the wagon, that acted as a counter, and walked over to my saddle bags. I got the package Mrs. Stuart had given me. I returned to the sergeant. "Would you offer my compliments, Colonel Walter, and give this to the General for me? I carried it up here from Mt. Airy, for his mother."

"You should do that sir," the sergeant said.

"I do not want to impose on the General, I just want to make sure that he receives this gift from his mother," I said. "Jim what do I do with the plate?"

"Suh, rinse it in the pan of water, and I will take care of it."

"Great stew Jim, thank you sir." I said. Jim smiled, the Sergeant looked up from his plate at me.

As I walked away I could hear Jim and the sergeant talking as they walked towards Jim's campfire.

About that time Major Harmon walked up to the fire. "Glad to see you made it back Colonel Walter."

"Thanks John. All go well with Major Hill?" I asked.

"Yes, he did have an inventory of goods, and we can start tomorrow to get these items out to the respective Carolina regiments." Harmon replied as he sat down on one of the logs in front of the fire.

"Sandie, I heard General Lee and some of his staff stopped by for a surprise visit with Mrs. Jackson." John Harmon said.

"True, the General was not here at the time," Sandie reported, "but, Mrs. Jackson did a fine job of entertaining General Lee. They had met last year in Winchester around Christmas."

About that time, the door at the house opened, the light from inside silhouetting the General, Mrs. Jackson, General Stuart as they came out on the small enclosed porch at the top of the steps. In a moment, the sergeant who had been with Jim was mounted and taking Stuart's horse to him. After the sergeant got there, he spoke with the three of them at length, pointing in my direction briefly. He handed Stuart a package, the two volumes of Shakespeare his mother had given me. After the Jacksons bid Stuart goodnight, he mounted his horse, turned and rode down towards us at the camp fire.

It was dark, and my first view of him mounted on his steed was somewhat startling. His cape spreading behind him, his long flowing dark beard a seeming pillow that held his face, his hair flowing from beneath his hat. Though he did not gallop up to me, but instead walked his mount towards me, he was quite a sight.

"Colonel Walter," Stuart said mounted on a beautiful horse.

"Yes," I stood up and saluted. He returned the salute.

"Thank you for bringing mother's gift with you from Mt. Airy. It was very kind of you, sir. How was my mother?"

"Seemed in strong health and good spirits," I replied.

"Fine. Again, thank you. Good evening, and good evening to this collection of vagabonds," he smiled and waved, Jackson's men chuckled, as he spun his horse and was off. Formality was not always present, I noticed. These men were like brothers, though there was never any doubt about who the leaders were.

A horseman coming into camp passed by Stuart and his companion, and headed directly to the horse line for the staff. He dismounted, and began unsaddling his horse. Jim went up to him and spoke, and then took a feed bag from the man and went and got some grain for the horse. The man then turned and walked towards us, taking his gauntlets off.

"Hello Holmes, how was your day?" Sandie Pendleton said.

The man walked up to the steaming pot of coffee and dipped his cup in. "Fine Sandie, and yours." He replied.

A barrage of "hellos" and "evenings" rained down on the man as he approached. "Dr. McGuire, may I introduce Colonel Walter." I stood, we exchanged greetings and shook hands. Dr. McGuire was a tall man, well over six foot, slim, and in his mid-twenties, dark hair and a full mustache. His blue eyes caught my attention. He was Jackson's physician and Chief Medical Officer for Second Corps. Like most of the rest of the staff, he was a Virginian, from Winchester.

"My name is Hunter," he said to me, "but for some reason Sandie prefers my middle name."

"It just has a sound to it," Sandie quipped, "there's just something about it."

"Doctor McGuire, I believe you need to take Colonel Walter to your tent," John Harmon mused, "He seems to be enjoying horse's tail." The others laughed quietly. Harmon was referring to the aches you enjoy when riding a horse for long hours when the exercise is new to you.

"How's the General and Anna doing?" Dr. McGuire asked.

"Very well," Colonel Darby replied as he strode up to the fire, "As you saw Hunter, J. E. B. just left, and he always brings gaiety to anywhere he visits. And Julia loves his beard!"

"But where was his banjo player?" Kyd Douglas asked. Stuart was known to travel with a banjo player who would keep him entertained as he rode. Stuart looked the part of a devil-may-care, gallant ladies' man, but he was a devout Christian and faithful husband. He fit the Christian mold for officers Robert E. Lee wanted in his Army.

So, this was most of Jackson's staff, his inner circle. Men who I had read about since childhood. These were the men who helped create the legend of Stonewall Jackson.

Jed Hotchkiss was the exception to the rule, a New Yorker by birth, he had lived in Connecticut before moving first to Pennsylvania and then into the Shenandoah Valley. Jed Hotchkiss, the map maker, was renown for the accuracy and the detail of his maps. And he had devised a color scheme to make his maps easier to read; roads were red, streams blue, woods green, mountains, hills brown. His work had been first recognized during Jackson's extraordinary Valley Campaign a year ago. The gathering of these legends had distracted me from my wet leg and foot, but suddenly I was reminded that my foot was wet and cold. And I was going to have to figure out what to do to dry these pants. ...

"Well, it has been a long day, I best get to bed," I said. With that, I rose, said good night to all, and left to find my saddle bags and bed roll over by Jim's wagon. The stars were out, the temperature cool, but not cold.

Jackson's Camp, The Yerby Home "Belvoir"
April 26th, 1863
The Sabbath

I woke up to the chatter and laughter of men sitting around the fire on the other side of Jim's wagon. By the sun, I guessed it to be about eight am.

I sat up, stretched and looked around, things were moving at a slower pace than I had seen yesterday. Jed Hotchkiss walked up to me, handed me a cup of coffee, "Morning sir."

"Today would be a good day to wash clothes, or take care of your horse, but we are off to church around 930 am." He said. "We will be headed over to Hamilton's Crossing for service." Hotchkiss, like all of Jackson's staff were devout Christians, most were Presbyterians.

Well, that told me what day it was.

Time to get moving I thought to myself. I looked over at the horses' line, one of Randolf's troopers had brought hay over in a wagon and was laying it on the ground in front of them. There was also a shovel leaning against the tree, along with a wheel barrel. So that's why there wasn't a stench from their days of deposits of manure I thought to myself, it was removed to who knows where.

"We'll move that line today," Hotchkiss said, "the smell of the urine is getting a little strong."

I rose and walked down to the creek so I could wash my face. I had forgotten how a soldier adjusts to living in the field. As an aviator, I didn't have to do that. I did it only once in my basic training as a lieutenant, and that was only for a couple days. It had been weeks since I left Hattie's farm. I was sure I smelled now, maybe I would take a bath this afternoon, I thought.

From the creek I went to Jim's wagon, where there was a pile of biscuits on a plate. They were cold, but edible, even tasty when you are hungry.

I decided to change into a fresh shirt for church. And then moseyed over to the campfire where the rest of the staff were fixin' to go to church. It wasn't long before it was time to go.

After mounting, we rode over to the house. "You ride next to me," Colonel Darby said.

A carriage was brought up to Belvoir. General Jackson, Mrs. Jackson and Julia accompanied by the Yerby's I supposed, came out the front door and down the stairs and climbed into the carriage. When all were settled, the driver, Jim Lewis, Jackson's man servant and cook snapped the whip, "Getti -up" he said, and the carriage jumped and moved.

We were lined up, two abreast behind the carriage, Colonel Darby and myself the first pair, with Sandie Pendleton and Dr. McGuire behind us, and then Major Harmon and Henry Kyd Douglas behind them. Lt. Morrison and Jed Hotchkiss were in front of the carriage.

The sun was up, and it was a beautiful spring morning. As I rode along, I made a special effort to enjoy the scents and smells, and the sounds of our entourage moving; the clomp of horse steps, the occasional whinny, and the jingle jangle of soldiers' wear, though I noticed none of the officers wore their sabers.

Men walked in groups, on both sides of the road, in the same direction as we, many carrying Bibles. When they looked up and saw the general and his wife, they smiled, waved, said morning General, or hello Mrs. Jackson. There was real adoration and joy in their voices. Many of them had never seen Mrs. Jackson before. Many tipped their caps.

We traveled northeast; it was about a mile to Hamilton's Crossing. Men were coming from all directions, on the roads, and even across meadows. Wagons were parked across the road. There was a tent, and the carriage pulled up to it. General Jackson got down, and then took Julia, while a silver haired man with a beard offered a hand to Anna to assist her coming out of the carriage. When I looked again, ... that was General Lee. Robert E. Lee, a man I had studied my whole life, a literal legend, a myth, I lost my breath. Phoenix jumped a little, sensing my strong emotional reaction to the unexpected sight of Marse Robert. There he was, a smile on his face, looking down, holding her hand, speaking to Anna. They turned with the General holding his daughter, and went into the tent. A sight I will never forget.

"Are you OK?" Colonel Darby said several times, louder each time, he had grabbed my arm and was shaking it. "Yes, sir," I said. He could tell I was moved. "We follow the carriage, and will dismount, and sit with the men, Colonel."

We dismounted and tied our horses to the carriage. Jim Lewis walked with us and we all sat as a group on some benches that seemed to have been saved for us, in the front. I looked around, and there were hundreds, maybe a thousand men all seated on benches in the open air, under trees. "General Jackson has done much to bring revelation and Christianity to his soldiers, Parks" Colonel Darby said.

Chaplain Beverly Tucker Lacy, who had most recently baptized little Julia, would be giving the sermon today. There was a small tower built, so that he could rise up, and be seen and heard by all the attendees.

As we sat waiting for the service to begin, I noticed the tent holding General Lee, the Jackson's and Yerby's, and others I could not make out was in the center facing us. A group of maybe 30 men sat to the left of the tent facing us, I assumed they were a choir, and to the right of the tent was a wooden tower which Lacy would ascend to speak to us. The entire chapel was a woods, a large pine woods, with no undergrowth, just a brown pine needle floor. And then rows and rows of benches.

After a few minutes Chaplain Lacy came out and stood, hands clasped in front of him, while a loud voice asked us to rise. Our first hymn would be *How Firm a Foundation*. The choir began, and within a couple of lines a thousand voices joined.

A man, a regimental chaplain I guessed, ascended the tower and asked those who had a Bible to open it to: "And we know that all things work together for the good of them that love God, to them who are the called according to his purpose." Romans 8:28.

Reverend Lacy ascended the ten-foot tower, and drew out some papers that were inside the drawer of the speaker's stand.

"Almighty God thank You for this glorious day, for Your Presence amongst us, and for Your Protection and love of this gathering of men striving to preserve the original intent of our Founders, who knew You and constructed our nation on the Rock, Your Word, the Bible.

Holy Father, we know You have a Plan for us, that all that occurs is Your Will, and that we are mere instruments. We ask that we be as strong as possible for Your use. Almighty God put aside our fears and wants, and place in our hearts love for You and the wisdom to see Your desires act to make Your Will on earth manifest."

For more than an hour, Reverend Lacy talked about Providence in its many ways, the Providence of nations and God's direction of kings and presidents, the Providence of individuals, and God's Walk with each of us, and His Plan for us, designed even before we were born. But it was his conclusion which stuck home to me, and to many.

"Lastly let us be thankful for the peace of Providence. Isn't it comforting to know that our welfare, our existence, our sustenance and our departure from this world are all in the Hands of God, all already planned. Can we not venture forth with courage knowing that none can hurt us, lest he be God's instrument? Let us thank God for His Mercy, His Gracious design for our lives. Amen."

Reverend Lacy descended from the tower and returned inside the tent to his seat. To complete the service, the choir stood and started, and the congregation followed and joined in on *Amazing Grace*.

I could sense the certainty of these men, their complete trust in God, and it explained how they could be here, facing an Army in every way superior, except one … in faith.

As with all other churches, some men moved quickly to head back home, but others remained to talk with one another. The folks within the tent spent some time visiting. In an almost leisurely way, Colonel Darby led us to the carriage. As the Commanders were in no rush, and about one thousand men were trying to head out, it was simply too crowded to attempt to move.

I watched to see if there were any other celebrities of the war I might recognize. About that time, Colonel Darby placed his hand on my shoulder, "Colonel Walter may I introduce General Fitz Lee." I turned, and his hand was already extended, "It is an honor sir," I said. He smiled, "Thank you, I am always curious to meet officers in Jackson's party. They are talented men, and unique men, everyone." General Fitz Lee was a nephew of Robert E. Lee and had demonstrated great skill as one Stuart's subordinate cavalry commanders.

Dabney and Lee chatted while I pretended to listen. After some time, Jim Lewis said loudly, "excuse me men, the general wants me to come and pick them up." The road was somewhat muddy, and no place for Mrs. Jackson. As we stepped away, Jim touched the flank of the horse on the right and the two began to pull the carriage forward and across the road. "Let's mount gentlemen," Colonel Dabney said aloud.

We formed as we had before in the road, and waited for Jim to pick up his riders, and then do a large turn to get back on the road in the right direction.

The trip back to Belvoir was peaceful. The rest of the day was taken up in maintenance of equipment and animals, and self. I did go down to the creek, and take a bath in a very cold creek. Which was more out of need, then desire. Late in the afternoon I received an invitation from Mrs. Jackson to join them for dinner. I wanted to be as presentable as possible.

I walked up to Belvoir a few minutes before six pm. This was my first opportunity to meet and get to know General Jackson. If I was going to be successful in my mission, I would have to learn about the General and hopefully get to a point where I can influence the events that will occur on the evening of 2 May.

There was a sentry at the bottom step. He gave a rifle salute when I walked past. Up the steps I went, and knocked. The door opened and a well-dressed older gentleman said "Hello Colonel Walter, I am Thomas Yerby, welcome."

"Parks Walter, sir."

We shook hands, "Come in Parks." I entered through the door into a hallway that ran the length of the house. As I walked in there was a woman, "This is Mrs. O'Neale, a friend from Fredericksburg, and the hostess for tonight."

She smiled, curtsied and extended her hand, "Good evening Colonel Walter, we are so glad you accepted the invitation from Mrs. Jackson."

"Good evening ma'am," I responded.

Mrs. O'Neale reached for my arm, "Let's go into the parlor and meet the General and his wife." I offered my arm and she led me into the parlor. Mr. Yerby followed us.

The General was standing near the fireplace, Mrs. Jackson sitting on the couch. She rose when I walked in, the general turned facing us.

"Anna, may I present Colonel Walter." Anna offered her hand. I bowed before taking the hand, then gently took her hand, "It is my honor Mrs. Jackson."

"You will please call me Anna," she said. She curtsied.

General Jackson walked to me, extending his hand, "Good to see you again Colonel."

I couldn't help it, I came to attention, then, after a moment, extended my hand. "My honor sir."

"Parks, isn't it?" He said.

"Yes, sir." I responded.

"Well Parks, it seems your wife and mine have spent some time together." He said with a smile on his face.

"Is that so," I looked at Mrs. Jackson.

"Yes, I had the pleasure of Jeanne Marie's company on the train from Greensborough to Richmond. And also the company of Jimmie

Earle and Micah. He was an excellent escort for you wife, and was very good with Jimmie Earle."

"Parks, I have heard quite a bit about you, sir." The general said.

The general looked at Mr. Yerby, "Thomas, it appears that Parks saved the life of Governor Vance." Mr. Yerby closed in to enter the conversation.

"Thomas, shall we move to the table?" My. Yerby said to General Jackson.

Jackson nodded, extending his arm, offering Mr. Yerby the lead. Mr. Yerby took Mrs. O'Neale's arm and they walked through the opening from the parlor into the dining room. He escorted her to one end of the table, pulled her chair, and she sat down. The Jackson's circled to the back side of the table, where the general assisted Anna in sitting. Mr. Yerby's pointed to the single chair opposite the Jackson's. The three gentlemen took seats.

It was a beautiful dining room, with a candelabra on the table, beautiful plate ware, glasses on the white table cloth. A painting hung on the wall, a very good rendition of George Washington.

"Before we begin dinner, shall we say grace," Thomas said rhetorically.

After the prayer, servants came into the room, one filling glasses with water, others carrying bowls of soup. On the table, was a plate with rolls, and a small bowel with butter. Clearly, the blockade had not yet had an observable effect on Belvoir.

Mr. Yerby looked at me, "Tell me about saving the Governor, Colonel Walter?"

"Please call me Parks, sir. It wasn't really as much as people make it out to be sir."

"Nonsense." Anna said.

"I appreciate your modesty, Parks, but if the story as related to me is true, I think it was a quite daring rescue." General Jackson said.

Anna related the story as it was told to her by Jeanne Marie, and actually it was a fairly accurate telling. And then she said something I did not know occurred. "General Stuart relayed to us last night that his mother said your heroism was reported in the *Mt. Airy Gazette*."

I think my mouth dropped open with that comment.

"Well done," Mrs. O'Neale said.

"Yes indeed," Thomas Yerby said, "seems we have a celebrity with us tonight."

I bowed my head, I really was overwhelmed. Given that every man I had met since I got back to this time had endured much more danger, shown much more courage than anything I had done in my entire life, my actions seemed nothing spectacular.

"Colonel, I appreciate your humility, but I also appreciate your courage, and decisiveness." General Jackson said quietly, looking directly at me. In his eye, I could see his mind working. He had made up his mind about me, I had met the standard.

'Thank you, sir," I said.

I turned to Anna, "So you enjoyed Jeanne Marie's company?"

"Yes, I did. We spent a night together at the Governor's mansion before I left to join Thomas. She was very good with Julia and very protective of us. Micah watched after our bags at every transfer. Together they made the trip much more enjoyable. And little Jimmie Earle sure is something."

"I appreciate those comments Anna, Micah was involved in the rescue of the Governor."

"Yes ..." Anna said.

"Tell me Parks, what did you think of Reverend Lacy's sermon?" General Jackson asked. The soup dishes had been removed, and the main entrées were being brought out, including a side of ham and vegetables.

"Would any one care for some wine?" Thomas interrupted.

Anna, and Mrs. O'Neale responded positively. General Jackson looked at me, "It's alright Parks, if you would like some. I just avoid alcohol; I like it too much." He smiled. General Jackson did not drink alcohol

"I will have one, sir." I said.

I then looked at General Jackson, "Sir, it was inspiring, but it always raises the question, how do we know the Lord's Will?"

"His Will unfolds, Parks. What happens is His Will."

"But can God allow someone to work against His Will, and if one does, is he placing himself on bad terms with the Lord?"

"Parks, your question is one asked of me all the time. I ask it of myself. And I will respond as I always respond, the duty is ours, the consequences are God's. We must seek God's Will in prayer, and then do what we feel is our duty as God has given us the eyes to see it. But we must trust and embrace what happens as God's Will," the general said with a sincerity and earnestness that was the core of personal essence.

Anna, reached for his hand, seeing the purity of her husband, knowing it is him, as he lives.

While the general was speaking, the servants were pouring wine into our glasses, and at that moment I needed a drink, one stronger than wine.

"I thought General Lee looked well today," Thomas Yerby said. His home had been used months earlier by General Lee when he was enduring some health concerns.

"Yes, he did look quite well," Mrs. O'Neale said.

We turned to our plates, filled with slices of ham, and boiled potatoes and carrots. It was a fine meal.

"Are operations about to commence?" Mr. Yerby asked.

The question seemed to bring discomfort to General Jackson. "I think we should talk about other things, it's so rare for me to have time with Anna." And almost as if that statement was a signal, Julia cried out from upstairs. General Jackson rose, "There is someone up there, darling." Anna said.

The general put his cloth napkin on the table, "I know, but I would like to check," as he left the table. Jackson probably knew he did not have much time left to be the father of Julia. Soon, Federal actions would force him to send his wife and daughter away.

"Will you be remaining with the General or heading back to Carolina?" Thomas asked.

Mrs. Jackson sneaked a look at me. "I don't know," I said. 'I have no orders at this point."

The general came back down stairs. 'She is fine."

General Jackson walked straight up to me, looking at Anna he said, "We are going to step outside for some air my "esposita," we shall return shortly." The general grabbed my arm gently and pointed to the door.

The guard came to attention and present arms, as the two of us descended the stairs and walked past him out into the yard. The moon was up, and the stars shone very bright. Even when I was in Area 51, the sky had not seemed so full, the velvet blackness seemingly holding God's glistening diamonds. A strange calm settled over us.

We began walking, side by side, not to any particular place, or for any specific purpose. Inside, the General had been cordial, and easy to talk to, but now, he seemed to be in a different state.

"Col. Walter, I sense something special about you, almost as if you are here to tell me something? I have learned in my life to continually watch for God's messengers, they have come to me more than once."

I was caught completely by surprise. What do I do now, I thought?

"Are you a man of strong faith, Colonel?" Jackson asked.

"Sir, I confess, …"

"We are strongly Christian here, Colonel. My duty is not just to command men, but to help men find their way to our Savior. I am blessed to be joined by a staff of Christians, and under the command of Robert E. Lee, who is comfortable with our Father." The General said.

"General, I want to tell you …"

The general almost said shush as he put his arm around my shoulder, "Colonel Walter, my religious belief teaches me to feel as safe in battle as in bed. God has fixed the time for my death. I do not concern myself about that, but to be always ready, no matter when it may overtake me. That is the way all men should live, and then all would be equally brave."

"God has fixed the time for my death." Echoed in my head as we continued to walk. Whatever I was going to do to attempt to save the general's life was not going to happen through a warning of events to come.

We continued to walk some distance in silence before the general spun around to walk back towards the house. It was weird because I sensed the general felt he had said what he had to say.

"Thank you for bringing the supplies, Colonel Walter, I must suggest you visit the North Carolina troops soon, as the spring campaign may be only days off." General Jackson said as we walked past the saluting guard and up the stairs.

As he opened the door, the General said loudly, "Anna, I believe the Colonel will be leaving us for the evening." In a moment, Anna walked in with my hat, handing it to me she said, "Colonel Walter, please express my best wishes to your wife, and thank her for her companionship."

"I certainly will," I said as I took her hand.

"I hope you had a pleasant evening; I know we did." The General said to me at the door as he shook my hand. "See you in the morning Colonel."

General Jackson's actions were truly odd. I didn't even get to finish my dinner as he rushed me away. I don't think he was disturbed by me, but seemed to know that we should not talk about the days to come.

As I walked back down to my gear near Jim Lewis' wagon I reviewed the night's events. The news about the story in the paper really shook me, but I did not realize until later in the evening that Nash might see that story. I laid down on the ground on my bedroll under the starlit sky thought about what I should do. I had to try to comply with the Governor's instructions. But what to do about my primary mission? A breeze blew across my face as I thought and fell off to sleep.

Jackson's Camp, The Yerby Home Belvoir
April 27th, 1863
Anna's Review

The day started early, first light. And Jim Lewis was up before me. He had coffee and biscuits ready when General Jackson came down from the house.

"Morning Jim," I heard as I rolled my blanket. "Mornin' sir," Jim replied.

"Morning Kyd," General Jackson said as Jim handed him his coffee. "How's the biscuits this morning?"

"Tolerable," Kyd said. The look Kyd got from Jim would have killed the average man. Kyd smiled.

I walked up to the board where the coffee and biscuits were sitting. I reached for both.

"Horses saddled?" Jackson asked.

I damn near froze. A lightning bolt struck through my head, my God, I forgot all about that. My heart was racing. I started to turn for the horse line.

Just before Kyd bit into his biscuit, he said, "Of course General." He slid an eye towards me. "All three taken care of." I relaxed. I owed him one.

"Good morning, Colonel Walter." General Jackson looked well, as he ate a biscuit and sipped his coffee. The white crumbs of the biscuit were collecting on his beard. A light seemed to emanate from his blue eyes.

"Morning, sir." I said.

At that moment three men walked up with their horses; it was Chaplain Lacy, Dr. McGuire and Sandie Pendleton. There was an exchange of greetings between all the men. Each man reached for a biscuit.

"We best get moving," the general said, "long day today, and we have to be back here before two." He finished his last swig of coffee and handed the cup to Jim. A private had brought up Little Sorrel. While Jackson mounted, the two of us walked briskly to the horse line.

I wasn't gonna need my bedroll. I placed it beside Jim's wagon.

"Thank you," I said to Kyd.

"No problem Colonel, you looked bushed last night, so I figured I would leave you sleep some." He would have had to been up an hour before me. At dark, dark thirty, to feed and saddle three horses.

We found our horses; they were side by side. Kyd's horse did have his bed roll tied onto the back of the saddle. Number one rule of war, always be ready for anything. I had to remember that beginning now. We mounted and turned together.

Jackson sat mounted on Little Sorrel when we rode up to him, his famous kepi pulled down over his eyes. "We are off to General Early's division this morning?" Asked the general.

"That's right, sir." Kyd said.

"Let's be off gentlemen." He spurred Sorrell to a canter, Kyd and I pulled up on either side of him. The three other staff rode behind us, side by side. It was just dawn; the sun had not risen yet.

We rode for a while in silence. General Jackson pulled a lemon from his pocket, cut a slice off and placed it in his mouth to suck on. He seemed deep in thought. "Kyd, when we get back to camp, please ask Sandie to bring me the morning reports from the respective divisions." The morning reports gave the "present for duty" strength of each unit, Jackson was curious to know if the men were returning from furloughs he had approved.

"Will do sir."

After a quarter of a mile Jackson turned to me, "General Stuart was quite touched by your effort to bring a gift from his mother. He is particularly fond of Shakespeare."

"Mrs. Stuart is a nice woman; it was pure accident that we were in Mt. Airy when she was. I had never met her before." I replied.

"J. E. B. said he got a letter from his mother a few days before, telling him of the coming gift. She had written him about your exploits to save the life of Governor Vance." Jackson looked at me.

I didn't know what to say. Maybe he didn't remember we talked about it the night before. Or maybe he was interested in hearing more about the incident. I just let it drop.

Jackson simply grunted "hmmm," and rode on.

The smell of wood smoke filled the air, as we rode closer to Early's camps. Small camp fires dotted the landscape. Row upon row of small two-man tents, laid out in straight lines and sprinkled with larger tents could be seen. Hundreds of them.

A trumpet sounded reveille in the distance. The sun was breaking above the horizon to the east. Thousands of men, and yet so quiet and peaceful, the first moments of an army's next day. The quiet would not last long.

Early's forces were spread along a rail line running into Fredericksburg, the same line Mrs. Jackson took from Richmond to Guiney Station. The rest of Jackson's Corps, three divisions, was off to the south watching to see if the Yankees might try to cross the Rappahannock River south of Fredericksburg on Lee's right.

"Sir, I have to depart here for Corbin's Hill, see you back at Belvoir." Captain Douglas said to General Jackson, he saluted and turned off to the left. We rode along, every man to his own thoughts this morning. Finally, off in the distance we saw a group of officers.

General Early and members of his staff sat atop their horses, on the road, waiting for us to arrive. There was a flurry of salutes, greetings and smiles between the two groups. The horses jostled around a little, snorting and shaking their heads. It was kind of amazing to me how two different animal groups greeted each other.

"Good to see you Jubal, thank you for entertaining us this morning." Jackson said. The two extended their hands.

"A pleasure sir, I am sure we will learn from the visit of you and your staff." Members of the two staffs were hooked up. Dr. McGuire was there to inspect the sanitation of the camp, and their field medical operations. Chaplain Lacy was there to visit with Regimental Chaplains, observe the morning Bible studies that had been implemented, and get a feeling for troop morale. And Sandie Pendleton was going to inspect the camps, and randomly take a look at the weapons and equipment of soldiers.

Looking at General Jackson, General Early announced: "With your permission sir, gentlemen we will meet at my headquarters for lunch at about 12:30."

With that, the paired staff members saluted the two generals, turned and departed for their respective areas. I was left with the two commanders.

"Jubal, this is Colonel Walter, he joined me a couple of days ago, after bringing up a wagon train of supplies from North Carolina, from Governor Vance for the North Carolinians." General Early reached out from atop his horse to shake my hand.

"Hmmm, I will have to mention that to Governor Letcher the next time I see him," General Early said. Clearly, he wanted to motivate the Virginia governor to do the same type of act of support for Virginia troops. "Would you like to ride the line, General, before we head to the headquarters?"

"At your convenience," Jackson said. We rode past men having breakfast, companies holding formation, with a sergeant laying out the activities for the morning, men airing out bedding, all activities of daily life in a military camp.

"Jubal, what have you observed from our friends across the way?" Jackson asked.

"Not much, sir, they don't seem ready to move against us."

"I hope no more of your officers have been duck hunting." Jackson said, referring to two Confederate officers who had been captured by the Yankee pickets, when their boat drifted across the Rappahannock while they hunted ducks. General Early made no reply.

We rode along, the two generals talking about the position, about actions by the Federals over the past days, and about the re-organization of the brigades. General Lee had decided to make a real effort to organize brigades by states, where possible. The thinking was they would fight harder if they were fighting next to their neighbors. Also, it provided a lynch pin for morale, states would compete against one another.

Eventually we ended up at Early's headquarters. General Early's staff had done a lot to organize a lunch for almost two dozen men.

"Perhaps you would like to visit Hoke's Brigade, Col. Walter?" General Early asked.

"I would sir."

Early called out to a junior aide, "Son, take Col. Walter over to General Hoke, will you?"

With that, I saluted the two, and we were off.

As we rode over, the aide told me that Brigadier General Hoke had just been promoted on April 23rd. He then went on to tell me of Hoke's rise from lieutenant all the way to his current position. "He is something to see when the caps start busting," he said.

It wasn't far, we were there in minutes.

As we rode up, a group of senior officers were sitting under the shade of the tree talking. It was not formal, the apparent leader white cotton shirt, gray britches, and black boots below the knee. The others, regimental commanders for 6th, 21st, 54th, 57th North Carolina Volunteers and the 1st Battalion North Carolina Sharpshooters, were in different stages of the uniform, some sitting, other laying back. But all shuffled to look more at work when they saw me and Early's young aide.

The leader stood up, a tall thin, very young-looking man, and yelled out "Hello Lieutenant, who do have with you there."

"It's Colonel Waler, general" he replied, and then turned to me, "… that's General Hoke, sir." We rode over to the horse line and dismounted. As we did that, the men at the feet of Hoke rose, brushing the grass and dirt off their legs and bottoms. General I thought to myself, he doesn't look old enough. …

We strode up, came to attention and saluted.

He returned the salute, his regimental commanders had gathered behind him. "We heard about your visit Col. Walter, been expecting you, sir" He smiled and reached out his hand.

"Then you know I am here on behalf of Governor Vance, to visit with you and your troops, and as many of those from North Carolina to observe and listen to your needs," I said.

"So we've been told. Let me introduce you to the regimental commanders." With that he introduced each slowly, giving us time to greet and shake. "You will only have enough time to visit with one regiment before we have to leave for lunch with Generals Jackson and Early."

"Colonel McDowell[4] and the 54th have volunteered to be your hosts for this morning. They heard of your of adventure with Thomas' Legion and saving Governor Vance. And since the Legion is part of the 54th, they thought it only right that they accept responsibility for you!" He said.

I stood there shaking my head. "This is remarkable," I said, "who could know the entire Second Corps of the Army of Northern Virginia would hear of a small affair near Mt. Airy, North Carolina?"

The men laughed, McDowell said, "Well it's a little bigger than that, we heard Hood's Texans are wanting you to go guard Galveston!" At that, there was an outburst of laughter.

"Col. Walter lets head out to my regiment." He grabbed my arm and spun me around.

"Please call me Parks."

"And I am Jim, or James." He said. Unusual I thought, most men don't offer two first names. "Bring your horse."

"I will have him back to you in plenty of time, Robert" McDowell

---

4 Information concerning Col. McDowell provided by North Carolina History written by Dr. Hill and Genl. *The Civil War in the East*

looked, waved at General Hoke, who returned the informal goodbye.

"So, tell me something of you, Jim" I asked, as we walked through a camp filled with tents. Men were doing odd jobs along the way, stretching out their bedding, shaving and washing, cleaning their weapons. Sergeants were briefing details of men; I heard one noncommissioned officer talking about some wagons of supplies they would be unloading this morning.

"Those are your wagons Parks. About me? Well, I am a few years older than the General. I am from Burke County, where I farm. I went to Davidson. Am married, and if you return to North Carolina, maybe you could see this to my wife," he said, as he reached to field desk in his tent and picked up a piece of paper. "This is a letter to my wife Julia and the children, Annie and Charles."

I had not been asked for anything like this, and didn't quite know what to do. My future was very uncertain, and even if I made it safely back to Hattie's what would I do with this letter? "Jim," I hesitated to take it.

"Parks, I am aware that each of us is a thin string when it comes to life, and our respective futures, but I have more confidence in you, than the mail system."

The look in his eyes told me he was determined. I took the letter, folded it, and put it in the pocket of my jacket. Letters in this jacket seemed to be a hallmark of my adventure.

He let out a sigh of relief, and thanked me. "Parks, I have had some junior officers and enlisted men brought up for you to visit with. I will step away so that they feel free to talk. I know the entire regiment will be happy to hear what you tell them. We are getting ready for a serious fight, and your presence on behalf of the governor could help raise the spirits."

"Be positive Parks, remember you will be the talk of this brigade, and more when you leave us."

"Aye sir," I said.

McDowell called his Regimental Sergeant Major over, introduced him and departed.

"Sir, right this way." We walked maybe thirty feet to a collection of maybe twenty men and Lieutenants who stood as I approached. I said, "Be as you were men, sit down please." And they did so.

The sky was clear, the sun up, but the Sergeant Major had set up the geometry of the talk so that sun was not in their eyes or mine.

"Good morning men," a reply from many, and a lot of smiles, I continued, "Governor Vance wants you to know the entire North State is proud of you, and follow your adventure with General Jackson. He and many Tar heels made an effort to collect and send supplies to you. I am told that among them is a special gift of honey and apple butter." The reaction was positive.

"I can tell you, that on my part, I don't know which honor is greater, representing the governor, or being with you. Each of you is a patriot, and a soldier of great esteem."

"The governor wants to know how you are, and should he be aware of any special needs?" With that I hope to elicit comments from the men.

One soldier said, "Tell us about saving the governor sir?" A rustle amongst the group seemed to echo the question.

"It was your Thomas Legion that did that." I said, "I ..."

"That's not the way we heard the story, Colonel ..." one soldier said.

"Men, let me say that each of you has endured much more then me, have shown more courage than I, the stories about me, are overblown. Now help me out here, and tell me what you want the governor to know."

One lieutenant stood up, "Sir, tell him, thanks for the supplies, and our love to our families."

"That's right." Another soldier said.

"We can always use canteens," one solder said

Another soldier said, "shoes, always shoes."

"And socks," another soldier yelled out.

At that point, the men all stood up, Colonel McDowell was walking up behind me. I turned and saluted.

"Be at ease men," the colonel said, "Parks, we need to be going."

"Yes sir," I turned back towards the men, "well thank you for the visit, and good luck."

One of the lieutenants called attention as we walked away. McDowell led me back to his tent, where he put on his blouse, and we mounted to ride to General Early's headquarters. When we arrived some of the separate staff officers were coming in, Jackson and Early were off on a walk. We saw them engaged as they came back towards the headquarters.

Early's other brigade commanders arrived, and after them, the remaining staff groups that had been conducting the inspection arrived.

Early's Chief of Staff had amassed cooks so as to make enough food for all the men present. The two wagons that had traveled to the Chapel at Hamilton's Crossing to pick up the benches we would sit on, were parked nearby.

As we sat there eating, I marveled at the fact we were not two miles from the Federal front line. But things had been quiet, not even shots fired between the pickets.

Sandie Pendleton came up to General Jackson to remind him of the time, and that we had to get back to Belvoir, to escort Mrs. Jackson to Hamilton's Crossing.

* * * *

Kyd Douglas had ridden to the west to Corbin Hall to gather up some women who were coming over to visit Anna, and then to accompany her to the Review that afternoon. General Jackson had stayed at Richard Corbin's home at Mossy Neck before moving to the Yerby's. While at the Corbin's, he had met little six-year-old Janie, and had spent Christmas with her and the family. A real connection had developed between the two. But Janie had gotten sick before Jackson left the Corbin's, and died shortly after. It was very hard on the general.

Captain Douglas, accompanied by Captain Stockton Heath escorted a number of women from Corbin Hall to Belvoir on the morning of the 27th. They would visit with Anna first, before they all left for the review later in the day.

It was Kyd's first time with Anna and Julia. Anna wanting to demonstrate family love for Douglas, passed Julia over to him. But he was not sure of himself with the baby. Julia sensed it, and grew cranky. At that moment the General walked in, returning from Early's visit. Sensing Julia's uneasiness with Kyd, Jackson called on the nurse, amidst much laughter by the ladies, to take the baby.

That afternoon was spent accompanying an ambulance carrying Mrs. Jackson and Mrs. O'Neal and Mr. Yerby to Hamilton Crossing for the Review by Colston's Division, and then returning. Their ambulance was followed by a carriage with the women from Corbin's. I had never witnessed a Review, and was not sure exactly what it would be.

Though some clouds had gathered around noon, almost on cue, as if God enjoyed a Review, the sky cleared.

It was impressive to see an entire division formed into regiments, by brigades across a plain. Colston's Morning Report had shown a little more than 6,700 bayonets present for duty.

Reviews were a kind of social event, both for the locals and for the officers of the Army and especially the Second Corps. The Corbin women were joined by what seemed to be hundreds of civilians from the local area came, dressed in their finest. And somehow, a band had been formed and played music as General Jackson, mounted on Little Sorrell, accompanied by General Colston, trooped the line, inspecting the units. As they rode by each regiment, the soldiers on command came to present arms.

The silver flash of the bayonets as they moved from order arms to present arms ... and back again. The sounds of the hundreds of men raising their arms at a time, and then the thud of moving them sharply back to ground on crisp orders is a sound a soldier will never forget. The battle flags and national colors flying, the sounds that accompany formations movements echoing. It was magnificent.

The rest of day was spent back in the yard at the Yerby's. That evening, around the fire, I got to spend time with Douglas, Hotchkiss, Sandie Pendleton, and the others listening to their stories and resting.

One thing I did not know at the time, and would not know until I got back to the 21st Century, Colonel McDowell would be killed at Chancellorsville.

* * * *

April 28th was another day of activity. Divisions were moving from their winter deployments on the Rappahannock miles south of Fredericksburg, closer to their December battle positions. Both Generals Lee and Jackson sensed activity by the Yankees. J. E. B. Stuart discovered Yankee movement north, east of the Rappahannock River.

I spent the day visiting North Carolina Regiments in Rode's Division. I inspected Phoenix's footwear as the veterans were sure ... battle was coming. I also cleaned my weapon.

General Jackson spent as much time with Anna and Julia as possible. He knew things were about to change and that they would have to be leaving.

General Jackson had received a gift, a beautiful bay horse named Superior. The horse was much larger than Little Sorrel and the General displayed his riding skill for Anna atop this gorgeous new mount. He galloped across the front yard for his admiring wife.

At the camp fire that night, speculation about the coming battle was the topic of conversation. Though many thought Hooker would move against our Army's left flank, none predicted what was about to happen.

At one point during the evening, I took the opportunity to speak with Dr. McGuire alone. I told him that my wife was supposed to have provided some new medicine to Mrs. Jackson when they visited. I advised him it was from Europe, and that it was supposed to be helpful with pneumonia.

Dr. McGuire was very interested. He said he had never heard of such a thing. He would ask Anna if he could see it, the next time he saw her. McGuire would not see Anna again, until after May 2nd. But she would still arrive in time to possibly make a difference, if the medicine were used, if Jackson were wounded.

I still had no absolute plan on how to prevent what was about to happen. It may be that Jeanne Marie's second option would be all that could change history.

"Belvoir"
Jackson's Headquarters
April 29th

I was up before the sun, I couldn't sleep. My knowledge of history is pretty good, and I knew things were fixin' to get exciting this morning — the Battle of Chancellorsville was about to begin.

The General's cook, Jim Lewis was already at work, a large pot of coffee was steaming over the fire. And you could hear him cutting meat on a wooden board. The smell of biscuits baking made me hungry. Because there was no sound, not even birds singing, the noises Jim made in his preparation of food were distinct.

I was shaving when a rider galloped into camp and was taken up the steps of Belvoir by Kyd to the General. I learned the rider was General Early's adjutant.

He wasn't in there long, before he re-appeared, mounted and quickly rode off. Kyd came down and went to Darby and Sandie Pendleton who were both dressing. General Early had sent his adjutant to advise Jackson the Yankee General Hooker was on the move, pushing across the river in force. The staff moved rapidly through their morning routine.

Sandie looked at me, "Be ready to go sir." He yelled to Captains Douglas and Hotchkiss and Lt. Morrison "Be ready to move." After rolling bed rolls, we all headed to the horse line to saddle our horses.

One of the orderlies at the horse line knew to saddle Little Sorrel, and take it up to the house. He was standing there, when the General came out. Jackson looked in our direction and headed to the road, assuming we would ride to him. We did.

We headed towards Early's division at a fast pace. The firing grew steadily louder as we moved closer.

General Jackson looked at Lt. Morrison "Joe, I want you to take an ambulance to your sister Anna, and use that to evacuate her and Julia back to the railroad station."

"Thomas, please, can't someone else do it, I should be here at my duty, sir." Being the General's brother-in-law, Joe Morrison did not want to be removed from danger because of that fact.

Jackson thought for a moment, he handed a note to Lt. Morrison, "OK, tell Chaplain Lacy to take an ambulance and take Anna and Julia to the railroad and give him this note for Anna."

Morrison took the note, "Yes, sir." He spun his horse and was off to Lacy.

We spent the rest of the day accepting reports and watching.

The Yankees crossed the Rappahannock and spread out in front of Early's division. Early's division was protected by the rise of rail line. It was a face off. General Sedgewick commanded the Corps facing Early. Federal artillery lined Stafford Heights on the other side of the river.

While there was activity in front of Early, the real action was to our left. Stuart had heard large formations of Yankees moving north on the opposite side of the river. But he did not know how many, or who. General Lee ordered General Anderson to ready his division to move west towards Chancellorsville.

* * * *

Back at the Yerby House the thunder of artillery firing shook the house and the glass in the windows. Anna had never experienced anything like it, and of course Julie was scared and crying loudly when Reverend Lacy rode up to the house. Jim Lewis was standing near the front door, as a guard.

"Jim, please go get us an ambulance to carry Anna and Julia to Guiney Station," Reverend Lacy said as he bounded up the stairs.

"Yes, suh," Jim said as he took off towards the ambulance park.

"Anna, we have to get you two to Guiney Station for the train back to Richmond," the Reverend said. He handed her the note from her husband. More cannon fire shook the house, putting an exclamation mark on Lacy's words; "Let's go."

Jackson sent one of his aides to Lee to inform him of the movements. Lee who had expected things to begin to heat up told the aide to tell Jackson:

"Well, I heard the firing, and I was beginning to think that it was time some of your lazy young fellows were coming to tell me what it was about. Tell your good general he knows what to do with the enemy just as well as I do." [5]

The day was spent running messages to Jackson's Divisions south of Fredericksburg. They needed to move north back to positions they had held before. Yankee observation towers and balloons on the high

---

5 Quote from *Stonewall Jackson & the American Civil War*, P.415 Lt. Col G.F.R. Henderson, C.B.

The Adventure – Stolen Days

ground east of the river were watching us. Off to the north we could hear cannons firing, J. E. B. Stuart's Cavalry was contesting infantry crossings miles upriver.

* * * *

Robert E. Lee

Catherine Furnace.
May 1st, 1863

April 30th had been a day of waiting for Jackson, the Yankees were moving, there was great energy on their side of the line. But, on our side it was a time to wait and discover their plans and directions.

By April 30, General Lee had recognized the threat from the west-northwest and had directed the divisions of General McLaws and Anderson towards Chancellorsville. Their job was to find and fix the Yankee forces coming from that direction. Lee had decided to leave only General Early with his division, reinforced to hold Fredericksburg. Jackson's Corps was pulling itself together.

The brigades of Anderson's and McLaws' divisions were engaged throughout the day with the advance elements of Hooker's Army. The firing was constant, creating great stress on each of us. The close proximity of the fighting, the inability to see anything because of the thick woods, created a sense of urgency that at any moment we might be overwhelmed. I could see it on almost every face, though not Stonewall's.

Late on the 30th, Lee directed : "General Jackson, I need you to bring up your Corps on the Plank Road behind and to the left of General Anderson."

* * * *

Jackson was up just after midnight on the 1st, and began to rouse his divisions for the march to support Anderson and McLaws. The troops were moving by eight o'clock.[6]

Jackson understood that the two divisions had created an impression in front of Hooker, that much more of Lee's Army was in front of him.

"Colonel Walter, the thickness of this wilderness is helping the few look mighty," General Jackson said to me, "Hooker's boys have stopped advancing because they don't know how few or big we are! Once again, God is with us." And there was a light in his blue eyes, the light I had read about in so many history books.

It took the better part of the day for the general to move his scattered divisions, more than twenty thousand infantry, as directed by

---

6 Pg 458, *Mighty Stonewall*, Frank E. Vandiver

Lee. Ambrose Hill's Division was first, followed by Generals Rodes' and Colston's Divisions.

General Lee caught up to Jackson and traveled with him for awhile. Satisfied with Jackson's plans and actions, Lee turned back to find Anderson and McLaws.

As the Corps closed up behind Anderson, Stuart came riding down the plank road around dusk.

"General Stuart," Jackson said as he came close, "Have you been up that lane to see what we can see?" Jackson was pointing up a trail towards Catherine Furnace. With staffs behind them, and grabbing a battery of artillery, the two headed up the wagon trail.

The one thing I had learned from riding with Jackson during battle, was that he led from the front, was fearless, never afraid to ride forward of the troops so he could see the battlefield better, and Little Sorrell responded each time, quickly. Joe Morrison, the general's brother-in-law was always on Stonewall's right.

The knoll that Catherine Furnace sat on was not large at all, but it did provide sufficient elevation to allow us to see large areas to north and west. Stonewall immediately pulled out his field glasses to scan his front.

Following the generals was an artillery battery of Stuart's cavalry. They quickly deployed on the ground, found targets and opened fire. The problem with that was that the Yankee artillery quickly organized counter-battery fire and we came under heavy fire within minutes.

The accuracy of the Yankee guns was terrifying. Rounds were whistling through the air, clumps of dirt flying up as cannon balls hit the ground. Except for Little Sorrell, the horses were rearing and winnowing. Kyd Douglas lost control of his mount when his reins were sliced by a piece of shrapnel; another piece tore a piece of paper from his hand. One of Stuart's aides was hit. I grabbed Little Sorrell's bridle, and with the help of Phoenix, jerked him around. Jackson spurred him, and they were off. The next instant a shell landed where Jackson had been. Had I just saved his life?

In moments we were back on the Plank Road. The incident, just another moment in battle for Jackson and Stuart, they turned west on the Plank Road and kept moving forward.

Ramseur's brigade was now in the lead on the road, and the command group trotted west looking for the forward troops of the brigade.

Jackson's entire Corps was now on the plank road, he was driving the Yankees back to Chancellorsville house with just his lead brigade.

"Stuart, we have got to find another place to see the Yankee line," Jackson said.

And so the day went, constant contact, nowhere to deploy a Corps on the attack.

The last meeting of Generals Lee and Jackson
Evening of May 1st, 1863

It was after dark when Generals Lee and Jackson met at a small clearing at the intersection of Furnace Road and Orange Plank Road.

When we rode up to the crossroads, General Lee was already there, sitting on a wooden cracker box near a fire with a map stretched out in front of him. I took the reins for Little Sorrel, and Jackson walked up to General Lee, saluted and took a seat on another box. They spoke quietly, looks of concern on both their faces. The situation was grim, Hooker's army nearly surrounded us, and Lee knew he was outnumbered at least two to one.

The fire light cast the faces of the two men in a very unique image. They spoke quietly, too quiet for me to hear.

The site of the meeting seemed Divinely inspired — two great men seeking salvation on this hallowed ground. The battle had gone well, to a point, but nothing had been found which could change the present situation. Greatly outnumbered, no weakness had yet been found to attack. Only Hooker's hesitation had prevented disaster.

After tying the horses to a branch, I had just sat down, my back against a tree, when I heard the recognizable thunder of a small group of horses headed in our direction from the west. When I looked, the silhouette gliding against the darkness was now unmistakable to me, it was General Stuart and his small band.

Stuart dismounted, and hurriedly moved towards the two generals at the fire, "I've found it!" He proclaimed, louder than I am sure the two generals expected. Stuart was animated, his hands flying in the air, occasionally pointing west.

General Lee calmed his young cavalry commander, and the three closed in a circle to talk. Stuart's gloved hands flew over the map as he continued his telling of his discovery.

"Sir their right flank is in the air, they are acting more like it is their rear area, than their flank." Stuart reported.

Lee and Jackson studied the map, it was a good day's march to cross in front of a large part of the Yankee Army in order to get their extreme right flank. "Is there a road to get there?" Jackson inquired of Stuart.

Stuart said there was a local farmer who knew a road that could get them there.

A plan was offered by Jackson, "I will take my entire Corps and attack."

General Lee inquired: "And what will you leave me."

Anderson and McLaws was all that could be left. And there it was. Two divisions would occupy Hooker's force for a day, while Jackson's twenty thousand bayonets marched to get completely around the Yankees.

* * * *

A damp coolness settled over the ground during the evening of the 1st after Jackson had issued his orders for the morning. General Jackson was not personally prepared for the change, Jim and his wagon were nowhere to be found.

The orders had been issued and the general looked for a place to sleep. Jackson did the best he could to use the clothing he was wearing to provide for his warmth. J. P. Smith, one of Jackson's aide de camps offered the general his cape.

"No thank you Lt. Smith" Jackson replied.

"Sir, I have to stay up in case riders come in, please take my cape, sir." Smith went on.

The general reluctantly took the cape, thanking Smith for his consideration. So, for a time, the general was somewhat protected from the weather. Maybe an hour later, I noticed the general got up and saw Smith sleeping nearby. He walked over and covered the lieutenant with the cape, then returned to his place on the ground, laid back down and went to sleep; exposed to the damp cold that would bring a cold in the morning. [7]

A small thing, but I did not think to cover the general with my blanket. Something I will ponder for the rest of my life.

---

7 P. 214, *I Rode with Stonewall*, Henry Kyd Douglas.

The Adventure – Stolen Days

The Great Gamble
May 2nd, 1863

It was about six thirty when I felt a push on my shoulder. I was asleep, sitting against a tree. The night had been very busy, things had to happen after Generals Lee and Jackson met, and it was hours before I got to dismount, take the saddle off Phoenix, tie him to the tree, and sit down next to him. Another push on my shoulder, stronger than the first, I had to look. It was Phoenix pushing his large head against me. The sun was just coming up.

Oh, my back hurt. I had to turn on my side to get a leg underneath me, and rise.

By now, I had learned how precious moments were early in the morning, and took a step to my saddle, reached down and grabbed a feed bag with oats, and put it over Phoenix' head and let it hang down to his mouth. I already knew today would be a very long day.

I reached into a saddle bag for one of the biscuits Jim had given to each of us a couple of days ago, and a metal cup. I then turned and stumbled towards the General.

"Morning, Parks," General Jackson said.

"Morning sir," I replied, taking a bite from the biscuit.

"As soon as you get something in your stomach, get on the road for General Rodes and tell him, I want to move as soon as possible."

"Yes sir," I saluted, turned and went back to saddle Phoenix and get on to General Rodes. I mounted, got out on the Orange Plank Road and headed down the road. Soldiers were waking, and standing, stretching, rolling a bed roll and getting themselves ready to move. Everyone had more or less fallen at their last position on the line last night. The orders that had gone out the night before had said be ready to move at first light. But, that did not happen, this entire wing of the army had fought well into the night.

The Fateful Volley
May 2d, 1863
Chancellorsville, Virginia[8]
After Dark, May 2nd, 1863

The Southern men who leaned against trees, resting on one knee were exhausted, exhilarated, frightened, determined. Most importantly, they were in full warrior spirit. They rested momentarily, in the dark, waiting. Some may have been thinking of what they just accomplished.

After several days of hurry up and wait, hearing the battle all around them, but not actually being too involved in it, now they were at the very center of its vortex. The day started with a twelve-mile forced march, beginning at eight o'clock. Once they got behind the Yankees, they formed in to three divisional lines of battle, brigades abreast, a mile wide. Three divisions of Stonewall Jackson's Corps deployed in three lines, one behind the other, a hundred yards between each line two ranks deep. They formed these lines in a thick wood filled with vines and brush. They were facing the entire right wing of the federal army.

They formed these lines in silence, making no sound. Surprise was the key to this operation, and all 24,000 Confederate veterans were savvy enough from their combat experience to remain completely silent. They waited patiently for the order.

The Federal's Eleventh Corps was sitting in front of them, completely unaware of Jackson's 24,000 bayonets preparing to burst upon them. Thousands of men of the Eleventh Corps were preparing their dinner over small fires. You were as likely to hear German as English. Their day had been quiet, uneventful. Their rifles were stacked amongst their tents. Men were relaxed, playing cards, or instruments, or just resting, completely unaware a mighty whirlwind was about to fall on them.

That had been four hours earlier, around five pm. But now, it was dark, the Confederate attack had been like a tsunami wave, completely overwhelming and literally washing away the Yankee line in blood and gray.

---

8 Much of the information, and some of the dialogue in this section was taken from *All Things for God, The Steadfast Fidelity of Thomas Jackson*, by J. Stevens Wilkins

The three waves of Confederates moved at a speed only dreamed of in tactics' classrooms around the world. Very few soldiers, in all of history, had ever participated in an attack so unexpected by their enemy. All of the Federals had been caught unawares, and facing ninety degrees in the wrong direction. The Federal line faced south, but the enemy burst upon them from the west. The first evidence of the attack was the sound of the rebel yell on the Federal's right; a stampede of deer, rabbits, raccoons, and birds who were flushed by Jackson's men rushed from the woods, harbingers of the Rebel charge. It was 5:15 pm.

At first, the sight of dozens of different wild life rushing towards the Yankees from the tree line was amusing. But the smiles of amusement changed to looks of disbelief, and then to terror as the gray ranks broke out of the woods.

Now, these Confederates had driven for more than a mile in to thick woods encountering and destroying small, rallying groups of Yankees again and again. As the Confederates moved further and further east, the sun moved further and further west, darkness settling over the battlefield. The chaos caused by a complete surprise attack only became more confused as visibility shrank first to feet, then to inches. Moonlight was blocked by the thick canopy over top of both the Confederate and Yankee forces. Only the Plank Road allowed the moonlight to break through and illuminate a thin sliver of the Wilderness.

These men, known as Jackson's foot cavalry had experienced many a forced march with their famous commander. They had known victory on many fields, and they had seen their general almost glow on the battlefield, as he directed the thunderbolts which were his man. They had seen General Jackson, like a Biblical figure sit atop his horse Little Sorrel, and raise his right arm to the sky during battle, almost guiding the battle with his mind.

As exhausted as they were, as hungry and thirsty, and sore as they were, they sensed from their commander that this fight could be the one that finally crushed the Army of the Potomac. They "field cleaned" their weapons, checked their ammunition, tried to eat something from a pocket, or find even a sip of water, while they waited for the order they knew would come, the command to continue on the attack.

On both sides of the Plank Road which ran east and west, hundreds of gray clad soldiers waited. These men knew the men standing beside them, they had all come from the same farms and small villages near Charlotte and Salisbury, North Carolina. They were neighbors, kin, friends, who had served together for more than a year. All were part of James Lane's brigade.

As they loaded their muskets, they heard a group of mounted officers' riding on the road between them. The sound was unmistakable, the clanking of swords, the clodding sound of walking the horses. It was not a large formation, twenty or so horses, maybe.

Amongst the officers and couriers some of the soldiers could make out Thomas Jackson their Corps Commander, wearing his famous kepi hat. Lt. Morrison, an aide, and Jackson's brother-in-law road near him. General A. P. Hill and some of his aides were in the group.

A second group of officers, including Dr. McGuire, Jackson's Medical Officer and Sandi Pendleton, Jackson's Assistant Adjutant, were about a hundred yards back down the road to the west.

"There he is," one private in the line whispered to anyone listening.

"Yes sirree," that be the Stonewall thar," another proclaimed with a tinge of delight in his voice.

"He's huntin' Yankees," yet another said as he took a bite of an early peach not ripe, but needed anyway.

"We be fixin' to finish this fight tonight, I reckon." The first said as the group of mounted men moved forward in front of them down the road bathed in a soft yellow glow.

Minutes passed, the fighting had died down to intermittent shots, some cannons firing, flashes of light and then the booms. Sounds of canister or mini balls sizzling above their heads, cutting branches and leaves.

Then there were the sound of hooves, many hooves thundering straight down the road towards the Confederate line. Though the men gripped their rifles tightly, they remembered the party that had gone out in front and hesitated to shoulder their arms. All of sudden, a mass of a Yankee cavalry milling around in the road, fired their pistols at the Confederate line. Surprised, the Confederates fired haphazardly, some aiming, some just firing. Company officers yelling, sergeants trying to regain control of their troops.

The cavalry realized they were engaging infantry, and way too many for them to get into a long gun fight with, they turned quickly, firing their pistols as they raced away. But, as the Yankee cavalry departed, heavy skirmishing opened hundreds of yards to their front. Tensions rose as the smell of gun powder wafted back through the woods to them. Men, tired, exhausted men tried to squeeze their eyes to see in the darkness.

Moments passed, the firing in front flared up from time to time. Then there were the sound of hooves coming down the road again. Yankee canons fired down the road, flashes blinding men, and the horses on the road seemed to rush forward.

A shot, then a spattering of shots, then a volley first from the Confederates south side of the road. Men fell, Thomas Jackson was hit in the right hand, losing the reigns. One of the couriers next to General Jackson fell dead. Little Sorrel, Jackson's horse, was hit, and spun and bolted toward the Yankee line. The General grabbed the reign with his wounded right hand and turned Sorrel back towards the Confederate line.

The mounted men yelled, "Cease fire, you are shooting into your own people."

But, Major John Barry, an officer of the line, yelled, "They are lying boys, pour it into them men." A second volley was fired, from the north side of the road, two rounds hitting Jackson in the left arm. Sorrel bolted again, a tree branch catching the General in the upper body, slapping his face, knocking off his kepi, and almost knocking him out of the saddle. Captain Wilbourn, an aide, caught Little Sorrell, pulling him into the woods. Private Wynn one of the couriers was able to bring Sorrel to a halt. Wilbourn and Wynn lifted Jackson from his horse and laid him beneath a small tree. Wilbourn sent Wynn to find Dr. Mc-Guire.

Immediately, Wilbourn began wrapping Jackson's wounds to stop the bleeding.

Lt. Morrison's horse had been shot from under him. Wounded and dead men and horses lay in the road. The groans of men, and the screeching whinnies of horses added to the cacophony of battle.

Wilbourn asked: "Sir, are you hurt seriously?"

General Jackson replied, "I believe my left arm is broken."

General A. P. Hill rode up, and dismounted, and knelt down next to Jackson: "I am sorry to see you wounded, and hope you are not hurt much."

Jackson said, "My arm is broken."

Hill asked: "Is it painful?"

"Very painful."

"Are you hurt anywhere else?"

"Yes, a slight wound in the right hand."

Hill sat on the ground next to Jackson, who was lying on his back, and placed his commander's head gently in his lap. Just at that moment, two Yankee infantrymen pushed through the woods, surprised to find their rifles pointing at the two generals. Hill looked up at them, and said quietly, "Take charge of those men." Several Confederate officers moved quickly forward, and took the weapons from the startled soldiers.

General Hill, as the senior division commander had to move, he was now the commander of Jackson's Corps, and the entire force was waiting on word to continue the attack. As he left, Hill said to Jackson; "I will try to keep your accident from the knowledge of the troops."

General Jackson nodded and said: "thank you."

Dr. Barr, from A. P. Hill's Division arrived and began work on Jackson. He said there was nothing more that could be done there and that the general needed to be moved to the rear.

Lt. Morrison went to the road, observed the Yankees positioning a section of artillery about two hundred yards down the road from their current position, and rushed back to the group gathered around the general: "We've got to get him out of here, now!"

General Jackson rose to stand, and was aided by placing an arm on the shoulder of an aide, and with Lt. Morrison at his other side, he made his way towards the road and then towards the Confederate line. A group of soldiers moving in the opposite direction were attracted by the large group of officers helping one man off the field.

One of the soldiers got close enough to recognize Jackson and exclaimed: "Great God, that's General Jackson."

As they continued down the road a litter team arrived. Jackson was placed in the litter.

Four men that included Morrison, Leigh, Private James and another lifted the litter and began carrying Jackson back towards the rear. Another volley of fire came from the Yankees. A piece of shrapnel hit James, and he went down; the front right corner of the litter fell, bringing down all the other men; Jackson landed on his broken arm, groaning in pain.

The Yankee artillery on the road opened fire, chasing the men carrying Jackson into the wood. As they attempted to make their way through the tangled wood, once again the General was dropped when a bearer got tangled in vines. Again Jackson fell on his wounded arm and moaned in agony.

The men scrambled to get back up. At that moment, General Pender rode up: "Sir, I am going to have to withdraw my men as the lines are tangled and disorganized."

General Jackson lifted his head and upper body and ordered "General Pender hold your ground. Hold your ground, sir."

Once again, the litter bearers started to move, and though very painful for the general, they finally got him out of harm's way, and to an ambulance at Stony Fork Road. Colonel Crutchfield, Jackson's artillery chief was in the ambulance with a leg would. Another officer, with a lesser wound volunteered to give up his place for the General. Meanwhile Dr. William Whitehead fixed some whiskey with water and gave it to the General to help him cope with the pain.

The ambulance began moving, but continued the torture as it had faulty springs, the patients feeling every jarring bump.

When the ambulance finally made it to Dowdall's Tavern, the group was joined by Dr. McGuire, Jackson's friend and personal doctor. McGuire spoke with Jackson who said he thought his wound was still bleeding. McGuire confirmed that it was, and that the General had lost quite a lot of blood. McGuire redid the tourniquet so as to stop the bleeding and provided more whiskey for the pain.

The wagon proceeded down the road and at 11 PM reached the Wilderness Tavern where a field hospital had been established. Jackson was moved to a tent, wrapped in blankets and allowed to rest. His pulse was too weak and erratic for any serious examination of the wound at that time.

Dr. McGuire checked Jackson's pulse every hour, and at 2 AM he found the pulse strong enough to examine the wound.

"Thomas, I am going to give you some chloroform which will put you to sleep, and then I am going to examine your arm."

"OK, Hunter."

"If I need to, may I amputate your arm?"

"Of course, Hunter, do what you think best for me." Jackson replied.

The operation to remove Jackson's arm was successful, and he is later moved to Guiney Station where he was joined by Anna his wife, and Julia his infant daughter.

For a time, General Jackson begins to recover. But a cold, turns into pneumonia, the eventual cause of his death. Thomas Jackson passes over the river on Sunday, May 10, 1863.

* * * *

I had separated from Jackson's command party because of Darby's orders to collect up those soldiers on the turnpike that could be sent forward. It was a moment I will never forget, when I realized I would not be near the general when the volley would be fired that would wound him.

But the orders were clear, "Move to the rear and push troops forward."

I was surprised to find so many men who had, for their own reasons, fallen out of the attacking columns. Yes, there were wounded scattered all along the road, and on each side, and yes some of those soldiers who were not wounded were caring for those down. But there were some, many, just sitting on the road, with their rifles between their legs.

Wherever I saw an NCO, a noncommissioned officer, I tried to encourage them to do their duty and collect small groups of soldiers and press them forward.

It was dark, and not easy to see. Phoenix kept us on the road. I was so tired. Days of combat tension placed a heavy burden on me. At this point, I had to begin my long return home; first to Charlottesville, then to Hattie's farm, and then back through space-time to Rebel Mountain. I needed to try to make some miles tonight, if I had stayed with Jackson through to the inevitable incident, I would not be able to make it Charlottesville by the time appointed.

Vicinity of Greenwood, east of Gordonsville, Virginia
May 3rd

I had only gotten a few hours of sleep the night before. The battle on the 2nd had required more human energy than I had ever expended before. I actually fell asleep before I hit the ground in the early hours of the 3rd. But after only a couple of hours, I was awake. I knew it was close to sixty miles between Chancellorsville and Charlottesville. Last night I had made it as far as Locust Grove.

It was still going to be forty miles to Shadwell, where the landing zone was. The question was could Phoenix, do it? There wasn't any time to think about it. I was mounted and riding before the sun up. We had about 18 hours.

Most of the day was riding hard, mixed with walking Phoenix, feeding him, watering him. But I had to keep moving. This was by far the most physically difficult part of the entire mission. There weren't any enemy soldiers, in fact few people anywhere.

As dusk came, I was within ten miles of the landing zone. All I could do was keep pushing Phoenix, and myself. We arrived in the general area around eleven thirty, and I was exhausted. I had to get my saddle bags off and go through them for the equipment I needed, and take the saddle and other rigging off a very tired Phoenix.

I was exhausted, but I had to check the landing zone, and place out my beacon and lights so that Jeanne Marie could find me.

Finally, I had to unsaddle Phoenix. ...

Hattie's Farm
Mt. Airy, North Carolina
12 am, 4th May 1863

Michael was standing directly in front of the *Alabama*, the cord from his headset hanging to one side one side of his head as he gave the hand signals, whirling the flashlights to his sister indicating she was clear to fire up the engine.

A low hum, quickly rising to a higher and louder pitch began when Jeanne Marie hit the ignition button. Jeanne Marie thought to herself, it was kind of surreal as the pitch moved so quickly while the blades themselves barely moved.

Meanwhile when she looked forward Michael was gone, she heard the side door slamming shut, and then static in her headset as Michael moved to the engineer seat and plugged in his cord, "hatch is secure, over" Michael report.

"Roger, strap in." Jeanne Marie said almost robotically as she focused on her dials and gages, the blades now moving more quickly overhead. She gave the throttle a slight twist to increase the flow of gasoline to the engine.

"All my instruments are up," Roger said as he hit his blue light which provided a glow over his area. Screens were flickering. An electronic compass dead center of the arrangement. "We are going to be bearing right as we lift to a heading of three five degrees true."

"Roger," Jeanne Marie was doing her final pre–lift check, as she increased the throttle and pulled back on the handset. The *Alabama* jarred, and lifted, slowly at first, then faster and angling forward to the right. The darkness of the surrounding trees, topped by a sky lit by a million stars.

They elevated quickly in a whirl of wind–blowing sounds never heard in this time in North Carolina. Their speed increased, both in gaining height and moving away from the barnyard. They were off, running without lights, except for those in the cockpit, and at Michael's station.

The days had passed quickly since Jeanne Marie's return from Virginia.

While Jeanne Marie was gone, Michael had realized that every gallon of JP4 fuel was vital for the *Alabama*, not just for the trip to pick up Parks, but for the flight home. He and George Washington had gone back to the original crash site of the vehicle Michael had flown and crashed. They were able to locate the fuel pods, and drain out about twenty gallons of JP4. They carried it in a wagon to the barn. George Washington did not go in the barn with Michael, and they never talked about it. Like other secrets, it was just one more George Washington would keep to himself.

It was a relief for Jeanne Marie when Michael advised her of his revelation, and ability to secure additional fuel for the *Alabama*. This unexpected flight really was outside the capabilities of a bird with an original range of 280 miles. Its capabilities had been increased in the years before the trip through many improvements made by Reece and the engineers back on Rebel Mountain. Heavy armor plating had been removed, an American fuel system replaced the original Russian system, and an advanced JP4 that could be used in a leaner mixture so as to burn less fuel per mile all had made this ad hoc addition of the mission possible.

Reece will want to know how important his innovations had been when we get back, Jeanne Marie thought.

"When should you pick up Park's signal, over" asked Jeanne Marie.

"Well, I am hoping fifty miles out, but we'll see," replied Michael as he monitored his screens. Without 20th century lights, GPS systems, satellites and beams on the ground, the two relied on the compass and the side view radar that provided a topographical look at the ground.

Jeanne Marie checked her clock on the dash, extraction was set for 1 am. The flight of 156 miles would not take an hour.

"I have the beacon, come right to four zero degrees, three zero miles out, over."

"Roger, four zero!" There was an excitement in Jeanne Marie's voice.

"I am gonna start our infra-red, and thermo scans to see if we have anything to worry about down there, Jeanne Marie," reported Michael. This was the main reason Michael had to go on the flight. Everything had to be done to conceal, or limit exposure of the *Alabama* at the landing zone.

After about twenty minutes Jeanne Marie reported; "I see, the lights," and *Alabama* adjusted in flight to head directly for the lights.

"Everything seems pretty quiet down there, I am not seeing any large bodies of men down there, just a herd of something off to the north," Michael reported to Jeanne Marie.

"On my way down, over" Jeanne Marie's voice was calm.

"Opening the side hatch," Michael reported. … Michael felt the *Alabama* meet the ground, it was a little rough. He looked out the door into the darkness seeing nothing. Out of nowhere, a saddle came flying into the bird, followed by a large man throwing in saddle bags. Michael awkwardly moved backward trying to drag the equipment.

Parks tried to yell over the blast, "I have to pick up the lights." He turned and disappeared into the darkness.

"Is he in Michael?" Jeanne Marie asked.

"No, he stepped away, hold on a minute." Michael replied.

Jeanne Marie saw a shadow step in front of the landing light directly in front of her, and realized what Parks was doing.

After collecting the lights, Parks returned to the hatch of the *Alabama*, threw the lights in and then jumped into the compartment and slammed forward the hatch.

"He's in," Michael yelled into the mic, "let's get out of here."

The bird lifted, even before Michael finished his sentence. The pick up was complete.

The *Alabama* rose quickly turning to the right for heading two one zero. Jeanne Marie took her up to three thousand feet and pushed the throttle forward.

Michael handed Parks, who was scrawled on the deck, and thrown back against the wall by the G forces from Jeanne Marie's actions, a headset.

"Test," both Michael and Jeanne Marie heard, as Parks spoke into the mic.

"Good to see you," Michael responded.

"Hi," Parks could imagine a smile on Jeanne Marie's face when he heard her voice.

"Thanks for the lift," he responded to both.

The flight southwest proceeded without incident, Jeanne Marie was amazed at the beauty of the stars, stars never seen in twenty–first century America because of all the ground lights. And after about an hour she picked up the chimney-like silhouette of Mt. Airy. It was this silhouette, recognized by Nash during the early planning of the mission that had led this entire effort through this area of North Carolina. I must have dozed for a few moments — but then heard.

"I have the beacon at Hattie's," Michael reported, "start your approach decline and prepare to turn left on my mark."

I don't recall the landing sequence at all. The last thing I do remember from that night is they helped me to a waiting wagon and I fell asleep.

Fixin' to go home
May 3rd, 1863

I slept most of the day on May 3rd. The past couple days I had not gotten much sleep at all. Jeanne Marie woke me about 5 pm.

"Time to get up sleepy head," Jeanne Marie was bending over the bed. Her hand was in my hair. "Parks, we need to get you up and packed, and get some dinner before we head down to the barn."

"Ughh, stretched out. I had no idea how bad I smelled. I had not taken a bath since Belvoir in the creek. I probably had an amalgam of scents on me including gun powder, smoke, and sweat.

I grabbed Jeanne Marie and kissed her. "Mrs. Jackson was very impressed with you," I said.

Startled by the kiss, or my comment I did not know which?

Her voice raised in pitch as Jeanne Marie asked "You met Mrs. Jackson?"

"I not only met her, I had dinner with the Jacksons and two other people at Belvoir." I replied. "Yes, the Yerby mansion, near Hamilton's Crossing, where the Jacksons stayed."

"OK, and?" She said looking at me.

"Well, you made a strong impression with her, as did Micah and Jimmie Earle." I went on, "And the story that was covered in the Mt. Airy Gazette, which Mrs. Stuart wrote to her son, the general about. And those things helped earn the General's trust."

"They knew about the story?" She asked.

"Yes, they did, and they told me about it. I can tell you, I was surprised."

"Well if I helped you, that's important." Jeanne Marie, got up, and turned away, but asked, "Did she say anything about the medicine I gave her."

"No she didn't," I said.

"Uh huh, OK boy let's get moving." She said

"Maybe I should take a bath," I offered.

"That wouldn't hurt. I washed your clothes today."

"You did?" I asked.

"I did, I threw them out the window last night," she laughed. "Pew. It was pretty bad."

"So, what do I wear to the creek?" I asked.

"I don't know, let me ask Hattie. She headed out of the room and down the stairs. In a few moments she came back up and headed towards Hattie's room. She came back with man's night coat and threw it on me. "Here ya go, now get moving." And she was gone.

I headed down to the creek and found myself collecting men and children from around the farm including George Washington and Micah.

"Thank you Micah, for all you did for Jeanne Marie, and Jimmie Earle." Just as I said that Jimmie Earle ran up to me, and jumped onto me.

"Hello Uncle Parks," he said.

"Hi, Jimmie Earle, how are you doing?"

"Well, I am fine, sir. How might you be?" He smiled.

"I am pretty good. Did you have a good time with Jeanne Marie and Micah?"

"You betcha, we did some really cool things." I put him down.

George Washington offered his hand, "Good to see you sir."

"I would say the same thing." Micah then offered his hand, "Great to see you Micah, and can I tell you that even General Jackson knows who you are?"

"He does?" Micah said.

"He sure does, Anna Jackson was very complimentary of you when she talked about you, and Jimmie Earle."

"She talked about me?" Jimmie Earle said, looking at Micah.

We were almost to the creek when Ruth came running up with my uniform and some underwear. She handed them to me. "Hello Ruth." I said.

"Hello suh, I am so glad you have returned."

"George Washington, I am going to take a bath, could you please have the ladies turn around and look away." With that there was a burst of giggles. Ruth turned and ran away as fast as she had come. The young girls who were standing around us, turned around.

"No cheating," said George Washington.

The kids kept asking questions, and I did the best I could to answer them. "George Washington, maybe we can talk. ..."

"There won't be much time, suh, we know you will be moving on tonight." George Washington said.

I took some time to bath, there wasn't a towel so I had to wait awhile, drying off. The kids picked up my socks, and the underwear.

George Washington told the kids to take it to the washer ladies.

We walked back to the house.

＊ ＊ ＊ ＊

I was surprised that Michael would bring Hattie and her two sons, Jimmie Earl and Karl David, down to the barn in the far meadow where the *Alabama* was settin'. I found it difficult to believe he would expose to Hattie and Jimmie Earl the reality of what we had done, and that all of us came from a different time. But Michael was proud of what we had accomplished, and he wanted his family to know what his role had been. He said he would make sure they would never speak of it to strangers, that it would be a family secret.

The moon was up when we headed in a wagon, and on a couple of horses out towards the barn. We would wait 'til the sun had slid behind the Blue Ridge before we cranked up the *Alabama* and made the last part of this adventure, the return to 2012, if we could.

The women and kids were in the wagon behind us, while Michael and I rode ahead and talked.

"I can't believe it, Parks, we done it." Michael was bursting with pride and joy.

"Well, it looks like it, maybe." I said.

"Looks like it nothin', you heard what they said, Stonewall had been wounded, but he was alive, and they thought he'd be back on the battle-field afore the next battle done come." Michael was beaming.

"I guess." I said. I still didn't know if I had done good or bad. How would God deal with what happened? And even more than that, what would America be like when we got back?

Time to start thinking mission planning.

"Sure hope we can find that window, if we don't I don't know what we will do?"

"Well, I think you will find it," Michael said, but if'n you don't, come on back this way. You should have enough fuel for that."

"Did you double check on the arc?" I asked.

"I did," answered Michael, I had to get on the computer on the *Alabama* to check it.

"I still don't understand how that works, Michael?"

"Well, it has to do with Alpha Mechanism, and being able to plot wear the opening of the worm hole will be in this time, and where it will be in the year, month and date we want to land in. There is a unique arc through the space–time dimension, and we don't have another one for ten years. We have to go now. Well, you have to go now."

"True, Jeanne Marie is sure this is it, we have to get out tonight, or the wormhole will be gone and we don't have any idea when it will show back up." I said.

"Hey everything has worked so far ain't it?" Michael replied.

"Yea, if you count bein' shot at by Yankees, fallin' in love with your sister, and your decision not to go back. Nash is gonna be heart broken." A lot had happened in these stolen days. Jeanne Marie and I had spent 24 days in this time, but only a few days will have passed when and if we returned.

Michael sat up on his horse, "Parks, I love my dad, but you can see what I have here. Hattie and the boys, and a nice piece of land. You tell dad, he swapped you for me."

"Michael !!!" I almost kicked him. "I ain't saying that."

"Ah, I am just kidden' ya. Just tell dad, how much I love Hattie and my children. Tell him, losin' mom when we did, and seeing him go through life alone made a real impression on me. I know what I got, and I can't leave it."

"You all could come with us?" I said.

"Naw, look at them boys. Imagine dealing with that?" You could hear the love and concern of a father, "No need for that. We got us a nice place, and if'n the South does win the war … well … we will be fine."

As he said that, the meadow came up on our left, through a tree line. I could see the barn down about a half mile, on the far corner of the wood line, down by a creek. The meadow was a mixture of green and gold.

"Umm, we gonna have a good hay draw this year. Look at that Parks. Too bad you can't stay and help me reap it. My horses, and Betsy my milk cow and her baby gonna have a good winter."

"The women are gonna have to go down to where the wood line intersects the road so they can catch the road down to the barn, but we can cut through the meadow," he looked at me, smiled and spurred his horse, pulling left, and the horse bolted and took off cross country through the meadow. I kicked my mount and we took off following them.

We flew across that meadow and actually caught Michael and his steed two thirds of the way across the meadow and beat him to the barn. Pulled up on reins just like in the movies, and dismounted before Michael got there.

Everything looked right. The doors were closed, nothing seemed different from when we left. I walked up, pulled one of the doors open. We were going to need all the horses and wagon to pull the *Alabama* out of the barn and get her to a clear place where I could get the blades free of interference. I looked at the wheels on that bird and thought, they thought of everything.

The moonglow provided plenty of light outside, but not inside. Michael lit a lamp outside, and walked in. He found another lamp and lit it and hung it on the wall. The light from the two shown on the nose and front half of the *Alabama*, the rest was hidden in the dark.

Just about then I heard the wagon pulling up. Michael walked back outside. "OK, boys, come here." I heard Michael call them. "Now you are gonna see something you just ain't gonna believe. Before you do, I need you to take an oath to me."

"An oath pop?" I heard Jimmie Earl say.

"Yes, Jimmie Earl, you know that's when we crosses our heart and calls on the devil to take us, if'n we break our word," said Karl David. You could kind of hear in Karl's voice he was going to be an attorney or something important.

"OK pop." The words echoed as one and then the other boy said it.

"OK, boys, here's the oath, ready?"

"Yessuh." In unison. The looked at each other and smiled.

"Take off your hats, cross your hearts and repeat after me," Michael sounded mighty official, "I promise not to tell anyone what I am about to see, and won't talk to anyone but family 'bout this, the family here right now." The boys echoed their father.

"Now cross your hearts again." Michael said. I guess they did, couldn't see them. Then I heard Michael say, "OK, you can look in the barn." And with that I could hear the patter of bare foot feet running towards me. When they broke around the door it was something to see.

Jimmie Earl just stopped flat footed just inside the door, his mouth wide open. Karl David, the older brother ran up to the *Alabama* and touched her flank. "Oh my gosh, what is this thing?" Despite it being dark, the boys could see most of her. I could not imagine what they were thinking.

"What do you think boys?" asked Jeanne Marie. "Dang I can finally get out of this outfit and into my flight suit." She walked right past Karl

David, pulled open the sliding side door, and pulled out her suit and boots. Like a cat, Karl David stuck his head inside the bird.

He looked up at me, "Is this an ironclad? We heard about these things, hey Jimmie Earl I think this is an iron clad."

Without looking Jeanne Marie called out "Come on over here Jimmie Earl, take a look at this monster!" She giggled. "I got to find me a place to change, and get out of this corset!" You could tell Jeanne Marie was ready to be done with her hoop skirts and long undergarments.

"Maybe over in that corner," I said with a smile.

She looked, "I ain't putting on no show husband." Then she leaned towards me and whispered, "ceptin' maybe for you." And she smiled.

About this time Michael and Hattie walk into the barn. Hattie kind of slowed her walk, acting as a drag on Michael, as she approached the bird. "My Lord Michael, what is this?"

"Jimmie Earl, come over here," I said as I took off my heavy wool Colonel's blouse. I handed it to him, almost knocked him down with the weight. "Would you do me a favor and put this somewhere, I have some work to do, and that's just too hot for me in here." Jimmie Earl took it and turned. I didn't watch where he went. Funny since I was looking forward to taking that back with me as a souvenir of this adventure.

I climbed into the bird and started looking around. When I cut on the electric power some lights came on and a hum from a small indoor fan over by the engineer's chair. The boys jumped, and I heard Hattie take a breath. "Hold on honey, it won't bite ya." said Michael. I guessed he said that to calm his wife Hattie.

I turned on the outside running lights to give us more light to work in. That really shook 'em up. Hattie put her head in Michael's chest. The boys ran to grab his legs. After being comforted by Michael, the boys sheepishly looked at helicopter and made their way over to me. I was inside the door of the cabin.

Cautiously, the boys stuck their heads back in the door, to see the little blue and red lights all over the compartment lit up and blinking. Meanwhile, I went forward through the hatch up into the cockpit to get the preflight guide.

"Karl David go get the wagon, and back it up to the door, we are gonna have to pull the monster out of it's lair." Michael told his son.

"Jimmie Earl, come here son." Hattie called. "Jimmie Earle I want you to take one of the horses and head home. I had something to give

Jeanne Marie as a gift. I left it on the bed, would you go get it for me?"

"OK momma," Jimmie Earl called "Titan." In a few seconds, Titan came up from the creek and little Jimmie Earl walked Titan over to a tree where he could climb the tree and then jump on Titan. "Let's go Titan." Titan took off along the road next to the wood line at a slow trot.

"OK Michael, let's get those ropes around the rear end of this baby and drag her out." As Michael and Karl David and I worked to get a rope harness securely around the bird and tied off to the wagon, Jeanne Marie walked around the nose carrying her dress and undergarments, and dressed in her flight suit and boots.

"Here ya' go Miss Hattie, a present from me to you."

Hattie looked at Jeanne Marie, and in the deepest of Southern drawl said, "well, look at you Miss Jeanne Marie, aren't you a sight?" And she giggled nervously. "I don't think I have ever seen anything like that, ma'am."

"Hattie, I feel right again, I can breathe. I am sorry but you ladies sure are wearing some heavy gear, and so dang hot." Jeanne Marie laughed as she lifted one foot to the deck of the bird and jumped inside. Jeanne Marie got in her seat, flicked on a reading light and pulled up her preflight guide and started going through it.

"Time is a clicking Parks," she yelled out.

"I know."

We finally got all the ropes secured. Michael told Karl David to get up on the wagon and be ready to move forward at a slow pace when he told him. "Are we ready Parks?"

"You ready Jeanne Marie?"

"Breaks off, let's roll." She yelled out.

"OK Michael." Just as I said that, I thought I heard a sizable body of horses at a distance and on the move.

"Pull her out Karl David"

"Giddy up," Karl David said, as he snapped the reins, they went taught and then, after a moment, the bird started moving out the door.

Once moving, it didn't take too long before it was pulled completely out and into open space in the meadow.

"Hold her up Michael, that's it. Let's get these ropes off as quick as we can. Jeanne Marie, get in the cockpit do the pre-start procedures and stand by to start up the engine. Wait 'til I wave to you."

"OK Parks," she yelled back.

As we started untying a removing the ropes, I saw movement in the far wood line, maybe a little more than a quarter of a mile away. As we cleared the last rope I heard the crack of a rifle, followed by a couple more. A second later, rounds smacked into the wagon, the horses jumped, I fell forward into the wagon bed.

"Get down Hattie," Michael called. "Karl, reign in, hold 'em tight." Michael reached into the bed and pulled out his carbine. With the wagon between him and the wood line where the shots came from, he looked for targets. Meanwhile, I grabbed my rifle and jumped out of the wagon onto the ground. I reached down to feel my pistol on the belt.

The high-pitched hum of a chopper's engine started, and the blade started to move slowly.

A second volley of cracks sounded, almost in unison, and again rounds splattered on the wagon. Karl David yelled out and fell off the front of the wagon. Released, the horses pulled forward and took off. Michael's carbine went off by accident. Hattie got up from the ground and ran towards Karl David.

From the woods, the yells of half a dozen men sounded and they broke through the wood line mounted, charging at us. "Bushwhackers." Michael sounded as Hattie grabbed up Karl on the ground. Michael was reloading. I took aim at one of the lead horsemen and fired. He fell.

There was no time to reload, I drew my pistol, they were closing on us fast, pistols drawn. "I count five coming." I yelled out.

They fired a volley, Hattie covering Karl was hit in the back, I heard the thump and her sigh. On her knees she fell forward on Karl.

Michael raised his rifle and we fired together. I think he got his, but I missed mine. Five kept coming but one was bent over and had dropped his pistol.

By now the blade was moving at an ever-accelerating pace and was almost there to full rotation, the engine roaring.

Michael was trying to re-load, I fired two shots from the pistol, but I don't think I hit anything. They were within fifty yards and still coming, when they fired another volley. A ball hit my left arm. They were screaming, "we are going to kill you all, and take your scalps."

I fired again, hitting one and knocking him off his horse.

Michael was having a problem, he was panicked. Hattie was moaning, Karl crying. I fired again, hitting another, but had only one shot left. But three of them were still mounted; the wounded man had drawn his other pistol.

All of a sudden behind me, and to my right, I heard a heavy caliber pistol fire … several rounds. Two of them struck home and those two men were blown backwards off their horses. It was Jeanne Marie and it sounded like a .45.

The wounded bushwhacker got off a round just before I fired and hit him in the face.

He fell dead. Michael dropped his rifle and ran towards Hattie and Karl. I turned to look at Jeanne Marie. She was standing, but there was a dark color on her olive-green flight suit down on her left thigh. She was hit. I ran towards her, I heard Michael scream, "Hattie."

Jeanne Marie was falling when I got to her, and I caught her and lifted her into the door of the chopper. "How ya doin' dead eye?" I said with a smile. I squeezed her arm. I was trying to make a joke more for me, than her.

She looked at me, in a daze, she was going into shock. I looked around and on the ground inside the barn I saw a piece leather, looked like a piece of rein maybe two foot long. I stepped away from Jeanne Marie, and she fell back. I could hear her head hit the deck of the chopper. I grabbed the rein up, ran it over and tied off her leg above the wound.

She was hurt bad, and I was scared.

I turned and Michael was running towards me carrying Karl in his hands. He had to yell to be heard above the noise of the blade. "Hattie's gone, and he's hurt, but not too bad. Shot in the arm."

I yelled back "Jeanne Marie …" and pointed to her leg because I was not sure she could hear me.

Michael put Karl in the bird, leaned into my ear, "get up there, I will take care of them and engineer." He pushed me.

I wasn't in my flight suit, but I climbed up into the bird, went through the hatch into the cockpit, strapped in, put on the head set and started looking at the controls and meters.

"Michael, this is Parks, over."

"Michael, this is Parks, over."

"Michael …"

"Parks, we are buttoned up, get us out of here."

With that I drove the power up, pulled on the stick, and applied pressure to the foot pedals and we started to lift. I was pointed in the wrong direction and had to pull her left to give me some distance to gain enough elevation to get over the far tree line, the one where the bushwhackers had come. We barely cleared it.

"Parks, this is Michael over."

"Go Michael."

"You are gonna have to get us to the mirror, I am gonna have to break open the med kit and stabilize Jeanne Marie, or we will lose her. I am sure she's in shock."

"Roger Michael."

"Once I get her set, I will try to do something for Karl's pain and then start working on the return flight protocols."

"Roger, Michael."

I searched my mind for the heading we had taken from the mirror to Mt. Airy. If I could remember it, I could add 180 degrees and get my back azimuth to the mirror.

"Parks, how is your arm?" There was a strain in Michael's voice.

"Don't feel a thing, you hurt? Over" I responded.

"No, not that I know of. Got an IV in Jeanne Marie, moving over to Karl, now."

"Roger" Just then I saw the paper I had written the first course on, 110 degrees east. I swung my nose to 290 west and took off. It was gonna take about twenty minutes to get to the area of the mirror. We were short gas because of the flight to Charlottesville and back. This was going to be a close-run thing.

And Michael would have to pin point the mirror, do the pre-reconfigure check list and be prepared to do the reconfiguration once we hit the window..

I had to keep the *Alabama* as low as possible. We had plenty of fuel, I kicked her hard trying to make time. Only then did I realize my running lights were on, I shut them off, but who knows if anyone saw us.

"Michael, got anything new on Jeanne Marie?"

Some time went by.

"Negative, Parks, how "bout your arm?"

"Startin' to smart some," I replied

"Be up to you in a minute. Over"

I couldn't pay too much attention to my left arm, trying to stay just above the trees with the terrain below rising and falling.

Michael's head stuck up through the cockpit. He tore my sleeve and started working on the arm.

"Uggh" I yelled into my mic. He didn't hear it, his headset was off. He just looked up and smiled as he dabbed some powder on the wound. It stung some, but he kept working and started to wrap the arm. When he was through he handed me a pill, and a canteen followed. After I took a drink he patted me on the arm, "ouch" and turned back down into the cabin.

A couple seconds later he came up on the intercom, "Parks, I am at station, will start working to find the mirror, you might have to give me a little elevation, it could be anywhere."

"Parks, how did the retraction of the blades work during the flight coming in? over"

"She handled it totally, it was very smooth which surprised me. But we were in a steep dive. Over"

"Might be a little shaky this time." Was Michael telling me he wasn't sure of what he was doing? Better not ask.

"Gotta beep, Parks, pull your nose up some. Over" Michael sounded surprised a little.

I pulled on the nose.

"Gotcha," I heard him say.

"Parks, adjust your course to 295 west, and start to climb, this baby is at 3000 feet and if you want to dive into it we need to get above it. She's about ten miles out. over"

Plenty of time to get to that elevation, I thought. I am going to stay down for a while longer, no reason to make our presence felt across all of south western Virginia.

"Michael once we get into the other side, you will have a good amount of time to deal with Jeanne Marie and Karl and try to improve their condition, or at least keep 'em stable."

"Roger, you should start climbing over."

"Distance to target? Over"

"Eight miles, over. Don't forget you are carrying some weight back here." We were both a little weak on our comm.s procedures.

Forgot about that. These could climb fast, but I had forgotten about all the gear in the cabin and probably close to 300 additional pounds of people weight. I started to climb. I wanted to get to about 5,000 feet at two miles out and use the 2,000 feet drop to build kinetic energy for going through the mirror.

"Michael, there's no glide on this thing, so you can't reconfigure 'til the very last moment, won't get a second chance if we miss the entry point."

"Roger."

In my mind's eye, I could see Michael checking his panels, and switches and looking at his procedures. I watched Jeanne Marie do it once on the ground, and could not believe the speed you had to do everything at. If you missed a toggle switch, that could be all she wrote. Once you cut power to the blades, it a race to get everything done in a matter of seconds.

That got me to thinking about my transition. In the first flight I had two hands, could do several things at the same time. This time, I have one good hand and a broken arm. I have to release the chopper control, grab the time ship control, and lower the computer flight screen all at the same time. If I don't and there is something just inside the window we'll hit it, and that will be that.

All I can do is lift my bad arm with my good arm, place my left hand on the screen, hold it 'til the right time and then pull it down by pulling on the broken arm with my body. I knew that was going to hurt like the dickens, but there wasn't another way.

I looked down at the altimeter and I am at 3,500 feet, true on 295.

"Distance to mirror? over"

"Four miles, over"

"Are we lined up Michael, over"

"Let me get a bearing check at two miles out, and a second at one mile, over"

"Roger"

"Two miles, come left to 294 west"

"294, roger"

I checked the altimeter I am at 4,900 and still climbing. We need that extra energy to push us through the window. I won't start my descent until a half mile out. 2,000 feet in half a mile, I am hoping that will work.

Time to lift my left arm. Can't mess around with it too long, because the one mile marker will come up quick and I will have to reset the course on final. Ouch, God that arm hurts, right hand lifting left over my head to the screen, flying direction with my knees.

"Your sliding off course," Michael's voice a little tense. "No breadth for error, get back on 294. Over."

My left hand is holding the screen, I am praying nothing happens, no bumps which bring it down early. I grab the stick and pull left to 294.

"One-mile marker, left to 293. Over"

"Roger 293, give me a course correction at the half mile. Will start descent there. Buckle in if you aren't. over," I said.

"Roger, commencing reconfig. prep."

"half mile …"I started my descent "293 true. Over"

"Starting reconfig, see you over there."

"Tell me the window intersect point over." I screamed.

"Window now"

I pulled back with my body, literally dragging my arm down, my left hand gripping the screen, I yelled in pain. My right hand switched over to the time ship controls, I had felt the blade disengage, Michael had done that.

In the back of the bird, Michael had to be working his tale off. Disengage the blade, and retract, engage the anti-matter power pack, energize the magnetic field, and bring up the neutron field, this time in positive harmonics and accelerate their spin. Then shut down the main engine. A lot to do.

The visual on the screen came up, there were objects on trajectories in all directions, at first moving slow, but increasing in speed as Michael brought our power up to 100 years per hour. The next ninety minutes would be all I could handle. On one axis I am trying to hold to a computer-generated course to Mayberry, Texas 2012. On the board I am watching for trajectories of foreign bodies which may intersect with my flight path, and on the other axis I am watching my true course through the Dark universe. No feet required for this part of the flight, just a second brain a couple of eyes and may be another hand.

The good news is the reconfiguration appears to have worked for the third time. One more time would be the trick.

We got through a fairly thick portion of time space, where there were a lot of objects and now seemed to be in the open field running. But I couldn't take the chance of getting distracted; there was just too much chance something would show on the screen, or multiple somethings.

The things on the screen weren't just moving in one line, but in time to, which made their trajectories herky jerky. And worse, it made mine the same. If we tried to add power to go faster, it could get past what I could handle. We were already approaching and passing objects on the screen at a very fast rate. A few of them I barely missed hitting.

"Anything on Jeanne Marie? Over"

"I was just checking her, I think the bleeding may have stopped, maybe her blood pressure is too low? I don't know. Over"

"And how bout Karl? Over"

"He is awake, I have a blanket on him. I think he will be OK. Over"

Because we were moving with time, things were going in the same direction, which really reduced their speed towards us. The ride back, in that way, was actually easier. It was more like passing cars going in the same direction. Yet, some of those cars were much faster and passing or coming in from one of the flanks. And every once in a while, one would be coming at us. In addition, there were some things which flashed and disappeared. I wondered if those were Super Nova, or something.

Then I felt a violent jerk, the entire craft shook. I tried to hold the controls but the pull by the ship was strong. "Michael, what's going on? Over"

The shaking stopped. "Sorry Parks, was checking Jeanne Marie and there was a fluctuation in the neutron field. For just a half second we lost it. I am checking the panels now, over."

"Roger Michael." I was in extreme pain. The flight to the mirror had been forty-eight minutes, the flight to the next window through the Dark Universe would be about ninety minutes. I knew Michael was busy but I wasn't sure I would stay conscience if I didn't get some pain killers.

"Michael you got any pain killer, or aspirin back there? over"

"Roger, up in a minute, over."

When he came up through the hatch I looked down on him over my left arm and noticed the shirt sleeve was shiny red, soaked in blood. He did too.

"Hold steady" he yelled. I could barely hear him.

He ducked back down into the cabin.

"Parks, your bone is protruding out of your arm. You are in bad shape buddy. I know, I am not supposed to tell you that, but since you are flying this contraption you have to know. I can only help if I lift your arm onto your lap, but it's gonna hurt plenty when I do, over"

"Understand, how 'bout the pain killer? Over"

"Probably better after I move it, than before. Over"

"Michael, under.....OOOUCH, AHHHHHHHHH" I thought I was going to black out. The pain was so powerful it was like a shard of glass driven into my eye! My brain exploded. I don't know how, but my right hand stayed on the time ship controls. Michael must have figured surprising me was better.

Once he got my left arm on my lap, the pain level dropped, a lot, and for a second I thought the pain was over. But, it kicked back in. Less than when he moved it, more than when it was hanging.

"Sorry Parks, I had to do that, now I have to wrap it again. I won't surprise you, but I have to try to stop the bleeding, over."

"Understand over, bring a rope with you if you can find one over."

"Roger, over"

The pain was pretty strong, it made it real hard to focus on the three screens in front of me.

Michael had to get back to his station, first to find the window, and then to reverse the reconfiguration as we passed through the window.

We blew through the mirror and out of the shaft in Rebel Mountain just as Michael finished reconfiguring the bird and engaging the blades. It was smoother than I had anticipated though we dropped sharply until the blades were rotating fully. We quickly lifted away from the tree tops.

But now, gas was problem. We didn't have much left, minutes.

Rebel Mountain, Texas
July 20th, 2012

"Michael, do you have any way to communicate with Nash? Over"

"I do have my cell phone. over"

"I need to know, do I fly to Three Pines, or do we make for the local hospital and do you have their radio frequency so I can get their attention about our two patients? Don't forget we are short on petrol, we can't dally, our gauge is in the red. Over"

"Head towards Three Pines and we can fly right over it to town. I will call dad, over."

"Roger."

Michael pulled out his cell phone and hit the number for his father. The phone rang less than once:

"Hello, Jeanne Marie?" Nash sounded excited and confused.

"Dad, this is Michael, not Jeanne Marie, Jeanne Marie is wounded."

"How can that be?" He said

"Dad, we can talk later, Jeanne Marie is hurt bad, and should we land at Three Pines, or go. ..."

"Go to the football field, I will make the calls down here." Nash said.

"Roger" Michael said, he clicked his communications toggle. And there, I could see the runway coming up, the lights just clicked on as Michael came up on the radio "Dad said fly straight to town and put us down on the high school football field. Over"

"Dad said he would notify the hospital and get an ambulance to the school as quickly as he could. Over"

We had been flying for almost two and half hours, most of it under the alternative power system in the Dark Universe, but we were low on fuel, The lights of the city came up quickly.

"Michael, I don't know where the high school is. Over"

"Due north from the County Courthouse over."

The lights of Mayberry stood out in the darkness and we were over them in just a minute or so after we passed Three Pines. I could make out the courthouse and saw red and blue flashing lights racing North on the road from the town square. I guessed they were rushing to meet us at the ad hoc landing zone Nash had directed us to. The school came up quick and the football field. I went past the field, then turned hard left circling back to it. I wanted to get down quick.

I approached the field from the north and looked to land on the fifty-yard line. I could see moving police lights making their way towards the field from several directions. The first car to the field stopped on the other side of gate, and I could see the policeman trying to unlock the gate. I was touching down when he finally got it open and was waving cars through. The ambulance followed two police cars as they raced the short distance to us.

My blades were still rotating, though the engine had been disengaged and I was going through the process of shutting her down.

In the back, Michael had pulled the door back and open. When I looked back, I could see him over Jeanne Marie. He was pressing on her chest in a rhythmic way. Was she gone? There was nothing I could do. The ambulance pulled up in front of me, the bright colored lights flashing and rotating, two EMTs got out and ran straight under the blades that were still moving. They must have had training on this kind of situation because they knew to drive up to the nose of the bird so the pilot would see them.

One, and the other EMT tech jumped into the cabin pushing Michael out of the way. The engine noise was gone; all that I could really hear was the quiet rotation of the blades, the sirens rising in intensity as more cars showed up. A vehicle without lights pulled through the gate where a policeman stood guard and drove right up next to the ambulance. I could see it was Nash, he jumped out of the car and walked quickly to the side door. The EMTs were just then pulling Jeanne Marie out the side door and placing her on an ambulance gurney one of the Policemen had pulled out and brought over to the *Alabama.*

Looking out my side window I could see one of the EMTs talking to Nash as the other was strapping Jeane Marie down on the gurney. The one talking to Nash was holding an IV bottle above Jeanne Marie. The talk was excited, but I couldn't hear anything, even after I propped the side window open.

The first EMTs hadn't even looked at me or Karl David.

A second ambulance was rolling through the gate. I hadn't moved my arm; it was in just too bad a shape to move it until an EMT got to me.

Just then I heard Michael scream. I turned and looked back in the cabin. He had lifted the blanket where Karl David had been resting. I saw nothing but a pile of gray white dust where I thought Karl David had been. "He's gone," Michael said turning to look at me. Michael reached down into the dust that was there, picked up a handful and lifted his hand from the pile; the dust ran through his fingers.

I looked through the open side window and I watched them bring Jeanne Marie around the bird and towards the rear of the ambulance. Nash followed them, got into his car and closed the door. He backed up and drove towards the gate stopping on this side. It looked like he was waiting on the ambulance.

I heard the ambulance doors slam as someone stuck their head up into the cockpit, he hit my arm. "Ouchhhhhhhhhhhhhh," I yelled. I starting cussing, using words I hadn't said in years.

"I am sorry sir, I will get you a pain killer before we do anything." Flushed with pain and anger I looked at his face. He was sorry and I could tell it.

Michael was sobbing in the back. He had frantically looked for Karl David when he found only dust under the blanket, but there was nothing back there. As cars pulled up on the bird more and more light flushed into the cabin. There just wasn't anywhere Karl David could have gone. I could only think we might have lost him when we lost the neutron field and at that point Karl David would have traveled more than one hundred years in time from his birth.

Michael had a really bad three and half hours, losing his wife, caring for his near dead sister and his wounded son, and trying to help me with my wound; all while acting as the engineer for a first time, one of a kind flight. I was surprised he was still standing.

When the EMT showed back up, I told him they needed to take care of Michael, all his wounds were internal. He had been under immeasurable stress for the last four hours.

I don't remember much at the helicopter after that. Once they gave me the pain killers I kind of blacked out 'til we got to the hospital. I came too in the ambulance once, for a moment. Michael was in with me sitting in one of the seats that drop down off the wall of the ambulance.

Sometime around 2 am I woke up. My left arm was in a cast. Michael was in the bed next to me in the same room. I hate hospitals. The room was dark but the door was open and the light from the hallway shown in at the foot of my bed. I could hear things going on. I was hooked to something. I went to get up and out of bed and found all kind of cords patched to me.

Sorry, nope, not doing this. I need to know where Jeanne Marie is and how she is? They had cut away my clothes and I was barefoot with one of those hospital gowns on that shows your butt. I finally was able to undo enough of the pesky cords and tubes to make my way out of the bed. My head hurt and I could not move the left arm. The hardness of the cast felt strange against my chest and belly. I walked slowly out into the hall and looked in both directions. There was a nurse's station to my right so I figured I would make my way to that. As I walked down the hall a man walked out of door on my right, it was Nash.

I bumped right into him. He was looking down. He looked up, saw it was me, and smiled. "Thanks for bringing her back. And for Michael. …"

"Nash if it wasn't for those two I wouldn't be standing here. How is she? I want to see her." I started to move around him towards the door. He raised both hands grabbing my arms, including the broken one. I pulled back in pain.

"Parks, she is resting. She has not come conscience at any point since the helicopter. She has lost a lot of blood. Michael did a lot, he stopped most of the bleeding and had an IV in her, though it ran out. The EMTs told me Michael was doing CPR on her when they got there. She was gone, but he kept the blood circulating 'til they got there. All we can do now is pray."

As we talked a short dark-haired nurse with a stern look on her pretty face came up the hall; "What are you doing out of bed? Turn yourself around mister, we are going back to your room." She said.

"That's my wife in there ma'am, I ain't leaving her!" I said.

"Your wife?" Nash and nurse said in concert.

"That's Jeanne Marie Laurent in there sir, what do you mean your wife?" The nurse said with a strange tone in her voice, "they said you were the pilot who landed the helicopter at the football field with Jeanne Marie and Michael in it."

"We eloped," I said.

"Parks, this is Denise, one of Jeanne Marie's closest friends. She would probably know if Jeanne Marie got married. And I kind of think I would too," said Nash.

"Well, it was her idea Nash, it's a long story. But Michael can verify it." I pleaded my case. I didn't want to go back in the room; I wanted to see Jeanne Marie.

"Denise, help me get Parks back to bed," Nash said. "He has had a tough time of it." The two of them turned me around and walked me back to the bed.

"Sir, you have to keep these monitors hooked up to you, Doctor's orders," Denise said with a little more feeling in her voice. She turned to Nash, "that girl will do the dangdest things, getting married without even telling me?" Nash smiled. Denise checked Michael and then left the room.

"Parks I will be with Jeanne Marie every minute, if anything happens I will come and get you, I promise. Get some sleep. You are gonna have to tell me about the bullet holes in the *Alabama* later."

I was asleep before Nash got to the door.

* * * *

About 7 am an aide brought in some trays. Hospital food, yuck. I needed some coffee and something solid, I was starved. Michael wasn't as picky, he dove right into the food. Nash walked in as the aide walked out. He walked over to the side of Michael's bed a big smile on his face, "How are you boy?" He spread his arms around Michael and pulled him close. "Wasn't sure how this was going to work out. I am glad you made it back."

The look on Michael's face changed from a smile to grief "I wasn't coming back dad, I lost my whole family last night. Nash was smart enough to know not to ask questions, but held his son as Michael cried. That lasted a couple of minutes. I felt like an intruder and wanted to get out of the room. I started disconnecting wires again.

Finally, Michael pulled himself together, "We will talk son." Nash said.

Nash turned towards me, "What are you doing?" He almost shouted when he saw me fussing with the tubes and cords attached to me.

"Nash I am not good with hospitals; I have to get out of here. And how is Jeanne Marie anyway?" I said with some doubt, I wasn't sure what he would say.

Nash looked at Michael, "Your wife is fine, Parks." Michael just smiled and started eating again. I think Nash saw what he was looking for. "She awoke just as the sun came up. She is weak, too weak even to talk much, but she did recognize me, and gave my hand a squeeze. And she asked about her husband." They came in to check her and told me the worst is over, but she won't be leaving the hospital for days."

"I want to see. ..."

Mark K. Vogl

321

"I will get you in there as soon as I can Parks, today for sure; maybe this morning."

"OK, now it's your turn to help me Nash." I said.

"How's that?"

"Let's start with, what day is it?" Michael's ears perked up. He was interested in that question too. "It's Sunday, July 21st. You two were gone about 72 hours.

"OK. Look I still can make Houston on time if I haul. ..."

"Yes?" Nash looked at me with an inquisitive look.

"You have to get me some clothes from the bunk house. I have to get out of here today. If I drive all night and all tomorrow I think I can make it." I was adamant. I had to get to NASA in Houston to sign in.

"Parks, I am headed to Three Pines, so I can get you some clothes. And I will talk to the doctors before I have them start checking you out. But, you don't have to drive all night, I have a short cut for you." Nash winked and you need to spend some time with Jeanne Marie.

"Nash one other thing."

'Yes?" He looked at me.

"Do you guys have a McDonald's here? I need a large hot coffee black, and a bacon, egg 'n cheese biscuit!"

Nash laughed. We don't have a Mickey D's in Mayberry, but I will see what I can bring you back from the house. "Bye Michael, you will get out today too." Nash left the room.

Michael laid back in the bed and seemed to relax. I think we both realized at the same moment what we had done and that we were back. Michael turned towards me, the best he could do all wired and tubed up in a hospital bed.

"We made it back in time for football," Michael said, "Hall of Fame Game isn't for three weeks."

"You got that right. Wonder if this TV works? See what we missed news wise."

It didn't take long 'til doctors and nurses came into the room and started checking me all over. When one was done with me, they'd move over and check on Michael. There was so much commotion and noise we couldn't hear the reporters, or really see the television. At one point there was a scene with Stars and Bars, the first national flag of the Confederate States of America.

Then Nash showed up, all fresh and cleaned up, in his white dress shirt, white slacks and red suspenders. He had a brown paper bag in his hand, "Here's your coffee and here's a roll with bacon, egg and cheese. Made it myself." He beamed with pride. "I buttered the roll before I put the fixin's in it."

I took a large gulp of hot coffee and though I burned my tongue, and the back of my throat, it sure tasted good. I then turned on the roll. I devoured it quickly, but when I looked up Nash had left. I sat back in the bed, drinking coffee and answering more questions from the doc. A nurse, not to bad looking I might add, was removing the wire and patches from my bare skin. She was a pretty brunette, and smelled good.

About that time Nash walked in with a stack of clothes and my boots. "Once you get dressed, come on down to Jeanne Marie's room," Nash nodded his head, "but Parks, she is still weak, so don't go telling her to go to Houston with you. She needs rest boy."

"Got it pops." I said and laughed. I liked Nash. We weren't really married yet, but that was probably happening in the not too distant future.

Nash had got me some tan slacks and Citadel blue alumni golf shirt. I usually wore dockers with this outfit, but maybe Nash was trying to remind me of something. Anyway, put on my socks and boots. "You coming Michael?"

"I'll be along after a while Parks, you go ahead," he replied.

I walked down the hall to the next room on the right and walked in. It was dark, Jeanne Marie was laying almost flat on the bed. She was talking to Nash when she heard someone at the door and turned towards me. She smiled. I walked straight to her, bent over and kissed her lightly, "How are you?" I said.

"I am here." She replied and smiled.

"You saved my life Annie Oakley," I said looking into her eyes.

"And you saved mine." A faint light started to glow. After a minute or so I stood up, looking for Nash. He wasn't in the room. "Jeanne Marie, I have to go, I have to go sign in at Houston. Astronauts aren't allowed to be late."

"I know, dad told me. It's OK. I am gonna take some time healing, mostly sleeping." She said. She reached for my hand with hers. Some needles stuck in her hand, blood and a second IV were running into her hand.

"Jeanne Marie, I will try to call you every night. I will get Nash's cell, and he can tell me how to get in touch with you."

"OK Parks. It's OK, I know you have to go."

"I will be back."

She smiled, "You better, I know where you are in Houston!"

I laughed and bent down to kiss her again. Looked in her eyes "be back in no time."

"Go on now, get going."

I touched her head, turned and walked out of the room. Nash was standing just outside the room with his back against the wall. He handed me a piece of paper, "Here's my cell and the house number." He said.

"Thanks for getting me out of here."

"Parks you can take the plane at the ranch if you want to?"

"No, I need my 'vette Nash. Don't worry, I have driven all-nighters before. Once I sign in I can get some sleep." I wasn't lookin' forward to the long ride, but one has to do what one has to do.

"Parks, listen, don't leave town the way you came. Take the road to Three Pines out of town and off Rebel Mountain. It will save you a few miles. Give me a call when you get to NASA so I can tell Jeanne Marie you are there safe, OK?' He said, unsure of himself for the first time since I met him. "Your 'vette is on the square, your duffel bag is packed and in the back seat. The keys are under the driver's seat."

"You got it, Nash." I said, "don't worry about your daughter's heart, I ain't playing."

He seemed to buck up some. He brought his hand out for a hand shake. I took it, and then pulled him in for a hug. "What an adventure," I said. I turned and headed to the elevators. Down one floor and out the front door I could see the steeple to the courthouse and headed in that direction. As I turned a corner, there was the square and my 'vette.

I walked up to the 'vette and was about to open the door. I decided I wanted to know. Did our trip to the past make a difference, did we change history? I looked up at the flag pole in front of the courthouse. I smiled.

I got in the car and reached under the seat, found the keys and fired up the 'vette. The engine roared. I backed up, took off around the square and out on the road towards Three Pines. The sun was up, it was a clear blue sky, but still a mild 75 degrees. I drove past Three Pines climbing to 80 MPH as the road curved and started down the mountain. Pretty soon I could see where the green of the mountain ended and the reddish brown of the desert started. I felt a bump as I drove off the macadam on Rebel Mountain and onto the dirt road in the desert. Instantly the temperature soared from 75 to more than 100.

I kicked another gear and was closing on 100 MPH. I decided I wanted to see the cloud of dust I was raising. But when I looked in the mirror, there was no dust, and no road. The road was there in front of me, but like before, not behind me. It was literally disappearing as I drove over it. After about four miles I came up on a highway. I turned right and started driving figuring I had at least eight hours to Austin. A couple miles down the road there was a mileage sign, Fredericksburg ten miles, Austin, 97 miles.

I thought to myself, Nash had said the shortcut would save me a few miles.

Fredericksburg – Spotsylvania National Battlefield
April 10th, 2035

I had driven Interstate 95 between Washington and Richmond many times in my life, with and without Jeanne Marie and had never really given much thought to Chancellorsville as I passed the exit for Fredericksburg. It amazed me now, that I had never come back here, or that my bells didn't ring every time I passed this area. But, they hadn't. I was always distracted by what ever adventure I was presently on at the time.

But this trip was planned. Jeanne Marie had wanted to tell our kids about our stolen days ever since the first was born. But, we had been very careful never to speak of it in their presence. This trip was intended to set the stage for the grand revelation to the four teenagers, Melissa, Michael, Micah and Nash. From here, we intended to drive to Mt. Airy, North Carolina, and hopefully find Hattie's farm. That's where we intended to tell the children the story.

And, from there, we would head to Charleston, for a vacation, and the graduation at THE CITADEL. Melissa was talking about applying there, and we wanted here to see the campus and the Corps.

"There's the sign, Parks," Jeanne Marie said. She reached over and grabbed my hand. Cars had changed so much in my lifetime. Most cars now drove themselves, but I was not one to allow that. As a pilot I was jealous of control of my speed and course. No, this car was a renovated, completely refurbished 1950s wood paneled station wagon. Not a single computer in this car. Still had a spare tire and a jack. I also had a tool box and a spare can of oil in the back.

The kids were busy playing with their gizmos, or typing notes to friends. They didn't even look up when we passed through the gate and pulled into the parking lot.

The Secretary of the Interior had personally called the national historian here to let them know I was coming with my family. I spoke with him at the White House, we were there for former President Trump's Medal of Freedom Ceremony. He was still a feisty man, very proud of what he and Melania and his family and administration had accomplished. The world was a different place, and he had much to do with how far it had progressed. One of his smaller feats had been the preservation of American history, including Civil War battlefields.

Michael who was learning about American history, asked the former President about the Yellow Journalism of his day, and that sure did set him off. But, despite the scars of those days, the former president seemed to have a strange feeling of affection for those in the media who had been so mean to him, for so many years. He was by no means perfect, but he had a huge patriotic heart.

"Good morning, Dr. Walter," the guard said as we pulled up to the gate. I still could not get used to doctor. "Ranger Taylor is waiting for you at the headquarters. He is very anxious to see you and Jeanne Marie," the Ranger touched his cap looking at my wife. "Oh, I am sorry ma'am, it's just he seemed very excited about the visit of you both."

Ranger Taylor I thought to myself. Interesting coincidence. But, why would he be interested in meeting us?

"You can see the center from here, sir, have a wonderful visit," the Ranger said as he handed me our ticket. As we drove away, I heard the squelch of his radio, "Dr. Walter is here, sir."

It had been 182 years since I had last been on the Chancellorsville battlefield. Parking the car, the memories swarmed me, and overwhelmed me. I was frozen for a moment. The kids quickly jumped out to stretch, and Jeanne Marie had opened her door and started to get out when she noticed my slight tremor, she stopped and grabbed my hand, "Parks, are you alright? Parks. ..."

Fortunately, the kids were too busy doing whatever to notice, "Parks," she shook my hand, "Parks, come to me. ..." She said.

I heard her, and it brought me out of whatever state I had been in. "I am OK, just lost my breath a minute." I lied. Pulled the keys out of the ignition, opened the door and got out. I always loved red cars. This station wagon was a deep maroon with a light wood paneling. It glistened in the sun and stood out like a sore thumb. I had thought cars were boring back when I met Jeanne Marie, and there had been little progress in the modeling of cars since.

"Well, lets go see what we can see," I announced to the clan, "and kids leave your gizmos here." A joint sigh was released by the four, as they tossed their electronics through the windows into the car.

"I told you he would do that," Micah said to Michael, "You owe me a dollar."

"OK, OK," Michael said, "When dad gives us our vacation money, I will pay you."

Melissa rushed next to my arm and grabbed it, she was almost as tall as me. "So, this is it, huh dad, this is where General Lee won his greatest victory!?"

"And, where we lost the war," I said. We had failed, and it was a failure Jeanne Marie and I felt every day. Nash had been disappointed, and after our return his health had soured. But worst of all, was Michael. He never recovered from the loss of his wife Hattie, and the death of Karl David in the *Alabama*. He was still in Mayberry, at Three Pines.

The walk across the parking lot was pleasant and quick in the cool sunny air. Spring was about to hatch, but not quite yet. As we entered through the front door, a large black Ranger in a starched uniform approached us. He was older, tinges of gray in his hair, and a broad smile I had not seen in an eternity. "Hello Dr. Walter, or should I say Dr. Walters, glancing at Jeanne Marie, I am Dr. George Washington Taylor, his hand extended. But, as he closed he spread his arms and gave me a big bear hug, and then moved to Jeanne Marie and did the same.

The kids looked on in surprise, what was going on? I could hear their minds clicking.

"George Washing Taylor," I asked. He tried to break away from Jeanne Marie, but she held on an extra moment. "Are you. ..." Jeanne Marie's voice faded to a whisper.

"I am," he said. "Maybe we should go to the conference room, I have a lot of things to tell you."

Jeanne Marie took his arm, and I fell in behind him, and the kids behind me, we walked down a hallway, and into a room painted gray, with large colorful prints of the battles that occurred here, Fredericksburg, Chancellorsville, the Wilderness, and Spotsylvania.

"Please take seats around the table." He spread his arm out.

My mind rushed, as I am sure Jeanne Marie's did too. This quickly spiraling toward the revelation we had planned for Mt. Airy. We both looked at each other. As the kids sat down, George Washington sensed concern, he closed the door and looked at us.

There had always been a degree of telepathy between Jeanne Marie and I. I can't explain it, I can only say that we appeared to be able to send thoughts to each other. The concern on our faces faded simultaneously as we both decided or accepted that George Washington might be the best means of announcing to the kids what their parents had done … if it came to that.

We smiled at each other, and sat down. "OK, George Washington, but let me say that while my kids know this battle inside and out, they are not aware of hidden stories of Chancellorsville."

"I see," said George Washington, a look of disappointment on his face.

"George Washington, I think God thinks you are right the person to tell them those tales."

"What are you talking about, dad?" Asked Michael.

"Yea, dad, what secrets?" Micah said.

"Hold on, hold on," I said, Micah speaking had hit a trigger in my head, George Washington had not known me or my family, I had to introduce the kids.

"Ranger George Washington Taylor, these are my children," I pointed to each as I called their name, "Melissa," she stood and smiled, and they extended their hands to shake, "And Michael," "And, Micah," a special smile came to George Washington's face, "and Nash."

"Well, it is a pleasure to meet each of you. Given what you know about your mom and dad, I know you know they are very special folks."

A look of pride came on each face, and then the look of, we know, we know already. They sat back in their chairs, and hung their heads. They didn't want to hear the same stories they had been told many times.

"But, I believe you don't know the greatest adventure of your parents life," he said. With that, four heads popped up, "what adventure?" Melissa said.

"Before we start, does anyone want a soda, or water?" Among a cacophony of Coke, orange, Dr. Pepper, "And you might want to take your jackets off." He pointed to the refrigerator in the corner, "help yourselves."

There was a scramble of kids towards the refrigerator. When they were done, I got up and helped Jeanne Marie take off her coat, and then got her a Diet Coke, and a root beer for me.

When every one was settled back down, George Washington sat down and looked at our kids.

"Many many years ago, your parents visited my family in Mt. Airy, North Carolina."

Looking at us, Micah asked; "What were you guys doing in Mt. Airy, North Carolina?"

"Your parents were on an adventure never attempted by man before, your parents and Michael."

"We have heard this before," Melissa said, "We are always being told our parents were pioneers, doing things never done before."

"Yes, I am sure that's true," George Washington said, "but your parents touched my family though many generations ago, what they did has been passed down through many generations to me."

"Come on, they have only been together since 2012." Micah exclaimed.

Nash was counting his fingers, "Yea, that's only 23 years."

"It is, normally," George Washington said.

"Normally?" Melissa said, her head tilted.

"Normally, but this is not normally. Your parents visited my great-great-great grandfather in 1863." The last word, "three" hung in silence.

Micah shook his head, Michael almost dropped his soda. Nash pushed his chair back. Melissa looked at Jeanne Marie, and then me.

"I was first told about your parents by my great grandfather, Micah's son, when I was six. It is a story and a secret that has been kept by my family, and told at reunions."

"I don't believe you," Michael said.

"It's true," I said quietly, looking at Michael. Jeanne Marie nodded her head.

An explosion of sound filled the room, questions burst from each mouth in rapid order, like several machine guns firing. Nash moved close to Jeanne Marie, seemingly in fear.

"Hold on, hold on," I ordered, "let the man tell you the story."

"When I was twelve, my grandparents showed me a letter, a letter about your folks. I brought it with me, to show you." George Washington opened a leather-bound portfolio, and there was a handwritten letter inside a protective plastic cover. The hand writing was obviously feminine and beautiful."

"I think it would be best if I read it to all of you," George Washington said. He reached in his coat pocket, and pulled out a pair of glasses. After fixing his glasses, he sat back in his chair;

Charleston, South Carolina, January, 1870
  Dear Hattie,
I am sorry it has been so long since I have written to you. The struggles of life consume much of my time and all of my resources. If it weren't for the overseas investments of the Trenholm's during the war, we would be in poverty. But, even with those investments, there is little to buy. The Yankees harbor and cultivate a special hatred for South Carolina, and

Charleston. Living in the country, and on your farm, I hope provides you both with safety from the carpetbaggers, and an abundance of food, and the necessities of life.

We had the great pleasure of a visit by General Lee, who was making what he said would be a last tour of the South. He talked about many things, including the great Virginia battles and of his right arm, Thomas Jackson. He had especially fond memories of the General and Anna in the days just before Chancellorsville.

I wanted you to know that he spoke of your brother-in-law, Colonel Parks Walter. He said that while most Southerners mourned the loss of Stonewall as a result of his wounding on May 2nd, that few knew he miraculously escaped death on May 1st because of your brother-in-law.

General Lee said that there would have been defeat, and not victory at Chancellorsville, if General Jackson had been seriously wounded or killed on May 1st, because there is no one else he would have trusted to execute the grand flanking movement that destroyed the Eleventh Corps, and almost the entire Army of the Potomac. The General said it was Divine Providence that brought Colonel Walter to the Army for those few days. And to this day, he mourns his disappearance.

My family is well, and I hope to be able to visit you soon. Please give my best and a hug to Jimmie Earle, and to all who remain with you on the farm. If Micah is still there, please give him my best.

Affectionately, Melissa

Once again, a letter from the past rocked my life, and that of Jeanne Marie. The letter was addressed to Hattie, who we thought had died in the gun fight in the barn, the night we escaped back through time to this reality. It appears Hattie had lived. Imagine Michael's response when we tell him.

Jeanne Marie was filled with excitement, tears in her eyes; "Hattie lived?"

"Yes ma'am, she did." George Washington answered, surprised, that we did not know. "She recovered and lived a long life, always looking for Michael to return with Karl David."

"Oh my God," I said. A bolt of sadness struck me, settling throughout my body.

"Whose Karl David?" Melissa asked, "And who is Melissa?"

"Dad, General Lee knew you?" Nash asked in astonishment.

"And you saved General Jackson, dad?" Michael exclaimed, bewildered, "How come the secrets?"

"Yea mom, how come the secrets?" Melissa poked her mom.

"And Uncle Michael was there? How 'bout grandpa Nash?" Nash said.

Jeanne Marie, was quiet, not her normal self, she was stunned by the whole thing. "Is your family still in the Mt. Airy area, George Washington? And what about the Taylor's?"

So many questions.

"We have some long drives coming up, to Mt. Airy, and then to Charleston, so there will be plenty of time to relate the whole adventure to you." I said to the kids. "And your mom has much to tell you."

"If you all are headed towards Mt. Airy, I can alert my family, if you want to see some of them?" George Washington offered. "They could show you the farm house, the cemetery … and other things."

'We want to try to find the farm, if its still there," Jeanne Marie said.

"It is." George Washington replied. 'Here are some pictures from long ago, I thought you might want to see. And here are some newspapers."

George Washington laid out some very old photos of the farm, and Hattie and Jimmie Earle, and the Taylors.

There was the newspaper with the drawing of Jeanne Marie and I. The kids couldn't believe it. They jostled and pushed each other, and I had to be sharp at one point, because these papers were so old and fragile, they could have been easily torn, or soaked with soda, destroyed.

Today was an amazing day. It was as if I were back in time again. The children were awe struck, and Jeanne Marie was so excited to call Michael and tell him of the meeting with George Washington, and that Hattie had survived.

This time it was me who reached for a hug from George Washington as we left. I had gotten his card, with his personal e-mail written on the back. We gave him our cell phones, and the phone for Three Pines, near Mayberry, Texas.

As we walked out of the park center, and towards the car, I had this feeling we were starting a new adventure. Life was filled with chances, opportunities, and this time maybe we would have some help. Maybe we could share this adventure with our children.

Creating this Tale

It was great fun to create this Tale, may be the biggest "what if" of the War for Southern Independence.

Much of that fun was the research involved in composing it. There were five primary areas to research; space — time and time travel, Mt. Airy, North Carolina and Danville, Virginia, the last days of Stonewall Jackson's life, the concept of Providence, and finally slave language, feelings, and experiences. To that end, there were many people, organizations and books who helped.

Frank O'Reilly, Lead Historian of the Fredericksburg and Spotsylvania National Battlefield Park was especially helpful with details of the battle and locations.

Great assistance was provided by the Historical Societies of Mt. Airy, North Carolina and Danville, Virginia. The primary source histories of Henry Kyd Douglas and Rev. R. L. Dabney, and especially *All Things for the Good* by L. Steven Wilkins provided insight into Thomas J. and Anna Jackson, and tiny Julia.

I received much help and encouragement from many people, but also benefited from the previous work of many. Melissa Attridge Ricketts was a late inspiration and motivation for the last half of the writing of the book.

The Federal Writers Project, through the *Slave Narrative Collection*, established by Franklin Roosevelt, was especially helpful in the creation of George Washington Taylor, Micah Taylor and other slave characters.

Though much effort was expended in an effort to keep the tale historically accurate, license was taken because dates or locations did not work out for the telling of this tale, but the reality, I believe, improved the story and gave readers a view of the era they may not have known about.

I have made great effort to introduce the reader to how different life was in the 1860s. Life was so different, much slower in some ways, much more physical in many ways and God much more present in daily life and decisions.

While slavery has been given a benign flavor in this work, do not mistake that for my hatred of the institution, and my life long belief that slavery is a sin. Our freedom, liberty, and rights come from God, and no man has the authority, except in the case of criminal punishment, to remove the freedom of any person.

Further, the South owes a great debt to our black ancestors who did not revolt against the South, but rather supported her in her effort for independence.

Mark's Other Books

Military Lessons of the Civil War, 2007

Rebel Mountain Reader, 2008

Because of Him, 2012

Southern Fried Ramblings, 2013

Confederate Night Before Christmas, 2015

The White House Reclaimed, 2017

Dixie's Best Kept Secret, 2021

CPSIA information can be obtained
at www.ICGtesting.com
Printed in the USA
JSHW041439020622
26479JS00003B/12